The Sweeter Realm

Book 2 of The Swan Knights Trilogy

STEFAN SCHEUERMANN

"The Sweeter Realm: Book 2 of The Swan Knights Trilogy," by Stefan Scheuermann.

ISBN 978-1-947532-93-9 (softcover); 978-1-947532-94-6 (hardcover); 978-1-947532-95-3 (eBook).

Published 2017 by Virtualbookworm.com Publishing Inc., P.O. Box 9949, College Station, TX 77842, US. ©2018, Stefan Scheuermann.

Centerfold of Rudolf's Map

Contents

Prologue

VERENA ELIZABETH KESSLER, a teenage American girl in Centennial Colorado, developed an obsession with King Ludwig II of Bavaria, who died mysteriously in 1886. She swore that Ludwig had something to say to her, but she didn't know what. In a visit to the castles and palaces of King Ludwig, Verena got her answers. She discovered a manuscript written by the King and left for the next Swan Knight, the next custodian of the portal to the Sweeter Realm, the hiding place of the Holy Grail.

Verena sat in a boat, on an artificial lake, in an artificial cave, built by King Ludwig outside of his palace, Linderhof, near a mural of the legendary Germanic hero, Tannhäuser. Linderhof valley is the home of the Grail Portal, the gateway to the Sweeter Realm, opened by the Grail Knight Parsifal in the year 515, after he was stabbed with a blade by an enchanted flowermaiden. Parsifal drank from the Grail and his wound closed. Before it did, a single drop of his Grail Blood hit the ground of the Bavarian valley. On the very spot, the portal to the Sweeter Realm opened. Parsifal took the Grail through the portal. The Grail fell to the custody of the Queen of the Land and Shallow Waters in the Sweeter Realm, where it remained for centuries, waiting for the day that God recalls it into service.

1

The portal opened each time Parsifal approached it and closed as he walked away. It did the same for every one of his descendants, all the way to King Ludwig II of Bavaria. From Parsifal to Ludwig, generation after generation, a Swan Knight was sworn into the service of the Queen of the land and Shallow Waters for the protection of the portal. To assist the Swan Knights, many fantastic creatures came through the portal, into Linderhof valley, first among them was The Ancient One, a giant swan who served every Swan Knight as teacher, friend, and counselor. It was he who took the Grail from Parsifal and gave it to the Queen.

But not all creatures of the Sweeter Realm are friendly to the Swan Knights. The Sweeter Realm knew its own share of war. Löwschock, the King of the Deep Waters, wanted the Grail for himself. During Ludwig's knighthood, Löwschock killed the Queen to get the Grail. But she had hidden it. In 1886, the King of the Deep Waters found his way through the portal and killed King Ludwig II on the banks of Lake Starnberg. After Ludwig's death, there was no Swan Knight, no Grail Blood to protect the portal — until it opened for Verena, opened by her Grail Blood. The portal pulled Verena into the Sweeter Realm, where she found a set of armor. The armor belonged to the third Swan Knight, Elsa, the granddaughter of Parsifal. Verena recognized it from its description in Ludwig's manuscript. She put on the armor. It fit her perfectly.

There, on the shore of the Queen's Lake, in the Sweeter Realm, wearing the armor of Elsa, the greatest Swan Knight, Verena met her first friends in the Sweeter Realm. They too recognized Elsa's armor. And seeing it on a human, on their side of the portal, the assumed her to be the heir of Ludwig. They declared her the Queen of the Land and Shallow Waters. Verena, who just days earlier was an ordinary American girl, about to enter high school, had no choice but to admit the truths before her. She found the manuscript that Ludwig intended for the next Swan Knight. She opened the portal with her Grail Blood. She found Elsa's armor and it fit her as if it had been crafted specifically for each contour of her figure. She is the Queen of the Land and Shallow Waters, and she is the Swan Knight.

She tells the following tale of the years after her passage through the portal, her war against the creatures of the Deep Waters, her attempts to locate and save the Holy Grail from those who seek it, and her efforts to unite the Sweeter Realm under the peace and love it enjoyed under the previous Queen.

CHAPTER 1

The New Queen

THE FIRST CREATURES I MET IN THE SWEETER REALM stood before me at the edge of the lake — my five, short, round, green-feathered little hosts, with their long, grey tails cutting into the sand behind them. Without noses or eyebrows, their pale-green faces still clearly expressed their ecstasy in meeting me. I told them that I did not recognize them from any description in King Ludwig's book. In choppy and antiquated German, they introduced themselves as "Friends of the Scheriers" and inhabitants of the Nomadic Belt that surrounds the Queen's Lake. The Scheriers, those first creatures, other than The Ancient One, to meet the Swan Knights, were my favorite creatures from Ludwig's history of the knighthood. Other creatures were more exciting to me, but none as comfortable, and I needed comfort. I begged my new friends to take me to the Scheriers.

I showed Rudolf's Map, the map of the Sweeter Realm left for me in Ludwig's book, passed down the line of Swan Knights from its creator, Duke Rudolf I of Bavaria. The creatures huddled around it and whispered, spoke, and argued over its accuracy. I pointed to the portion of the map labeled "The Scheriers" and asked them to take me there.

"No Scheriers live there anymore." The leader told me. "They have been run into Unicorn and Eulesänger land. They hide in the marshes and many roam the Nomadic Belt."

Any regal air expected of me with my new title could not hide my disappointment, or the sigh that it pushed from my lungs.

In a rush to retrieve my spirits, he continued, "I know a pair of them. They have lived for many months in a cave near here."

My spirits revived at the thought of meeting them, and my recovered posture and smiling face brought nods and giggles to my little green friends.

I got one syllable of my next request out of my mouth before I was interrupted, "Plea—".

"We can take you to them, Your Majesty," one of them said.

The others repeated those words in a celebratory tone, slowly morphing the proclamation from plain speech to song, until all five of them sang it as the only lyrics in a long song they seemed to all know. As the obvious delight in my face grew brighter, and turned to laughter, their song grew louder and more musically complex.

I asked the leader his name. He looked puzzled. He huddled with the others, whispering heatedly with his friends. The whispering stopped and the huddle broke.

The leader stepped to me and said, "We have decided to call me Cort."

"Okay," I hesitantly replied, "then I will also call you Cort."

I reached my hand out to shake his, as I said, "It is nice to meet you, Cort."

Cort stuck his hand out in imitation of mine, but not reaching to shake my hand. The others did the same.

All of them, including Cort, repeated in varying tones, "It is nice to meet you, Cort. It is nice to meet you, Cort."

This went on for a few minutes. It began to unsettle me. Their voices, their appearance, their behavior, as they turned to and away from each other and me, with one hand extending forward, repeating my words, was so foreign that it frightened me and sent chills down my body. I was not afraid of the Friends of the Scheriers, but their bizarre, foreign behavior was so peculiar to me that it unnerved me deeply and reminded me how far I was from home. The trees on one side of me, the lake on the other, and as friendly as they were, even the little green-feathered beings in front of me set me into panic. I felt sickeningly disconnected from everything I had known. I wanted home. I wanted away from those strange little creatures. I began to hyperventilate and shake. Cort stopped the imitation ritual when he noticed my uneasiness.

He yelled at the others, "Stop! You are upsetting the Queen."

They all froze as they stood, their hands still extending forward. They stared at me in mortification. Cort looked sharply down at his hand, realizing that his imitation of my attempted handshake upset me. He snapped his hand to his side and growled at the others until they did the same. Cort stepped up to me and snuggled his face against my knees. Through the armor, I could feel his good-will and loyalty. The others joined him, rubbing themselves against my legs, lowly humming tunes that began disconnected and individual but slowly blended into concerted harmony. Their caresses seemed to activate the armor's Scherier magic. A warm wave of well-being washed away all of the loneliness and panic that had seized me.

The Friends of the Scheriers were content to cling to me and hum. And I was content to receive their embrace. The warm but bizarre display of affection seemed to last for hours. Yet, I dreaded its ending. In the shortest of moments, they became as comfortable and familiar to me as they had been peculiar and foreign.

The setting sun behind me began to shine off of the Queen's Lake, into the eyes of my new friends and subjects. Their squinting eyes were my first realization of how much time had passed since I came through the portal. With my heels against the dark water of the lake behind me, and the last of the sunlight hitting the trees in front, I was taken by sudden terror.

My nerves were fragile and my emotions erratic. But there was wisdom in my instinctive apprehention of the lake behind me.

As an intense fear of the waters to my back raised the hairs of my arms to brush against the inside of the armor, Cort told me, "Please, my Queen, we must leave the shore before the sun does. There are safe places, secret places in the woods. Let us please be your hosts and servants. We will take you to the Scheriers tomorrow."

I followed my five little friends along the shore, until the forest to our right grew thicker and darker. I glanced over the darkening lake. Only the slightest remnants of the daylight reflected from its surface. When I looked down to my friends, I saw that they had turned to stand at my feet, facing me. Four of them stepped toward the woods and disappeared as quickly, fully, and mysteriously as they had appeared to me earlier. Only Cort remained.

He stood still and whispered, cordially, but as if afraid of waking someone, "After you."

He gestured in the direction where his friends disappeared and he bowed low to me, replacing his face with the bony tail behind him. I took only a few steps into the trees, then looked back for the Friend of the Scheriers. He was gone, along with any sign of the lake or the entrance into the woods. Although I had only walked a few steps into the trees, the woods behind me seemed to go on, as if I had walked for hours from the lakeside. I turned back to the direction I was walking. There were no little, green creatures. There was nothing but dark forest on all sides of me.

I felt alone, lost, and scared until a voice that sounded mere inches from my face said warmly, "Please, please, keep walking."

I resumed my hesitant paces, forward, in the direction of the encouraging little voice. Suddenly, the trees cleared in front of me, giving way to a perfectly round patch of bright green grass, about ten yards in diameter. The grass and the trunks of the surrounding trees seemed to be lit by warm, orange firelight, but without the flickering of flame — and there were no torches, no candles, nothing that I could see that would be putting off the light. Nevertheless, the clearing was brightly and warmly lit. The light did not penetrate past the nearest circle of trees. I saw nothing beyond it. I looked up and saw no stars, no clouds, not even the branches of the surrounding trees reaching across the top of the cozy circle. I felt utterly enclosed from whatever was beyond the little round clearing in the woods.

Gathered in a semi-circle around me were the five Friends of the Scheriers. Behind them stood a second row of the same creatures, about thirty of them bunched in tightly together, all staring at me in wonder and holy reverence. I stared back, scanning my eyes back and forth across their lines several times, before they erupted simultaneously in a chaotic chorus of questions. Some spoke German, some spoke in language I did not recognize. I understood none of them. Some spoke calmly, some frantically, some fearfully and some excitedly. Their voices rushed at me so suddenly, so loudly and disordered that it startled me and began to unravel my already loosely bundled nerves. Cort noticed my agitation and hushed the

9

crowd. The clearing fell dead silent. I looked all around me, afraid of what attention the ruckus may have brought to our little hiding place.

He assured me, "No sound escapes the circle."

In disbelief, I rolled my eyes across the tree trunks surrounding us.

Cort turned to the others, and rallying them with his waving hands and his raised tail, he asked loudly, "Isn't that right?"

The outburst of cheers reverberating off the wall of the tree trunks around us was deafening. I had seen and read enough magical things since I awoke that morning that I thoroughly believed their boast. I joined in their loud celebration with an awkward laugh of my own, which grew louder to match the noise of the group. My hosts cheered and sang, clapped and slapped their hard tails against the floor. They taunted the world outside of the clearing, a world that could neither see nor hear anything inside of the wall of tree trunks surrounding us.

The exuberance settled into calm conversation. The Friends of the Scheriers wanted to know everything about their new Queen. So, I told them about me. The portions of my life that were ordinary and mundane to me captured and held their attention. My description of a grocery store and my excited summary of the finer qualities of my dream car widened their eyes. They asked many questions and I answered openly. I told them of my family, of my parents and little brother. I tried not to cry, but I did not know when or how I would see them again and my emotions swelled beyong my ability to contain them. As I cried in description of my family, the Friends of the Scheriers huddled tightly to each other. They rubbed those nearest them, kissed them, and wept with me.

The cry did me good. I recovered and moved on to other facets of my life. In the middle of an explanation of my class schedule in eighth grade, I yawned. Cort apologized on behalf of them all for wearing me out and keeping me up late. He slapped his boney tail on the grass behind him and all of the Friends of the Scheriers gathered to lay in a circle in the middle of the clearing, leaving a space amid them all just large enough for me. Cort gestured for me to take my place of honor and protection, so I obeyed and laid down in the center of the circle. By the time I settled into a comfortable position, the Friends of the Scheriers had gone stone still and soundly asleep, wearing the pleasantest expressions on their sweet, innocent, and devoutly loyal faces. At the time, I could not understand how my appearance in their world energized them with such hope.

There were no sounds from the Friends of the Scheriers, no sounds from the forest around us. The absolute silence was both calming and refreshing. It allowed my mind to wander through my memories of the day, from my first breath of Linderhof air as I stepped off the bus, to the scowl and scream of the portrait of Ludwig in the palace, from discovering the manuscript (which still held tightly to my hand, more like an appendage than a possession), to The Ancient One and the many details of the Swan Knight history. As I thought about the Swan Knights, I caught myself gently stroking the armor above my left shoulder with the fingertips of my right hand, while my left thumb rubbed Ludwig's book.

I thought about the hands that had touched the armor — Elsa, Lohengrin, and the Brunnen who caressed it to a deep black brilliance. I thought about The Ancient One, who took it from Bechtold and brought it through the portal. The Ancient One — I pondered him deeply, reinacting in my mind many of his heroic scenes from Ludwig's journal. I began to regret his loss and long for the comfort he had given to my ancestors. Of all the revered hands to touch the armor I wore, it was the feathers of the great swan that I wanted to feel brushing against me in an encouraging stroke. Only then, as I imagined his feathers against my shoulder, did it strike me that I still wore the armor as I laid in perfect comfort. The armor held me as softly as the flannel pajamas that still sat folded on the corner of my bed in the hotel room in Füssen.

I relished the sensation of comfort, letting out a long, vocalized sigh that was cut abruptly by yet another sudden decline in my erratic spirits. My heart was suddenly and sharply stabbed by the thought of my family, how sickeningly worried and frightened they must have been. Were they still searching for me? Had they returned to the hotel? The violently squeezing pity I felt for them settled quickly as I resumed the gentle stokes to the armor. The magical qualities of the Scherier's ore, gifted to the infant Elsa, had lost none of its potency during the armor's long sabbatical from service.

I looked at the pleasant, loyal faces around me and I could vividly recall Cort's voice proclaiming me their queen. I did not authentically see myself as a queen or a knight. But I wanted to. For much of that night, as my mind spun around the events of the day, I believed myself again at my desk or in my bed at home, drifting through one of my fantasies. They were not much unlike what I had lived that day. I startled and jolted many times when snapped back to the moment only to find that the scenery of my wildest dreams truly surrounded me.

I missed my family. But it had only been hours since I had seen them, and I did not believe at the time that our separation would be long. I was curious about the Sweeter Realm and its creatures. My heart was reluctant to disengage from the fantastical; and my vanity was caressed by the adoration I received from the Friends of the Scheriers. My resolution to honorably fulfill my roles as the new Swan Knight and Queen made palatable the sacrifices those roles required and calmed any agitation still clinging to my consciousness, enough for me to take a few deep breaths and join my little friends in sound slumber.

CHAPTER 2

The State of Affairs

I AWOKE SEVERAL TIMES while Cort and his kind still slept incrusting me from the strange world that awaited me outside of the safe circle clearing. I had no way of determining time. The circle maintained its warm brightness, as if the grass put off its own light. No light and no sound from outside showed itself within. Small thoughts of panic crept into my head through the night, always defeated by my unexplainable trust in the little creatures who adored me so. As each wave of comfortable trust washed away my concerns, I fell back asleep. This cycle continued for a span of time unnoticeable by the senses and immeasurable in my mind. Finally, I awoke to find most of the Friends of the Scheriers gone from the clearing. The half dozen or so that remained bustled about, meticulously setting an assortment of foods on one end of the circle.

With an inexplicable need to see him, I asked, "Where is Cort?"

His voice appeared exactly as his image did, materializing out of thin air as he entered the clearing. He held a fruit which he broke over his knee. I recognized it from its description in Ludwig's journal. It was the fruit that the Scheriers brought to Elsa and Cunrad in celebration of their wedding.

As Ludwig had described it, it was "a flat round fruit. Its casing looked like baked bread, but was not edible. The inside was pure black with white seeds. The meat of the fruit was so soft that it was almost easier to drink it from the casing than to hold it in the hand. The black fruit was bland, but the seeds were sweet and piquant, releasing onto the palate almost more flavor than it can tolerate."

Cort set the Scherier fruit beside the other foods and said, "Please my Queen, permit me to share with you your first meal in your queendom."

"Of course, of course" I repeated several times until he gestured for me to sit on the ground in front of the offerings.

Rather than obeying, I decided to test my authority. I gestured in return for Cort to take his seat first. His eyes widened and he jumped to where my hand had ordered him, lifting his legs and landing on his round rear end. His bony tail bounced a few times in the grass behind him. I sat beside him and stared at him until he took a piece of fruit and handed it to me. I laughed. He laughed in response. We enjoyed a long, leisure meal alone together while others of his kind came and went with additions to the meal. Some of the foods were familiar, fruit-like or vegetable-like, but not exactly like anything I had known — a fruit that looked like a small apple in shape and color, but fuzzy like a peach and more like a grape in consistency, once I bit into it. Some of the foods were completely strange to me. In fact, I could not tell if they were breads or meats, plants or something else entirely. Although my palate was surprised by many of the flavors, it was never displeased. I enjoyed the meal thoroughly and I enjoyed the warm company.

During the meal, Cort and I spoke of trivial things, mostly comparing the foods to the comparable flavors from my world. As we sat digesting, the conversation slowly dipped into deeper topics. I was very curious about the seemingly magical properties of the clearing in the woods — how it is that sound cannot escape the inner trees, what it is that causes the light. I don't know if his answers were science or myth, but it all confused me, so I let it go.

I asked about his name. He told me that his kind do not have individual names, nor do they have a name for their species. He saw my Swan Knight armor when he first beheld me. He knew that the Scheriers were dear to the Swan Knights. That is why he referred to his kind as Friends of the Scheriers. They are indeed friends of the Scheriers. Cort knew the importance of telling me that immediately.

He had never considered a name for himself until I asked for it on the shore of the lake the day before. That is why he huddled with his friends and decided on his name, for my sake, because I asked for one.

"Why the name Cort?" I asked him.

He answered in a soft and humble voice, while his eyes looked up adoringly at me, "We thought it would please you."

He held his breath, and his stare, as still as a statue until I assured him that his name pleases me perfectly well.

We winded much of the day together, sitting in the circle. As we did, and my comfort with Cort came in balance with my burning curiosity, my questions reached for the many mysteries left unanswered by Ludwig's manuscript, slowly touching darker and darker topics. Eventually, I asked about the war — what had happened after Löwschock went through the portal, into Linderhof, how each species had fared, and how things stood then. Since I closed Ludwig's book and opened the portal, I had assumed that Löwschock died with Ludwig, or that he was dead at the bottom of some lake or another in southern Bavaria. Cort told me that the King of the Deep returned through the portal about thirty-five or forty years after he left to kill Ludwig.

"You mean he's here? Now?" I asked in obvious and terrified dismay.

"He stays mostly in the Waters these last several years. The war has been hard on him too."

I felt my blood freeze at the thought that Löwschock could be stalking me. My heels had dipped into the water of the Queen's Lake. He most likely knew I was in the Sweeter Realm.

"How did he get through? Who opened the portal?"

"He came through with a man clinched in his claws. Somehow, he found a child of Parsifal. He dragged the man to the portal point and used his Grail Blood to come home. Once through, he tossed the man aside and sped to the Waters."

"What happened to the man? Who was he?"

"He had little life in him when the Zweigwesens found him. Their medicines kept him alive for several months. His name was Hubert. He told the Zweigwesens that he was a visitor in the home of a Bavarian farmer named Gruber, not far from Munich. A monster attacked the farm, calling for Hubert by name. Poor Hubert watched as Löwschock slaughtered the entire household, before grabbing him with his claws and dragging him to Linderhof. Until he died, in a Zweigwesen healing center, in the heart of their capital, the man thought that he was in a nightmare. He begged himself to awaken. He had never heard of the portal or the Swan Knights, never imagined anything as terrible as the King of the Deep Waters. As the Zweigwesens nursed his body, his mind slipped away. His body had nearly recovered when his soul left, too tortured by what he had witnessed to live on."

I thought deeply and silently on what I had just heard, then said in a half-whisper, "The poor man didn't even know he had Grail Blood."

I thought about my father and brother, about all of the bearers of Grail Blood, spread throughout the world. Aside from the ability to open the portal, is there a difference between us and everybody else? The Ancient One used to say that the Swan Knights stand out from the rest like veins on the back of the hand. Who was Hubert? Was he a good man, a husband, a father, a brother? These are the questions that rang in my head for weeks after my breakfast with Cort.

Cort gave me updates on the condition of the Land and Shallow Waters, each species, each city, each homeland, to the best of his knowledge. Things were bleak. The war raged violently when Löwschock returned after being trapped in Bavaria for so long. He was furious to have returned without the Grail or any notion of where it was hidden. With Ludwig dead, he believed the entire Sweeter Realm to be his inheritance. He swept across the Land and Shallow Waters to claim it, to annex it into his own kingdom.

For about seventy years the violence continued. Löwschock seemed determined to kill every living creature in the Sweeter Realm. There was no old swan, no Queen, no Swan Knight to stand in his way. Cort admitted that Löwschock could have been defeated if the creatures of the Land and Shallow Waters had united. But such was not the way in the Sweeter Realm, and they had no leader under whom to unite. The sweet creatures fought bravely and made Löwschock and his army pay for every city they destroyed, every heart they stopped.

Terror was the King's primary weapon. He made sure that there were always surviving witnesses to his brutality. He made parents watch as their children were eaten in ceremonial meals. He maimed many, sending them to their homes brutally broken and disfigured. But the King fought unaware of the multitude of his enemies. The armies of the Deep were greatly outnumbered. When Löwschock realized that he did not have the numbers to win decisively, he retreated to the Deep with what remained of his armies.

That was at least twenty years before I came through the portal. That is how things sat. The creatures of the Land and Shallow Waters were too terrified to rally themselves or attempt a return to normalcy. They just survived, not rebuilding, not electing a new leader. They abandoned all that they had known for fear of disturbing the border to the Deep and recalling Löwschock's ambitious wrath. All assumed that the King was rebuilding his numbers for a final and decisive war. Their fear of that assumption crippled them.

As Cort told me the state of things, the full weight of my position as Queen settled upon me. I am the exact sort of disturbance that the creatures feared, the exact sort of thing to recall Löwschock from his uncertain, unsteady peace. Since my earliest days, I had fantasized about being a queen. But none of those dreams elicited the deep chills of horror that Cort's report injected into my marrow. As Cort described the brutality of Löwschock, with his signature bluntness, I never wanted my mother and father so badly. I wanted to return to Linderhof and find my parents calling for me, to run into their arms and put the whole Swan Knight business behind me, to go north with my family and walk the streets of our ancestral home with my father, to return to my house in Centennial, Colorado, go to high school, grow up with Birgit, graduate, marry, and have a predictable, settled, boring life. Even the little annoyances of my previous life seemed as sweet to me as my mother's homemade cheesecake.

As I thought of my family, of home and my life there, my sunken spirits must have been readily apparent to my new friends. I sat in a nightmarishly dreamy state while Friends of the Scheriers crawled on and around me. By the time Cort recovered my attention, my little friends had removed Elsa's armor from me. There I sat, in my worn and comfortable jeans and my soft, cotton shirt, as Verena Beth, the same old Verena Beth, not a knight and not a queen. In a tone of pungent compassion, Cort told me to sleep and dream of pleasant things.

In a single, low, and drawn out note, he sang, "Schlafen Sie gut" (Sleep well). The song appeared to beckon the others, who materialized before my eyes. They all joined Cort in a lullaby. The song began in German, but drifted in and out of my understanding. The notes, the words, their sweet voices, all seemed to gently stroke me and rub my temples and weigh my eyelids. I swear to this day that I began dreaming before I fell asleep. With the clear vision of my friends before me and their voices ringing clearly and consciously in my ears, I dreamed of pleasant things, but not of my home and my family, not of Birgit and my school. I dreamed of the Swan Knights, of Lohengrin and Elsa, of Otto II and Agnes, of Tannhäuser, Brunhilde, and The Ancient One. I dreamed of the magically seductive touch of the Brunnens and the sweet song of the Eulesängers. I flew on the Wühlenvogels and rode on the Unicorns.

In my dream, I rode to the top of a hill on a Unicorn with whom I was deeply in love. I was fully-clad in Elsa's armor. A white figure awaited me there, a soft but manly figure. He was too bright to look at for long. He was more feeling than visible. I dismounted the Unicorn and joined him. I closed my eyes in defense against his brightness. He wrapped his arms around me and kissed me tenderly on the nose. The kiss seemed to last for hours. It was broken by cheers. When I pulled away from him, the hill we were on was surrounded by the lovely creatures of the Land and Shallow Waters. They adored me and celebrated me. The bright man at my side whispered in my ear, but I could not hear him over the cheers of the crowd. I shook my head and gestured to him to repeat himself. He whispered again to me but I still could not understand him. I felt that his words would be the sweetest sentiments ever spoken to me, if only I could hear him clearly.

I shouted to him, "I can't understand you."

He leaned into me again. But before he could repeat himself, I awoke to Cort, inviting me into a new day.

"I am sorry," I told him, "I must have dozed off."

"Dozed off? You have slept through the afternoon and night and into the next morning."

I stood quickly and reached for the armor. It was already being handled by the Friends of the Scheriers, who were strapping it to me before I realized I was standing.

"I thought we might take you to the two Scheriers." Cort said.

I eagerly darted my eyes to the wall of the clearing, as if my vision could pierce its strange threshold by simply desiring to do so. Within a matter of seconds, I played out furious debates in my own mind, whether to leave the safety of the clearing to meet the Scheriers. In such cases, the imaginary voices in my head are all mine, bickering back and forth between my options. The voices in this debate were not mine, nor did it seem that I thought them before hearing them. I felt like an audience to a debate between others. It all felt detatched from me and out of my control — and it perplexed me and provoked me.

I eased my way to the center of the circle, trying to be as far from the surrounding forest as possible.

Cort prodded me for an answer to his question, "You know, the ones I told you about?"

22

Still dazed, I answered in confusion, "The two Scheriers? . . . Oh yes, the Scheriers who live near here, yes, please take me to them."

My curiosity faltered and was evicted by extreme discomfort at the strangeness of my surroundings and company, and a desperate desire to be home, with my family. My anxiety must have been flamboyantly demonstrated in my expression. Cort noticed, sat down, and suggested that we talk more. I obeyed with a sigh of relief as I sat beside him. It took hours of careful conversation on his part to coax the terror out of my heart with light subjects of talk and question about the most peaceful and mundane parts of my life. It worked well. His sweet voice and his authentic smile lightened my thoughts. By the time the day ended and we all set ourselves back into the sleeping positions of the previous two nights, Cort had long lost any traits of a stranger. We giggled and chatted like old friends. When it was time to sleep, the Friends of the Scheriers sang to me again.

When I rose in the morning to the same bustling circle of servants, eagerly placing my breakfast, the Sweeter Realm felt more like home, the silly little creatures more like family. None of the fears and morbid regrets of the day before hung on me. I had dreamed of home, of family and friends, but with my new friends seemlessly stitched to my old life. I dreamed that Cort was in my German class, that he lived with me and went to school with me each day. The warmth of familiarity and kinship that Cort wore in my dreams seemed to glow just as brightly from him when my eyes first caught him that morning.

Even now, I still believe that the dreams of the previous two nights were planted in my head by Cort and the lullaby of the Friends of the Scheriers who sang with him. It worked. I was strengthened, emboldened, and ready to wear my responsibilities to the Sweeter Realm like a crown, a thorny crown, if that be its nature. The comfort and safety of the circle clearing, that shield behind which I hid the day before, seemed drab and trite to me, like walking the halls of a school you have long graduated from. I was ready to leave it and meet the creatures I had read about, and to serve their interest in any way I could.

CHAPTER 3

First Thing's First

I WAS EAGER TO LEAVE THE CIRCLE, and Cort and his friends were eager to lead me out. We returned to the shore of the Queen's Lake and resumed my course of travel, away from the portal point, with the lake to our left and the woods to our right. I caught myself often staring across the lake, trying to reconcile the serene placidity of the surface with the furious chaos I knew dwelled beneath. Cort led the party, walking a few feet in front of me. The rest of them followed behind me. The four other Friends that I met on the beach were joined by thirty, the same smiling, singing faces that had eaten, slept, and spoken with me for two days in the circle clearing.

As we walked, the only sound was my own footsteps. Even they were much softer than I expected, sounding like little more than socked feet walking across a hardwood floor. Cort marched along proudly, glancing over his rounded shoulder from time to time, with a look of slight concern, until he saw that I still followed. Then he returned his focus forward with a wide smile.

We continued in this way for at least an hour, until the thick woods to our right opened into a sparsely wooded and slightly hilly landscape. We turned to our right and hiked up and down the small, low hills, away from the lake, until we reched what appeared to be our destination. In front of us was a small hill, or more of a large mound, only ten or twelve feet high, poking out from the ground and covered in grass. It had a sharp, vertical, dirt cliff on the side that faced us. We walked straight at the side of the mound. Sporadic rays of light shot down on us through the broken canopy of the sparse woods, shaking and vibrating from the high breeze above us. I stopped and watched Cort walk directly against the dirt wall. He stopped with his nose against it.

He turned to me and said, "Please wait here."

He walked forward and disappeared into the wall of the mound. The rest of us waited, as directed, until Cort stepped back through the wall and beckoned me forward. I stepped forward while the rest of the Friends of the Scheriers remained still. I turned to them inquisitively. They looked up at me excitingly but did not move.

I turned back to Cort when he called to me, "Please My Queen, come, meet the Scheriers."

This was all the coaxing I required. I walked toward the wall of the mound. As I got close, I realized that it was not a wall at all, but an entrance to a cave. Just as I was about to reach my hand forward to touch the wall of dirt, my eyes perceived the dimensions of the tunnel. My hesitant steps turned quickly confident and excited. I walked beside Cort as the tunnel sloped downward, turned to the right, and opened into a large, cozy, well lit room. The walls and ceiling were rounded, blending seamlessly into each other. It was all dirt, but made softer, cleaner, and more comfortable by the light. The light came from several rusty, dented, antique oil lamps, resting on flat-surfaced mounds of dirt, rising up from the floor to serve as chairs and tables. Standing on the table in the center of the room were two Scheriers. Ludwig's descriptions were not wonderfully vivid. The image in my head from the Swan Knight history was not exactly what stood before me.

They were flat-bodied, almost like the end of a cricket bat, or more like a Sunday paper still in the bag — long and rectangular. Their bodies were the length of my leg from knee to heel. They had thick, course, white hair that covered every part of them but their faces. Four thick, stubby legs held their flat bodies just a couple of inches off of the table. From the flat rectangle of their bodies protruded a thick neck, which rounded slightly from the flatness of the torso as it lifted their heads into the air. There was no hair on their heads and faces, just soft, pale skin. The cutest little ears protruded from their heads, soft and fleshy, and shaped exactly like human ears, only small, about the size of one knuckle of my thumb. Their faces came to a point, like a trout. Their eyes were deep black and their mouths were wide, in the form of a radiant smile at the sight of me. They had two small slits for nostrils, but no noses. I couldn't have said how I knew, for there were no designators of gender, but I was certain that one was male and the other female.

The Scheriers stared at me in astonishment.

"I told you." Cort boasted to them.

The male Scherier stuttered, "You . . . you are the Swan Knight!"

The other responded, "Of course she is. Look at her. Oh thank God, at last, the Swan Knights have returned."

They both exploded into questions about Ludwig and my relation to him. They kept firing their questions at me, not inhibited by my inability to answer. Finally, I threw Ludwig's journal beside them on the table. They stepped slowly away from it, as if afraid that it might awaken and bite them. I opened the book to the end and read to them Ludwig's decision to abdicate his throne, his plan to enter the portal and assume his duties as King of the Land and

Shallow Waters, Löwschock's appearance, the pursuit to Neuschwanstein, Ludwig's arrest and his decision to face Löwschock on the banks of Lake Starnberg. I closed the book and told them what history knew about the death of their Swan Knight and King. They cried heartily, as if they had wrestled with him the day before. The spirit of the company sank so low, I decided to revive them with further reading. I opened the book to Lohengrin's first introduction to the Scheriers. I read several of the happier passages from the Swan Knight history. As I read, the two Scheriers pulled themselves tighter into each other's embrace. The male began stroking the ear of the female and releasing a pleasant little sigh with each stroke.

The female snapped herself from her dreamy state and sharply scolded the male, "Rüdiger, stop that!"

She curled her head around to bury it beneath her belly. Muffled, through her body, she continued, "Not in front of the Swan Knight."

Rüdiger tugged at one of her front feet and answered, "Lina, she is a child of Elsa. She wears the armor that Lohengrin made."

Lina uncurled herself, thinking suddenly of the Scherier stone and its ability to soothe the soul. She walked to the edge of the table, right in front of me.

She reached her small hand forward and said, "The ore."

She stopped short of touching me until I invited her with a nod of my head. She stretched her hand forward and placed her palm flat against the armor over my belly.

She hummed a sweet and increasingly softened, "Hmmm."

Rüdiger crawled over the top of her and laid flat on her back. He placed his hand right above Lina's.

He harmonized her hum with a soft, "Ohhhhhhh."

As soon as Lina pulled her hand from the armor, she realized that Rüdiger was laying on her. She yelled at him. He pulled away from me and yelled back. The two of them started wrestling on the table. They fell onto the floor and continued wrestling, unfazed by the fall. The wrestling transitioned from aggressive to playful until they both stopped, let out a long sigh and began laughing together. They laughed until Cort cleared his throat and gestured to me.

"Uh, the Swan Knight," he said rather indignantly.

"Oh . . . yes . . . sorry . . . my Queen", the Scheriers alternated in sheepishly apologetic tones.

Cort interrupted them saying, "Rüdiger, Lina, this is Verena, Swan Knight and Queen of the Land and Shallow Waters."

The Scheriers lowered their chins, turned their heads to one side, closed their eyes, and touched one ear to the floor. I recognized this from Ludwig's description as the formal bow of the Scheriers. I returned their reverence with a low bow of my own. When I recovered my posture and looked to the Scheriers, they were in full flight, leaping at me. They hit me in the chest and knocked me to the floor, laughing and expressing such devoted affection, like they had known me since I was a baby. I was drawn in by their playfulness, their innocence, and an undeniable authenticity. Their laughter pulled giggles from me that were so instinctual and uncontrolled that they seemed more like echoes of the Scheriers' laughter than anything coming from me.

I wrestled around the floor with them, pulling their playfully scrambling bodies from my neck and shoulders, tugging on their legs, and rolling across the floor with one or both of them held tightly to my chest. Like only Scheriers can do, they infected me with their spirits — until Cort announced that he had to leave.

I stuttered in a frenzy, "What? You can't leave me. You can't. I order you to stay with me."

"Of course I am with you. I will serve you and the Land and Shallow Waters by announcing your arrival. The creatures need this news. You will bring us together. You will bring us back. Please allow me to serve you in this way. You have Lina and Rüdiger now."

I picked him up and kissed him on his pale green forehead. I was comforted by his loyalty and assurances.

"You are my first friend here," I whispered to him. "I cannot disappoint you." With shaky hesitation, I continued, "Do what you think is best."

I immediately regretted giving my consent. I put him down, knelt in front of him and bent low to give him another kiss. The Scheriers could tell how much he meant to me and how much he did not want to leave me. They praised Cort for his goodness, his friendship, and for bringing me to them. They assured him and me that they would guide me from there, to wherever I needed to go next. I trusted them. The Scheriers were dear to me before I set eyes on them. Ludwig endeared them to me as I sat in the boat of the Venus Grotto.

Cort looked solemnly at me and said, "The Sweeter Realm will celebrate the day you came through the portal. They will celebrate the day I met you near the lake . . . for thousands of years to come."

With a face that looked like it was about to erupt with tears, he dropped his head and gave me a slow and shallow

31

bow. He turned and left the room. I stared into the tunnel long after he was gone from view.

I only turned to the Scheriers when I heard Rüdiger say, "Now that you are here, we can rescue him."

Lina startled me with a sharp and hissing shush aimed at Rüdiger.

Keeping his head facing me, he turned his eyes to Lina, then back to me.

"Whom? Whom can we rescue?" I asked.

He looked tentatively at Lina again. She stared Rüdiger down with a threatening gaze.

Nevertheless, he answered, "The Ancient One, of course, with you here, we can mount a rescue."

I could not believe my ears. I was hesitant to allow myself to hope that The Ancient One could still be alive.

I lost my balance and stumbled backward, weak-kneed, until I hit my back against the wall. To the obvious effects of Rüdiger's news, Lina gave him a deep growl.

In almost unconscious disbelief, I asked, "The Ancient One? . . . the swan? . . . the teacher of the Swan Knights?"

Rüdiger responded to each with a nod of his head.

"I thought he was dead."

"He is dead, Your Majesty, long dead . . . God bless him." Lina responded to me while maintaining her scowl at Rüdiger. "Don't you go wasting the Queen's time with your rumors."

"They are more than rumors, Your Majesty," he defiantly retorted, stepping forward and raising his head in confident posture.

Lina and Rüdiger continued to argue, forgetting that I was there.

"Where did you hear that? Who told you that he is still alive?"

"My father told me. He heard it from the Old Digger, and he would know better than anyone."

"How would the Old Digger know better than a blind rock? I wouldn't trust him to lead me to his own cave."

The Scheriers argued in this way until Lina pushed Rüdiger and he pushed back, and the two began wrestling across the floor. I began to allow myself to consider the possibility. If there is a chance that The Ancient One is alive, captured and imprisoned somewhere, then we must set him free. I grew to love the swan as I sat in the shell-shaped boat and read his story. Each episode in the Swan Knight history endeared the old bird to me more. When Ludwig's journal reported his death, I could not read on for several minutes, until my eyes stopped welling with tears. Here I stood, in the Sweeter Realm, wearing the armor of his dear Elsa. I felt like I owed everything to him, like he had taught me since *I* was nine years old, like I was his First-in-Training, though I had never met him.

To the growling of the wrestling Scheriers, my mind mused on the possibility of meeting The Ancient One, of rescuing him. I pictured him in front of me, exactly as I had imagined him while I read the history, until Lina and Rüdiger, as one big, white, hairy, wrestling ball, rolled into my legs. They broke from each other and looked up to me. My newly erect posture and smiling face clearly spoke to them the thoughts in my head.

I looked down to them and proclaimed, "We must rescue him. We must try. Now, we must go now."

Lina, in a sympathetic and sorrowful tone, reminded me, "My Queen, there is no army, no unity. We are scattered and broken. Most are afraid to step into the light of day. How can we rescue The Ancient One — *IF* he lives — with nobody but a couple of Scheriers and a few dozen nomads? There is so much to do, so much you must do as Queen."

"No", I said sharply, startling the Scheriers, "First thing's first. We must have The Ancient One. I am lost without him. I need him if I am to . . . I need him."

My sternness muted Lina. She nodded in obedient deference.

I looked to Rüdiger and asked, "Where is he?"

"He is most certainly dead, my Queen and Swan Knight." Lina said in a formal tone, with her head turned downward, avoiding eye contact with me. "I do not want to waste the Swan Knight's time or risk her life in vain."

I looked to Rüdiger. My smiling excitement had turned to fierce resolve. I repeated my question to him, "Where is he?"

Rüdiger crawled up my leg and leapt from my waist to my chest.

With his feet on my belly and his left hand holding tightly to the swan figure on my right shoulder guard, he brought his pointed face right to mine and whispered, "He is not dead. He is in the Shallow Waters of the great lake, in the Queen's old jail."

Lina lifted her eyes from the floor, to look directly at me, and said, "If he was there, he is surely dead by now. Nobody would survive so long there, not under the cruel watch of Löwschock. He is dead. Besides, there are no more Shallow Waters. The entire lake belongs to Löwschock, so even if he is not dead . . ."

My posture slouched as I continued Lina's thought, just above a whisper, " . . . he might as well be."

Lina swirled her head and looked at me with a mixed expression of sympathy and relief.

I asked out loud, but more to myself than to the Scheriers, "If he is there and he is alive, is there any way to retrieve him?"

"Please don't try, my Queen," Lina begged. "Right now, we do not have The Ancient One. We have not had him for over a hundred years. But we have you. We cannot lose you now, now that you have finally come. That would break us once and for all."

I took a moment to consider the case. The Scheriers stared silently at me, waiting for my decision. The Ancient One was seen almost a century and a half earlier, dragged into the Waters by Löwschock. It is unlikely that he survived. He was most likely eaten in a ritualistic sacrifice. If he did survive, imprisoned in the Queen's Jail, in the Shallow Waters, the task of freeing him seemed impossible. The full weight of each of these considerations piled upon me as they entered my mind, until they buckled my knees and dropped me to the floor. I bit down hard on the inside of my cheeks until I realized the damage. I touched my hand to my mouth and pulled it back to reveal the blood that my teeth had drawn.

"Oh my sweet girl," Lina said. "Here, sit here and have a drink."

Rüdiger snapped at her, "Look what you've done. She was excited. Now she's bleeding."

Lina growled at Rüdiger and dove at him. They resumed their wrestling. I looked at the blood on my hand. It was the first time I had seen my own blood since I knew that it came from Parsifal, that it was Grail Blood, enhanced by the Cup of Christ. I stared at it. Everything else in the cave faded from my mind and vision, including the two wrestling Scheriers. As I stared at my reddened hand, I didn't see it as my blood. I saw it as Elsa's. I saw it as Hildemar's, as the blood of Ludwig the Crusader, and that of Otto II. I saw it as the same blood that flowed from the arrow wound to Adolf, inflicted by his uncle's assassin.

A surge of righteous duty flowed through me as I continued to stare at the blood on my hand and to draw in my mind a clear line between that enchanted blood and the heroes who shared it. Waves of chills lapped across my body in steady repition, as my mind connected the blood I saw with the stories I had read. That blood — my blood — was from Parsifal. Of that I became keenly perceptive. The Grail Blood in my hand had opened the portal, just as the Grail Blood had for centuries before me. For the first time, I felt as much a Wittelsbach as a Kessler, as much a daughter of the Portal Valley as of Centennial, Colorado. These feelings manifested themselves in the form of intense love for The Ancient One, as if all of the Swan Knights swimming in my veins shouted their love and gratitude for the venerable teacher simultaneously.

With teeth clinched tightly in determination, I stood sharply and firmly erect. This caught the Scheriers attention. They froze their feud as if a bright light shone harshly down onto them from my commitment.

Responding to the obvious change in me, Lina asked, "What is it, my Queen?"

"Come. We must gather creatures of the Shallow Waters, all who are loyal to The Ancient One and to the Queen."

As I mentioned the Queen, my thoughts were on Kandake, the Queen killed by Löwschock and buried at the portal point in Linderhof. It was only when the Scheriers responded by lowering their turned heads and touching an ear to the floor that I remembered that *I* was their Queen, at least they considered me so.

I continued with more authority in my voice, " . . . to me, those loyal to me and The Ancient One, and brave enough to risk their lives to free the swan, knowing he is likely dead."

I added that last part while looking at Lina, to vindicate her position, to show her that I was not ignoring her opinions and her concerns, rather weighing them fairly against what could be gained for us all by freeing The Ancient One.

36

She acknowledged me by responding, "We will all be brave enough if you are standing with us."

Lina insisted that I sit and receive the offer of a drink that she had made earlier.

My patience slowly overcame my desperate resolve, as Lina said to me, "After all these years, surely little could be lost if you sit with us and share a meal and some conversation before we begin. Eat, my Queen. Rest with us while we discuss our strategy."

I could not argue with her reasoning. She pulled something from a small jar, wadded it and handed it to me.

She instructed me to place it against the wound in my mouth, saying, "This came from the Zweigwesens. It will fix you right up."

I followed her instructions and felt an immediate warm tingle in my cheek. It spread to cover the entire right side of my face. I patted at the side of my head to determine if my hand would feel the same warmth. To my palm, my head was quite normal. When my mind returned from the spreading, tingling warmth, back to the wad of medicine in my mouth, I noticed that it was gone — dissolved or swallowed. I could not say which. In either case, the bleeding had stopped. The pain was gone. The warm tingling subsided and my cheek was quite normal, as if I had never bit myself.

I sat and ate. I got to know my new Scherier friends. I came to admire them even more than I did after reading Ludwig's journal. We ate and drank and plotted, all the while a knot remained in my stomach as I considered the wise and wonderful Ancient One, trapped for so long in a jail beneath the surface of the Queen's Lake. I loved him and my desperation to free him, to see him, gnawed at my insides. Despite the pull at my gut, I sat and listened to Rüdiger and Lina speaking passionately, received their gracious service, and watched their petty disagreements turn to rolling and spinning bouts of Scherier wrestling.

This went on well into the evening. As it did, each little experience of them drew my spirits more deeply into the Swan Knighthood and the many stories in which the Scheriers figured so prominently, stories that had adhered themselves so seamlessly to my identity that I could not easily differentiate between them and the stories of my own life. I began to feel like a Swan Knight, in the old lodge at Linderhof, keeping company with Scheriers like the earliest Swan Knights. This dissolved — one thin layer at a time — my homesickness. The company of Rüdiger and Lina became so pleasant and soothing, in such a strange and mystical way, that I gladly accepted their invitation to spend one night in their cave before embarking.

We talked well into the night. We never determined a time to sleep, never bid each other good-night. I must have dozed off in mid-conversation, in the middle of some funny story or some oath of devotion from the smiling and laughing lips of the Scheriers. With no idea how long I had slept, I awoke to a scene similar to that which saw me to sleep. The Scheriers were still telling stories and bustling about their cave. I'm not sure if they slept at all.

A serious and focused mood rose with the sun. Without outward coordination, our hearts were synchronized in their determination to rescue The Ancient One. Lina served us breakfast. I have no memory of the food. Our minds and conversations that morning were on the swan. Rüdiger bounced around with enough excitement for all three of us. Lina was weighed with worry. I was still swimming in my images of The Ancient One from the stories in Ludwig's book. We brought three hearts of very different shades to the table that morning. But they were united hearts — beating in unison and pumping blood in a unified direction.

CHAPTER 4

A Humble Beginning

AS I ATE AND PLANNED WITH THE SCHERIERS, and as our plan seemed increasingly reasonable, I grew impatient to begin — more than impatient — desperate, as if each passing second inflicted more pain on The Ancient One and decreased our chances of finding him alive. These were not reasonable fears and I knew it. But my reason could not convince my pulse to slow or my breath to deepen. It could not stop my legs from jigging and my eyes from shifting. As Rüdiger's contagious excitement and confidence spread to me, and our strategy unfolded, my spiritual irritation and impatience grew almost intolerable.

Our plan was sound. We would search every shallow lake, every pond, pool, and puddle for wet creatures loyal to the swan. He had been their King. He had been their teacher and friend. And the love of the creatures of the Land and Shallow Waters seemed to have an endless shelf-life. We also knew that Cort went before us, spreading news of the new Queen and the return of the Swan Knights. I trusted Lina and Rüdiger, and they spoke as if they knew every watery hole in the Land that might unfold a friend. It was the Shallow swimmers we would need. Only they could free The Ancient One from the Queen's Jail.

As my confidence grew, my heart and mind were already on the paths of the Sweeter Realm, moving from pond to pond. My eyes hurt from their desire to see the great swan. They darted randomly and unconsciously toward the tunnel to the surface. As I returned my eyes to my friends, I found Lina, standing on the table.

She walked slowly toward me and said in a grave tone, "You are ready to go, and we are ready when you are. But I beg you to go carefully and quietly. Let us pray that you can surround yourself with friends before Löwschock knows you are here. Calm yourself. Be like a breeze blowing through the Land, picking up dust. We are not ready for war. We would not win."

Rüdiger replied through a laugh, "What are you talking about? We have the Swan Knight."

His laughter transitioned abruptly to passionate, wide-eyed enthusiasm as he continued, "She has the blood of Otto I, the Red-Head. He defeated an entire army with his axe."

"Yes, my Love. I remember him well. But *she* does not have the Swan Knight training and she is in a strange new place."

I interrupted, "That is why I need The Ancient One. Who else would train me? And get me ready to . . ."

I wasn't sure what I would be trained to do, what was expected of me as Queen, what was a Swan Knight's duty on this side of the portal. I considered the inevitable prospect of facing Löwschock, as Ludwig did, which only made more desperate my desire for the swan. The thought sobered me from any intoxication of excitement.

I cupped Lina's pointed face with my palm, and I told her in a tone as grave as hers, "I'm scared to death. But I know what we have to do. I will do it as quietly and as carefully as possible. And I beg you for your guidance along the way."

This relieved her concerns enough for her to rest back on her legs and lift a slight smile to me. In that single, slight, sweet smile, commitment and adoration was expressed more vividly than the most eloquent poet could describe in twenty pages of writing. Rüdiger waddled beside Lina, crawled up onto her back, and laid his head between her shoulder blades. He released a long and blissful sigh that ended in a short, vocalized hum. Lina joined him with a short hum of her own.

Rüdiger drew a deep inhale and disrupted the soft moment with a sudden and awkwardly loud proclamation, "Alright, shall we get started?"

Lina and I looked at him, then looked at each other and smiled, both in agreement with Rüdiger, that there could be no good reason to delay the plan.

We all walked through the tunnel and exited through the side of the mound, where I had entered with Cort. Cort had been busy. As I emerged from the Scherier cave, several curious creatures waited to meet the new Swan Knight. They were spread haphazardly across my field of vision, some in clusters and some standing alone, some eagerly near the entrance to the cave, some shyly peering from behind trees.

I saw some of the creatures I had hoped to see — a couple of Zweigwesens ready to render first-aid to any scrapes or bruises I may have sustained in my first few days in the Sweeter Realm, three more Sheriers, climbing over and under each other with such frantic anticipation that I could hardly tell whose leg was whose, which little ears belonged to which set of arms. There were more Friends of the Scheriers, but not Cort. I saw small birds circling low, just inches off the ground, but they were not Eulesängers. I looked to the sky in hopes of glimpsing a Wühlenvogel. But a strange and dreadful instinct pushed my eyes quickly downward. I wanted to see the Brunnens, to experience the seductive charge of their beauty and the softness of their touch for myself. None were there at the entrance of the cave.

All eyes were on me, some fixed and frozen, some scanning me up and down, many breaking their stares as soon as my eyes met theirs. Suddenly, all heads turned to the distance, off to my right. My eyes followed theirs and I saw two figures round the side of the Scherier's mound. One was a Unicorn. He was light grey with a salt-and-pepper mane and beard. His horn was thicker than I had imagined the Unicorns' horns, thicker than Ludwig's sketch from Gessner's book. A faint hint of bluish-grey peeked through the brilliant white of the horn, from the deep recesses of the spiral. He walked beside a figure unlike anything described by Ludwig.

It was a man, neither young nor old, or rather both, covered in white feathers. His feathers rested camouflaged against his pale skin. He walked with erect posture upon two short, steeply bowed legs. He stood no taller than the breastbone of the Unicorn, four or five inches shorter than me. He was unclothed but covered almost entirely by his feathers, which were small and downy from the base of his neck, across his head and under his eyes. The rest of his face was bear, exposing his pale, almost sparkling and glowing white skin. His nose did not protrude from his face, but hung from its base between his eyes, a flat and loosely flapping piece of flesh that dangled just above his mouth, shaped like a flattened bell. When he turned his head quickly, it swayed back and forth, hitting against his bright cheeks. From the base of his neck through the rest of his body, his feathers altered in size and shape, large and course down his back, smaller and finer across his belly and chest, and shorter and more rounded on his arms and legs. His hands and feet were as fleshy as his face, with soft, downy feathers on the tops of his feet and the backs of his hands.

The white-feathered man had an obvious intimacy with the Unicorn. They walked toward me in a unified cadence, exchanging smiled glances at each other between their inquisitive stares at me. The creatures between us scurried out of their way, making a corridor for the two of them as they approached me. As they walked to within a few feet of me, I nearly fainted from the beauty of the Unicorn, sobered only by the almost goofy awkwardness of the feathered man's shape and dangling, flapping nose. I looked at the Unicorn and found myself unable to draw deep breaths. I focused my eyes on the tip of the horn, inviting the sacred communication that had tingled my imagination as I sat in the boat and read the Swan Knight history. My eyes begged the Unicorn to lower his head and touch my chest with the tip. Instead, he raised his head further, tilted his head slightly to his right and eyed me up and down with his left eye.

The feathered man said, "I am Felix and I am at the disposal of you, Verena, Queen and Swan Knight."

Rüdiger, ever-proud of all his connections, boasted, "Felix is a Federman. The Federmensch live in the Nomadic Belt."

I shyly looked down to the Unicorn's front hooves and spoke through a widening smile that I could not restrict, "Cort has been busy, hasn't he?"

Felix replied, "Oh yes. He must be halfway to Brunnen land by now."

The Unicorn added, "He speaks very highly of you, so highly in fact, that many do not believe him. They do not believe you are here, yet here you are."

He let out a quick huff, ruffling his shaggy beard, eyed me head to heel, and added, "It has been a long time since I have felt that armor riding upon my back."

"You . . . you knew Elsa?"

"I knew her. I served her. I loved her. And here you are, through the portal and wearing her armor. Whose child are you? Where do you connect to the line of Parsifal?"

"I don't know."

He slowly lowered his horn. Time seemed to slow as I eagerly invited the connection ritual. It seemed to take hours for the tip of the horn to point directly at my chest. I leaned forward but did not make contact with the tip. Felix placed his right elbow on the base of the horn and draped his forearm toward the point. He slowly wrapped his fingers into the deep recesses of the spirals and closed his eyes. I looked to the tip of the horn and watched it creep slowly forward until it touched the armor, in the center of my chest, just beneath my collarbones. Nothing that I had read or envisioned, seen, heard or imagined, could have prepared me for the experience.

I felt probed, as if everything beneath the walls of my skin was being painstakingly evaluated. I felt my thoughts being pulled from my head, my feelings, hopes, fears, and desires exiting my body through the point of connection. When the shock of the sensation wore off, I consciously released all that was me, allowing it to flow freely from me, through the horn. The Unicorn's eyes remained open, peering at my lower half through his long eyelashes. I knew this as I gained flashes of his thoughts. Felix obviously shared in the Unicorn's experience. His eyes remained closed as his head swayed back and forth. His lips parted slightly as my deepest secrets flowed through the horn and down his arm, into his head.

A surge of thought flowed in my direction. I did not know what to make of the sensation until images of the Unicorn's life began to fill me from toe to scalp. My mind tried to sift through the Unicorn's thoughts for something of his feathered companion. But nothing from Felix came through. All I saw of him was through the thoughts of the Unicorn. I saw hundreds of years of friendship between the two of them, millions of bright and intimate memories dumped into me through the small point below my collarbones.

I saw Elsa through the memorialized images in the Unicorn's mind. I felt her ride upon my back as I relived those moments of his life. I felt Hildemar run her hand down my neck. I heard the hearty laugh and pure singing voice of Otto II. I felt the worry and anger as the Unicorn recalled Tannhäuser's flight through the portal. I cried as I experienced the midnight departure of the company of creatures from Linderhof to the Black Forest. This Unicorn was left behind and bitterly missed the friends he saw through the portal that night. He was chosen to go to the Black Forest, but committed himself instead to the protection of the portal. He thought that it was what Elsa would have wanted from him.

Some of the thoughts and memories seemed directed to me through the connection. Many seemed to pour into my head on their own, through some backdoor, not through the horn. It felt like I was connected to the Unicorn for centuries, like I had lived a dozen lifetimes, with the full memories of each, by the time he pulled his horn from my chest. His name is Acheriel, and he had been dear to many of the Swan Knights, and many of his own kind. He had been dear to The Ancient One.

When he raised his head to make eye contact with me, our gaze went so deeply into each other's eyes that the connection of the horn felt unbroken. I turned my head to Felix. He stood with his mouth wide open, staring at me and barely breathing.

Acheriel interrupted the silent awkwardness, informing me, "You connect to the line of Parsifal through Else, the daughter of Stefan, Count of Zweibrücken, son of King Rupert."

I responded in a thoughtful trance, "The Counts of Zweibrücken . . . my dear Ludwig."

"Yes."

Reclaiming myself, I asked, "You could see that — where I came from?"

"I saw much, and much remains hidden in that stubborn Wittelsbach blood of yours."

I demurely turned away from him to set my eyes back on Felix, whose astonished gaze and shallow breaths had not changed.

I gave him an inquisitive look and asked, "What is it?"

His adoring glare was only broken by a few blinks of his eyes, until I repeated my question.

He closed his gaping mouth, swallowed a couple of times and said in a hoarse whisper, unlike the smooth voice he spoke with earlier, "You are beaut . . . you're beautiful . . . I mean to say that there is a magnificence to you that you do not yet understand, a purity and a fierce nobility that somehow hides beneath your—"

Acheriel interrupted sharply, "Felix! Not now. Surely the Swan Knight must be eager to begin."

In our connection, Acheriel had clearly seen the most pungent thought on my agitated mind — rescuing the swan.

Rüdiger interjected, "She is going to rescue The Ancient One!"

The proclamation unsettled the air around us all. There was a strange mix of excitement, fear, and uneasiness, bouncing off of the gasps and gestures of the creatures gathered around us.

Acheriel looked at me and asked, "Is she? Is this what she wishes?"

"More than anything," I answered. "I would not know where to begin without him. And . . . and he will have to train me . . . and . . ."

I was clearly searching for excuses for my decision.

Acheriel relieved me, interrupting, "If that is the Queen's decision . . ."

He looked down to Lina and raised one bushy eyebrow.

"It is," Lina answered with surprising confidence and authority.

Acheriel nodded slowly and said, "We are your servants, my Knight and Queen. We will rescue The Ancient One, if the rumors are true. Tell us the plan."

I did not have a chance to answer. Rüdiger climbed up the back of my left leg and mounted himself upon my right shoulder, staring straight into Acheriel's eyes. In language and gestures so dramatic that he nearly fell from my shoulder several times, he described our plan to rally the creatures from the Shallow Waters and bring them to the Queen's Lake.

Acheriel thought for a few seconds, then announced, "I can think of no amendments. Let us get to the business of gathering allies from the Shallows."

He dropped to his front knees, lowering his shoulders to the height of my hips, and said, "May I please carry the Grail Blood again?"

It took a few seconds for me to realize what he was asking.

When it dawned upon me, I stuttered, "Wha. . oh, me, right, yes."

I stood beside him and awkwardly lifted one leg, repeating quietly, "Um . . . um . . ."

I heard Felix's voice behind me, stronger and recovered, "Allow me, my Queen."

Before I realized that my feet were off the ground, I was seated on Acheriel's back. I looked to Felix, whose hands were just withdrawing from my leg and side. He had hoisted me like I was nothing, like I was Brunhilde in a great mood. But behind the power, I felt a gentle adoration that made my head swim. As he looked up at me, it dizzied me and stopped my breath for several seconds, until the wave passed when he turned away.

Acheriel stood fully erect, lifting me high above the creatures around me. I was sitting on a Unicorn. The realization of that fact provided the final brushstroke of the picture in my mind. I was really there, in the Sweeter Realm, wearing ancient and magical armor, mounted upon a mythical beast of such magnificent beauty. Acheriel felt like a throne to me — the Queen's throne — my throne. The powerful sense of Providential destiny stiffened my spine. One week earlier, I sat at my desk in Centennial Colorado, doodling pictures of unicorns, a mythological creature I did not believe in. The confidence swelling my mind — coming from the faith of the creatures around me, the effects of the Scherier ore, and probably a bit of psychological shock — was a *naïve* confidence, with no realistic notion of what I faced. The realistic fears and doubt I had felt earlier were entirely gone.

I ran my right hand down the side of Acheriel's neck and said, "Let's go."

"Where do you wish to go, Verena, Queen of the Land and Shallow Waters?"

I looked to Rüdiger.

He said, "She has appointed me guide. I know every pool, pond, and puddle from here to Eineklaue."

Acheriel asked, "Are there any impediments?"

Lina answered, "Fear . . . Terror . . . The creatures of the Shallow Waters have been mercilessly brutalized."

She looked at Rüdiger, to me, then to Acheriel and continued, "Finding them is not the challenge. Rallying them from their hiding places will be difficult enough.

Convincing them to charge into the Queen's Lake will take some doing."

Many low murmurs filled the trees around us, as each attendee whispered their doubts to those nearest them. A single voice pierced them all, stabbing through them before muting them entirely, beginning low and increasing in volume. It was Felix.

In a cemented stare into my eyes, he spoke directly to me, "You will rally them. We must present you to them, to them all, in a manner to revive their faith and their zealous devotion."

Acheriel nodded his head as he said quietly, under his breath, "Yes, yes."

Felix continued, "We will form a procession and parade you in gallant, valorous splendor past the pools and ponds that hide the Shallow creatures. They will see you. Oh, they will see you and hear your voice, and be reminded of better days. Their hearts will have no choice. With one glance at your . . . at your . . ."

He choked on his words, cleared his throat, let out a quick sigh, pressed his right fingertips firmly against his lips, and stared at me. He dropped his hands to his side and swirled his head subtly.

He struggled to continue, "They will see your . . . your radiance, your majesty . . . your . . ." He drew a sharp inhale, and continued slowly, " . . . your beauty."

My flattered ears consumed each word directly from his lips, reddening my complection. My head wanted to turn away from him in embarrassment, but my eyes would not allow it.

Felix seemed to regather himself, standing more rigidly and nearly lifting me off of Acheriel with his eyes, saying, "They *will* follow you, my Queen."

The absolute homage and obedient adoration coming from him was so unique to me, so unlike anything I had ever experienced — magnified by the surroundings and the events that brought me there — that I was paralyzed. The only part of me not stone-still was the water welling in my eyes as I stared at Felix. He broke the stare when he lowered his head in a reverent bow to me. Only then did I realize that I was not breathing. My sudden gasp was loud and dramatic, an obvious reaction to Felix. The creatures around me noticed it. They noticed the almost tangibly dense air between our gazes.

I shook it off and covered it up, scanning the creatures around me and asking them, "We will need help. Are any of you willing to come with us?"

Acheriel huffed and chuckled and answered for them, "That is why they are here. They are yours. We are *all* yours."

The creatures began mumbling in agreement, "That's right." "He's right." "That's why we are here." "We are yours."

They grew louder, more confident and more exuberant in the exclamations of devotion, until they grew to a clamor that was more shouting than speaking. The shouting slowly soothed and blended until the entire company around me, different creatures of different shapes and sizes, united in a single, pure note, holding it in flawless pitch. It grew quieter until it hushed entirely and gave way to absolute silence. After a few seconds of silent pause, one by one, the sound of inhales and exhales broke the silence and the scene returned to normal.

Acheriel carried me away from the Scherier cave, around to the slope under which it was dug, to the top of the mound. There were still trees around us, but every inch of the mound was lit with sunlight, as if the light passed unhindered through the trunks, branches, and leaves of the scattered trees. The entire company of creatures followed. Acheriel closed his eyes and held his head high, pointing his bearded chin straight upward, so that his horn ran beside my head. He hummed a low tone for several seconds. He lowered his head and told me that his family will be joining us soon.

I don't know how much time passed. I sat on Acheriel atop the hill that held the Scherier cave beneath its shell; and the company of creatures milled about in hushed conversations. I alternated between scanning the excited faces around me and clinching my eyes tightly in thoughtful attempts to savor the moment and secure it firmly in my memory. I opened my eyes to a blinding brightness to my right. It was a Unicorn, entirely white. The beard, the mane, the hooves, even the deep recesses of the horn were dazzling white. It was rubbing its horn against the horn of Acheriel.

"This is Prische," he said with a joyful giggle in his voice. "She will be your ride."

I stared at her in a stupor. Her whiteness made her look like pure light, without physical form. Thoughtlessly, I reached for her, as if to verify that she was real. She stepped toward me and touched her neck against my outstretched hand. She was quite solid, quite real. My very slow stroke turned to a slight squeeze of my hand, then a few gently pats, all performed in the same mindless trance.

Acheriel snapped me back to sound consciousness, "Yes, she is real. I had the same reaction when *I* first saw her."

Just as before, Felix lifted me off of Acheriel and onto Prische before I realized he was near me. When I turned to him, he was backing slowly from me with a widening smile and widening eyes. I looked at the creatures around us. They all stared with fixed eyes and many gaping mouths, all except Lina, who climbed up Prische, carrying my helmet. She handed me the helmet and I put it on my head to the accompaniment of scattered oohs and ahhs. Acheriel backed slowly away from me, nodding his head, very subtly at first, almost unnoticeably, but increasing as he stepped backward, then rearing up and landing with a forceful huff, ruffling his shaggy beard.

Then he stood perfectly still, staring at me on Prische's back, as he said, "The pure blackness of your armor against Prische's whiteness is the most breathtaking sight my old eyes have ever beheld. Felix is correct, young knight. They *will* follow you."

Rüdiger wanted everybody to remember that he and I shared a special relationship, that *he* told me that The Ancient One still lives, that *he* has been appointed to lead the expedition. He gathered everybody's attention and announced that *his* Queen is ready to begin, that *he* is ready to bring me to the pools and ponds that hold the creatures of the Shallows. He asked the others if they would not mind kindly filing in behind me while he leads the way.

"Wait." The pure voice of Felix rang out from behind me. "We must stage the procession precisely, to present her to perfect advantage."

Rüdiger acknowledged, "Yes, yes, that's right."

Felix stepped back and began pointing and directing the creatures into the order of the procession. As he did, another Unicorn joined. He gave a quick horn rub to Prische and Acheriel, then took his place near the front of the procession. Felix meticulously placed each member of our party. Once he was done, they stood two by two, in formal pageantry, with Prische and me in the middle. Felix stood beside Prische's rear, left hip, in a position subserviently supportive to me. He called to Rüdiger, asking him to please lead us to the creatures of the Shallows. Rüdiger and Lina stood side by side, at the front of the procession. Lina began walking carefully, darting her eyes in all directions. Rüdiger waddled in the most regally triumphant march that a Scherier body can manage. We all paraded behind them.

We took several steps forward before Felix halted the procession with a yell.

Staring at my left leg, he said, "We cannot begin like this."

He stepped up to me and rubbed the white feathers of his right upper arm against my left leg, wiping some thick, tar-like smudge from my armor, just beneath my knee. When he stepped away from me and resumed his position at my side, the black smudge he had wiped from me clung to his white feathers. An ugly, black stain ran across his upper arm, just above his elbow, demonstratively contrasted against his white skin and feathers. I didn't know whether to thank him or pity him. He caught me staring at the black stain on his feathers. I must have worn my thoughts clearly on my face.

He gently lifted a slight smile and said to me, "Oh, don't worry. I assure you my . . . my Queen, they will not be looking at me."

He turned his face forward and signaled Rüdiger to proceed. We walked down the slope above the Scherier cave, into a more densely wooded patch of forest. We seemed to be moving aimlessly. There were no pools or ponds, no other signs of life. I began to feel ridiculous parading around in such pageantry, for nobody to see. In fact, there was little to draw my attention; so I caught myself staring at the dirty smudge that tarnished and defaced the otherwise gleaming whiteness of Felix's arm.

I wondered if Rüdiger knew where he was leading us, until we intersected with a path and took a hard right turn onto it. The path led us into thicker woods. As we walked, the canopy of the forest closed over us and it darkened the path. I had just reached forward to stroke Prische's white mane when she abruptly halted. I looked ahead and saw

Rüdiger gazing into a puddle no larger than the turkey platter my mother used on Thanksgiving.

He tapped his fingers on the edge of the puddle and yelled, "Come out! The Swan Knights have returned. Come, meet Verena, the Queen."

I let out a heavy sigh, quite telling of my confused frustration. I drummed my fingers on the side of my helmet. Rüdiger stood against the puddle, excitedly repeating his proclamation.

I shook my head and whispered, "Seriously?"

It was loud enough to elicit some uncomfortable fidgeting from the creatures around me. Prische stood still and erect, eagerly awaiting what would come out of the little puddle. This aroused my curiosity and silenced my frustration. Rüdiger stopped yelling into the puddle. He stood with his nose just above the water for at least a full and silent minute. He began to slowly back away. The entire procession took a few steps backward in response. I strained my eyes to see if anything came out of the puddle. After waiting like that for several awkwardly long moments, I saw ripples in the water. Rüdiger stood his flat body high on his legs. He held his hand up, as if holding something in his palm.

He said, "You see? Isn't she magnificent?"

"Isn't who magnificent?" I asked myself.

Then I realized he was not talking to me. He was talking about me — talking to whatever small thing he held in his hand.

He dropped his hand and returned to all fours. I saw a flicker of blue in the dark air between us. As I strained my focus, I saw a tiny creature flying toward me. It was no longer than two inches. Its body was tubular, with one large eye at the front end. It had wings that connected to its tubular body from end to end. The wings were long, but not wide. Its wingspan was no more than an inch and a half, but the wings fluttered quickly and carried the tiny creature to a landing on the tip of Prische's nose. Prische forced out a squealing greeting that the little creature seemed to understand. In response, it rubbed itself against the Unicorn's nose. It walked up Prische's face, on hair-thin legs, until it nestled into her mane, staring at me with its one large eye. I stared back and raised an awkward wave with one hand. Thin lids closed over its bulging eye. It let out a squeal of its own, like Prische's greeting only infinitely fainter. Fifteen more of the little creatures emerged from the puddle and flew toward me.

They landed all over Prische's face and head. Some flew past me, to Felix's outstretched hand. One landed on my leg. I offered my palm and it climbed into my hand. I held the creature a few inches from my nose. If eyes can truly smile, this strange little creature did — a wide, delighted smile with its one bulging eye. Its wings continued to slowly flap as I held it. Hints of florescent green rippled across the blue of its wings. I could not imagine these little creatures defeating the knobby-headed serpent or the King of the Deep. But I was so surprised to find such beauty in such a small, strange little creature, hiding in a puddle on the side of a path in the woods, that I thought nothing of the daunting prospects ahead, or of the inauspicious beginning of my attempt to gather creatures to rescue The Ancient One. A deep and immense intelligence shone from the creature's single eye, captivating me, as if my own eyes were listening for it to speak to them.

Lina shouted from the front of the procession, "You can speak to her. She understands German. We call them Pfützeschilfs."

I gave the creature an awkward but cordial greeting and asked her if they would be willing to join us in gathering wet creatures to rescue The Ancient One from the Queen's Jail. She answered me in the same faint squeal. An undeniable excitement in her rapid waving wings and affectionate rub against my palm spoke clearly to me what her squeal did not. They were with us. It was a humble beginning to our plans. Sixteen little swimmers, no longer than my middle finger, would not rescue the swan. But it was a start, and it encouraged me to press on. I was inspired by their bravery. And I was embarrassed by my own doubts in the dutiful little Scherier who called my new friends from their puddle.

These many years later, the Sweeter Realm is not as peculiar to me as it was that day. But it is just as wondrous. There is still immense beauty beneath the most mundane puddles. My introduction to the Pfützeschilfs was one of those moments in my life that altered me to the core. I began that day to expect wonderful things at every turn.

CHAPTER 5

Voices of the Past

WE MOVED ON PAST THE PUDDLE, with our new companions traveling on the heads, shoulders, and backs of the party. We marched along the same path, following Lina and Rüdiger, who halted our progress each time their bickering turned into an impromptu wrestling match. I rode on Prische with a Pfützeschilf always on me. They were very curious about me and took turns examining me closely. They spoke, their same faint squealing, but try as I could to discern any recognizable syllable, it did not resemble language to me. I spoke to them in German, and they understood, reacting in accordance to my words.

The experience with the puddle affected me. Every few minutes, my eyes darted to the ground to make certain we were not walking through another colony of fragile little creatures.

Prische sensed my thoughts, as Unicorns do. She said, "You may relax, Your Majesty, I will not trample any of your subjects."

That simple reassurance settled my nerves and allowed my mind to return to the task of absorbing the truth of my new life.

We passed many puddles, smaller and larger than the hiding place of the Pfützeschilfs. At each, I expected to stop and meet new friends. But we walked right past them. I turned and watched as they went by. The forest grew thicker and thinner. The path became narrower and wider. Finally, it ended as it opened to a clear valley that dropped sharply in front of us. The forest around the path had grown so thick that very little light made it to the floor. It was like night. I had no idea where the sun was in the sky until the woods and path ended at the rim of the valley. The warm orange of a brilliant sunset washed the entire basin in front of us. Either from fear or excitement or the degree of the slope into the low valley, the entire procession ran from the end of the path, out of the thick forest, to the center of the clear valley.

We broke formation and huddled tightly. Acheriel declared that we would remain there for the night. I was deeply unsettled by the declaration. The valley was a deep basin. There was no shelter, no trees or rocks or cover of any kind.

"Here?" I asked. "We're sleeping here?"

I thought about the secret and snug circle clearing where I stayed with Cort and the Friends of the Scheriers. I longed for it, or something like it. I had never felt so vulnerable, so exposed. I ran my eyes quickly over the rim of the basin, waiting to see fierce enemies barreling over the horizon toward us.

Felix, silent and stealthy as always, appeared to my right side and took my hand, startling me. I jumped in fear as I snapped my head to face him. My heart was soothed by the sight of his awkward face, but soothed all the more by his gentle rub of the top of my hand as it laid against my leg. He lifted my hand and held it in both of his.

He told me, "No creatures of the Deep will find us here. They do not come here. That is why we chose this place to camp."

He told me an ancient story from the earliest pages of Sweeter Realm lore. The valley basin, the very point upon which we stood, was once the bottom of a lake, deep and rich and teeming with life. According to the legends of the Waters, a giant Land monster once rambled across the Sweeter Realm, eating the creatures of the Waters, clearing one lake after another, consuming every living thing within. The swimmers of the Sweeter Realm retreated from his path until all remaining, in the entire Sweeter Realm, had gathered into the lake where we stood. The giant began to drink the lake. The swimmers gathered at the deep center as the water receded. The giant drank the entire lake and ate every creature within. No wet creatures survived. The first age of the Waters came to an end.

A single weed poked from the center of the empty lake-bottom. After the giant had eaten the last swimmer, he plucked the weed and threw it into his mouth. His stomach was filled with every wet creature in the entire Sweeter Realm. It could fit no more. The weed got caught in his throat. The giant choked on the weed. He fell flat on his back and died. The weed rooted itself to the back of the dead giant's throat. It grew until it consumed the entire monster. It grew tall and beautiful, wearing a single scale from each wet breed eaten by the giant. But the weed grew thirsty at the bottom of the empty lakebed. It began to spread in all directions, in search of water, carrying the scales of the dead swimmers with it. It spread across the Sweeter Realm until it touched every body of water. It deposited the scales in the lakes, pools, and ponds, where they grew into new creatures and dawned the second age of the Waters.

Felix added, "This basin is sacred to the swimmers, from the Deep and the Shallow Waters. They revere it, but it terrifies them. The creatures of the Deep will not chase us here."

After a moment of pondering the myth, I thought about the Pfützeschilfs. They are creatures of the Waters. Are they not terrified of the basin? By the time Felix finished the story, the sun was quite low, barely peeking over the horizon, and the Pfützeschilfs are small and difficult to see. My queenly instincts overcame me and I walked from Felix, through the company, looking for my funny, one-eyed companions. They were nowhere to be seen. I walked up to Acheriel and stroked the side of his neck. I noticed that his shaggy beard and mane rustled in the breeze — only there was no breeze. I looked closer and saw the Pfützeschilfs, hiding in Acheriel's hair, shivering and terrified. I knew just what they needed. They needed the Scherier ore — my armor. I held both palms out toward the Unicorn's face. The Pfützeschilfs left the shelter of the Unicorn hair for the protection of their Queen. I laid down, flat on my back, and allowed the Pfützeschilfs to spread out across my body, laying on the armor. They were soothed by the magical properties of the Scherier ore. They nestled upon it as I sang to them a lullaby that my mother used to sing to me. It was in English and none in the company understood the words.

I looked straight to the emerging stars above as I repeated the lullaby, over and over, until I knew my little swimmers were asleep. I turned my head to both sides and saw the rest of the party, gathered near me, scooting nearer and nearer to me, and dropping off to sleep, in comfort and faith, as I sang. I continued singing until I neither saw nor heard any movement in the camp. I stopped my song and closed my eyes, praying that I would deserve the faith placed in me, that I was not leading these kind creatures to disappointment and death.

I prayed for their welfare, "Please do not let me be the ruin of these creatures."

Through the almost silent whisper of my prayers, I heard voices. Acheriel and Felix were talking quietly about how the Pfützeschilfs came to me, how I soothed them to sleep with my armor and my song.

My heart pounded with humble pride and gratitude when I heard Acheriel say, "You are right, Felix. She will be the salvation of us all."

Still staring straight upward, I strained my ears to hear more. I wanted to hear more. I needed to. No more words were passed between Acheriel and Felix that night. They fell asleep with the others. Acheriel's words seemed to echo off of the stars above.

"You are right, Felix. She will be the salvation of us all" were the words that sang *me* to sleep, as they bounced from my head to my heart and back again.

I dreamed that night, ordinary dreams about my ordinary life in Colorado. I dreamed that my alarm was going off in my bedroom, but I could not find it to turn it off. I grew nervous and agitated as I searched for the clock, afraid that my parents would be angered by the noise. I awoke with the Pfützeschilfs gathered tightly on my chest, speaking to me, each single, bulging eye looking directly at my face. As I surfaced from dreaming to awake, I realized that the sound of the alarm in my dream was the squealing song of the Pfützeschilfs. The agitation of the dream evaporated quickly. The song, although not particularly pleasant to the ear, was joyous and hopeful. It was loving and grateful — and they sang it directly to me. I wanted to kiss them all, but feared frightening them or hurting them.

I simply smiled and said, "Good morning."

I saw a heart-warming sense of hope in their expressive eyes, as they responded to my words with rapid, energetic blinking. One at a time, they flew from my chest to the Unicorns and other creatures.

I sat up to find, at my feet, a selection of foods, similar to those I had enjoyed with Cort. I still don't understand where the food came from. My fellow travelers carried no packs or bags. They carried nothing in their hands as we walked from the Scherier cave to the dry lake basin. But there it was, a meal fit for a queen, served and set elegantly at my feet. Nobody ate with me. None of them ate at all, at least not while I ate. I sat up, looked at the food, and said "Thank you" in every direction, not knowing exactly who had served me. I offered some to several of my companions as they walked by me. All declined. I knelt in front of the food and began nibbling tentatively. Several Friends of the Scheriers watched, wringing their hands in anticipation of my approval. The food was delicious. My tentative nibbling turned to ferocious devouring. The Friends of the Scheriers smiled and joined in the bustle of the company.

While I ate, several conversations were being held, between various groups of various breeds. The Unicorns knelt on all four knees, in a perfect row, with their heads lowered until their horns were just a few inches from the ground. They appeared to be in intense prayer or meditation. Lina and Rüdiger sat facing each other, their long flat bodies perfectly erect. They were involved in some ritualistic and seemingly choreographed hand slapping, similar to a human child's "Patty-Cake", only the ritual was not playful. It seemed quite serious. They alternated between looking intently into each other's eyes and closing their eyes and lifting their pointed faces to the sky, while continuing their hand-slapping ritual with perfect precision.

I finished my food, leaving before me the casings and peels of the various fruits. I didn't know what was expected of me. Was I to clean up after myself? If so, where would I dispose of the mess? Was I to be waited upon like I was in the circle clearing? I sat in front of my breakfast mess and looked around me, waiting for some indication of what I was supposed to do. As I ran my eyes over the creatures around me, while they were deeply involved in their morning routines, I forgot about expectations, about my dreams and my fears. I only saw the beauty of my companions. There was an undeniable simplicity about their lives. But behind the simplicity was intense intelligence and a degree of goodness, of honest morality that struck me with awe.

At that moment, as I admired my friends, I would not have given them up for anything. Even if a portal to my own bedroom had opened in front of me, with every wish I had ever wished waiting to greet me to an ideal life on the other side, away from these creatures, away from the Sweeter Realm, I would not have passed through it. Oh, I missed my family terribly. But the purity of my companions hooked me, mind and spirit. In that moment, I committed whatever remained of my life to the service of those sweet and noble creatures, as their Queen, their Swan Knight, as whatever they needed me to be.

I began to feel like one of them, to see the lake basin, the hills around us, the dark path we had walked, the circle clearing, even the dark and mysterious Deep Waters, as my home. In a flash, my thoughts returned to my breakfast mess. I looked to the ground in front of me. All casings and peels were gone, even the bits of food I had dropped on my lap were wiped clear. A few feet in front of me stood three Friends of the Scheriers, in a low bow, holding their positions, with the exception of tiny, quick glances up to me to see if I was pleased. I thanked them and held my hands out, inviting an embrace. They rose from their low bow and stared at me.

I curled my finger in invitation and said, "Come on. Let me thank you."

The one in the middle took a small step toward me, looked to her left and right, at the others, then back at me. She lifted a wide smile and jumped into my arms. The other two laughed and jumped onto my lap. I fell to my back, wrapped my arms around them all and rolled back and forth. I closed my eyes and savored the warmth of love coming from my three friends. When I opened my eyes, Rüdiger's face was right against mine, nose to pointy face. He stood near the top of my head, looking down at me, so he appeared upside down. He smiled and jumped on the pile. Lina followed him. I don't think they meant to, but Rüdiger and Lina knocked all of the Friends of the Scheriers off of me. They tugged on my arms and pushed against my face, enticing me, or rather taunting me to wrestle. I rolled around the ground with them, pulling on their arms and legs, squeezing them against my face, and placing quick occasional kisses on their backs. They laughed such hearty and authentic laughs that they pulled almost identical laughs from me. We sounded like three laughing Scheriers.

The wrestling slowed and came to a stop, with me on my back, Rüdiger on my belly, and Lina on my chest. I looked around us and saw that every creature in attendance stood in a circle around us. They smiled. Some shed tears. Some hummed soft, contented tones.

Lina drew my attention back to her, as she held my chin in her little hand and said to me, "Verena, oh my dear Swan Knight, thank you for coming back to us. We have been so lost, so scared without you."

Her words drew me instantly from the light mood I was enjoying. The crushing weight of my responsibility to them, and of the perils we faced together, fell on me so hard that not even Elsa's armor could warm my spirits. I winced and contorted my face, trying to hide the swell of emotion that overcame me. I failed. The creatures around me were so much more adept than I — the strength and skills of the Unicorns, the knowledge of the Zweigwesens, even the little Scheriers and Friends of the Scheriers could dig caves and create safe circle-clearings and find food.

"What could I possibly do for them?" I thought loudly behind my silent lips.

I felt like a fraud. I felt utterly unbefitting the honors, faith, and services they had given me. I sat up and erupted into full, shaking sobs, wetting poor Lina with my tears. She wiped them from me lovingly. I was afraid to look up at the creatures around me. I did not think that the sight of their Queen in such broken fear and such fragile confidence would hold their spirits high. I could not help it. I lifted my head and looked around me. They all stood where they had, still wearing their wide smiles and looks of adoration. I was confused. Acheriel walked up to me and lowered his horn to me. I grabbed the horn and he lifted me to my feet.

While I held his horn, Acheriel spoke to me through the silent connection of the Unicorn horn, "Your sobs have not frightened them. They have encouraged them. Your tears show them how much you love them and how seriously you take your sacred post, as a child of Parsifal and as the Queen of the Land and Shallow Waters."

I thought to him, "But what if I can't help them?"

The thought was interrupted by a surge of mind and emotion, coming to me, from Acheriel, through the horn, the sentiments of which cannot be put into words. But they were thoughts of faith in me and faith in the Grail Blood, faith in God and faith in the brave love of my subjects. The surge sternly hushed my doubts and exiled them to some deep corner of my mind. My vision, which had been blurred by my welling tears, cleared in an instant. I thought about Irmengard, as I pulled Acheriel's horn to my mouth and sank my upper lip into a recess in his spirals, holding a long and grateful kiss.

As I thought of Irmengard, the great-great grandmother of Else of Zweibrücken, where I connect to the Grail Blood, I strongly felt her maternal embrace. As I kissed the horn of a Unicorn, the way she did when she entered the Black Forest, I became a Swan Knight. I felt the plight of Rudolf I, of his son, Adolf, Irmengard's husband. I thought about Irmengard's twin boys, slaughtered in the attack on Einigkeitstadt, the Wühlenvogel city in the Black Forest. I thought about The Ancient One, carrying the boys' bodies through the forest — not with the vague and hazy image that was in my head as I read that part of the Swan Knight history, but with the clarity of first-hand memory. I felt a proper Swan Knight's love for the great teacher and my desire to rescue him swelled inside of me, into an absolute necessity, mandated by the very blood in my veins.

All of these evolving thoughts flowed into Acheriel while my lips remained embracing the spiraling horn. I ended the embrace with a quiet and subtle kiss as I withdrew my mouth from the horn. I looked into Acheriel's face. My own emotions and determination reflected back to me through his committed eyes. He had felt everything I had just thought.

He said to me, "The Grail Blood flows zealously through you, young Swan Knight. Irmengard was dear to us. You are dearer. Your Grail Blood flowed through the portal to us, guided by The Holy Redeemer himself. Trust your blood. Trust those who have passed it through the centuries to you. Have faith, my Queen. Your greatness is just beginning to blossom."

I believed him. That is, I decided to try to believe him. Still soaking in the pool of what I had just experienced, how could I not? I was surged with such ambitious and confident energy that I felt like my skin was trying to march up the side of the lake basin and continue our quest without me. The voices of every Swan Knight shouted from my blood and echoed off the walls of my veins.

I still failed to envision exactly how I could be of service to the strong, intelligent, magnificent creatures around me, what heroic deed I could perform that they could not. But I decided to believe Acheriel and I allowed his words to caress and soothe my worried mind, "Your Greatness is just beginning to blossom." The abilities that would be discovered and fostered in me over the next couple of years were at that time unfathomable to me. But Acheriel said that they would come and I was in no position to disagree.

I looked around me and announced to the statue-still creatures, "We have work to do. Let's go."

They all scrambled and bustled into the formation that Felix had meticulously set the day before. Once the procession was in order, Rüdiger looked back to me from the front of the line. I nodded to him, and he and Lina began our march from the bottom of the basin, toward the green, sparsely-wooded hills beyond.

CHAPTER 6

Connections and Collections

THE CARAVAN IMMERGED FROM THE RIM of the dry lake basin, exposing to my eyes a hilly, grassy landscape with few trees. The grass stood almost belly-high to the Unicorns, burying the Scheriers and Friends of the Scheriers. The only indication of Lina and Rüdiger was the wave of displaced grass at the front of the procession. The two Zweigwesens, who stood no taller than my armpits when I stood beside them, barely poked their heads above the grass, just in front of Prische and Acheriel, until one climbed atop the other. The brownish-orange hair from the legs of one blended seamlessly with that on the head and shoulders of the other. I could not tell where one Zweigwesen ended and the other began. They appeared as one tall, thin branch, towering out of the tall grass.

My heart warmed as I was cuddled with familiarity. By that point, the stories of Ludwig's journal felt like my stories. Each reminder of the Swan Knight history brought me a sense of home. My natural, unintentional smile grew so wide that it began to hurt, as I stared at the Zweigwesen connection, uniting my imagination with my senses. I drifted into deep imaginative memory, recalling the concert for the newlyweds, Otto and Agnes, and laying the sight before me against the backdrop of Albert's battle and the large Zweigwesen tree formation.

I had noticed something in my two Zweigwesen companions. I noticed it as soon as I saw them outside of the Scherier cave. They were more serious than the others. Deep commitment radiated from there course, bark-like hair. They did not stare at me like the others did, as if they had already known me. They marched impatiently and were restless when we were not in motion. Of all of the creatures in Ludwig's journal, the Scheriers, the Unicorns, and the Zweigwesens were all that I had met at that point. I knew the Scheriers, especially Lina and Rüdiger. I laughed with them. I wrestled with them. I connected deeply with Unicorns. Although I only rode on two and had only met three, I felt the strength, the support, and the loyalty of the entire Unicorn collective.

I did not know my two Zweigwesens and I wanted desperately to speak to them of the Swan Knight history, of Milli and the medical manuscript, of young Elsa and the toy Unicorn, and of Albert's Battle. But I found their focus intimidating. Perhaps they were at the portal that Christmas night, with Nethe and Lohengrin, in front of the dancing ribbons and lamp-lit tree. The image of that night pushed my emotions over the edge and I let out a half-giggle, half-cry. Without touching me with her horn, Prische knew. She galloped ahead, to the right of the Zweigwesens, until I was almost face to face with the top one. He turned to face me. His companion beneath continued to march forward on the heels of the Friends of the Scheriers in front of her.

I stared at the Zweigwesen, inviting his return glance. He could not have missed the horn and head of Prische, out in front of us. But he continued to look forward.

I said, "Hello, my friend."

He turned quickly and sharply to face me. My widening eyes must have betrayed my alarm. He just stared at me.

The woody flesh around his eyes began to swell. The slight features of his face betrayed deep sadness. When his eyes had swelled nearly shut, he dropped his head and let out a long, low, vocalized sigh. My compassion threw my arms invitingly toward him without consulting my mind. No sooner did my arms stretch to the limits of my reach, than Prische lowered and twisted her head to the side, and lifted the bottom Zweigwesen from the ground in mid-step with her horn.

The two broke their seamless formation. The lower one sat on the horn and the upper one jumped to sit straddling Prische's shoulders, facing me. I wrapped one arm around him and extended my other arm to the one still holding to the horn. She cartwheeled down the Unicorn's neck and landed in a straddle directly behind her companion. I wrapped my arms around them both.

I burned with questions for them, but did not know how or when to disengage from the embrace and spark conversation. They wrapped their arms so tightly around me, not seeming to want to let go. I resolved to hold them until they released the embrace, determining that my questions would keep until then. So, I allowed my hands to settle some points of curiosity. Their hair, though course and appearing to the eye to be as rough as bark, was surprisingly soft. I caught myself subconsciously stroking them and twisting their hair between my thumb and index finger.

During the morning ride, I discovered that Ludwig's journal tucked snuggly beneath the bottom of my breastplate, freeing both hands. I took advantage, pinching and massaging the Zweigwesen hair with both hands. They responded from time to time, startling me by rolling their long, hard, splintery fingers against the back of my armor. I thought about the duality of those fingers, how they have killed and how they have healed. I think now with immeasurable gratitude of how useful Zweigwesen fingers have been to me, in both respects.

The conversation with the Zweigwesens had to wait. In the heart of the embrace, we rounded the top of a low and shallow hill.

The procession stopped and Rüdiger drew my attention to a small lake in front of us with a hardy, "Ha ha, there it is, right where I left it."

He ran ahead, ignoring Lina's sarcastic response, "Oh yes, right where *you* left it."

The Zweigwesens released me and dismounted Prische and stood beside her, lovingly running their deadly fingers across the side of the Unicorn.

The lake, though small, no larger than a soccer field, looked deep and filled my imagination with the horrors of what could wait beneath the surface. I reached forward to Rüdiger, who was barreling toward the shore alone. Felix settled my nerves.

He said, "This is a shallow lake. A dozen Zweigwesens, standing one atop the next, in the deepest center, would poke from the surface for all to see."

Acheriel added, "Many from the Shallow Waters of the Queen's Lake settled here when the war began, those fortunate enough to escape the angry, jealous claws of Löwschock."

Lina contributed her doubts to the conversation, "It will not be easy to convince them to return to the Queen's Lake. They suffered greatly there."

Prische took a few steps toward the lake and said, "Let them see you, my dear, with your hair flowing from beneath Elsa's helmet. You will remind them of the stories that The Ancient One and the Queen used to tell them of the early Swan Knights. Nothing could endear them to the mission better than seeing you, the Swan Knight and Queen."

I put the helmet on as I thought to myself, "I hope that Cort has come through here and prepared them for me." I dreaded having to explain who I am and why they should risk their lives to follow me.

I submitted to Prische, acknowledging the fact with a few pats on her neck. She carried me down to within twenty feet of the shore. Rüdiger stood between us and the water, alternating his excited glances between me and the surface of the lake. As nervous as I was to meet the creatures of the Waters, I could not help but be entertained watching Rüdiger grow impatient. He ran several steps toward the shore, tapped his fingers on the dirt, and ran several steps back to me. He glanced at me apologetically, then repeated the routine several times.

Finally, he ran to the very edge of the water, looked back at me and said, "Give me a moment, lovely Queen."

He ran into the water and disappeared beneath the surface. I didn't know Scheriers could swim. He had been under the surface for several minutes before I began to worry for him. In my fear, I seized a painful grip on Prische's mane. She huffed and shook her head until I let go and apologized. I looked back up the hill at the rest of the party. None seemed concerned. I asked Prische to call for the Pfützeschilfs and ask them to go in after him. She squealed for them and they responded, landing on me and on the Unicorn. I waited for Prische to give the order.

She reminded me, "You are their Queen. They await your request."

I asked them to look for Rüdiger and bring him back. They jumped into the air from where they had landed, flew over the edge of the lake and dropped straight down into the water. I watched eagerly for a few seconds before I saw Rüdiger's head poke through the surface, near the center of the lake. He shouted something, but I could not hear him well enough to understand before his head dropped under the surface again. Small ripples on the surface ran toward me from the spot where Rüdiger had appeared. The ripples grew as they traveled toward the shore. They were clearly not caused by a single, flat Scherier.

The Pfützeschilfs immerged first, crawling onto the shore on their hair-thin legs, then flying onto Prische and me. Rüdiger followed, waddling onto the beach with his signature triumphant march. Around twenty creatures followed him, immerging simultaneously, side by side. They were the length of my arm from fingertip to elbow. I recognized them immediately from the drawing in Ludwig's book. They were the Vogelkrötes, those Shallow Water creatures that Conrad Gessner saw from the shore, who enticed him to enter the water. They looked exactly like the drawing, from the pointy, fleshy cap on their heads to the long, spiny tails. The familiarity of their appearance comforted me, along with the knowledge that they were not friends of the Deep. They had been residents of the Shallow Waters of the Queen's Lake, and loyal subjects of Kandake.

What I did not know at the time is how social they were and how well-informed the Queen had kept them of the goings-on in Linderhof. They knew well of the Swan Knights. They knew of Elsa and her armor. They knew of my dear Ludwig. As soon as their long tails cleared the water, the entire line of them froze at the sight of me, mounted high on a brilliantly white Unicorn. It was nice to see that some things are universal, on both sides of the portal. Their astonished reaction was very human. Their eyes widened and their jaws hung open.

Their looks of wonder settled into slow, tentative steps toward me and whispered comments to Rüdiger, who stood between me and the approaching line of Vogelkrötes.

I couldn't understand the low whispers, but Rüdiger responded to them with, "That is what I tried to tell you" and "Of course she is. She is Verena, our Queen", with bits of self-promotion added in, like, "That is why I brought her to your lake."

Rüdiger's words and my eager smile seemed to warm them. Their slow and tentative walk sped as their tails began to wag. Their rigid paces loosened as they rushed toward me. They surrounded Prische and looked up to me, waiting for me to speak. I introduced myself. They all began shouting their introductions, in cordial German, but simultaneously and with excited speed and high-pitched voices, so that I could only respond personally to a few of them.

I patted Prische and commented to her, "Well, this is progress. There are many of them, and they are larger than my finger."

One of the larger Vogelkrötes answered in a silky-smooth, tenor voice, "And you have the Schildbüffels. They are big."

Answering while trying to piece the German words together in my mind's eye, I stuttered back, "The . . . Schild . . . büffels?"

"Yes," he answered, "Bechtold and Hildemar."

Rüdiger interjected, "Named after the children of Elsa!"

I had just formed my lips into a circle, beginning the word "who", when my eyes were drawn to the broken surface of the lake in front of me, broken by two large creatures. Two bulbous, shelled creatures walked slowly from the edge of the water. They had the shell of a turtle, but rounder and bulkier. They were roughly the length of our kitchen table back home, which seats four. Four thick, stubby legs extended downward from the shell, with crusty, black, cloven hooves. Their heads looked like a buffalo, thick and wide, but with the spiraling horns of a ram. They walked at a turtle's pace toward me.

I thought about how slow they were, and how quick and furious the rescue would have to be.

Acheriel, who had stealthily walked up beside me, responded to my silent thoughts, "They are among the fastest creatures in the Waters, and their shells cannot be broken by anything known in the Sweeter Realm. These are the exact sort of allies you seek."

"I wish we had more than two of them."

"Many more still live in the Shallows of the Queen's Lake. They burrow into the lake bed. Perhaps these friends can draw them from their hiding, for the rescue of one they honor and adore."

"They know The Ancient One?" I asked.

"All swimmers of the Shallow Waters know him and love him. Whether killed or abducted, the swan was on the Queen's Lake that day for one reason . . . to tend to the needs of the Shallow swimmers. He knew how they suffered and his sacrifice was for their sake."

My army of swimmers was growing, with promises of many more to join. My confidence swelled on the shore of that small lake. Rüdiger told me that there were many more lakes and ponds like that one, holding the exiled subjects of the Queen. I could almost feel The Ancient One's embrace — hear his voice. Those gentle musings were interrupted by the greeting of the Schildbüffels. In the prejudice of my closed mind, I expected their address to be low and slow. They spoke quickly and in a pitch not much lower than the Zweigwesens'. They began by telling me how much they adored their old Queen, Kandake, a fellow creature of the Shallow Waters.

I understood. I did not expect to replace her. Nevertheless, as they continued a long, animated, adoring chain of her merits, I began to feel like a fake. The Swan Knight history is filled with stories of her goodness, her wisdom, and her magnificent beauty. There I sat, high upon a Unicorn, bearing Kandake's title, wearing the armor of the greatest Swan Knight. Perhaps "fake" is the wrong word. I felt like an accident.

I listened to the praise of one predecessor, while itching to rescue another. My mind got lost in the sea of praise for Kandake. Prische shook and stirred me back to the moment.

I looked down to the Schildbüffels in time to hear Hildemar say, "As true as she was, as pure and as noble, as lovely and majestic, you are much lovelier. Thank God you are here now, when we need you the most."

I felt the color rush to my face in a fevered blush, as the surrounding party spoke their concurrence. I did not know what strength and beauty they saw in me, but the sincerity and the intelligence in their eyes convinced me that they were right. They knew Kandake, and they held me to her level.

I only wondered, "How well do they know me? If they knew me thoroughly, would their faith falter?"

The Unicorns seemed to see right through me, and they still had faith. That thought, above all, dampened my doubts.

The rest of the procession joined us by the lakeside in time to add their praise to the others. It was overwhelming, almost embarrassing. I was never a child who lacked self-esteem. But the lakeside rally humbled me tremendously. The zeal of the party was formidable. I would not have wanted to face them in battle.

I didn't want the enthusiasm to settle before we resumed our mission. So, I ordered the assembly of the procession. Felix placed the Vogelkrötes and the Schildbüffels into their place in the formation and I yielded the reigns to my two faithful Scheriers. Lina and Rüdiger led us along the shore, to the other side of the lake, and up a hill beyond.

We meandered for hours through low-rolling, grassy hills. I wondered why our path was so indirect, and I asked Felix.

"Rüdiger is keeping us as far as possible from the Deep Waters," he replied calmly.

"The Deep Waters?" I questioned. "I thought the Deep was in the Queen's Lake."

"If only they were so limited. There are many deep lakes. Each contains a border between the Shallow and the Deep, between your realm and Löwschock's. Sadly, those borders are no longer stable, no longer peaceful. The black of the Deep has pushed upwards in most lakes. It has entirely consumed some. Rüdiger knows the state of things. He will guide us well."

Felix's eyes had lost none of their adoration. I felt safe while his gaze was so fixed on me. He was never far from me and I knew that he would risk his life for mine. But that was not the sourse of the comfort. There was something else — his eyes gave me a glimpse into a bright future, not one I could see or describe, with clear images and thoughts, but one I could feel with a warm sense of satisfied well-being. The feeling left me when his gaze left me, and found me again when I caught him staring at me again.

Felix's eyes and their aura were ripped from me with the excited shout of Rüdiger. The procession stopped with the halt of our two Scherier guides. They ran from the head of the line to join me. Lina jumped into Felix's arms and Rüdiger climbed up Prische's leg and stood erect on her head, hugging her horn with both arms.

"Over that hill," he began while releasing the horn with his right hand and pointing toward the front of the procession, "is a nice lake, a fun lake with many friends of mine. They too believe in the swan. We have often talked about it. Come! Meet my friends."

"No, no, no, no!" Lina protested as she leapt from Felix's arms, onto my lap, facing her lover. "You know that lake has Deep Waters. Verena in not going near it. She can wait right here on Prische."

Rüdiger sighed and rolled his eyes, then said, "Ohhh, the Deep is small in this lake. You know that. There are many more of ours than of his. Let's bring the Queen. She will rally their hearts."

Lina retorted, "If they are such good friends of yours, they will come at your request. We have no need to take Verena any closer."

Rüdiger looked at me, then to Felix and back to me. I widened my eyes, shrugged my shoulders, and tilted my head, as if to say, "Leave me out of this argument."

Rüdiger continued shifting his eyes between Felix and me until Lina drew his attention to her with a low growl. He recoiled and hid as much of himself as possible behind Prische's horn.

"I will go get my friends," he said with a sudden surge of confidence. "Verena, you stay here and keep Lina out of trouble."

Lina sat high on my lap and folded her arms in self-congratulations. Prische lowered her head and Rüdiger ran down her face, dismounted her, and ran over the low hill in front of us.

Rüdiger was not twenty seconds from our sight when we heard his cry. There were no words, nothing to the specifics of his dismay. He only cried, loudly, with mournful anguish. Instinctively and in concert, the entire company ran over the hill. Felix, with his short, bowed legs, kept up beside Prische with his right hand holding my left ankle. Within seconds we were atop the low hill. Directly in front of us was a large pond. The late afternoon sun was bright behind us, but it did not shine off of the water. A few inches of water around the edge was clear.

Beyond that, the water was black. It did not look like water at all. And it absorbed the sun, rather than reflecting it.

Acheriel was the first to break the astonished trances of the company, speaking over Rüdiger's continuing sobs, "The Shallows of this lake are gone, consumed by the Deep Waters."

Rüdiger stood at the water's edge, dipping one finger into the thin ring of clear water, then retracting it quickly. He repeated this ritual, taking a few quick steps right and left before tentavively testing the water again.

"Rüdiger, you get away from there!" Lina shouted in the loudest whisper her little throat could manage.

Rüdiger backed slowly from the water, still staring at it. His walk looked struggled, not as if he tried to stay but was pushed away by fear — more like he tried to leave but was held by the love of his wet friends. I was so fixated on Rüdiger that I did not immediately realize that I too moved slowly from the water. Prische and the entire company scooted away from the pond like a teenager sneaking out of the house in the middle of the night.

When we reached the top of the hill behind us, we turned and ran quickly, not in regal procession, but scattered in bunches, until we were several small and rolling hills from the pond. We settled in a tight circle in a small and shallow valley. Felix stood firmly at Prische's left side, with his right hand resting on my lower back and his feathered chest pressed against my leg. It was only through the panic in my friends, there in that shallow valley, that I first realized their fear of Löwschock and the monsters of the Deep.

Acheriel broke the tension, being the first to speak, "Well, we were bound to see such things. We knew this was happening. We knew this would not be easy."

I believe he intended to continue. But he was interrupted by the cry of Rüdiger.

"They are dead! My friends are all dead!"

I looked around for the distraught little Scherier. He and Lina were on the edge of our circle. He was curled in a ball and Lina wrapped herself around him. I could not tell whose hair was whose. They looked like half of a large, white, hairy walnut shell, mounding up from the grass.

"You don't know they're dead," Lina's voice rose from the mound of hair. "With any luck, they have rescued the swan already."

Rüdiger's head emerged from the pile of hair and Lina peeled herself slowly from him, as he said defeatedly, "You saw the Deep Water, black, cold, and furious as ever. My friends are dead."

"Lina is right." Prische interjected. "Your swimmers could have escaped to any of a dozen pools and ponds near here."

Rüdiger looked at Prische as she spoke, but turned his eyes to me when she finished. He stared at me, waiting for me to add my opinion. I didn't know what to say. I had no strong feelings one way or the other. And the terror exuding from the entire company still held me in shock. I lifted my eyebrows and a subtle smile to Rüdiger, and gave him a slight nod. It was enough for him. His spirits recovered in an instant, as if I had guaranteed his friends' safety.

Fully, however inaccurately, relieved of his fears, Rüdiger asked Felix to reassemble the procession.

"We have many more friends to gather," he said to Felix, but in a voice intended for all to hear. "And perhaps we'll find my missing friends along the way."

As his enthusiasm rose to its peak, the rest of us pulled ourselves up to meet him half-way. I caught myself dreamily watching Felix meticulously place the company into order. My eyes fixed on the black mark on his arm. I saw nothing but the stained feathers. But through them, I saw all of him. All of his self-denying, protective and loyal goodness seemed fully represented in those soiled feathers.

The reformed procession, with all of its pageantry, was not for the rallying of swimmers. It was for the rallying of our own hearts. We sought no more Waters that day. In fact, our path of travel was guided only by a desire to avoid water. We found a nice hill, large enough to hold us all and high enough to give us a commanding view of the area. With about an hour of daylight still ahead of us, we clung to that hill. It gave us a good defensive position and we were loathed to leave it.

We camped there for the night. I don't think the Unicorns slept. They positioned themselves in sentry posts along the perimeter of the company. I don't think Felix slept either. He sat beside me when I laid down on the soft grass. Each time I stirred from sleep, I looked to him. He sat or he stood in his place beside me, sometimes staring at me, sometimes straight to the sky. As the sun set and the sky grew as black as the pond, I felt surrounded by danger. My restless mind learned a new level of terror that night. I saw the black water myself, witnessed the fear it elicited in the company, especially the swimmers. What little sleep I got was no relief from the fear.

I dreamed of water that night, dark, cold water — no serpents, no monsters, just cold, black water, creeping from the Deep pond, up the hills between us, encircling our hill and my company. I awoke several times from my dreams of the black water, only to stare up at the black sky, equally scared of it, as if Löwschock himself could crawl out of the air above me and drop onto us.

CHAPTER 7

Perilous Passageways

AFTER HOURS OF RESTLESS DOZING in and out of nightmares, I slept soundly through the end of the night, waking to a bright morning. The sun washed our hill and every hill around us. It dispelled the sense of dread that had tightened and loosened its pulsing grip on my throat for most of the night. It was hard to tell if the brightness in the air came from the sun or from the rebounded spirits of the creatures in our party. Such resilient things they are. By the time my eyes adjusted to the new day's light, my friends were bustling about the hill with no signs of the previous day's sorrows.

Rüdiger was very excited to show me the next spot on our mission to find friendly swimmers. It was a small pond surrounded and protected by a wide band of thick forest. He used to visit it when he was younger. It was a common place to visit, outside of the Nomadic Belt, just inside of the Zweigwesen homeland. The pond was a popular gathering place because of the Shallow Water creatures who called it their home. They are called Glühenchor. They are pack creatures, never found alone. The Glühenchor are light blue or green, soft and fleshy, without scales, oval-shaped, like a rugby ball, and about the same size. They have a long, thin neck, no thicker than my thumb. The neck

83

is a little longer than the body. At the end of the neck is a tiny head, round and flat, like the lid of a two-liter soda bottle. The eyes are on top of the head, the mouth underneath.

Every evening, at sunset, the Glühenchor create a humming sound with an organ in the middle of their bodies. It is not singing. It sounds more like muted violins. As the sound organ of one of them senses the musical vibrations of the others, the Glühenchor begin to glow. The glow can be seen rising from beneath the surface along with the rising musical tones. Visitors from all over the Sweeter Realm used to gather around the pond to watch the evening concert, to hear the music and watch the pond light up. Intense and shifting harmonies, simultaneously soothing and stimulating, captivated the creatures gathered around the pond. If enough visitors gathered, and the Glühenchor felt like it, they would rise to the surface and send their music and their light bouncing off of the nearby trees. When a visitor steps into the water during the song, the musical vibrations travel through the body and the light awakens the skin and seems to be absorbed through the pores. It is a divine experience.

The pond held many wonderful memories for Rüdiger. He took Lina there when they were young. He could not wait to show it to me. We bypassed closer bodies of Shallow Waters so that we could arrive at the pond before the music began. Rüdiger wanted to introduce me to the Glühenchor personally.

"Oh, they will give their best show yet, when they know they are giving it to the Queen," he assured me.

We arrived at the band of forest before midday. But the woods were so thick that the company could only remain in procession by following a twisting maze of a path, which winded and circled through the forest, around the pond, until it came to an abrupt end, surprising the eyes with the sudden appearance of water. We worked our way slowly through the maze, arriving at the pond in the late afternoon, having paused and rested a few times during the slow walk along the path. There was no sign of the Glühenchor. This did not surprise anyone in the company. They gathered around the pond and waited patiently, having no expectation of seeing them before scheduled. The day passed on with casual excitement; and the sun fell low in the sky.

Lively conversations lit the air as the sunlight slowly faded. A Vogelkröte commented about the lateness, drawing every eye to the pond. Rüdiger and Lina ran to the edge and called for the musical creatures. The pond was still.

"Come, my Queen, step into the water. They will sing for you. Feel the music climb up your legs."

My curiosity was certainly piqued. I hopped to my feet and stepped into the pond.

I turned back and asked, "How deep is this pond?"

Someone in the party shouted back, "It is no deeper than your shoulders."

I took a few steps farther, until the water was just above my knees. A few of the Vogelkrötes followed me and jumped into the pond. Some Pfützeschilfs flew from the shaggy hair of the Unicorns and dove into the center of the pond. One of the other Scheriers waddled to the edge, sniffed the water, and then dove in. I did not feel comfortable walking farther toward the center. When I strained my eyes to see into the water, I caught glimpses of the Scherier and the Vogelkrötes darting playfully beneath the surface, but saw no Glühenchor or any sign of them.

Without any warning, a fountain of pitch-black water shot straight upward, high above my head, from the center of the pond. Although liquid, the water landed on us like hail — hard, cold, and painful. The temperature of the pond plummeted instantly. It chilled my body and spirit, and dropped me to my knees so that the water was higher than my waist. I struggled to get back to my feet and I walked out of the pond. Once I had, I looked around and saw that none of the creatures who had entered the pond with me had come out. The Unicorns had run to the water's edge with expressions of concern. The Zweigwesens grabbed me by the arms and held me on my feet while inspecting me for injury. Other creatures in our company cowered behind each other. It was clear from their reaction that this incident was both unexpected and something to be feared. My mind went to those of us still in the pond.

I ran a few steps back into the water, which by that point had returned to stillness, but remained black and ice-cold. I fought the chilling effect of the water, while I tried to see through the opaque surface any sign of my friends. Ripples broke the surface, followed by splashes. The splashes pushed against my legs the twisted and broken bodies of several Pfützeschilfs. My heart broke as I reached down and lifted one from the water. Terror still showed in its frozen, lifeless, bulgy eye. I looked back to the center of the pond. Amid the chaotic splashes, the violently broken body of the Scherier floated to the surface, followed by the mutilated Vogelkrötes.

The water suddenly calmed, leaving the bodies of my friends, twisted almost beyond recognition, sitting upon the glass-smooth surface like hors d' oeuvres on a platter. My instincts arrested my reason and I pushed toward the center of the pond to retrieve the bodies of my friends. The floating white body of the Scherier contrasted intensely with the blackness of the water. As I reached for him, the light of the evening sunset disappeared in an instant. I was under the water and sinking quickly, being pulled by a cold, black current, sucking me downward.

I have no idea how far downward I was pulled, but it was deep. The pond seemed to have no bottom. I swam as frantically as I could against the current, which seemed to have a conscious grip on me. But I continued to sink downward, unable to slow my descent in the slightest. For the first time in my life, I thought I was going to die. I was so convinced that I would never make it back to the surface, that I almost stopped struggling. I felt hands grab me and fins slap at me, and a hard, crusty body brush against me. I stopped paddling upward.

I thought about Conrad Gessner and his abduction. I tried to brace my spirits to be yanked deeper still by whatever had grabbed me. I was pulled, but not downward. The hands lifted me upward, toward the surface. The fins and paddles lifted me from beneath. Something large and hard pushed me upward in quick and frantic bursts. When I breached the surface, and I was no longer blinded by the blackness of the water, I saw the figures I had felt. It was some Vogelkrötes, a Schildbüffel, and Felix. They rushed me to the shore, onto the land, and dragged me several yards away from the pond.

Once the shock of my assumed death faded enough to allow the flow of emotion, I curled into a ball and cried. I had no notion of my surroundings until I felt like I was in motion. I opened my eyes and saw trees moving past me. It was only then that I realized that I was curled in Felix's arms and he was carrying me quickly away from the pond. I was not wearing my armor, but I gave no thought as to where it was. My body was still frozen. What little I felt with my skin was sharp and stabbing — except for those parts of me touching the feathers of Felix. Those few parts of my flesh rested soundly.

I dropped my head against him and surrendered myself to his care and the care of the herd of creatures rushing through the woods beside us. They did not travel in a regal procession, but in a panicked and disordered frenzy, through thick woods that were little lit by the fading dusk. I must have passed out. I did not open my eyes again until I was no longer in motion. I felt warm and swaddled, but thoroughly exhausted. I don't know how long my fingers were stroking the feathered arms of Felix before I realized that I was still in his embrace, as he sat on the ground.

The Federmensch can raise and lower their body temperatures at will. Felix warmed himself and held me until I awoke in his arms. The night was dark around us. I looked through eyelids that seemed to weight a ton and saw the hazy images of the Unicorns. I heard the voices of Lina and Rüdiger, but could not tell what they were saying, or even if they were speaking German. I suffered a violent flashback of the floating bodies on the pond. My heart jumped instantly to my throat and I began to hyperventilate. Felix's feathers surged with new warmth. His arms squeezed me more tightly and he pressed his face against the top of my head. The terrible images in my head dissolved and I fell back to sleep.

I awoke in the same position, still held in Felix's arms while he sat. The infant morning was bright enough for me to see my surroundings. We were on a treeless hill. Acheriel and Prische were gathered near us, speaking with three new Unicorns, while four more stood in protective positions around the party, facing outward. About ten more Zweigwesens had joined and gathered with the two from my procession. I wanted to rise, to talk to them all about what had happened at the pond, what it meant, and what we should do next. But I was afraid to leave Felix's embrace, as if the warmth of his feathers controlled my very heartbeat.

I didn't have a choice. He stood up and set me on my feet. Once he assured himself that I could stand securely, on my own, he stepped away from me and signaled for the

Friends of the Scheriers to bring my armor. I found myself locked in a stare at Felix's awkward face. Such nobility shone from him as he directed the creatures to strap me into my armor. The black stain on his white arm decorated him like a hero's medal, earned by such a small act — the simple wiping of a smudge from my armor. My eyes stayed with the stain while Felix's heroic blemish darted through the air, as his arms commanded the movement of others.

Before I knew it, I was fully clad and facing directly into Acheriel's shaggy eyebrows.

"I am so sorry," I told him. "How disappointed you must be. You did not need me last night. You needed Kandake. You needed a real Queen, a real Swan Knight. I am so sorry that I am not what you expected."

He answered, "You are everything we prayed you would be."

His answer stunned me. I just stared at him in disbelief.

He continued, "Without a thought of concern for yourself, you ran toward the bodies of your friends. You nearly sacrificed yourself just to save their bodies from the dark, cold water."

"But Felix and the others . . . they had to dive into that water and save me."

"They simply performed the duty they have sworn themselves to, to serve you. And they are grateful for the opportunity. They believe in you. And they believe in your decision to rescue the swan."

I looked down to my feet and thought hard on what he said. The incident with the small pond killed several of us, and it nearly killed me. We needed to gather many more allies before charging into the Queen's Lake.

Acheriel interrupted my chain of thoughts, speaking to ideas I had not spoken.

He said, "We cannot gather more Shallow Water creatures."

I thought, "Why not?" But before my lips could form the first sound, he answered.

"The pond was part of the Shallow Waters, no deeper than your shoulders. It had been that way as long as any of us could remember.

"But it was deep," I snapped, "very deep. The current pulled me down so far before . . . before they saved me."

"The cold black water that chilled you so deeply was the waters of the Deep. The eruption from the center of the pond, the current that pulled you down, those were not natural events. They were an attack, and an attempted abduction. I have no doubt that those currents would have pulled you to Löwschock."

I thought the question, "But what killed the Scherier and the others?"

The moment the thought entered my head, Acheriel answered, "You were not alone in that pond. Who knows what manner of wicked beast swam around you? Perhaps the King of the Deep himself killed our friends."

I involuntarily exhaled all the air in my lungs. My bones ceased to hold me and I dropped to a seat on the ground. I shivered violently as I thought about Löwschock swimming inches from me, those claws that killed the Queen, those arms that abducted The Ancient One, that beast that killed Ludwig. I shook so badly that I thought I might throw-up.

I watched two shiny, spiraling horns extend under my armpits from behind me. They lifted me to my feet. As they were in contact with me, they spoke feelings of comfort to me, but with a strong underlying concern. Once they released me, the two Unicorns who lifted me walked to either side of me.

Acheriel said, "Come with us. We must discuss our options."

I followed Acheriel, boxed in by the same two Unicorns and a third behind me. I felt like I could not have escaped them if I tried. But I did not feel imprisoned by them. I felt protected — guarded. I followed them down the grassy hill upon which I had slept in Felix's embrace, around to the right, along an empty riverbed, to a tall, thick, gnarly dead tree. Six more Unicorns waited there for us.

A short, brown Unicorn, with a particularly bushy face, spoke to me as if continuing the conversation I was having with Acheriel.

She said, "My Queen, we can no longer trust any body of Shallow Waters. The armies of the Deep either dug the old pond deeper or tunneled to connect it to the Deep of some other lake. The same could be with any Shallow lake, pond, or pool. We cannot risk another loss like yesterday's. We cannot risk the Grail Blood."

Prische took over, "We believe that only the Grail Blood can find the Holy Grail. We have searched all of the Lands and Shallow Waters. Kandake hid it well."

Acheriel continued, "She hid it for you to find. The Ancient One is important, but we think we must find the Grail first."

"No", I screamed. "I can't find the Grail without him. I can do nothing until I have him."

I heard Acheriel's voice say, "She is certainly a Wittelsbach." But I did not see his mouth move.

Prische spoke, "We do not have the forces to raid the great lake. With the Grail, we could succeed."

My face grew stern, to match my heart. I was angry at the Unicorns. I understood their point, but they did not understand mine.

Again, they answered my thoughts, as the bushy brown Unicorn said, "We do understand, Swan Knight, but it is our holy duty to advise you."

Despite their insights, I believe I surprised them with my response, as I pointed toward the hill and shouted, "They dove into the cold Deep and saved me, perhaps from the grip of Löwschock himself. You have lived with these creatures for centuries. How could you know so little about them? They are strong and brave, loyal and committed. How dare you underestimate them! I need the swan. My heart tells me . . . my blood tells me to rescue him. This must be done first, and if we can gather no more allies, it must be done now. Let us leave for the Queen's Lake and do what I know must be done."

The sudden exertion of my will exhausted me. I wobbled on my feet. My heart felt like it was knocking against my ribs and my hands shook.

In a softer, more reverent and deferential voice than I had heard from her yet, Prische asked, "Are you certain that this is what must be done?"

I answered, "I can hear the blood of Ludwig telling me so. The blood of Parsifal and Elsa is screaming in my head, 'Rescue The Ancient One!' — *I* trust it."

"And *we* trust it," the brown Unicorn replied.

The others all huffed and nodded in agreement.

The truth is — I did not know The Ancient One except from Ludwig's journal. My unyielding desire to have him came from somewhere. My love for him, even as I read his stories in the Venus Grotto, was the united love of many Wittelsbach, many Swan Knights, gathering at the walls of my blood vessels, infiltrating my muscles and my brain, and manipulating me. Also, I missed my mother and father. Even as I read about the old swan, I was struck with familial, habituated feelings. He is much like my parents — a strange combination of them both.

With the thoughts of my parents, I grew weaker still. Thoughts of home and of the Sweeter Realm swirled indistinguishable in my head. With the expressed support of the Unicorns, I lost all strength and my shaking hands spread through my body. I sat down against the old tree. I turned my head to the side and leaned my ear against the thick bark. Something tickled my ear, a hair that had wiggled its way through my own hair to touch lightly in my ear. I pulled away from the tree, rubbed my ear, and turned to face the trunk. I looked closely. The tree trunk was not covered in bark, but in coarse hair. I knew immediately what it was. They were Zweigwesens, connected to each other, in the formation of a tree.

So vivid were the images depicted by Ludwig that my heart and head were soothed instantly by the intimate familiarity of the Zweigwesen tree formation. I felt like I had encountered an old friend or relative, some precious loved one that I hadn't seen in years.

I reached forward, gave the thick-haired tree a gentle stroke, and said, "Hello, my friends."

Suddenly, dozens of eyelids opened, all across the tree. A single voice, from high in the tree replied, "Hello, Swan Knight."

One at a time, Zweigwesens broke from the formation, starting with the high branches above and working downward, until there was no tree, only a crowd of lovely Zweigwesens, encircling me closely, some with wide smiles, some with swollen eyes.

One spoke, "We agree with the voices in your Grail Blood. Let us get the swan. He has suffered too long."

I thought, but most definitely did not speak, "If he is still alive."

Acheriel said, "If your blood tells you he is alive, I trust it, as if Elsa herself told me."

I was not irritated by yet another penetrating Unicorn insight into my thoughts, but I was agitated.

I stood quickly, and in the tone of a Queen, not to be denied, I asked, "How do you always know what I'm thinking, before I speak? Am I that easy to read? Am I really that simple?"

Prische answered from behind me, "We have wondered when you would ask that question. You have often thought it."

Acheriel added, "You are not simple, My Queen. In fact, I have never met a more complex mind. But we Unicorns hear what is in your head, not in words, that could be recited later, but in thoughts and feelings."

"Like Elsa?" I said tentatively, almost in a whisper.

"Like none since Elsa. Like none but Elsa."

"But Elsa also saw *your* thoughts, and I cannot."

The brown Unicorn answered, "You haven't seen it because you haven't sought it."

I stared into Acheriel's eyes, trying to see more deeply. All I saw was the rich depth of his eyes through his shaggy eyebrows. I closed my eyes and reached my right hand up for his horn.

"No!" He snapped. "You do not need the horn."

I withdrew my hand and ran it down the armor of my left upper arm, silently begging Elsa for help. This was the proof I needed to bury my doubts. I would believe in myself, believe that I belonged here, that I deserved their reverence, that I truly own the armor, that I would find the Grail and save them all, if only I could connect with the

Unicorns as Elsa did. That was the evidence I needed that Grail Blood really flowed through me.

I thought about Ludwig's journal and the Swan Knight history. The Journal! In a panic, I realized that I did not have it, that I have not had it since we left the pond. One of the Zweigwesens, one of the two that joined me outside of the Scherier cave, held it in front of me, as if *he* heard my thoughts. I took the book, pushed it to my face and inhaled deeply. I parted my lips slightly and pressed them against the leather. With my lips firmly against the book, I thought about the many Swan Knights whose lives I had come to know, whose traits I had come to love, and with my lips still pressed against the book, I mouthed the words, "Help me."

I began to see the Unicorns, not just the ones surrounding me, and not as I imagined them when I read the journal — more like memories of feelings. I lowered the book from my face, but kept my eyes closed in probing concentration. I felt the affirming thoughts of the Unicorns around me. Then, I felt the surprise of Unicorns far away, ones that I had not met. They sensed my curious mind reaching for them — and they answered. I heard Unicorns far away ask me if I required them to come to me. I invited them all. Acheriel joined in the long-distance mental conversation. He reminded me and the others that we must embark immediately for the Queen's Lake, and that we did not have time to wait for others to join. I felt the whole collective concur.

I believe that I sensed every living Unicorn simultaneously. In one long and rushing, consuming wave, the entire Unicorn collective rode into my mind — their thoughts, their fears, and their hopes. I did not have a tight grip on their thoughts. They flew in and out of my head before I could grasp them. But they *were* in my head. That moment changed me forever. I have often been slow to grasp the full scope of my existence since I came through the portal. But there have been moments that have shoved that realization into my hands and squeezed my fingers around it. That was one of those moments. I sighed and allowed myself to bathe in the thoughts and feelings of the Unicorn collective, swirling and indistinct as they were.

CHAPTER 8

The Return of Elsa

MY CONNECTION TO THE UNICORNS had its limitations. I felt them all and they all felt me. But the thoughts, poignant as they were, were often hazy and difficult to articulate. Needs and desires came through clearly. I no longer had to open my mouth to call them to me, especially those nearest me. I did not yet have Elsa's control. They read me well, but I could not place thoughts in their heads and their thoughts were swirling, misty clouds in my mind — beautiful, intoxicating, but chaotic and impossible to decifer into coherence. So spoken language was still the vessel of planning.

I called the Unicorns around us to gather at the top of the hill, where the rest of the party still waited. I did so with a thought and I thrilled in the ability. I reached my mind for all of the Unicorns that were within a few hours ride of us. I concentrated on my desire to gather them and I strained to project the thought outward. We waited on the hill for several hours. The company grew restless, but I kept my concentration on the exploration of my new ability.

While we waited on the hill for more Unicorns to join us, and hours passed in an instant, I alternated between thinking directly to a particular Unicorn standing near me, to broadcasting general messages to them all, from communicating with the nearest to connecting with the farthest. I did this for several hours, interrupted occasionally by the presentation of a meal by the Friends of the Scheriers, until we were set upon by a herd of about sixty Zweigwesens.

They had come from a Zweigwesen settlement not very far off. A few of the Unicorns rode out to meet them. I remained on the hill and concentrated, trying to experience the interaction through the thoughts of the Unicorns. The thoughts were hazy as I stared out toward them. I closed my eyes and focused. I did not see what they saw. Nothing of their sensual perceptions translated directly. But their thoughts on what they saw, heard, and felt were getting clearer to me, allowing me to paint a picture in my mind. As the hairy brown Unicorn began to speak to the Zweigwesens. My perception of the event blurred. I felt the words of the Zweigwesens twice, like an echo. My heart skipped as I realized the nature of the phenomenon. It was not a repeating echo of the Unicorns' experience. I felt the thoughts of the Zweigwesens before they spoke, *then* I felt the thoughts of the Unicorns as they heard the words of the Zweigwesens.

As this realization dawned on me, the Unicorns perceived my excitement. I believe the Zweigwesens did too. They all ran up the hill to me.

One Zweigwesen came to me and said, "We heard your call from our village. The one you call Cort told us that you were here. We were waiting for you to come to us. We all felt your call. You are really here. You wear Elsa's armor and speak to us as she did. Thank God you are here, Swan Knight."

The Zweigwesens joined with their kind from our party, attaching to each other, some in simple embraces, other in the formation of complex architecture. The greeting ritual was fun to watch. I don't know if I sensed their love for each other through some ability of my Grail Blood, or if the love of the scene around me was self-evident through the senses. But the warmth of familial adoration replaced what the lowering sun took away.

Once all greetings and introductions completed, the hill was filled with a massive company. The nearby Unicorns that I had summoned joined us on the top of the hill. We gathered what remained of our Shallow Water friends in the center of our company. To my own intense shame, I realized that our company was not complete. Bechtold and Hildemar, our Schildbüffels, were not with us. A tyrannical panic seized me. I scanned the area, feverishly volleying my eyes across the company and back again.

I felt Prische, specifically Prische, reach into my head to discover the sourse of my agitation. In a moment she knew what I knew and she passed the information to the Unicorns in our company. Felix stood near Acheriel and grabbed the horn of his old friend. A similar panic took him. His movements mirrord mine. He looked frantically across the hill for the Schildbüffels. They were not there. They had never convened with the company after the flight from the Glühenchor pond.

Upon that realization, Felix darted down the hill, to the edge of the thick woods between us and the pond. Acheriel took a few quick steps after him.

"No!" Felix demanded. "Your place is with Verena. The Queen is in your care."

Felix turned from us and disappeared into the woods. I ran down the hill, to the tree line. My vision saw little deeper than the first few trees of the thickening woods. I turned to Acheriel, with fear in my heart — fear for Felix. Acheriel turned his head to his right and left. One Unicorn on each side of him nodded and huffed in unison and sprinted down the hill. They disappeared into the woods in pursuit of Felix, in search of the Schildbüffels. I called for them. I don't know if my screaming voice reached them or if they received my frantic thoughts through their minds, but they reappeared at the base of the hill.

"Take the Zweigwesens with you," I suggested in a soft cry, not in the determined dictates of a Queen. "You might need them."

I felt the Zweigwesens brush past me, the two that had been with me since the Scherier cave. They mounted the Unicorns, and the four of them disappeared.

The night was right around the corner. I had no faith that my company would be fully united before the hill went dark. Still, I prayed for it. The sun set fully with no sign of Felix, the Unicorns, Zweigwesens, or Schildbüffels. The minutes of fading dusk flew in seconds. After the sunset, they dragged for hours. Thick clouds covered the sky, hiding the moon and veiling the only accurate measure of passing time. I cursed the clouds. I needed to know how long they were gone, as if such knowledge would serve any good.

Acheriel stood stoicly above me as I sat near the base of the hill, staring fruitlessly into the dark woods. He gave me security but little comfort. Felix, whose warm feathered arms I most desired, was the primary source of my concerns. My only comfort came from my dear Scheriers, Rüdiger and Lina. The night exposed to me a side of Rüdiger I had not yet seen. He was nurturing, even more so than the ever-maternal Lina. He snuggled onto my lap and nestled, as if trying to burrow into my abdomen. He spoke kind words to me, flattering words of encouragement. He complimented my courage and my goodness. He spoke to me of his reaction in meeting me for the first time. Lina draped herself in absolute stillness around my neck, moving only her mouth in occasional, subtle concurrence with Rüdiger's impassioned sentiments.

The Scheriers were an effective adhesive in holding my spirits together that night. I thoughtlessly ejected them from my mind and body, in a sudden jolt, when I received the touch of Acheriel's horn just below the back of my neck. He had remained in communion of thought with the Unicorns on the expedition to find the Schildbüffels. They had caught up quickly with Felix. And when they found Hildemar and Bechtold, Acheriel invited me into the union with the touch of his horn.

The Schildbüffels were alive; but Bechtold suffered an injury to his right rear leg. In fact, it had been nearly severed by the bite of Deep monster, suffered while he rescued me from abduction. I stood, breaking the connection with Acheriel's horn. I sought the Unicorns with my own mind, with my own abilty. I found them. They praised me for sending the Zweigwesens. Our two branch-like medics treated Bechtold, secured the leg, and guaranteed his full recovery in time.

Time — it was a commodity with which I did not feel abundantly blessed. I had been housing in my skull a sharp desperation to free The Ancient One. But that did not matter when my friends immerged from the threshold of the thick woods. Felix carried Bechtold over his head. The Schildbüffel must be five times the weight of a Federman. Felix held him high above his head with a rather triumphant strut. Bechtold's bandaged limb was plastered to his shell in what looked like a sticky cacoon.

Hildemar waddled behind them, followed by the Zweigwesens riding high on the shoulders of the Unicorns. In the arms of one of the Zweigwesens was a Vogelkröte, one that I saw surface lifeless on the blackened pond. She lived, and Hildemar rescued her from the water and dragged her with the limping Bechtold through the woods, until discovered by Felix and the others.

The survival and recovery of my friends had simultaneous and polar effects on my spirits. In one hand, I felt less vulnerable. On the other, I was intensely sensible of the danger the swimmers faced in our plan to gather wet creatures and rescue the swan. The Unicorns were right. We could not risk more lives diving into the Shallow Waters in search of allies. The company deserved to know. But this was not the time, while creatures of many shapes and sizes pushed to tightly encircle our returning heroes. Bechtold was tired and in great pain. He spoke little. But Hildemar told their story with vivacious animation. The Vogelkröte smiled wide at the sight of the gathered company, then fell asleep in the arms of a Zweigwesen.

We spoke nothing of plans that night. I had no idea how much of the night had passed. For once I was the example of calm reason. I kissed the Schildbüffels, gently ran my fingers down the back of the sleeping, bandaged Vogelkröte, and thanked the Unicorns and Zweigwesens. I walked slowly to Felix, whose exhausted eyes still glazed with adoration as they locked on my approach. I simply patted him a few times on the shoulder and begged him to get some rest. I settled on the grassy hill alone, curled up and closed my eyes. I heard the company quickly calm and follow my example.

I awoke before any of them. So I was the first to see another dozen Zweigwesens join us from the northeast, their orangeish-brown hair made oranger by the sunrise. They carried large baskets of food for the company. The baskets were filled with light, crunchy, dried shells of a plant. They reminded me of locus shells, but fist-sized and purply-brown. I took pride in waking the company while helping to pass out the food.

After breakfast, the company became restless. They wanted to know where we were going next, what we were doing. Acheriel told me that it was my voice that must inform them. I told them that we could not risk their lives in the Shallow pools and ponds. Our search for more help was over. They looked at each other and at me. Some were confident and resolved. Others were terrified.

A Vogelkröte asked me, "Are we enough? The largest and fiercest of Löwschock's army are in the Queen's Lake."

Bechtold said, "Many more of us still survive in the Shallow Waters of the Queen's Lake, on the sands near the shore, where the icy-black of the Deep has not fully spread. Many of my own kind lay hibernating, buried in the Shallow banks. They will join. They will see Verena standing on the shore and they will join."

Acheriel thought to me, but did not speak, "You must try to communicate with them, through the water. Rally them to join our friends when they dive into the great lake."

This was the first Unicorn thought to come to me in complete clarity. I responded by thinking clearly but in silence to the crowd, until Prische reminded me that I must *speak* my thoughts to the others. I announced to them all that the bravest creatures on either side of the portal stood before me, that their love for each other and for The Ancient One would defeat any fountain of black water or any scaled monster that will be waiting for them.

I believed my words as I spoke them. But during the breath that followed, I began to doubt. My very marrow chilled and shivered with the sudden memory of the icy-cold currents that dragged me downward from the surface of the pond. I must have broadcasted my fears to the Unicorns and to the handful of Zweigwesens nearest me. They sent me a warm wave of confidence and support that my armor seemed to receive like an antenna.

I passed that warmth to the company of Shallow swimmers in an unguided effusion of my love for them. I spoke of the swan and of the Grail. I spoke of Kandake and how proud she would be to see the unity of our little band. Those who were around for the exodus to Einigkeitstadt, who celebrated the swan's holiday there, nodded in agreement. Confidence and fear ran neck-and-neck in a race for their hearts. They were scared. But they were in love and they were committed.

One of the Zweigwesens tending to Bechtold shouted, "I hope your excitement will keep for a few weeks."

The creatures went silent.

"A few weeks?" I repeated with an inquiring tone of confusion.

"Three weeks at least, if you want this Schildbüffel on the campaign. He should move quite normally in three weeks. Until then, he cannot move."

This was a blow indeed. The thought of three weeks on that hill shook me on two counts. First, I illogically feared that three more weeks, added to more than a century, would spell the end of the great swan. Second, our hill pressed against the band of woods that surrounded the treacherous pond. I felt exposed and in danger.

One of the new Zweigwesens to the hill spoke of a similar hill not more than and hour's march away. It has an advantageous view in all directions and is distant from any body of water. We agreed to gather there and wait out the recovery of Bechtold. Felix carried the crippled Schildbüffel, without rest, to the new hill. We spent the entire afternoon recovering from the march. Most needed it. I did not. The hour of travel passed comfortably for me on Prische's back.

Calmness covered the hill. The Zweigwesens built a bed for Bechtold's recovery. The Scheriers began immediately but passively burrowing into the hill. They spent the rest of their day digging a small cave, little more than a hole, where I could sleep in greater protection for the three weeks. When they finished, it looked rather like a grave. Recent events had brought my mortality keenly to mind, making rather rancid the idea of slipping into the ground. They were proud of their efforts. They gifted the hole to me with all of the ceremonial grandeur befitting their love for their Queen.

When the time came for me to employ the gift, I dreaded it, but dared not refuse. Neither could I not lay in it like a body being put to rest. I got in, but I sat against the wall of the hole and slept in a seated position. Before I fell asleep, I heard the huffs of the circle of Unicorns that guarded my bed. In truth, I felt safer in that little hole than I had felt since I left Cort's clearing. I silently contrasted my previous sense of exposure to the hidden and guarded Scherier hole. The thought comforted me. I was comforted further when Lina and Rüdiger asked to sleep with me. They held each other so tightly that they appeared as one thick cylinder of white fur. United just so, they snuggled onto my lap, against my belly. Their lovingly dug hole lost all sense of morbidness and death. It was warm and filled with love. It was protected by fiercely loyal horns and brimming over with the shared adoration of its three occupants.

I awoke and rose with the addition to our group of more Zweigwesens. The empty, grassy fields surrounding our hill were no longer empty. The hill was skirted by a belt of gnarly trees — Zweigwesen tree formation. Any enemies approaching the hill would have to work their way through the hairy sentries. The prospect of waiting there for Bechtold's recovery seemed much less daunting. Running my sentimental eyes across the Zweigwesen trees, the stout Unicorns, the brave swimmers, my powerful Federman, and loyal Scheriers, swelled my heart with admiration for the creatures around me, and for the place they call home.

We passed the three weeks together. The days lasted forever. I grew dangerously comfortable and patient. I savored my company. I spent most of my time in light-hearted conversation with Lina and Rüdiger. When not with them, I regaled the others with stories from my life or readings from Ludwig's journal. Felix rarely left my side. He spoke little. But when near me, very near, his feathers rose from his body to reach for me. I don't think he knew it was happening. I often leaned in, more desirous of the connection than he could have been. The memory of sleeping in his arms gave me an itch I was afraid to scratch.

In those weeks, Felix lost all of his physical awkwardness in my eyes. Although he stood nose high to me, his merits towered over mine. The few words he shared were austere and deeply philosophical. Much of it went out of my reach. I often wondered how the creatures of the Land and Shallow Waters could revere me while I stood in comparison beside such a wise and wonderful Federman. They saw something in me that I could not.

CHAPTER 9

Decamping

ACHERIEL AND PRISCHE TOOK IT UPON THEMSELVES to explain the reverence paid to me, often referencing Elsa and the springing of her unique abilities from inside of me. They encouraged me to seek the connection of the Unicorns. I broadcasted my own thoughts all too easily, but struggled to extract thoughts from them, even when they offered them freely.

These efforts were the smaller part of my desires. I spent most of my time strengthening my bond with the creatures, learning from them and inadvertently stitching them tightly to my affections. I fell in love during the three weeks on that hill. By the end, when Bechtold waddled around the hill as easily as Hildemar, my drive to free the swan was less selfish than before. I wanted him for their sake, for Rüdiger and Lina, and for the swimmers, who had long deified him. I knew what his return would mean to the creatures whom I loved more deeply with every passing hour on that hill.

For a few days, I anticipated the order to continue our mission, expecting it from Acheriel or Prische, or from the shaggy brown Unicorn. They were antsy. They grew sharp and impatient in their communication with me. One afternoon, I spoke to Lina about it.

She told me, "We don't know why you wait."

"Wait for what?" I asked.

I did not need her answer. As I finished the question, the answer struck me. The order to rescue the swan was given by me. The order to resume must also. I stood with abrupt determination and marched to the top of the hill. I passed a circle of Frends of the Scheriers. I asked them to bring me the armor. As I walked, my thoughts drew nearer to The Ancient One. My need for him regained its full potency. The Unicorns felt my sense of resolution and followed me to the peak of the hill. The Zweigwesen tree formations broke and mixed into the gathering company.

Standing at the crest of the hill, a halo of space surrounded me. The gathering company left a ten-foot perimeter between me and the nearest circle of them. They stared wide-eyed in anticipation. The Friends of the Scheriers breached the halo and strapped me into my armor. I spoke while they worked, beginning with a summation of some of the swan's more heroic moments from the Swan Knight history. The words flowed from me without premeditation. The topic was inspiring, so I easily whipped them all into a frenzy of brave devotion to the cause.

As I spoke of the Queen's Lake, of Löwschock and his serpents, my voice shook and apprehension crept from my depths to expose itself demonstratively in my palsylike mannerisms. Lina broke from the crowd. She climbed up my leg and stood on my left shoulder, leaning with both hands on the top of my head. She reached down and rubbed my ear, lowered her head and kissed my scalp in slow but repeating kisses. Rüdiger appeared from the crowd, ran a few circles around my legs, stopped, and stood in a noble pose against me. He repeated this several times until Acheriel and Prische joined on either side of me. With the addition of each of my dearest ones, the audience cheered.

Felix joined last, walking from behind me to stand pressed against the right side of my back, with his left hand on my left shoulder.

We stood there and received the raucus cheering until the sun set behind me and the hill grew dark. That night was not about the band of friends at the crown of the hill. It was about the swimmers, about those in our party who would be diving into the Queen's Lake to rescue The Ancient One. For the rest of us, our job was to keep them safe, warm, and comfortable while they rested for the dangers ahead.

The Zweigwesens formed into four large trees, surrounding the hill. Their eyes remained open. All other creatures gathered around the swimmers and huddled tightly to them. They were protected. They were warm. And they slept soundly. Before they settled, Lina came to me, looking for Rüdiger. My eyes knew where to turn before my mind could give the situation a single thought. They shifted thoughtlessly to the center of the swimmers. Of course he was there, rallying them with his signature excitement, speaking reverently of The Ancient One, telling tales of the Old Digger, of meeting me and convincing me to rescue the swan, but most importantly, expressing his contagious confidence into every ear in the group, one at a time, as if each repeated sentiment was a secret between one Scherier and the one swimmer he spoke to at that moment.

The Friends of the Scheriers removed my armor and placed it meticulously in a neat pile. My mind was swimming with memories of the three weeks — and fears of the next day. My fears triggered something in my subconscious, bringing my thoughts into a vivid recollection of being pulled downward by the icy-black currents in the Glühenchor pond. My body seemed to direct itself, taking me where it needed to go to recover from the recollection the way it recovered from the event. I walked up to Felix, ready to assume my place in his warm embrace, as I had slept in recovery on that terrible night.

I was not chilled to the bone. I was not in need of his warmth. I don't know why I went to him to be held while I slept. It was my body's natural inclination as it walked free of my mind's control. I stood directly in front of him, looking him squarely in the eyes, before I realized what I was doing. I felt my blood rush to my face. He had to have seen me blush, but he did not know why. Mortified, I turned quickly to the Unicorns, afraid that they sensed my thoughts. Some slept. Some talked. None seemed to notice my embarrassment.

Felix looked at me with the most sincerely devoted expression and asked, "What can I do for you, my Queen?"

From the tender but passionate allegiance in his eyes, I knew that he would have done whatever I asked, fling himself from a cliff or hold me while I sleep. Still swimming in the terror of recollection, I almost asked him if I could sleep in his embrace. Although I know he would been honored to do so, I was too embarrassed to ask.

I simply stuttered, "I. . I only . . . I just wanted to thank you for saving me from the pond."

He tilted his head slightly to the side and his grave expression told me what his mouth did not, "I am faithfully yours. I would do anything for you."

These words ran through my head as my imagination pulled them from his eyes. At the end of a long train of imagined expressions of devotion from Felix, my mind added, "And I love you."

I shook my body to expel the thought from my head. Felix saw it. He could not have missed it.

He asked me, "Are you well? Are you cold?"

He leaned forward as he asked the questions, as if eagerly anticipating my answer. I gathered my freely swimming thoughts and caged them behind my reason. I told him that I was well and thanked him again for his service to me. I wanted to thank him for holding me and warming me, and remaining so near me while we lived on that hill together, but I was afraid I could not do so without opening the cage and freeing my fanciful imagination again. I told him to get some rest, assuring him that the next day's perils would surely require his strength and his warm feathers. He acknowledged me with a low bow and settled against the base of one of the Zweigwesen tree formations.

I pushed the Federman from my mind and focused on the swimmers. I walked among them, stroked them, sang to them, and whispered encouragements until the last of them was asleep. I did not sleep in the Scherier hole that night. I dared not hide away like that. I laid down near my armor, among the Friends of the Scheriers, beside Rüdiger and Lina and the other two Scheriers in the party.

If I did dream that night, the dreams were buried beneath deep sleep. It felt like I had barely blinked my eyes when the sunrise cast its orange glow on the hill. I looked to the Zweigwesen tree formations. Their eyes were still open, still blinking. They held their post through the night and kept us all safe. Felix still sat leaning against the base of the nearest Zweigwesen tree. I looked at the swimmers. They were so beautiful in the soft sunlight. I thought about the dangers they faced. I knew that it was unlikely they would all live to see the next sunrise. I cried for them. It started as a welling of tears in my eyes. My face felt swollen. As the first few swimmers began to wake to the dawn of what might be their last day, my breath followed my eyes. My chest shook as I cried in silence, still staring at my beautiful and brave swimmers.

I tried to weigh their sacrifice against the gain of The Ancient One. But in truth, I did not know if the rumors were true. Plunging into the Queen's Lake was almost certain death, for a prize that might not be there. As more of the swimmers awoke, and they rubbed and kissed each other, my silence broke. My emotions swelled, shoving me into a full cry, with loud sobs. It woke the rest of camp. They stared at me, some in shock, some in pity, some in support. I just looked at my swimmers and continued sobbing — until a soft-feathered arm wrapped around me.

Felix gave me a tight squeeze around my shoulders. There was an intimacy to the embrace that did not exist before our awkward encounter the night before. I suspected that he knew of my desires more than I cared to reveal. But before I could relish the embrace, he broke from me and directed the Scheriers and the Friends of the Scheriers to strap me into my armor. The Scherier ore comforted me, allowing my mind to focus on the mission at hand — returning to the Land and Shallow Waters its greatest treasure, its one indispensable citizen — The Ancient One.

The company surrounded me. Those who could not send their support through thought did so through the light of devoted eyes and the fires of passion that provided that light. We gathered tightly on the top of the hill and prayed. We begged God's blessing and protection for our swimmers. We prayed for The Ancient One, that he might keep his strength and courage for one more day. Some of us ate. Some didn't. I didn't think much about Felix. When I did, I wanted desperately to be by his side. I wanted his warmth to rescue me from my fears, the way it rescued me from the cold. But those thoughts were fleeting. My mind was on being for the company whatever sort of Queen or Swan Knight they needed me to be.

CHAPTER 10

The Gates of the Enemy

WE TRAVELED IN A DIRECT LINE TO THE QUEEN'S LAKE, not in a meticulously placed procession, but in groups huddled tightly, not marching regally, but pressing forward as quickly as we could while keeping the band united. Acheriel led the way. I rode beside him on Prische. Felix was just behind me on a tall, light-grey Unicorn. As determined as we were, we moved slowly for a Unicorn, not exceeding the top speed of the Schildbüffels.

We kept a safe distance from any body of standing water, no matter how small, until we came upon a brook. It was clear and shallow. We could see the bottom as if no water flowed over it. The swimmers took the opportunity to refresh themselves. Most of the Zweigwesens napped, having remained alert through the night. I just sat near the bank and stared at my swimmers, relishing their pleasure in the water, trying to brand their faces into my memory, so I could speak vividly of them when they are gone.

I heard a humming that I thought came from the Vogelkrötes. Rüdiger heard it too and recognized it immediately.

He shouted at me, "Your Majesty, the Glühenchor!"

I jumped to my feet and scanned my eyes up and down the brook. Upstream, to my right, riding the light current of the clear, shallow brook, were the Glühenchor. Nine of them, in no particular formation, traveled the current toward us, while six Scheriers ran along beside them, three on either side of the brook. Lina recognized the Scheriers. She called them by name and ran to them, diving into an immediate four-Scherier wrestling match with the three on our side. The three from the other side leapt over the water. Rüdiger met them in mid-air. Those four fell upon the other four and my worn heart laughed spiritedly at the sight of the giant rolling and bouncing ball of wrestling Scheriers.

I thought about the children of Elsa, of Bechtold's letter to Hildemar, from the Swan Knight history, when he detailed the events of the valley competition, when the race was interrupted after one Scherier bumped another and the wrestling started. The entire competition came to a halt while they laughed at the spectacle. My brave company enjoyed a similar distraction.

The Glühenchor stared at me. I believe they were making their music and glowing, but the noise of laughter drowned out any soft tunes and the sun shined off of the Glühenchor backs. I called sharply for Rüdiger.

"I thought you wanted to introduce me to the Glühenchor."

Rüdiger and Lina crawled out from the ball of Scheriers.

"Right, yes, I apologize, my Queen."

The new Scheriers joined behind Rüdiger and Lina, and the other two from our party stood with them.

Rüdiger began in a lofty, courtly proclamation, "Verena, Queen of the Land and Shallow Waters, may I introduce to you —"

He was interrupted by one of the new Scheriers, who shouted out in excitement, "The Swan Knight! Look everybody. It is the new Swan Knight!"

The formal introduction was shattered in classic Scherier style. They all jumped on me. Some kissed my face. Others rubbed the armor and hummed. The nine Glühenchor formed a semi-circle around us. I stared at Rüdiger, who stood at my feet, rubbing my armor and humming.

"Right, yes, my Queen, these are the Glühenchor. In the evening, you know, after we rescue The Ancient One, they will play their music for you and light your beautiful face with their glow. You just wait. It really is something to see."

I allowed a few more moments of rest for the swimmers, while the Scheriers and the Friends of the Scheriers caught our new friends up on all that had happened and all that was planned. I spoke with the Glühenchor. Those nine were all that survived of the more than forty who lived in the blackened pond. They escaped to the brook and had lived in its flowing waters since. I did not have to ask them to join our mission. It seemed understood among them. They made their way to the other swimmers and joined in the last few moments of relaxation before pressing on. While they did, I sat. I sat and held Rüdiger on my lap. Lina spoke with the new Scheriers while her husband fell asleep to the slow, mindless strokes of my fingertips through his fur.

It was his contented hum that drew my attention toward my legs, to the blissful smile of the sleeping Scherier. I resumed my gentle strokes across his back, but with intention, with mindful sensations of his soft fur, his warm body, and the boundless spirit that rested peacefully on my lap. I thought hard about Rüdiger, as I ran my fingers through his hair more for my pleasure than his. I caught myself holding my breath as I pondered him. My lungs pleasured equally in his goodness. They forgot all about their primary function. I caught myself holding my breath as my eyes, my fingertips, my heart and my head basked in his faith, his bravery, his love and kindness, his loyalty and his intelligence.

My body demanded its next breath, which it drew furiously, as if to scold me. Only then did I realize the depth of the trance. As the shock gave way to an elevated adoration, my stroking fingertips continued sensing so much more than the soft fur of a Scherier. They savored his goodness. That moment holding Rüdiger while he slept on my lap altered me forever. It made me more aware, more receptive to experience the comprehensive beauty of others.

Rüdiger awoke gently and calmly, simply lifting his eyes to me and releasing his signature hum with the slow blinking of his contented eyes. He gathered his wits and energy simultaneously and hopped from my lap, eager to proceed.

I drew the company to attention and led them with Prische, Acheriel, Felix, and the other Unicorns beside us. The morning sun was getting high in the sky. The brook divided the sparsely wooded hills of our morning hike and the flat, thickly wooded forest that continued to the shore of the great lake. Although I feared our destination, I took comfort in the thick woods. They reminded me of the bright circle-clearing and of my loyal friend Cort. Only then did I realize how much I missed him. As we rode slowly through the thickening woods, I prayed for Cort. My prayers obviously did not go directly to God. They made a few stops in the minds of the nearest Unicorns, including Prische and Acheriel, who joined their prayerful thoughts to mine.

The woods grew so thick that the sun made little progress through the canopy above. I knew that several hours of travel had passed, but I did not know how late it was. I began to worry for the swan, worry that we would arrive just moments too late, that after more than a century in captivity, he would perish just as my heroic swimmers found him. Prische's pace picked up in accordance to my subconscious desires. I don't think she knew that I controlled her tempo with my anxiety.

Acheriel thought to us both, "The Schildbüffels."

I looked behind and saw them lagging. Prische slowed her paces, which slowed the company following behind.

I heard a shout from the back of the company in Bechtold's voice, "Thank you, Your Majesty."

I shouted back, "You're welcome."

Waves of giggles rippled back and forth among the creatures between the Schildbüffels and the Unicorns.

The thickness of the forest lightened, allowing the sun to reveal itself. It was not as late as I had imagined. This relieved me tremendously. The warmth and the light of the sun would be our allies in the struggle ahead. The lightly wooded forest opened to a very sparsely wooded field between us and a broad band of beach. On the other side was the lake. I did not recognize the scene from my first day in the Sweeter Realm. I had never been there before. I pulled the journal from its place, tucked into my breastplate. I pulled out Rudolf's Map and tried to compare landmarks.

A single thought rushed into my head from Acheriel, "Much has changed since that map was drawn."

I acknowledged the futility of my attempt by folding the map, wedging it into the book, and tucking the book back under my armor. It didn't matter what the map said. The Unicorns knew where the Queen's Jail was. They led us to the lakeshore at the closest point to the jail. We walked to the water's edge. The company behind me parted, allowing the swimmers to work their way to the lakeside.

At the mental prodding of Acheriel, I presided over a prayer for our rescue party. A dead silence followed the chorus of "Amen". Nobody moved. Few breathed. A single voice broke the silence.

From the middle of the huddled swimmers, a high-pitched Vogelkröte voice shouted, "Let's go get the teacher!"

It was followed by the rising squeal of the Pfützeschilfs, then the soft, muted hum of the Glühenchor, added to the cheers of the Schildbüffels and the rest of the Vogelkrötes. The swimmers dove into the water while the company of Land creatures cheered them on, Rüdiger most exuberantly of all. I sat high on Prische, as close to the water as possible, so that they may see me. I looked into the water, and through the water I saw several Schildbüffels emerge from the shallow sands and join my friends as they swam toward the center of the lake.

I thought. I thought hard, trying to connect with the creatures of the Shallow Waters who were still living in the Queen's Lake. I felt nothing but the vigorous fervor of the swimmers already on our mission and the support of the creatures on the shore. This was enough to encourage my spirits. They looked like a mighty force as they disappeared beneath the ripples they created with their entrance into the water.

Once all sight of them was gone, the crowd on shore settled into silence. I watched the low waves lap against the sand and rocks. The tension of anxiouos anticipation bound tightly the minds of the Land creatures. We were blind to the progress of our friends, blind to whatever might await them. I thought about how clear the water was on the very edge of the lake. This gave me hope, not just for our mission to rescue The Ancient One, but for the future of the Sweeter Realm. Just as the stress of blind fear slowly released its grip on my throat, allowing my breaths to tend gradually toward normalcy, my heart was viciously squeezed by the sight of blackness creeping from the center of the lake to consume the clear water on the lake's edge. The entire lake grew deep black. Just like with the pond, ripples turned to splashes. We all watched in horror as bodies flew from the water. They were too far out for me to see them clearly, but the violence of the scene was clear enough.

A Schildbüffel flew into the air and reentered the water with a tremendous splash. Smaller swimmers flew out of the water, not in flailing panic, but with the lifeless limpness of death. Bodies began to fly toward us, as if thrown at us by our enemies. A Glühenchor landed right at Prische's feet, twisted, mutilated, but still wearing on its lifeless little face a scowl of courageous defiance. This spurred Rüdiger into action. He jumped into the water and disappeared beneath the black surface. Lina and the rest of the Scheriers followed. I shouted at them, ordering them, demanding that they return to the shore. The thought of losing my Scheriers overwhelmed my desire to rescue The Ancient One. I wanted to abandon the rescue and save whom I could.

Vogelkröte bodies flew at us, landing on and around us. Scherier bodies, mangled and deformed, hit the ground with a sickening thud. The Zweigwesens immediately tended to the bodies, but none who flew ashore were still alive. In a frenzied panic, I studied the bodies of the Scheriers as they landed on the sand on all sides of us. My fear for Rüdiger and Lina crippled all other thoughts, all other hopes. I broke into a mix of screaming and crying, shouting at the water, alternating between cursing the enemy and begging for my friends to come back to me. The rest of my party stared out to the water in silence.

I dismounted Prische. I was ready to run into the water to save them. The collective thoughts of every Unicorn in the Sweeter Realm reproached me sternly and ordered me onto Prische. My desperate compassion for my friends was more powerful than my connection to the Unicorn collective. I did not realize how much I loved my suffering swimmers. I did not know how much I could love until I saw them dying in front of me. But dear as they were to me, shattered as I was by the sight and sound of their lifeless bodies at my feet, when the Scheriers dove in, and broken Scherier bodies flew ashore, my fear for *my* two Scheriers numbed me to all other pains.

My legs ran toward the water, but my body did not move. It was only when I looked down at my legs that I saw Felix's feathered arms wrapped around my waist, holding my feet off of the ground. In an instant, he threw me back onto Prische. He was right. The Unicorns were right. I could not save them. So, I just stared, grinding my teeth together in silence, wetting my neck and chest with my tears.

The violently splashing water calmed slightly. A low grumble followed the calming, coming from far into the lake. There was a distinct hatred in the sound, a bitter anger. It grew louder until it ended with a burst of splashing from the surface, about forty yards out. From the splashing, I saw a flash of white, a creature flailing and fighting to stay above the water. The white creature, still flailing about, began to ride a wave toward me. As it came closer, I knew what it was. It was a swan, riding on a row of four or five swimmers. I had no time to greet, inspect, or admire the swan. As they came ashore, a fierce eruption of black water shot from the surface of the lake, like at the Glühenchor pond only infinitely bigger.

Two Zweigwesens grabbed the swan and pulled him onto a Unicorn. The swan continued to flap his right wing. The left wing was gone. In its place was an oozing, bloody stump. The very moment the Zweigwesens secured the swan onto the Unicorn and held him tightly, the Unicorn raced away from the shore, toward Zweigwesen land. I watched them ride toward the thick woods. I looked back over the water. The violence increased. I screamed for my friends to leave the lake and follow me. Prische rushed her Queen away from the icy-black waters, into the safety of the woods.

I yelled at Prische, "Where are you going? The Scheriers! The Swimmers! Go back!"

With haunting calmness in her voice, she spoke in response, "They will either escape the lake or they will not. We can do nothing for them from land, nothing but save the old teacher and their Queen."

The Unicorns carried as many Zweigwesens and Friends of the Scheriers as they could hold. The rest ran behind us. I grabbed one Zweigwesen as we rode by him. I lifted him onto Prische's shoulders, dropped my chest down on him, and pinned him securely to the Unicorn.

I have no idea how long we rode like that. I watched the daylight disappear before we stopped in a lightly wooded portion of forest. We were met by dozens more Zweigwesens. They quickly formed into trees of protection around us, so dense, so close together that I could not see the forest beyond them. The moon shone brightly, high in the sky. It gave off enough light for me to see my friends clearly.

I shouted, "Where is The Ancient One?"

From ahead to my right, I heard in the voice of a Zweigwesen, "Here, my Queen."

I followed the voice, through a circle of gathered Zweigwesens, to the swan, The Ancient One, the teacher of the Swan Knights. His wounded stump was already tended to. A green paste oozed from beneath a leafy bandage. He was also chewing a spiraling, twisted bar of brown and green. He was calmer, no longer flailing about.

But his head was low. He followed the instructions of his caregivers, receiving their aid, but saying nothing, and never lifting his head from its low hang toward the ground.

I asked, "How is he?"

"It is an old wound, but one that was never allowed to heal. The wing was torn off with violent fury. The bone is splintered and the flesh is tattered and infected."

"Will he be okay?"

"Of course, my Queen. He is with us now. But we will want to get him to our city, as soon as we can be moving again."

"I leave him to you. Do what you think is best."

I closed my eyes and summoned Acheriel. He was with Felix, between our camp and the Queen's Lake, searching for survivors of the rescue. Within an hour, he was at my side. I committed him to the welfare of The Ancient One. The Zweigwesens were in charge and Acheriel was to serve them in any way they needed. I did not pass his orders through our silent connection. I yelled them loudly enough for the Zweigwesens to hear. He answered me loudly, with the same intention.

Several hours after our ride from the lake, survivors began to trickle into our gathering. A few Friends of the Scheriers waddled into camp. Two Glühenchor crawled to us, broken, but alive. The Zweigwesens took them immediately and tended to their injuries. Felix walked stoutly into the camp, carrying a single Scherier. The Scherier had a few Pfützeschilfs huddled in his thick hair. They too were attended, but not before I asked the Scherier about Rüdiger and Lina. He was exhausted out of reason. He had been running from the lake all night, until he was found by Felix. Every time I mentioned Rüdiger and Lina's names, he whimpered. With every whimper, every moment he did not answer me, despair consumed and digested my hope. I'm afraid I grew impatient as my panic set in. I yelled at him. I would have grabbed him and shook him, if the Zweigwesens had not swooped him from Felix's arms and carried him away.

I was at my wit's end. Prische suggested that she and I continue where Acheriel and Felix left off, that we ride toward the lake and guide our friends to the Zweigwesen camp. It was a good plan. And action of any kind was better than staring into the darkness, waiting and worrying. I asked Felix to join his old friend in caring for the swan. Prische lowered her horn. I grabbed it tightly and she flicked her head, tossing me behind her. It was a clumsy effort, but I landed on her back and we darted into the darkness, toward the lake.

We rode the very route that took us from the lake, following Prische's own prints. Signs of the chaotic escape were all around us, from dislocated flora to trails of blood. The high moon was setting and the thickening forest grew dim. Prische slowed her pace, not to better find her way. She could have sprinted it blind. She walked tentatively, with eyes and ears on high alert for signs of our friends. When the moon set entirely, we were at a near standstill, taking only a few steps per minute, listening and praying.

I grew nauseous, worrying about my favorite two Scheriers. I should not have left the lakeside until all of my surviving friends were in front of me.

I growled under my breath, more to myself than to Prische, "Why did you rush me away from the lake. I should have stayed with them."

A few bursts of breath broke through my attempt to not cry, followed by my airy, cracking lament, "Oh my Scheriers. Where are you?"

Prische defended her actions, insisting, "Only you can find the Holy Grail. There is nothing in the Sweeter Realm more important than your blood, nothing and nobody worth risking you."

I whispered defiantly, "They are. My Scheriers are."

Prische let it go and we resumed our search with full concentration.

I spoke their names aloud but to myself, "Rüdiger. My sweet Lina and Rüdiger. Where are you? Please come to me."

I closed my eyes and thought about them, trying to commune with their minds. All I felt was terror and loss, and I was not sure whether it was mine or theirs that I felt. We searched like this all night. The hour before dawn was a hellish eternity. We saw nobody, no friends or foes. In the first hints of the new day's light, Prishe shushed my mumbling. She heard something far beyond the reaches of my own ears. In an instant, I knew what she heard. She sent the experience to me.

"That's it!" I shouted. "Those are Scherier footsteps."

Prische ran toward the sound. A dark silhouette of a small creature appeared between the trees. It was Lina. She was limping, but with determined strength. Another figure was behind her. My eyes could not focus clearly, but it was a Scherier, dragging itself behind Lina. I found them. I found my sweet friends. As we got closer I could see Lina's face. I could see the white Scherier fur behind her. Prische, having keener eyes than mine, stopped suddenly and gasped. I saw what she saw, not in a picture from her eyes, but in the sorrow from her mind at what that picture was.

It *was* Lina. And it *was* Rüdiger behind her. But Rüdiger did not drag himself. Lina dragged him. As we drew closer, the morbid scene came clear. Rüdiger was mangled, twisted, and broken. When Lina saw us, she stopped sharp, stared at me, and began sobbing. She held Rüdiger's hand. Behind them were the bloody drag marks in the dirt. I jumped from Prische and ran to my Scheriers. I knelt down beside them.

"He's alright. He'll be okay. He's alright." I said in increasing volume, through an increasingly high-pitched and broken voice.

Lina could not answer. Her sobs had taken control of her. She knew what I tried to deny — Rüdiger was dead.

He could not be otherwise. He was as broken as a body could be. I reached for him, withdrew my hands, then reached for him again. I couldn't touch him. I was afraid to touch him. His eyes looked at me through slightly parted lids. There was no life behind them, none of the excitement they always wore, none of the love and devotion that always shone upon my face when he looked at me.

Lina finally burst a single word through her heavy sobs.

"Verena!" she cried, in a tone that begged me for something I could not give.

I looked at Lina. Her poor spirit was as broken as her lover's body.

"Oh, my love," I said to her, as I pulled her to my chest.

She held to Rüdiger's hand and pulled his body onto my lap. I held Lina with my left arm and pulled Rüdiger to my chest with my right.

"I love you both so much," I said, as I alternated kisses between them.

I caressed the top of Rüdiger's head with my thumb and repeated, "I am so sorry, my sweet friend. Forgive me. I am so sorry."

Lina nestled her face against my chest. But no ancient ore could soothe her. It was my love and comfort she sought, not the magical properties of my armor. I stood and placed Lina gingerly on Prishe's shoulders. Lina held tightly to the Unicorn's white mane. My teeth grinded together in fury. I wanted to walk into the lake and kill them all. I ordered Prische to take Lina to the others to be treated for her injuries.

"And Rüdiger?" she asked.

I snapped back bitterly, "There is nothing their medicine can do for him. He is dead."

"Are you telling me to leave you here alone, with no idea what followed us into the woods?"

I held Rüdiger's lifeless body as gently as I could, as if I could damage him further. A clear memory jumped into the front of my mind, suddenly and without warning. It was a memory of the day before, stroking Rüdiger's fur as he slept on my lap. The memory was pushed from my head by a long chain of memories, of snapshots of Rüdiger, each pushing the last from my mind's eye, all the way back to my first sight of him in his Scherier cave. That first image of him left my mind, leaving me only the vision of the moment — the mangled body that I held in my hands.

Intense shame exploded just behind my eyes, bringing with it a headache that almost matched the pain of my heart. It was ignited by a single thought, a single memory. It was of Acheriel, suggesting that we search for the Grail before rescuing the swan. Had we done so, and things went as they did at the lake, he could have been saved. Losing Rüdiger was more than I could bear. I turned my head from a fixed stare at the ground to my left. I looked into Prische's face, closed my eyes and turned away from her. My thoughts turned to Löwschock and all I had read, heard, and seen of his vileness.

My fury swelled and I growled through my teeth, "If there are others to save, I will save them. If there are others to find dead, I will find them. And if the creatures of the Deep find me, God help them."

Prische began another protest to my orders, until I sternly shouted, "Go!"

She sadly turned her head from me and galloped away with Lina.

I stood alone in the woods, holding against my chest one of the dearest hearts to ever touch mine — dear to me in the extreme, but still and lifeless. I walked toward the lake, stroking Rüdiger with my fingertips and begging him under my breath for forgiveness. I told him how brave he was, how much I loved him, and I promised him that I would care for Lina as long as I lived. As I walked toward the lake, I cared less and less how long that would be.

I saw disturbed soil, tracks, broken and bloody branches, but no creatures, dead or alive. The forest was eerily quiet. I walked slowly, but with a steady and determined pace. I paid no thought to the passage of time. The sun traveled high and I pressed on. Finally, I came to the shore of the lake. My determination to face the enemies of my friends fled me when I caught sight of the lake. Anger and revenge turned back into fear as my eyes found the pitch-black water. None of the blackness had receded. I could not see the ground one inch into the lake, like it was a sea of ink.

I was struck by the calm peacefulness of the scene, in light of what had just happened there. None of the bodies that had been thrown ashore, that had been thrown at me, were still there — none of them. The lakeside showed no signs of life *or* death. I assumed that the bodies of my friends had been taken and eaten.

I stroked Rüdiger's head as I said aloud, "Gessner's serpent got his precious Scherier meat, but he did not get you."

The thought of my friends being eaten did not twist my guts and grind my teeth together. It sank my heart. I asked myself why I was there, why I was not with the others, leading them and tending to the injured, and offering them the comfort of their Queen. I thought about my parents and wished for them, knowing what a comfort they would be to all the good creatures.

I looked down to Rüdiger's body, then up to the sky, and I said to my loyal Scherier, "I am so sorry this happened to you. You are the bravest and sweetest . . . the best that the Sweeter Realm has ever had. I love you my friend, my Rüdiger."

With that, I accepted his death. The body in my arms was just his body. I had said goodbye to his spirit. And I begged him to watch over me and Lina. I begged him for his blessing. And I begged my Ludwig to take him in and love him as I do.

I summoned the Unicorns to get me. Within seconds they were there, seven of them. They had stalked me, and my mind and heart had been too full to notice. Holding the body of my friend low to my waist, I mounted a Unicorn and rode back to my worn and weary subjects.

As I rode away from the lake, no words and no thoughts passed between me and the Unicorns that rode with me. I felt my heart being probed by them. I did not shut them out, but I did not invite them in either. About halfway back to the Zweigwesen camp, I began to think about The Ancient One. It was Rüdiger who insisted that we rescue him. And Rüdiger was proud to sacrifice himself to do so. He dove into the water so bravely. Now, The Ancient One is free. He is warm and dry and surrounded by friends. Oh how my dear little Scherier must have been smiling down on us all. The thought lifted my spirits and set the losses into perspective. The Sweeter Realm needed the old swan, and his freedom could not have been purchased at too dear a price.

When we got back to the camp, it had been fully struck. Nothing remained from the night before except a few Zweigwesens. They started to tell me how things stood, but their voices slipped into a tunneling haze as I reached my mind for Acheriel. I saw everything. I leaned down and kissed the shaggy mane of the Unicorn that held me. In a quick thought, I sent my orders. The Zweigwesens were scooped up by the other Unicorns and we all raced to

Zweigwesen land, to the Zweigwesen city where The Ancient One waited to be reunited with the Swan Knighthood.

CHAPTER 11

Secret Errands

WHEN WE ARRIVED IN THE ZWEIGWESEN CITY, a corridor of Unicorns and Zweigwesens ushered us to an altar they had erected for Rüdiger. We rode pass the buildings of the Zweigwesen city. They were nothing more than tree trunks leaning against each other, forming wooden tents. The trees were alive and still rooted to the ground, planted in a circle and growing in toward each other, bending to near horizontal at the top. Some were very tall, like a three or four story building. There were many trees between each building, blending them all together so that you could ride quickly through the city and not necessarily realize that you were in a city.

Prische met us at the city's edge and escorted us to within a few feet of the altar. I dismounted the Unicorn and walked to it. As I reached my dead friend toward it, I dreaded laying him down and letting go, knowing I would never touch him again.

I placed him on the altar, ran my fingers through his fur one last time, and stepped back. Lina jumped onto the altar from behind me. She kissed and rubbed her lover. She whispered something in his ear, pulled away from him, and giggled. She patted him a few times, leaned forward, and whispered to him again. Then she tilted her head to the side, rested her ear on him, and cried. All in attendance watched in silence for several minutes as her crying winded down.

She pulled away from Rüdiger, lifted her head to us, and said, "Alright, I'm done."

She leapt from the altar into my arms. Two Zweigwesens passed us on either side, carrying torches. They lit the altar and we all backed away.

As the flames grew to light the body, Lina whispered, "Goodbye, my lover."

I followed with, "Goodbye, loyal friend."

Cresting surges of similar sentiments flowed over us in whispers from the crowd behind us. I followed a single strand of smoke as it rose into the sky. I stared at it until it dissipated, then I kissed Lina and handed her into the arms of a nearby Zweigwesen.

My heart could not remain at the altar. Besides, I had put off my introduction to The Ancient One for long enough. The gathered crowd behind me formed a corridor as I turned from the fire and walked toward the heart of the city. The nods and gestures of the city inhabitants led me to a large building. When I entered, there on a thick pile of long grass, sat The Ancient One. His long neck ran along the grass bed beside him. His head rested on the bed, beneath the bandaged remains of his left wing. His eyes were closed.

An attending Zweigwesen told me, "He has slept since we left the camp."

A suggestion that I speak to him entered my mind from Acheriel, who had walked up behind me and tapped his horn to my shoulder.

"Teacher," I whispered.

I did not mean to whisper, but my voice was still affected by the emotions of the funeral.

I cleared my throat and repeated, "Teacher."

He opened his eyes and lifted his head, displaying an encouraging improvement in strength. His head wobbled a bit, until he blinked his eyes a few more times and stabilized. He looked at me, and in an instant, a tide of energy coursed through him. His eyes grew wide and light seemed to shine from them.

His head lifted high and he stood to his feet and croaked through a raspy voice that had not been used in many decades, "My Elsa, you have come back to me."

It was a mix of emotions for me. While I was honored to be addressed so, by one who knew Elsa well, I was afraid to tell him that Elsa was dead, and all I had to offer in her place was Verena Beth from Centennial, Colorado.

Acheriel answered, "Teacher, this is Verena, a child of Rudolf, and our new Swan Knight and Queen. She has come through the portal."

Clarity and focus returned to the swan's eyes. Along with it came a vivid picture of the struggle to free him, and the heavy weight of what was sacrificed. He winced with the realization. But the weight did not crush him.

He looked me up and down. He was not disappointed.

After a minute or so of sweeping his eyes up, down, and across me, he spoke, "My child, you are the very portrait of my dear Elsa."

He paused and continued, "As good as it is to be free from the lake, warm, dry, and among friends, it is much lovelier to see the Grail Blood inside of that armor again. I helped design that armor, you know."

"I know," I whispered as I pulled Ludwig's journal from under my armor.

I handed it to him and said, "This belongs to you. It is your story more than anyone's."

I placed the book in front of him.

He asked, "What is this?"

"It is how I know of you, how I have come to love you. It is the story of a wise and magical swan, and everything he has meant to my family, written and left for me by Ludwig II of Bavaria, King and Swan Knight."

As he flipped the first few pages, I explained how I came to Linderhof, how I found the book in the boat, how I suspected that I was not alone in the grotto that day, but shared the room with the Brunnen who took the journal from Ludwig.

"Ludwig made some changes to the valley," I told him, "but I will let you read about that."

His eyes widened further. I watched them devour the familiar handwriting. He shook in a half-giggle, half-cry, as he unfolded Rudolf's Map with his trembling beak. I signaled for Acheriel and the Zweigwesens to follow me out of the building to allow The Ancient One to read and reminisce in peace.

"Swan Knight," The Ancient One called to me. "Please, stay with me. Your lessons begin now."

The others left the building. I removed the armor and sat down beside my teacher. We took turns reading portions of Ludwig's journal to each other.

We sat for several days in this way, with Zweigwesens coming in and out with medicines and fresh bandages, and the Friends of the Scheriers serving and removing food. The swan and I read through the journal. Ludwig had skipped many wonderful stories in his need to finish before his death. The Ancient One elaborated on the stories included and told many that were not — in great and animated detail. It pained him greatly to read about Ludwig's last years. He asked me for all information I knew about Ludwig's death. I told what little I knew. He asked me who the Swan Knight was after Ludwig. As far as I knew, there were none, not until me. This agitated him. His feathers fluffed as he pondered the empty valley. But

Ludwig's writing brought him more joy than sorrow. And he was delighted to discuss it with me.

Life and brightness returned to him with every recollection of his favorite topic, the Swan Knight history. We laughed together and we cried together. His stories adhered my spirit more tightly to my bloodline. He is a vivid and colorful storyteller. He spent almost three weeks telling me stories of the Knights before me. He retold the lives I had read, but through eyes that had witnessed the events. Each chapter, each anecdote, pumped vigor into his healing body.

By the time he was finished teaching me the history, I believed in who I was and why I was in the Sweeter Realm. He knew my doubts, and he told each story with a specific rhetorical end, to thoroughly convince me of my place in the glorious history of Parsifal's children. We lost many brave friends to recover The Ancient One. But the creatures of the Land and Shallow Waters valued me, and I had no value without him.

I didn't need to learn the Swan Knight history as so many had, from the beginning. I only had to fill in what Ludwig had left out and add my own story for the keeper of the history. The Ancient One was very interested in my past. He asked questions and I answered. I was embarrassed to answer his questions with the drab and mundane truths about my life. He had raised the most heroic figures in Germanic history and legend. It pained me to talk about my town, my school, even my family, in the midst of studying about Elsa, Veronika, Tannhäuser, and Otto I. My family, my stories, did not stick out like veins on the back of the hand. I mentioned that regret to the swan.

He countered, "Of course they do."

He took the stories I told him, and without bending a single truth or elaborating upon a single fact, he constructed a narrative of my life that fit seamlessly into the Swan Knight history. I, my parents, even Karl, took our place among the protruding veins in Ludwig's book. As he read my life back to me, as it will be taught long after I am gone, I swelled with pride in myself, my family, and our secret heritage. I thought about how proud my father would be to know of the holy magic under his skin. My eyes remained dewy for days as that thought dominated all others.

In the weeks that I studied the history, the teacher rarely left the Zweigwesen building. When he did, he did not go far, and he sneaked out when the city was quiet. I believe he was embarrassed about his wing. Each time he returned to the cover of the building, he did so with great relief. He was never relaxed while others were around him. Oh, he was quite comfortable with me, but all others, even his oldest friends, unsettled him with their company. When others were in attendance, he turned his healing stump away from them.

There was no sense of urgency in his teaching, no time tables discussed. He was focused entirely on me. He seemed to forget the rest of the Sweeter Realm and its concerns. He rarely allowed me to leave his side. I wondered about my friends, Lina, Felix, Acheriel, and Prische, and how Cort fared in his travels. I had not seen Lina since the funeral. Prische and Acheriel offered to take me riding, but I was not permitted. Felix poked his head in from time to time, but was quickly brushed away by the swan.

A few days went by after he taught me the full history, days when I learned nothing. I began to feel restless, like I was shirking my responsibilities.

Finally, The Ancient One told me, "Send your Federman to see me. I must speak with him alone. We can go no further with your training until I speak to him."

The order excited me on two counts. It suggested that progress of some kind might be soon at hand. And it gave me an excuse to seek out a friend I had come to cherish deeply. As busy as my mind was during my lessons, I thought often of Felix, especially at night, when my memory of his service to me, after the incident at the pond, was most pungently on my mind. After the worst, the most terrifying experience of my life, he warmed me and comforted me. I slept like a child in his arms. It was hard to shake that memory. Even when warm and comfortable, I felt cold and lonely at night, and I craved his warm feathers.

I used the swan's order as an excuse to take the Unicorns up on their repeated offer. I invited Felix to ride out of the city with me, on my two favorite Unicorns. My entire association with them all had been urgent and dangerous until after the rescue. That ride was leisurely and light-hearted. The sorrow of our losses still hung on us. But there was a relaxed sense of hope during that ride. We laughed together. We spoke of no rescues and no losses, no needs and no dangers. I was without the armor, but the light-hearted conversation provided what the Scherier ore did not.

I brought up the subject of The Ancient One. I told Felix that he must speak to him alone. Then, I expressed my observations and suspicions to my friends. The swan avoided contact with others and I believed it was his wing that inhibited him. They told me how majestic he was in flight — when he could fly. We all agreed that he did not feel whole and his disfiguration and inability to fly probably troubled him more than he let on.

He was a bird who could not fly. But I didn't see him as handicapped. None of us did. His ability to fly had been such a trivial part of his character, insignificant to his overall greatness. What he had offered the Swan Knights, what he offered us all, didn't come from his *wings*. It came from his mind. It came from his heart. And those things were still intact and phenomenally strong.

We broke from our ride and rested under a tree, debating what we could do to convince The Ancient One of the facts I just detailed. Felix kept quiet while the Unicorns and I submitted and withdrew ideas. Finally, I looked to Felix. He wore a somber expression, as he sat staring at his feet, with his arms folded, stroking the feathers on the backs of his upper arms, tenderly and mournfully, as if telling them goodbye.

I asked him, "Are you okay? What's wrong?"

He turned to me slowly, as his eyes began to smile. His mouth followed in kind.

He said, "Leave the swan to me. I know what he needs."

I could tell that he had no intention of sharing his plan with the rest of us.

I said, "Come now. You're not going to keep secrets from your Queen, are you?"

Acheriel and Prische volleyed suspicious looks back and forth between us. I did not try to keep them out of my mind. This new intrigue made Felix all the more alluring and I did nothing to hide the flirtatiousness in my voice and manner.

I continued prodding, "Come on, why can't you tell me?"

His face grew somber and he winced as if in pain. This threw a heavy pall on the air around us.

He said, "It is personal. You will all know soon. Right now, it's personal. And I must reconcile myself to it before I talk of it."

There was such seriousness in his voice, in his face. It frightened me, in such contrast to the moments earlier. I felt a heaviness come into my chest and it startled me. I hated leaving the subject like that but did not know what to say.

Prische felt the awkwardness in the air, and just as it got unbearable, she said, "Well, then we will leave the matter in your capable hands, Felix. Let us know if we may be of assistance."

Not another word was said on the subject. I turned the topic back to the cryptic mandate of The Ancient One. We were all intrigued. We can go no further with my training until he speaks with Felix. The mystery put a delightful little itch into our minds, and it distracted us back into a more jovial air. We all decided that we could not wait to get to the bottom of it. We broke our little meeting and rode back into the city with hearts almost as light as when we rode out.

The Unicorns dropped us off at The Ancient One's building.

I poked my head inside and said, "Um, here's my Federma . . . Here's Felix."

I stood just outside of the entrance. I heard Felix tell The Ancient One how much better he looks, how very glad he is that the old swan managed to survive for all of those years.

Felix asked, "What happened to your wing?"

The Ancient One did not answer right away. I could not see what happened between them, but the long silence was uncomfortable — for me.

The teacher broke the pause, asking, "So Felix, what do you think of our new Swan Knight?"

My eyes widened involuntarily, as if doing so would help me to hear better. Felix's response reminded me of when I first met him, when he stuttered outside of Rüdiger and Lina's cave, staring at me. He told The Ancient One how inspired he was by me, how the first sight of me stirred his heart into zealous action, powered by hope. He called me beautiful. Every drop of blood in my body gathered just under the surface of my face. As badly as I wanted to hear more, I could not bear it. I walked away from the building, cupping my hands over my mouth. Felix's opinion of me was no secret. But hearing it from his mouth, especially to The Ancient One, whose respect and affection I desperately desired, was more than my ears could handle. I walked several laps around the city, alone, never taking my palms from my face.

At the end of each lap, I made a wide arch around the entrance to the swan's building, staring for signs of movement, but not daring to get close enough to hear what was obviously not meant to be heard. Finally, at the end of a lap, Felix stood outside the entrance. He waited there for me.

When I approached him, he said in a teasing tone, hinting at something that he believed would please me, "*I* have been sent on a special errand . . . to retrieve something for *you*."

"Will I be surprised?"

He tilted his head and his eyes glassed over with adoration, as he said, "Not if you truly know yourself. But then, *I* can't imagine that there is anything you don't deserve, that there is any wonder you would not make more wonderful."

I slight blush came over his pale face.

He recovered quickly, shook himself from his fixed stare, and said, "And now, my Queen, I am off on a sacred errand . . . on two, two sacred and secret errands."

With that, he ran from me at amazing speed. He disappeared around a Zweigwesen building and was gone from my sight.

CHAPTER 12

The Gifts

FELIX WAS GONE FOR FIVE WEEKS. As attracted as I was to the mystery of his departure and to his secret meeting with my teacher, I did not have time to mourn his absence or ponder his cryptic parting words. The Ancient One kept my mind full and active. He refused to burden me with the perils at hand. He would not speak of the Sweeter Realm or of Löwschock.

"Your mind is not ready," he said, "to address those issues. If you consider them now, you will paint them with the brush of your current understanding. Once your understanding improves, it will be too late. They will already bear the mark of your current judgment. That could be tragic."

It was a frank assessment of the situation, and I was not insulted by it. I truly was unready. This life had been so recently and so suddenly thrown on me. I tried to yield to his wisdom. I tried not to apply his lessons to the burdens of the day. He trained the Swan Knights. His résumé gave him irreproachable authority in my mind.

We combed through the Swan Knight history together — moment by moment, incident by incident, extracting the judgments and decisions of each figure, evaluating them for their wisdom or their folly. He asked me to judge them, to say what was done wrong or right, what lessons were to be learned from each action of each Swan Knight.

"If we rolled them all into one," he often said, "they would make the perfect leader. That is what you must become. You must be the best of each of them. Your actions must be guided by the lessons you learn from the Swan Knight history."

I certainly saw the wisdom in that, and I bent my mind and my will toward that end, though I did find rather daunting the challenge to become the very best of every Swan Knight. I held them all so high above myself.

By the end of the five weeks, I was beginning to satisfy the swan with my progress, enough for him to ask me to judge *him*. He asked me to point out his mistakes during his many centuries with the Swan Knights. We were beyond the awkwardness that would have elicited in me several weeks earlier. I answered honestly, giving respectfully stern criticism to the mistakes that he had made. He smiled at me. His eyes lit. And he told me that I was ready for the next phase of my training. His approval was the greatest energizer of my commitment.

The swan knew how attached I had become to the creatures I had come to know, especially those involved in the rescue. He also knew how badly they needed my attention. With nothing else to do until Felix's return, The Ancient One sent me into the city to reconnect with my friends. I sought Lina first. I worried for her. We spent the whole day together, mostly alone and entirely focused on each other. The day was one long, seemless conversation, speaking more of the past than the future, and memorializing with bright tenderness the friends we had lost together.

Lina spoke easily of Rüdiger. She shed the occasional tear and she pressed herself tightly against me. But she talked of her husband with more laughter and smiles than cries. She missed him terribly and I regretted the many weeks I had left her alone. My studies had taken my mind away. Lina reawakened my heart to tender and vibrant love that had begun to sleep undisturbed inside of me. The Ancient One was right. My love for Lina, my loss of Rüdiger, my enigmatic emotions for Felix, all looked very different to me once painted with the brush of my studies.

The very next morning, Felix returned to the Zweigwesen city. I had gone for an early morning ride, not on Prische. She and Acheriel were back in Unicorn land, tracking the progress of my friend, Cort, who worked tirelessly to prepare the Land and Shallow Waters to rally behind their new Queen. I rode that morning on a light-brown Unicorn. His coat was much softer than the hair of any creature I had felt. He told me that he had just returned from the Brunnen homeland, from a city called Saint Hildegard. The Brunnens had bathed him and brushed him with their soft fingers. Stroking his fur was like running my hand through steam, that soft and that warm.

When we rode back into the city, the Zweigwesens seemed more than usually delighted to see me. They grinned, as if they knew a secret I did not. That was exactly the case. Felix was back and in conference with The Ancient One. He had returned with the two sacred and secret treasures he had promised.

I entered the Zweigwesen building and saw my two, dear, feathered friends standing side by side. On the floor in front of them was a blanket with something long and slender beneath it. The Ancient One beckoned me closer. Two opposing forces fought over the attention of my eyes — my curiosity at the item beneath the blanket, which was clearly being presented to me ceremoniously, and my desire to arouse my spirits with the sight of my awkward little Federman.

When I drew within a few feet, The Ancient One announced, "This is why I had to speak to your dear Felix."

I began to say, "He's not *my* dear Felix."

But I only got as far as, "He's n . . ." before interrupting myself for fear of my dishonesty being too apparent.

I allowed him to continue, "An item, an artifact of infinite value has been waiting in the Sweeter Realm for you, waiting for nearly five hundred years."

I tried to subdue the smile that seized authoritarian dominance over my face. It was pointless. The wait, the mystery, the blanket, The Ancient One's introduction of this gift all combined to swell me with fevered anticipation. He could have removed the blanket to reveal an ordinary banana, and I would have believed it the greatest artifact in history. But he did not reveal a banana. He grabbed the corner of the blanket with his beak, flicked his long neck to the side, and revealed a sword — a shining, spiraling, Unicorn-horn sword. I had recently combed through the Swan Knight history. I knew in an instant what was being gifted to me. It was Albert's sword, the sword that Albert V fashioned from the horn that the Unicorn lost during Albert's Battle.

Ludwig's journal made no mention of what had become of the sword. The Ancient One left that out of my recent lessons, so that the gift would be a surprise. It was time for him to tell me the sword's story.

"Albert carried the sword for many years. He touched it to his chest or to his forehead when he was lonely, or when he simply yearned for the connection with the Unicorns. But such a peculiar item drew many questions, many unwanted examiners, and it was an unveiled window into the most sacred secret in history. One day, he gave it to me and asked me to take it through the portal, away from curious and probing human eyes. I hid it carefully, fully convinced that it would serve the Swan Knighthood someday. That day is now, my dear."

I stared at it, not daring to reach for it, or even step closer. I was drawn into a trance by its beauty.

The Ancient One snapped me back, saying, "Well, take your sword, Verena."

I answered in a reverent whisper, "This gift is too dear. I cannot accept it."

"It is not a gift, Swan Knight. This was Albert's sword. It belongs to your family. It belongs to you. We simply held it for you. It is a Swan Knight's sword, and you are the Swan Knight. Take your sword."

I picked it up as gingerly as my shaking hands could. I held it as I would hold a fragile artifact, not a weapon of war.

Felix blurted, "Well, give it a swing. Let's see how it suits you."

I gripped the handle with my right hand, let go with my left, and waved it in front of me.

Felix teased me, "Come on, give it a real swing."

I waved it over my head. The sword seemed to choreograph its own dance. Without thought, I swung it and I spun in place. I felt more graceful than I had ever felt in my life. For several minutes I danced around with the sword. Felix just smiled. The Ancient One laughed, not the laugh of ridicule, but the loving laugh of a parent watching a child take her first steps.

The Ancient One leaned to Felix and spoke, clearly with the intention of me hearing him, "Like the young Red-Head with Cunrad's axe."

For a moment, those words made me feel heroic. Visions of Otto I, the savior at Verona, danced through my head. I stood still, except for a little twirling of my wrist, on the hand that held the sword, as I envisioned the famous battle.

I stopped abruptly and looked at Felix, remembering his parting words, and I asked him, "What was the second errand? What else have you brought?"

He smiled, then turned his head to the entrance of the building and whistled. It was a loud and forceful whistle. It lifted his flap of a nose off of his upper lip. A Zweigwesen responded, walking in with his arms full, full of brilliantly white feathers. Felix pulled the item from the Zweigwesen's hand and held toward The Ancient One a wing with straps. He had fashioned a wing for our noble friend.

I was so delighted with him, so proud of his thoughtfulness. I ran to him and threw my arms around him, thanking him. When my hands touched his back, I discovered the origin of the feathers. Felix's back was bare. In place of the feathers of his back were sores, still raw and tender.

I pulled away from him and said, "Those are your feathers, the feathers from your own back."

Felix gave a timid nod to me, then looked to The Ancient One, reached forward, and offered the wing to the teacher. The Ancient One bowed his head in shame.

He held that pose for several seconds, then looked up to Felix and said, "I do not know what to say to you for this gift, for this sacrifice."

I said, "That is so wonderful of you, to tear out your own feathers to make him feel whole again. How long will it take for your feathers to grow back?"

Felix responded only with a timid and humble glance to the floor in front of him.

The Ancient One answered my question, "They will never grow back. His feathers do not grow back. That portion of his body will never again bear feathers."

Felix had permanently disfigured himself so that The Ancient One could have two wings. He knelt down and

148

fastened the wing to the swan. Once Felix stood, the old teacher looked whole again. I would not have known that anything had happened to his wing, but for the straps that held the prosthetic in place. The gift, the gesture, the sacrifice already shone brightly in my eyes as the noblest act. When I saw The Ancient One's face, as he bent his long neck around to admire his new wholeness with delight, pride, and immense gratitude, the sacrifice shone all the nobler. Although the new wing would not return to him his lost ability of flight, it made him look and feel whole.

The youthful glee in The Ancient One's face and the overall sense of health and happiness glowing from his full form released from my lips a question that had been lingering on my gums for weeks, "What happened to your wing?"

I regretted the question as soon as I asked it. I regretted for two reasons. I did not want to hurt my cherished mentor, to remind him of terrible times just as he recovered. I was also afraid to hear the story. I wasn't sure my heart could handle the horrible imagery that was certain to accompany the tale. Nevertheless, I had asked the question, and I waited with held breath for the answer.

"Löwschock ripped it off. After several years in the jail, he came to me, and without a word, he grabbed me by the neck and wing. He squeezed his claw shut on my wing, breaking it, but not severing it. I wish he had severed it. Instead, he pulled and twisted my wing, yanking on it until the bone fully shattered and the flesh fully tore. He held my wing high above his head. He brought his face to mine. With one claw he held my head, so I could not look away. With the other, he ate my wing, chewing it slowly, crunching and grinding away. I watched my own blood run down his chin. Several times, he stopped chewing to open his mouth and show me clearly the wadded mass of my former wing rolling around in his mouth. He did not threaten me or ask me questions. He simple finished eating my wing and left. Every time the wound began to heal, one of his monsters would hit me in the splintered bones and reopen the wound."

"How long ago?"

"One hundred years, maybe more. By then, I had already lost all sense of time."

"And they have been reopening the wound ever since?"

The Ancient One nodded his head with a wincing grimace.

I was right to regret asking the question. His answer horrified me more than anything I could have imagined. My violent shivers and crawling skin must have been visible to him. At the same time, he seemed slightly relieved to have told the story, once he recovered from reliving it. I became nauseous. I fought it back, not wanting to show such weakness. To relieve myself, I sent the thoughts to Acheriel and Prische. It was much to burden them with, but I could not bear it alone. I felt instant relief as they sent waves of sympathy back to me.

The story of the lost wing made Felix's gift all the more precious to me. It made *him* more precious to me. No longer was there the barren reminder of that horrible, violent act perpetually at the swan's side, in the form of the stump. In its place was a beautifully feathered wing. The Ancient One's story brought the weight of Felix's sacrifice into balance with the effect of it.

I held Albert's sword in my hand, the result of another violent amputation. The severed horn, the severed wing — we had survived both of those terrible events. But as I held the sword and looked at the prosthetic wing, I thought of our dangers. I thought of the violence that was surely mounting against us in response to our attack on the lake and the freeing of Löwschock's prized prisoner. I suddenly felt unsafe in the Zweigwesen city. The city had been destroyed in the war, destroyed and later rebuilt once Löwschock retreated back to the Waters. If it could be destroyed, it could be destroyed again. Nobody knew the condition of the Deep armies. A chill flew over me that I could not mask.

Without having shared the evolution of my thoughts, or the reason for the shivering of my whole body, I blurted out, "We have to leave here. We have to hide."

The Ancient One and Felix did not doubt or question me. Both had come to admire and trust the infant abilities that were just coming to life inside of me.

Felix asked, "Where can we go?"

In a rush of recollection, I thought about the homes that the Wühlenvogels burrowed beneath each homeland, those replicas of each breed's portion of the underground city in the Black Forest. They dug them before The Exodus — exact replicas of the living quarters that each breed would have in Einigkeitstadt, build so that they might get used to life in those conditions before undertaking their commitment to Rudolf I, the Rightful Swan Knight.

I asked, "What about the Einigkeitstadt replicas, beneath each homeland? Could we go to one of them, continue my training there?"

"That might work," The Ancient One commented.

"No," Felix quickly retorted, "Löwschock may not know about them yet, but the Wühlenvogels know of them, and they are with him now."

"They are what?!" I shouted.

"The Wühlenvogels swore an eternal oath to the Queen, when she saved them from the lake. When the Queen died, their allegiance passed to the swan. Upon his presumed death, it passed to Ludwig. When the portal sealed, we all assumed Ludwig's death. The Wühlenvogel oath had to pass somewhere. They felt honor-bound to maintain their allegiance to the monarch of the Land and Shallow Waters. The Land had no monarch. When Löwschock returned and took control of all of the Waters, he was all that they had. So they reluctantly transferred the oath to him. They have no affinity for the King of the Deep, but the Wühlenvogels are strange creatures. They are strangely bound to him by a since of honor that clings to the memory of a dead Queen."

"Perhaps," the swan said, "if they knew that she is here, that a new Queen of the Land and Shallow Waters has come, one who stands in Kandake's place, a cousin of Ludwig, their loyalty will find its way back where it belongs."

"Perhaps," Felix responded.

The Ancient One knew of my connection to the Unicorns, and of the progress I had made in developing Elsa's skill.

"Reach for them," my teacher instructed me. "Try to connect with them. Tell them that you are here. Claim the loyalty that your blood and your title should ensure."

"I will try to."

I sat on the floor. I handed my sword to Felix, not wanting to betray my Unicorns by connecting to the horn while communicating with the Wühlenvogels. I closed my eyes, imagined the Wühlenvogels, and tried to limit my thoughts to the simple message, "I am here."

The Wühlenvogels did not meet the Swan Knights until long after Elsa. They did not communicate with her the way that the others had. They heard me. That is, they thought my thoughts. But my message was confusing to them. They did not know who I was or why they all had the same bizarre dream about a young human woman declaring herself to be here. They spoke in private to each other about it. But none knew what to make of their shared experience. I tried every day to reach them. But I did not get across to them that I was a Swan Knight, that I was the Queen of the Land and Shallow Waters, and that their oath of allegiance belonged to me.

Over the next few days, many Wühlenvogels broke from their ranks, from the ranks of my enemy, and openly defied the oath. They did not fully understand my message, but the appearance of a human in their collective thoughts harkened them back to better times. Their affiliation with Löwschock grew rapidly repugnant. Most tried to push me from their minds, as hard as I tried to stay in. Fortunately for the creatures of the Land, Löwschock had not yet called in their allegiance. But that was a situation certain to change after learning of my presence in the Sweeter Realm. I wanted to continue reaching for them, but the desperation of our situation demanded the distraction of immediate action. We decided to take up in the underground portion of the Brunnen homeland. I called for Unicorns. They responded and were proud to serve as transportation, as beasts of burden, and as protection for their Queen.

CHAPTER 13

The Fall

THE ZWEIGWESEN HOMELAND BORDERS both Unicorn and Brunnen lands. The Brunnen homeland is farther from the Queen's Lake and has the Unicorn homeland as a shield. Not only that, but we could no longer trust the Shallow Waters. The incident at the pond taught us that. There are Waters Shallow and Deep in every homeland. But the Brunnens have an intimate connection to their water. They feel it. They connect with it somehow. And they would know if the darkness of the Deep infiltrated their shallow lakes and ponds. The Brunnen homeland it had to be.

Despite the fearful and desperate nature of our planned voyage, I was ready to see more of the Sweeter Realm, more of this place everybody was calling *my* queendom. I was particularly eager to meet the Brunnens. We planned to travel north and pass through a range of mountains on the border of the Nomadic Belt. From there, we were to turn east, toward the main Zweigwesen medical center, a place they call Heiligborke. From Heiligborke, a short, flat, and easy walk northeast would take us to the Zweigwesen capital. It was decimated by Löwschock's army. But in the quiet years since, they have slowly revived a small portion. I was promised a grand reception there. A dense forest stands between the Zweigwesen capital and the border of the Brunnen homeland.

I sent several Unicorns to inform the Brunnens and the Zweigwesens to gather in the dense woods, to clear them of any dangers, and to serve as escorts for our party, from Zweigwesen to Brunnen land. The Unicorns told them to prepare to receive their Queen and their former King. Cort had already spread word of my coming and reports of the swan's rescue were crossing every natural barrier in the Sweeter Realm. The rescue of their former King, so soon after the arrival of their new Queen, surged the kind creatures of the Land and Shallow Waters with hope. Had I any doubt about the decision to rescue The Ancient One, and the tremendous sacrifices to make it happen, it was dissolved by the effect his freedom had on the creatures.

The Brunnens were honored to receive us and to host my training. I could not wait to meet them. I was deeply attracted to the rumors of their allurements — the beauty, the touch, and the voices that drew seasoned knights to their deaths, that captured the heart of Tannhäuser, that almost enticed Hildemar to remain in the valley and forgo her own wedding. My curiosity burned inside of me.

I could not picture them from the stories of The Ancient One and the descriptions of Ludwig. I asked Acheriel to think of the Brunnens, to imagine them as vividly as he could. He obeyed and I invaded his mind. But my connection to the Unicorns brings me their thoughts, not in pictures or in any other snapshot of their senses. It comes to me in their mental interpretation of what comes through their senses. So I did not *see* the Brunnens through Acheriel's thoughts. I saw his admiration of their beauties. I saw respect. I saw friendship. I saw his hopes for them and his fears for them. But I had no clearer picture in my mind of the creatures with the notoriously seductive powers.

Our procession from the Zweigwesen city was meticulously arranged, but not for a regal spectacle, as before. It was arranged for my security and for the security of The Ancient One. Our two lives seemed to be all that mattered to anyone involved. I rode on Acheriel, the fastest, wisest, and most trusted of the Unicorns in our company. Prische rode beside me, and I cherished our conversations as we traveled. But optics were of no importance to this caravan. The Ancient One, who in previous centuries would have flown above the company, rode on a large, dusty-white Unicorn with a dark-grey mane and beard. She seemed to know the swan well. I wore my armor and sword, but not to impress and rally. I wore it for its intended purpose, to protect my body from injury. I even wore my helmet, which to that point had been more often carried than worn. And I was surrounded on all sides by bodies willing to serve as shields against an attack on me. All pains, all arrangements were bent around our protection, mine and the swan's.

I thought about the pain that Felix must have suffered, and the disfigurement he would carry for the rest of his life, just to bring comfort to the teacher, just to ensure that he is at his best. I had no doubt, as I mounted Acheriel, that he and the others would do that and much more for me, if circumstances demanded it. I looked around me and saw the dearest hearts, all of them superior to me in so many ways, all willing to endure anything for my well-being. It was humbling, almost unnervingly so.

Felix took up a position as he had before — just behind me to my left. Although there were Unicorns with no riders, Felix walked. I had spent enough time without his company. I wanted him by my side. I wanted to talk with him. I asked him to ride beside me. He began an explanation of the strategic value of his position in the caravan. Rather rudely perhaps, I interrupted him and told him in a mock authoritative voice that his Queen demands his attention. I was making fun of my position. He took it seriously. He mounted Prische and rode beside me. I was happy to have them both by my side. I asked many questions about his people, the nomadic band of Federmensch, who drift along the northwest shore of the Queen's Lake, on the opposite side of the lake from the portal.

He spoke of his childhood and his family. He told me of their history and customs, their cuisine and their music. He sang for me some of the popular songs of his people. I tried to keep my eyes on his face. He stared deeply into my eyes while he spoke to me, never breaking eye-contact. So he noticed every time my eyes were drawn to his bare back and the sores that had not yet healed. He demonstrated a visible discomfort each time my eyes drifted there. He was quite pleased with his sacrifice and gift. But that is not to say that he did not keenly feel the loss of his feathers.

He felt incomplete without them, but his wholeness was less important to him than the swan's. He was embarrassed each time he caught me staring at his back. What he did not realize is that I did not see deformity in his missing feathers. I did not see his body at all. I saw nothing but the nobility of his heart in my glances to his backside. With each subtle dart of my eyes from his face to the sores on his back, his beauty shone all the more brilliantly. All physical awkwardness, from his sharply bowed legs to his flapping nose, from the dark stain that still marked the feathers of his upper arm to his bare back, became admirable and attractive traits in my eyes. When I met him, he was covered in brilliantly white feathers. In the many weeks that followed, he gained a dark and apparently permanent stain on his arm and he lost the feathers of his back. There was no angle from which I could look at him where some "ugliness" did not declare his goodness.

However honored he was to ride at my side, I was surely more honored to be so near *him*.

I was so engrossed by my immediate company that I paid little attention to the changes in the scenery. The flat and thickly wooded forest surrounding the Zweigwesen city gave way to open and slightly hilly plains. In the distance ahead of us were mountains. I was quite accustomed to mountains, having been raised in Colorado. But these mountains were very different than the ones I saw from my bedroom window back home. Even from that distance, they spoke of experiences, of wars and peace, of cozy homes and midnight rendezvous. The sun reflected golden off of them.

As we drew closer, and the scale of the mountains became apparent, I asked Acheriel, "Shouldn't we have gone around them?"

He answered, "That would have been much easier. But there is a lookout point we wish to show you, to give you a better understanding of the area. You may find yourself alone and we'd like you to know your way about."

Well, there was certainly no arguing with that. As I said, all of my safety concerns were considered. The reasoning for our mountain pass having been made clear to me did nothing to settle the dull, but increasing sense of dread that the mountains elicited in my mind as our approach raised them higher and higher in my vision. I began to fear for the company, for my friends. I did not hide my mind from the Unicorns.

Prische felt my thoughts and answered, "I have spent much time in these hills. They are not far south of the Unicorn homeland. There is nothing there that should worry you, unless you are scared of heights."

I assured her that I spent much of my childhood looking through the window of the family car while my father sped through the high, twisting roads of the Rocky Mountains.

She continued, "Then you will be fine. There are some treacherous passes, but stay close to me, my Queen, and you will be well."

I have never been afraid of heights. Still, her comments gave me comfort — too much comfort as it happens.

We were still a few hours from sunset when we reached the foot of the mountains. Still, there seemed to be a general, unspoken understanding among the company that we would camp there and begin our climb in the morning. I was certainly not ready to argue with their collective wisdom. I winded the last hours of daylight sitting in light and easy conversation, with Lina on my lap and Felix at my side. Acheriel and Prische were never far, and the newly whole swan felt confident and comfortable enough with his new wing to mingle through the company, answering question, catching up with old friends, and of course teaching. I saw little of him that evening.

I loved The Ancient One, more deeply with each day under his tutelage. But I was subordinate in his company. I relished the conversation of friends, with no expectation of learning, no tests, no questions. Felix and I spoke with the intimacy and comfort of old friends. Lina laughed and wrestled with us. I fell asleep huddled tightly around Lina, with Felix so near me that I almost thought I felt his feathers tickle lightly against me through my armor.

The very moment the sun broke, the company was animated with commotion, efficient and focused. Fruits were handed to me by who-knows-whom, from every direction. Before my eyes had acclimated to the light, we were again in motion, marching to the slope that loomed tauntingly before us. As we entered the mountains, we worked our way around the highest peaks, cutting wide curves to remain in the valleys. Eventually, we climbed. We followed a natural path that took us up a slope so steep that it was unsafe to ride the Unicorns. Frankly, I was glad to be on my feet. I had sat all morning and my legs needed to feel useful. I found the hike refreshing at first, but it continued much longer than I thought it would. I looked ahead as we climbed, but I could not tell where the mountain peaked.

As we climbed above the neighboring hills, I paused, turned, and stood with my back to the slope. The views to my right and left were breathtaking, unlike anything I had seen in pictures, film, or the wildest reaches of my imagination. In look and in spirit, the expansive landscape within my field of vision was different — ancient and magical, mystical and richly intruiging. I could see for miles across Zweigwesen land. I strongly sensed the unfamiliarity of the scene, so very unlike my home. The newness, thc alien strangeness of the sight did not sicken me or frighten me as it did in my first few days in the Sweeter Realm. It intoxicated me and filled me the desire to fly from the path and soar at great speeds over the many mysteries that my queendom waited to show me. I wanted to consume them all as quickly as my full mind could receive them.

A few deep and contemplative breaths later, I was prodded to continue climbing. The steady incline of the mountain became too sharp to hike. We encountered a well-worn path that centuries of use had cut into the side of the slope, beginning quite narrow, but growing wide enough for three Unicorns to walk shoulder to shoulder. The path did not climb, but worked its way around the right side of the mountain, so that to our left was the mountain side, and to our right was a steep drop that grew steeper as we walked.

I was not afraid of heights, but the steep drop to our right was severe and daunting. I had hiked some impressive peaks with my parents, but never had I felt so high, so disconnected from the safety of solid ground. This sensation grew to fear, which grew to near panic as the path began to narrow. We had to walk it in single file. Prische noticed me glancing down the drop and shuddering with chills of anxiety. She talked to me, easily pulling my mind from its fears with stories of ancient Unicorn rituals.

She spoke of a Unicorn holiday, similar to Halloween, when the dead are recognized and honored. When she spoke of a ritual not dissimilar to Trick-or-Treating, I got excited — too excited. I turned quickly to her, to share with her the similarities between our childhood experiences. I slipped and fell off of the path. The drop to our right had become a vertical cliff. There was nothing for me to step on, nothing to grab, and nobody beside me to prevent my fall. There was nothing between me and the ground far, far below me.

I fell face first, but turned quickly to face upward and watch the path and my friends fly quickly above me. I anticipated the deadly blow of the ground beneath me, as the dwindling vision of my friends shrunk to nothing in front of me. But the ground would not come. I was terrified, but not like in the pond. I had experienced so much since then. I feared more the effect of my death on the creatures who had to watch me fall and shatter on the ground. In those moments of rapid-fire fear, pity for The Sweeter Realm was my dominant emotion.

I saw a flash of white feathers catch the sun, descending toward me.

I thought, "The Ancient One cannot fly. Maybe he can glide with his new wing. But he could not hold my weight and his."

I entirely forgot my own peril and sank into sickening panic as I realized that it was Felix, shooting at me like a feather-coated arrow.

"You cannot fly!" I shouted up to him.

162

As he closed the gap between us, I saw no fear in his face, only brave determination, and perhaps a slight twinkle of love peeking out through his eyes. The few seconds that passed during the fall felt like an hour, plenty of time for hundreds of thoughts, fears, and regrets — and pinching, twisting, biting love, love for many, from the many strange facets of my life — to bounce around my head.

Felix caught up to me, grabbed me, and spun himself beneath me, just in time to hit the ground flat on his back. With my back against him, I felt the weight of my own body crush every bone inside of him. Every crushed bone, every shattered tendon, every punctured organ, sent its signature vibration through me in morbidly vivid detail. I gasped desperately for breath.

Still looking to the sky, my backside pinning the crushed body of my dear, brave Felix against the ground beneath us, I drew enough air into my lungs to painfully whisper, "I have killed you."

I laid on him with no idea of my own injuries, and terrified to imagine what Felix looked like beneath me. I tried to roll off of him, but I could not move. I tried and struggled until I was able to make small movements of my arms and legs. I could not imagine that he lived. Yet, I still wanted desperately off of him for fear of hurting him further. After what seemed like ten minutes of rolling back and forth, I managed to rock myself off of Felix and onto my side.

He was not dead. He stared straight upward, with his eyes wide open, his neck and lower jaw convulsing fruitlessly in attempts to draw breath into his smashed lungs. His convulsions slowed until they stopped, and his crushed and ruptured body laid there, perfectly still, with his frozen eyes wide open. I cried as deeply as my struggling lungs allowed. Through the half-vocalized whisper of my damaged throat, I scolded him. I thanked him and scolded him again. And I kissed him. I kissed him all over his face, chest, and shoulders, as his blood escaped from beneath his body and ran onto me.

More and more air entered my lungs, and my voice regained some strength, combining to send my raspy screams and sobs echoing off of the cliff beside me. I felt for a moment that the cliff mourned with me, that my echo was its cry joining mine. Crying, breathing, screaming, hurt my chest and throat. It felt like the flesh had been burnt off of me, and my charred bones were being stabbed at with a knife. But that was not the worst of my pain. Felix had saved me again, not from my bravery, like before, but from my thoughtlessness and clumsiness — and this time it broke him. I stopped scolding him and occupied my dry mouth entirely with kissing him. When I pulled my head away from his, my eyes caught the black stain on his arm. Every drop of his goodness and purity rushed into my pathetic heart at once, nearly stopping it with grief.

I rolled away from him, buried my face in the dirt and repeated, "Not my Felix. Not my Felix. Please don't take my Felix."

Suddenly, I felt myself being handled and rolled over. Several Zweigwesens, more than my watery and weary eyes could count, surrounded me. They removed my armor, poked me and probed me, squeezed me and pulled on me. They spoke quickly in Zweigwesen. From between two of them, I saw more Zweigwesens lifting Felix. They did not poke and probe him. They simply lifted him and carried him away.

I erupted into frantic sobs and tried to speak to them, "Not yet. Please don't take him yet."

I tried to order them, "Let me say goodbye to him." But the order came out as a jumbled mess of tears and nondescript syllables. I tried to gesture an order to bring his body back to me, but all of my limbs were firmly secured by Zweigwesen hands. Felix was out of my sight, leaving my senses to focus on my own physical pain. Every aspect of my total being, body, mind, and spirit, were being twisted, crushed, and tortured beyond bearing. I passed out. And the swirling morbid thoughts of my tortured mind decorated the walls of my dreams with terrible images and torturous memories.

CHAPTER 14

St. Hildegard Cathedral

MY DREAMS WERE TRULY WRETCHED. There was no gradual building of the horrors, no slowly increasing suspense, at least none that I remembered. I dreamed that I was in the forest between the Queen's Lake and the Zweigwesen camp where we gathered after the rescue. I was walking beside Lina, on her left side. She dragged Rüdiger's mangled body behind her. I tried to comfort her and tell her that I love her. But the words came out in English. In my dream, I could not translate my thoughts to German and she could not understand me.

Lina slowly pulled ahead of me. Try as I did to keep up with her, I could not. I pushed hard with my legs but could not catch up with the slow march of a Scherier dragging another. I shouted for her to slow down, to wait for me. But the mourning little Scherier dwindled in my vision, her sobs growing as faint as her image. I did not know why I moved so slowly. I looked down to my feet. They looked normal, pushing each step forward with great effort, as if pushing a car uphill.

My right shoulder started to ache, then my elbow and my wrist. I looked to my right arm and found that it was behind me, pulling something. Horror struck me. It was Felix. I was dragging Felix's body behind me through the

167

forest, crushed by my weight, exactly as I had last seen it, still wearing his final expression. Suddenly, Lina was beside me again, but on the other side of me, still dragging Rüdiger. I stared at her as she looked straight ahead sobbing. I became aware of a dragging sound on my other side. I looked to the sound and saw my mother walking beside me, dragging the twisted body of my father. He was wet. A steady flow of water oozed from his mouth and nostrils. I could hear my brother Karl crying, but I could not see him. His cries echoed off of the trees so I could not tell his direction. I called for him. But my words came out in a language I did not know. It sounded like Zweigwesen, but I did not know for sure.

I felt a sudden pain in my left arm. I looked quickly to it, but it was gone. In its place was a bloody stump. All sounds in my dream were drowned out by the crunching, chewing sound of Löwschock. I couldn't see him, but he sounded close. And I knew that the crunching sound was my left arm between his powerful jaws. The crunching got louder and louder, until it hurt my ears. I wanted to cover my ears, but my left arm was gone and my right still dragged Felix. I squeezed my eyelids as tightly shut as I could, trying to block out that horrible sound. The sound stopped.

I opened my eyes and Lina and my mother stood staring at me, directly in front of me. Prische rode up behind them. Lina turned and climbed onto Prische's back, laying sideways across her. Still dead and mangled, Rüdiger's body crawled up Prische to lay on Lina. My mother followed, laying on the Scheriers. My father followed and flung himself across my mother. I heard his broken bones snap and grind as he moved. I climbed the pile and set myself, belly down, across my father's cold, wet, dead body. I felt Felix climb on me and lay across me. There was no warmth in his feather, nor were they simply cold. They were frigid, as if creating cold. And they were not soft. They were prickly and they scratched and dug through my armor and into my skin.

Prische shouted to the pile on her back, a pile of the living and the dead, "It is time to put you underground."

I tried to wiggle free from under Felix, but I could not move at all.

I shouted to Prische, "No! I order you, no! I don't want to be underground."

She replied in a calm and confident voice, "But Verena, that is where you are going. It is where you belong."

She moved forward, beginning with a slow walk, but quickly increasing speed until she was in a full gallop.

I felt the bodies beneath me, both the living and the dead, crushing under my weight. The weight of Felix's body pushed the breath from me. I could not draw it back in. The motion of Prische's full gallop bounced us on her back, crushing us all and digging Felix's feathers into my flesh. As his feathers dug into the back of my neck, I saw my blood drip down the pile beneath me. It joined blood that was not mine. Lina was being squeezed dry by our collective weight. Soon, Prische was entirely red with our blood.

She ran toward a sound, a single voice that split into two, and then three, and then a full chorus. They were beautiful. I tried to whisper to the voices, to take Felix's body off of me. I whispered and whispered, until I awoke from the dream.

I awoke from the nightmare, but did not open my eyes. I was lying down, afraid to see where I was and what terrible things were around me. I spent the next several seconds convincing myself that it was a dream, wondering how much was dream. Would I open my eyes to a Sweeter Realm where Felix was still dead? Would I open to the shell-shaped boat in the Venus Grotto at Linderhof?

Perhaps I fell asleep there. Maybe I would see the hotel room in Füssen, or my own bedroom, or the ceiling of my classroom, where I passed out staring at the portrait of Ludwig.

The answer came while my eyes remained shut.

I heard a Zweigwesen tell another, "She would not have survived if the Federman had not broken her fall. We owe everything to him."

I *did* fall. And I did crush Felix. That was not a dream. I squeezed my eyelids more tightly together, and I began to cry. I thought of Felix, of everything he had done for me and been to me since I met him outside of the Scherier cave. I thought about his kind voice and his awkward face, his warm feathers and his powerful arms. My cries began as small bursts of air popping from my nostrils. I tried to hold it back. As the pitiful emotions translated into sobs, the valves of my face opened and I cried heartily, through a wide-opened mouth.

I kept my eyes closed. I tried to connect my mind to Acheriel, but he was not near, and I did not have the strength to reach beyond my immediate setting. My hand turned instinctively to my chest, to rub the Scherier ore of my armor. My armor was off. I felt only the cloth of my shirt.

I heard a Zweigwesen voice say, "Do something. Soothe her."

With that command, I became intensely curious. My crying sputtered to a quick halt and I opened my eyes. I was in a room with high, arched ceilings, and intricately ornate support columns. The room was not large. It was no bigger than our living room back home. There were two Zweigwesens by me, one at each side. I was on a table, or altar or some kind. At my feet stood three Brunnens. They were so immensely, indescribably beautiful. The very sight of them filled my eyes with such sweet and soft beauty. My sense of sight was so overwhelmed that all other pains and all other concerns shrunk into the background of my mind.

I thought to myself, "No wonder Ludwig's description was vague. There are no words."

They were tall, nearly eye level to a Unicorn. They looked like fountains of water shooting up from the ground — or more like women, pale blue, phenomenally beautiful, and covered in several inches of water, flowing up from the ground to consume them, naked yet clothed by the water, so that they were unexposed. The water draped on and around them like a large cloth. I thought about Elsa, reaching for the Brunnen, expecting to push right through her and pull back a wet hand. The Brunnen was solid and dry.

The Brunnens at my feet swayed slightly back and forth, with a very natural flow, as if blown by a breeze. Only, we were indoors and there was no breeze. Their skin rippled in the direction of their movements. The rippling darted back and forth as they changed the direction of their sway.

I spoke to them, "You are the Brunnens. You are so beautiful."

They stopped swaying and smiled at me. In their stillness, the wall behind them came visible through their bodies.

The same Zweigwesen who gave the previous order, implored them, "Sing to her, will you?"

One of the three Brunnens began to sing — one voice harmonizing with itself through two Brunnen throats. It was very briefly the most nurturing, cradling, maternally soothing sound my ears had ever taken in, until the other two joined her. The three of them stood at my feet and filled the chamber with the sounds of many voices, reverberating around the high-ceilinged room. I stared at them and allowed my eyes and ears to celebrate their beauty together.

A third sense joined the celebration. No sooner did I hear a fourth Brunnen standing at my head, then I felt her touch.

She cupped my scalp with her long, soft palm. I felt like my entire body was cradled in her hand. She lifted her palm so that only her fingertips touched me, right above my eyebrows. She ran her fingertips down my face, over my eyelids, forcing them shut, then parting her fingers around my nose, and reuniting them on my upper lip. I opened my eyes again and saw her delicate wrist just inches above my eyes. That tender, pale arm looked as soft as her fingers felt on my face.

She lifted her index and little finger, so that only her two middle fingertips touched me. She ran those longways, across my upper lip, back across my lower lip, then back again between them. I felt like I could have parted my lips and sipped her directly into my soul. I almost tried. Her Brunnen fingertips were the softest things I could ever have imagined, until she stopped singing and leaned forward with a quiet "ssshhhh" and kissed my eyelids closed again. Kissing first the left, then the right, she seemed to suck all negative thoughts from me.

I thought about the Welf knights, lured to their deaths in the woods around Linderhof.

I thought to myself, speaking the words with my tongue, inside of my closed mouth, "Those poor men did not stand a chance."

She continued to kiss my face, all over. Although she was only one, I felt like I was being kissed by six Brunnens simultaneously. I felt my worries and my consciousness being pulled from me by the suction of each kiss, until I fell asleep. I dreamed that I was being held and kissed by dozens of Brunnens. Then, the Brunnens became Felix, holding me on the hill after the incident with the pond. Only, I was not cold. I was not scared. Felix stroked my cheeks with the downy feathers on the back of his hand.

When I awoke, the Zweigwesens were gone, and so was the Brunnen who had kissed me. The other three still stood at my feet singing to me.

I was not certain of the extent of my injuries from the fall. My heart was broken by the loss of Felix. Guilt crushed my spirits as surely as my thoughtlessness crushed his bones. That torment had overpowered any pain my body felt. The Brunnens had soothed my spirits enough for me to perform a self-evaluation of the condition of my body. I ached all over. Let there be no mistake about that. But I was okay. I wiggled my fingers and toes. I took deep breaths without severe pain. Felix had saved me.

I sat up slowly, looked to the high-arched ceiling above me and silently thanked Felix. I hoped to God that he knew that he saved me, that the knowledge brought him some comfort in those moments when his body slowed its futile attempts to draw air, and that he felt my eternal gratitude before his connection to this world was severed. The Brunnens continued to sing. Their sacred harmonies lifted my spirits to a higher plain, so that I believed that God heard my prayers more clearly, and Felix did too.

I sat up and spun around so that my feet hung from the table. My three serenading Brunnens halted their song and reached for me. I was afraid that their touch would lull me back to sleep. As soothing and pleasurable as the touch of a Brunnen is, there was too much I needed to know, too much I needed to do.

"No, no, no," I told them, as I gestured them away, "Where is the swan? Where is Acheriel? Get them for me, please."

They nodded and walked through the exit of the room. The exit had no door. It was two thin trees, no farther apart than the span of one of my arms. Yet I could see nothing between them, nothing through them. The Brunnens walked between the trees and disappeared. I gingerly got to my feet. They hurt. My ankles and knees, my hips and back, all felt like they needed to pop. I was barefoot, wearing only my jeans and shirt. The floor of the room looked like marble, but felt like soft sand. I followed the Brunnens, between the two trees and out of the room.

The doorway opened into a large chamber. It looked like an old cathedral, complete with stained glass, an altar, and high, arched ceilings. The walls looked like stone meant to imitate wood, or wood meant to imitate stone. There were no seats, just a long and open floor. The altar sat centered on an elevated stage on one end of the chamber. It was a large altar, of the same stony-wood look, large enough to have filled my entire bedroom back home, corner to corner. The room I had just exited opened into the larger hall near the altar, just off of the stage. The lighting was dim and the room was long. I could not see the far end clearly. The room was empty of all creatures but me. That is, I could see nobody. But soft chanting echoed from the walls and ceilings.

The chanting sounded prayerful. The harmonies covered a great range, from very high, as I had heard from the Brunnens so far, to much deeper than I would have imagined a Brunnen could sing. Although deep, the low voices were still undeniably feminine. I was so enraptured by the depth and beauty of the singing that I did not take note of the words until a few struck me as familiar. They were singing in Latin. As determined as my mind had just been to find my friends and ask my many questions, I could not walk away from the music. Along the sides of the long chamber were many pairs of trees — entrances to side rooms, like the one I had just left. I assumed the voices came from one of them, but dared not investigate. I just stood and listened.

The chanting ended naturally, brought to a perfect, long-held, softening note, with a broad depth of harmonies.

When it stopped, I walked toward the far end of the hall. I stared at the wall nearest me as I walked. The lower part, just beneath the stained glass, hosted some exquisite art — paintings directly onto the wall. It was Christian art, Grail art, figures from Grail legend, from the Swan Knight history, and from the Bible. I saw my armor in one of the paintings. It was Elsa, mounted high on the shoulders of a Unicorn, charging across the valley in one of the battles that Ludwig had left out of the book, but one that I learned well from The Ancient One in the weeks that I studied the history.

My steps were slow, as I walked toward the end of the room. My joints hurt badly. But they were not the reason for my tentative steps. I feared my clumsiness and I walked in fear of somehow causing damage to the beauty around me, the way my clumsiness caused damage to Felix. I did not stop, but I walked slowly enough to appreciate the art and identify the scenes they depicted. When I reached the far end, one painting remained unfinished. I recognized the scene from the little that had been completed. It was our assault on the Queen's Lake, our rescue of The Ancient One. It was exactly my perspective, had my spirit taken three steps backwards and viewed me from behind, staring out over the lake after the swimmers dove in. I wanted to know who painted this vivid recollection of that moment. No Brunnens were there, but it was a precise recreation of my memory of the scene, except for the backside of my own image in the middle of the painting.

Next to that painting, there was room for one more. A last painting had been framed, but no images were inside. I wondered if the space was held for an event that had already taken place, or for one that had not. I stared at it until I imagined within its borders my image of Felix, diving toward me as I fell. Those last moments, before he caught me and spun us around, froze in my mind, with that sparkle of loving devotion in his eyes. He must have anticipated the end of his heroics. But no fear came from his eyes — only love and devotion, and perhaps some pride in his sacrifice. The image branded itself to my memory, and I stood at the end of the cathedral staring at the picture in my inner-eye, as if I held a clear photograph to my face.

My thoughts progressed to the following moment, when we hit the ground. I shoved the memory from me in such a violent fit that I swayed and almost fell. I gathered myself, shook free of the rancid thoughts in my head, and returned my mind to the beauty that my eyes were still covetously consuming.

Two tall, thick trees stood side by side, embedded into the wall at the far end of the room from the altar. They rose to the top of the high ceiling. This was clearly the entrance to the cathedral. Just to the right, an inscription was carved into the wall. It was in German, but written with the Brunnen alphabet, so I did not understand it at the time. In German, it reads, "Heilige Hildegard, Bitte für Uns" (Saint Hildegard, Pray for Us).

I walked between the trees and found myself in a densely wooded forest. There were no buildings around me. I thought this a strange setting for a grand cathedral. I turned my head to look behind me. There was no cathedral, no building at all, just two large, tall trees, the same two I had just walked between. The trees of the Brunnen homeland are unlike any in the Sweeter Realm, unlike any I had seen. They were straight, narrow, and tall, like pines. But rather than bark, thick and rough, the trees appeared to have skin, soft, human-like skin, smooth, lovely, dark-brown skin of the purest complexion.

I ran my hand across the tree, gently with my fingertips. The coating of the tree reacted as skin would, twitching and contracting. Tiny bumps rose from the smooth surface, in reaction to my touch. I stuck my head and shoulders back between the same trees. I saw the interior of the cathedral. I pulled out again and saw nothing but forest, all around me. I walked around the trees, to the other side of them — nothing but forest.

I had seen some strange and wonderful things since entering the Sweeter Realm, but nothing so magical. I walked between the trees from behind them. There was nothing but forest around me. From the front again, I walked between the trees and entered the cathedral. When I exited again, there was a host of Brunnens before me, amid them was The Ancient One and Acheriel.

"We have brought them, Your Majesty."

I could not tell if one Brunnen spoke or several. I thought the words, "Thank you" but did not say them. Instead, I asked about the cathedral.

The Ancient One answered, "You are in Saint Hildegard, a Brunnen city on the southern end of the Brunnen homeland. There are buildings all around you, each with entrances like the one you have discovered."

I asked him to explain the magic. He looked to his right and left, to the Brunnens around him. He shrugged and said that it was beyond his understanding. I looked at the Brunnen nearest me and raised my eyebrows, as if to say, "Well?"

She said, "Most of these trees are simply trees. Many are the doorways to our various buildings."

She pointed to her right and said, "Our primary meeting chamber is right there."

Her hand drifted farther to her right as she said, "And I was born there, in that building beside it."

I scanned my eyes all around me. There was nothing in the woods I saw that indicated anything but a forest, a beautiful, thick forest, with tall trees, with deep-brown, fleshy bark.

"How does it work?" I asked.

Several nearby Brunnens took turns explaining the phenomenon, which like Cort's explanation of the circle clearing, sounded quite scientific, not magical at all, nevertheless well beyond the reach of my understanding. Many of the words I did not recognize. Perhaps they were scientific or architectural terms that my study of German never covered. Perhaps they were antiquated terms, no longer in use, or new words, added to the German language, specifically for the Sweeter Realm. To be frank, the creatures of the Sweeter Realm spoke much better German than I did, when I first came through.

When my mind grew tired of trying to understand the phenomenon of the Brunnen buildings, and I became content to leave it as a wonderful mystery, I returned to the matters at hand. Acheriel stood before me. He and Felix were very close friends. The moment that the first thought of apology entered my head, Acheriel assured me that the accident was not my fault, and that my entire queendom had been praying for me.

The Unicorn entered my head so freely. I needed to be more guarded. The guilt I felt over Felix was an intensely powerful emotion. It was not easily kept within the cage of my private thoughts. I didn't want to share it with the Unicorns, not with Acheriel, or even The Ancient One. I constructed strong mental walls around all thoughts and feelings regarding Felix. My guilt was too powerful to share, too piercing to even consider. So I buried it — deep and unapproachable, even for me. Acheriel felt my aching heart, but he did not understand its source, and sensing my vicious guarding of that part of my mind, he did not ask. He probably could have probed those thought by force, if he wanted to, or simply unlocked those gates with a single touch of his horn to my chest. But he would never do such a thing, not unless he believed my life depended upon it. So Felix, my guilt and my gratitude for him, my love, all remained locked away inside of me. I did not speak of him for fear of breaching that gate and releasing the beast inside. And nobody spoke of Felix to me.

CHAPTER 15

The First Celebration

THE MYSTERIES OF ST. HILDEGARD were a well-timed distraction to subdue the swell of crippling emotions over the loss of my beloved Federman. I asked for a tour of the city. The Ancient One may not have understood the science behind the hidden buildings, but he sure knew the city well. He presided over the tour, stepping over the words of the many Brunnens who tried to aid their Queen in the tour of *their* city. I followed him between trees that simply led through the forest, and between trees that opened into magnificent buildings, though none as magnificent as the cathedral.

It was very confusing, and I thought that I'd never learn my way around. I asked if there was a map, or if one could be drawn for me, so that I would see the city around me that everyone else seemed to see, not just a haphazardly scattered bunch of trees.

The Ancient One answered, "The Brunnens can make you a map, but you will have little use for it. You will be spending your time beneath the city."

I looked to the ground between my feet.

"That's right," he continued, "the Wühlenvogel constructs are directly beneath us, beneath the sacred Brunnen city of St. Hildegard."

My face must have lit the trees around me. I stood above an exact replica of the Brunnen portion of the Black Forest city. I badly wanted to see it.

"But first," the swan directed his student Queen, "we must get you back into your armor. You should never be above ground without it."

He hollered something in what I imagined was a crude slaughtering of the Brunnen language from a beak never designed to speak it. The surrounding Brunnens giggled, while several approached from behind me and strapped me into my armor.

"Every morning," my teacher dictated, "we will join the city in their morning prayers, in St. Hildegard Cathedral. Afterward, you will receive your moral schooling. From there, we will go underground, where you will receive the Swan Knights' training."

Since my first day in the Sweeter Realm, when I met Cort, I had been called a Swan Knight. Yet I had not sworn the Swan Knight's oath, or been asked to. I had not been sworn into the service of the Queen. But then, I was the Queen, and the first Swan Knight not to serve under the reign of Kandake. Nevertheless, I wanted to be sworn into the knighthood by The Ancient One, like every Swan Knight before me.

"How long will the training take? How will we know when I am ready?" I asked the teacher.

"Come now, my dear, I have been training Swan Knights for fifteen hundred years. You are not my first student."

"Forgive me, I should trust you."

"You are also not the first Swan Knight to ask me that question. It is further proof of your Wittelsbach blood, if any were needed."

My mortification at insulting the wise old teacher was replaced by a cresting of intense pride in my relation to the Wittelsbach, certainly the intended result of the comment.

"But before any of that, we celebrate." He continued, "We watched you slip on the narrow path. We saw you fall off the cliff side. In helpless dismay, we watched, all except your Felix. Thank God for him. Thank our beloved God for him. Here you stand before me, alive and well, wearing the armor forged by Lohengrin, ready to begin your training and resume the holy oath of Parsifal. Tonight we celebrate. You will meet new friends, new loyal subjects. We are all in need of celebration, my dear, and you give us the first good reason to sing, dance, and laugh in many long years."

Acheriel added, "The Brunnens are notoriously pious, and St. Hildegard is something of a cloister, a convent, dedicated to their patron saint. But when they celebrate, they do so in legendary style."

"Yes," the swan added, "tonight marks the beginning of your training. These are your first steps toward your destiny and our salvation. This day will be a holiday in the Sweeter Realm for thousands of years to come."

Such talk seemed a bit much. I still doubted my ability to bring about all that was expected of me. But my hidden, walled thoughts of Felix, and of what he sacrificed so that I could become what he assumed me to be, injected a confident, energetic sense of duty down my spine, stiffening me with resolve. My remorse over his loss had been like a chained anchor. It wrapped around my neck, strangled me, and held me to the ground. But hearing the talk of Acheriel and The Ancient One, Felix's sacrifice gained purpose in my mind, and I was determined to live up to it.

I needed something, anything to shake off the last chains of guilt, so I could engage my training as was expected of me. I was ready to celebrate, but much more ready to begin my training, to watch myself, as if in a mirror, evolve from what I thought of myself into what they all thought of me. I was tenaciously resolved to make that happen. I stepped forward and kissed The Ancient One, with a kiss that told of my commitment and my obedience.

I grabbed Acheriel by the horn and sank my lips inside of the deep folds of the spirals. I did not expose my walled regrets and worries. I sent him a clear and powerful thought of appreciation and love. Only my deepest feelings for him surged from my grateful heart, through my lips, into the horn, and up to the mind of the noble creature. When I opened my eyes, I saw the fine hairs, from his horn to his nose, rise and shake with his tingling skin. And in that subtle physical reaction, I knew what my love meant to him. I was humbled beyond expression.

My preparations for the celebration were simple. The Brunnens took me between two trees, into one of their gorgeous buildings, where they bathed me and polished my armor. In one of the rooms, a portion of the floor was set for my nap. It was not bedding or a mattress. It was a portion of the floor that sank down. The same marble-looking floor transitioned seamlessly into a rich, bright blue. The texture looked like a wad of chewed gum. I expected it to be gooey and sticky. It was soft and felt more like a cloth balloon. The Brunnens set my armor in a pile beside the bed.

The moment I laid down, I felt held. There were no covers, no arms around me, yet I felt encompassed. They sang me to sleep. I take keen note of my dreams. I believe them to be powerful tools in understanding one's self. But my dreams that day, as I rested for the celebration, to the dulcet harmonies of Brunnen lullabies, were so many, and varied so greatly in subject and setting, that I failed to set any of them to memory. Sufficed to say, they were happy, hopeful, exciting and energetic dreams. They were healing and forgiving. And I believe them planted there intentionally by the songs of the Brunnens, who stood by me while I slept, ensuring that each dream bathed in the healing waters of their magical melodies.

I awoke from the nap with few of the aches and pains I had earlier. Soft light came into the room from high above. It did not look like sunlight. It had the orange hue of torchlight. I rose to absolute silence. No sound of any kind was in the room with me. One Brunnen stood near the two trees that marked the entrance to the room. In the silence of the room, my light and easy breaths sounded thunderous. My heartbeat, though calm and gentle, seemed to echo off of the walls. I sat and stood slowly. The Brunnen smiled at me with an expression that made me feel loved.

In the softest possible German, she spoke with the musical tones from her own language, "Your celebration will begin soon, Swan Knight. Let us get you ready."

She patted her hand against the wall a few times. Three more Brunnens entered the room. Two of them took the armor, which was polished to such an unearthly gleam that it seemed to reflect light from no particular source. Bright greens, blues, and purples rode in waves across the pitch-black metal, brightly, as if it sat under the direct sunlight. As they placed it on me, I had never felt so honored to wear it.

Once the armor was on, all but the helmet, which sat in the corner, all four Brunnens began to touch me, pick at me, pinch and rub me. They pulled gently at my hair and rubbed my cheeks with their fingertips. I felt my blood respond to their touch, rising to the surface of my skin and coloring me with a natural blush. For several minutes they went on in this way, until the tall one asked me to kneel down in front of her. I obeyed unquestioningly. When I was on my knees, she stepped up to me so that her bare belly was within a couple of inches of my nose. She hummed

185

softly, and her belly went flat and clear. I began to see through her. She hummed more loudly and her belly turned silvery and as reflective as a polished mirror. I saw my image clearly in her flesh.

I don't know how they did it, with all of their pulling and prodding, rubbing and squeezing, but I looked so beautiful in that reflection, almost like a Brunnen. I didn't look made-up, with caked-on cosmetics. No, I looked very much like me, but like a heavenly, exalted me, as if I had died and returned as an angel. My image of myself had already transformed entirely since I had come through the portal. Now, on top of the titles and the adoration, I was beautiful. I felt like I belonged among the Brunnens. Tears welled in my eyes. As I watched the reflection of the tears, escaping my eyes and running down my cheeks, the Brunnen's belly mimicked me. Her pale, silvery, reflective skin began to ripple downward. She resumed her normal appearance, like a heavenly woman wearing a layer of running water.

She offered me her hands. I took them and she lifted me to my feet. I stared slightly upward to her face. Her cheeks looked so soft, so divine.

I was struck deeply by the beauty of her face, and I was about to tell her so when she told me, "My Queen, you are so very beautiful, more than any creature I have ever seen."

This was quite a powerful compliment, coming from a Brunnen. I believed her. I felt truly beautiful, and I could not wait to appear like this in front of The Ancient One, Acheriel, and the others. As I followed behind the same Brunnen, with the other three behind me, out of the room, into the main bath hall, and out into the open forest, I thought about Felix.

There was an excited bustle around me, but I did not notice it at first. It was late and dark. The space between the trees was warmly lit by flickering firelight, from high above, coming down through the trees like sunlight, but I could not see the source.

I thought, "I wish he could see me like this . . . could have seen me . . . before he . . ."

Thank God my thoughts were interrupted from going down that path, interrupted by a familiar, joyous little voice.

"Verena, Queen of the Land and Shallow Waters," Cort announced as his little green legs shoved him from a crowd of his own kind, where he had been regaling them with tales of his travels.

It was good to see him. It was Cort who had received me into the Sweeter Realm, Cort who led me to safety in the circle clearing, Cort who shared with me my first meal as a Queen. So much gratitude for him had been buried beneath the many experiences since I had seen him last, so much gained and so much lost, so much learned and so much forgotten. Afterall, it was Cort who introduced me to Lina and Rüdiger. Seeing him hurled lively and pungent memories of my dear Rüdiger through my head — his excitement to rescue The Ancient One, his arguments with Lina, his wrestling, and his rare, rich, and pure loyalty. All of my love and appreciation for my little green Cort rushed from my center to my extremities. I squealed with excitement as I lifted him up and kissed him.

He interrupted my kisses, saying, "Verena, you are different."

"How so?" I asked, rather puzzled and a little concerned.

"You are one of us now, a creature of the Sweeter Realm. You speak with the voice of a Unicorn, touch with the fingers of a Brunnen."

Tears filled his eyes, as he continued, "And I can read the emotions of your eyes, like you were one of my own kind. You were foreign when I met you, a stranger in a strange land. Now you belong to the Sweeter Realm. You belong to us."

He stared into my eyes for a few seconds longer, then he turned his head to the crowd around us, his little legs still dangling beneath him as I held him to my face, my fingers wrapped around his bulbous torso.

He shouted, "She is here, everybody, Verena, the Queen of the Land and Shallow Waters, and she is ours, our Queen, one of us, a creature of the Sweeter Realm . . . with Grail Blood, a creature Swan Knight . . . She is ours."

He turned his head to face me again, and his voice quieted to a whisper just loud enough for me to hear, " . . . our Queen, our friend, *my* dear friend."

"I am that," I responded in a matching whisper, "I am very gratefully that. Cort, I am so happy to see you again."

I pulled his little face to mine and kissed him again. The Ancient One's voice rang out, but I could not see him.

He announced, "Swan Knight, it is time for your celebration to begin."

I tucked Cort to sit in the crook of my left elbow. He perched there with regal pride.

I yelled in response to my teacher, "We celebrate the swan tonight. There would be no hope for any of us without him. There would be no Swan Knighthood. There would be no Verena."

A deep Unicorn voice bellowed out from the dim light, "Yes! Here's to the swan and here's to the Queen!"

The crowd erupted into cheers as I felt myself swept by Brunnen and Zweigwesen hands. Little Friends of the Scheriers pushed at my legs, and the entire company flowed like a stream, between two tall trees, into the city's main gathering hall. Prische stood at the head of the long, high room. She waited for our entrance. Her stateliness, her magnificent whiteness drew all eyes to her. She had obviously been bathed and brushed by Brunnen hands. She shone like my armor, reflecting light from some unknown source. The crowd went silent, captivated by her appearance and waiting to hear what she had to say.

"We are right to celebrate. The swan is free after all of these desperate years without him. Most of us believed him dead, yet here he stands with us, continuing his sacred duty to God, teaching the Swan Knights."

The crowd clapped, sang, and whistled. Prische bowed her head.

When she raised her horn again, the crowd went silent and she continued, "And the Swan Knight is here, where we need her, among us, in our hills, our forests, our homes. She *is* the Queen. She communicates with the Unicorns, as Elsa did."

There was a collective "Ooooh" from the attendees.

"She has shared her thoughts with the Zweigwesens, without opening her mouth."

Several of the Zweigwesens agreed, nodding their heads and whispering their experiences of hearing my thoughts.

Prische continued, "But she is not meant to save us by herself, to face our enemies alone. She is here to speak for us, to unite us, but not to fight for us or die for us. Our enemy gathers as I speak. They are angry and hurt. They are vengeful and hateful. Please do not fool yourselves. We have Verena now. We have the swan. And we could not hope to win without them. But we must be prepared for tremendous sacrifice. Our freedom . . . peace in our lands will come at a frightening expense of blood . . . our blood. Let us celebrate our Queen. But let us offer her ourselves as her weapons against Löwschock and his monsters. We cannot celebrate Verena, if we are not willing to give her our lives, and the lives of our loved ones."

A very resolute silence stole the room. Prische walked from her position at the end of the hall. The crowd parted as she came to me. She stood right in front of me. She lowered her head enough for me to grab the base of her horn and wrap my fingers in the recesses of the spirals. I lost control of my face. It did not feel like part of me. The sensation spread to my entire head. My mouth opened and Prische's voice came from my lips. I felt the strange vibrations in my throat of another's voice being manufactured through my body.

I felt my jaw move as she announced from my mouth, "Every hair on my coat, every spiral of my horn, every thought in my head and feeling in my heart belongs to you, Verena, Queen of the Land and Shallow Waters."

None but the Unicorns had witnessed such a strange phenomenon since Irmengard. Most had *never* seen anything like it. It was clearly Prische's voice, in a seamless continuation of the first part of her speech. Only her mouth was still and mine moved. The crowd allowed the moment to sink in, the silence of the room only being broken by a few heavy sighs and gasps. Then, a little voice shouted out from the crook of my left elbow.

Cort yelled, "And every one of my toes, and every one of my feathers is yours, Verena, Queen of the . . ."

His proclamation was drowned out by a sudden and simultaneous eruption of like-minded oaths and offerings by every creature in the room.

The zealous and excited oaths blended naturally into the events and conversations of the celebration. But Prische had focused the minds of the party. This was not a party. It was a celebration, one with a distinctly determined purpose. Never had I felt such a sense of unified commitment, of unified existence, among a crowd of individuals. Prische's speech drew much of the attention from me and placed it where it belonged, evenly spread among a company as single-minded as they were fearful, as determined as they were in love.

There was a great deal of singing, of dancing, of storytelling, and conversation. There were debates and competitions. Many came to me asking me to read their minds. Those endeavors were not entirely without success, intentional and unintentional. During a conversation with several Zweigwesens and a Unicorn, I thought about Cort. I wondered where he was.

"I am here, Verena," he loudly answered my mental summons.

With the Unicorns, there was no effort. My greatest effort went into blocking from them those thoughts I did not wish to share. Prische's possession of my head, as she spoke through my mouth, widened the mental path between us, between me and all Unicorns, near and far. My connection to the Zweigwesens was still dreamier, less conscious and more emotional. With the others, pieces came to me. I was rarely able to put together enough to make a complete thought. But I enjoyed trying, and they reveled in every little fragmented success.

The evening was a trove of joys and pleasures, with one small bitter ingredient — the conspicuous absence of Lina. I had not seen her since the fall from the mountain. But dear as she was to me, the celebration was a parade of distractions and demands on my attention. I was hardly allowed three consecutive breaths without answering a question or telling a story.

The celebration did not wind down, as celebrations do. It was brought to an abrupt conclusion with an announcement from The Ancient One that the Swan Knight needed to rest for an early start to her training. There were no moans, no reluctant agreements. The entire company gleefully acknowledged the truth of the announcement with excitement about the future.

The Ancient One and two Brunnens escorted me out of the building, back into the flickering, fire-lit forest. Acheriel stood, offering me a ride.

One of the Brunnens said, "We have accommodations for her very near here."

"Nevertheless," he replied with a rich and genteel voice, "I beg to carry her."

"Of course you can," I said, "anytime and always."

The Brunnens lifted me upon Acheriel's back. He took the few dozen or so steps to the trees that marked my lodgings. I wanted to apologize again to him. I knew how much he loved Felix, how many hundreds of years they had been friends. But I swallowed the thoughts and I shielded them from his perceptive mind. I dismounted him, kissed the side of his head, scratched him behind his ear, and followed the Brunnens between the trees that opened to my sleeping chamber. The entire floor was like the bed in the bath house. The Brunnens stripped me of my armor and asked me if I wanted them to stay with me, to sing me to sleep. I begged them to. As I settled into my sleeping position, they had just begun a song. I tested my growing powers. I thought to them of a song my mother used to sing to me. Their song continued, but they blended in and out of my mother's melody, until I fell asleep.

CHAPTER 16

The Swan Knight Training

IN THE MORNING, I AWOKE TO A MUCH BRIGHTER ROOM. The sunlight poked through high, arched, open windows. The walls were lit brightly enough to see the art painted upon them. Scenes from my life before the portal were depicted, but the only clear images were of me. The artists saw into my memories and captured the thoughts and feelings of the moments depicted, but not the visual details. A younger me held a blurry image I knew to be my father, as we sat in a boat together. It was a fishing trip I made with him when I was nine years old. The boat did not look at all like the boat my father rented that day. It looked like the shell boat from the Venus Grotto at Linderhof. Despite the inaccuracies, one glance at the painting returned to my heart a vivid torrent of memories.

The Brunnens of St. Hildegard were perceptive. They too had been practicing, reading the thoughts of their Queen when I broadcasted them unwittingly. They could not dig into my thoughts as the Unicorns could. But when my emotions were high and my thoughts were weighty and tenderly profuse, they received them like antennae. And they reveled in an ability they only had with me. But it was only hazy, scrambled thoughts that they perceived. They had to paint the images from their own assumptions. Still,

193

the sight of the paintings gave me great confidence that I would someday commune with them fully, and perhaps feel them all, know the thoughts of all of them, at once. With that warm hope, a Friend of the Scheriers walked between the trees that brought him into my building. He handed me a piece of paper, or something like paper. It felt sort of rubbery. On it, The Ancient One had written his meticulously plotted calendar of my training.

I had thought that my studies were over, that I would be flinging swords and learning to do tricks on the backs of Unicorns, like the son of Duke Ludwig II, who died in the tournament in Nürnberg. The paper detailed a schedule that did not excite me: Mathematics, Government, Philosophy, Music, German, Latin, and each known language of the Sweeter Realm. Sprinkled sparingly within this rigid academic schedule was Sword Combat and Riding.

I thought to myself, unguarded at first, but quickly walled away from probing minds, "Am I going to kill Löwschock with mathematics, or vanquish the knobby-headed serpent with the Zweigwesens' native language?"

In my head, I quickly revised the teacher's plan, dosing it heavily with swordplay and Unicorn stunts.

I held the swan's plans in front of my face, and only lowered it when I heard him enter the room, saying, "We have spent enough time above ground. Come, dear, quickly to the underground constructs."

He whisked me away so quickly that I did not have time to pitch my amendments to his curriculum. A couple of Brunnens grabbed my armor, my helmet, and my sword. The three of us followed the swan, who followed a third Brunnen in a weaving pattern, around tree clusters, to the outskirts of St. Hildegard, to a large stone. Behind the stone was a hole in the ground, with steps leading downward. The hole was large enough for a Unicorn to squeeze through it, crouching down and bending its knees. We all followed the lead Brunnen into the hole and down the steps. We were entirely below ground, but the brightness of the sun seemed to penetrate the dirt. A dim, dusk-like sunshine lit the passage, with no torches, no flames of any kind.

The steps took us downward for what seemed like six or seven floors of a normal human building. It opened to a large, wide cave. No sunlight came there. Torches hung mounted all over the walls and ceilings of the cave. Dozens of stalactites hung from the ceiling. Only, they were not natural stalactites. They were carved into the structure by the Wühlenvogels. Each was in the shape and dimensions of a Wühlenvogel, in different positions, some connected to the ceiling by a wing, some by the chest or back. Dozens of stone Wühlenvogels protruded from the top of the cave, each holding a torch in its claws. Each torch was lit, casting its necessary light onto the village below, but also lighting the statue that held it. No doubt the Wühlenvogels who constructed the village carved those hanging sconces to represent their kind to advantage. But the torch light upon them made them look fierce and frightening, especially in light of their new affiliation.

The steps continued downward, steadily winding along the wall of the cavern. Beneath us were the tops of buildings, small, square buildings, with flat roofs.

"Those don't look like Brunnen buildings," I commented.

"They are not Brunnen," The Ancient One said, "They are Wühlenvogel buildings, made for Brunnen comfort . . . an exact replica of the Brunnen portion of Einigkeitstadt, our secret underground city beneath the Black Forest. I have never been here. But I know it well. I spent many years in those buildings . . . well, in their twins, south of Heidelberg. Your studies will take place here. You will eat and sleep here. Everything but your moral schooling and the riding lessons will happen down here."

Unguarded, I sent out my disappointment like a powerful radio signal. He must have sensed my thoughts.

He responded to them, "Oh, you will be fine. Remember, the children of Rudolf I lived in Einigkeitstadt for six human generations. You can train here for one year."

"A year?!" I thought, "I had no idea it would be so long."

The academic schedule that I had found slightly irritating when I first read it, became intolerable as I considered the timetable. When would I see the light of day? When would I be bathed by Brunnens, and rocked to sleep by their lullabies? When would I see Cort and my other friends? More importantly, would the troubles of the Sweeter Realm wait a full year for me? These were serious questions and they needed answers. I intended to have them, as soon as we were off of the steps and settled into the Wühlenvogel buildings.

My irritation about my training took a back seat to my wonder in my surroundings. The cave was gigantic. There were about a dozen buildings inside of it, most small and humble, but one very large building in the center. It doubled as the house of prayer and the meeting hall. I imagined the Black Forest volunteers bustling around the buildings and alleys, preparing themselves for the exodus from Linderhof to the Black Forest. It must have been a difficult adjustment, from the tall, wooded, airy, sunlit Brunnen cities, to the small, square, clay buildings of Einigkeitstadt.

I said in a low whisper to myself, "If they can adjust, and live there for six generations, I can study here for a year."

We made our way down the steps, to the floor of the city. The large torches on and near the ceiling of the cave were so high above us, that they appeared as mere specks of light. Einigkeitstadt was much bigger than this. Each breed of volunteers had a portion this large or larger, except for the Eulesängers, whose portion of the city was quite small.

I thought about the Black Forest city, how it has sat there beneath the forest for hundreds of years. Nobody has discovered it. What would they do if they did discover it? What would they think it was, with monuments to the fallen, a giant Unicorn altar, and inscriptions in German as well as in the languages of the Sweeter Realm? The scientific community would be in an uproar. As these thoughts entered my head, along with an image of the scale of Einigkeitstadt much nearer reality than what I had in mind when I read Ludwig's book, I gained a new respect for the Wühlenvogels, doubling my fear at the thought of facing them in battle.

I said, "I wish they were with us, fighting as ferociously for us as they fought for Irmengard and the children of Adolf."

The Ancient One, having witnessed that battle first-hand, knew what I referenced and answered me with a frightening hint of desperation in his voice, "You must keep trying to get through to them. Reclaim their loyalty from Löwschock."

Frustrated and scared, I asked, "How could they have abandoned us?"

"In their eyes they did not. They lost their Queen. It grieved them terribly. In the many years of devotion to the Queen, they became defined by their oath. While I was their King, they adored me and obeyed me. When the Land and Shallow Waters had no Queen or King, their honor dragged them into a reluctant loyalty to the King of the Deep. But you have a much more legitimate claim on their devotion. You must demand it."

197

I shook off the overwhelming, almost crippling, cumbersome sense of daunting duty, as the Brunnens gave us a tour of the city. The Ancient One pointed out the subtle differences between the replica and the actual city. The rooms had been fitted up by the Brunnens with every amenity they thought we would find useful during my training, from tools and literature, to art supplies and food, to a comical, but admirable attempt at clothes for me to wear. I was the only creature in the Sweeter Realm who wore clothes. They made me clothes, from God-knows-what material, in a mix of fashions between my own jeans and shirt and the many fashions they had seen through their association with the Swan Knights.

Several dresses, several shirts, and several pairs of pants laid neatly in a pile, inside of the building and room designated as mine. The comical hybrids of fashions from the Brunnens' many centuries of human contact focused my attention from wandering despair. If an archeologist were to unearth my new wardrobe, they would have no idea from which era it had come. I held them against me, modeling them for the Brunnens, who waiting eagerly for my approval. I praised them for their fine workmanship and thanked them repeatedly. In fact, I was glad to have them. I had come to believe that I would wear my same jeans and shirt indefinitely — until they wore out and fell off of me. Now, I had a large selection of new clothes — something for any occasion.

In my sleeping room, an elevated platform that had been built by the Wühlenvogels was demolished. Two corners of it remained in tattered condition. It had been a sleeping platform. The Brunnens, not wishing to offend the Wühlenvogels, slept uncomfortably on these platforms for six human generations. The Wühlenvogels would have gladly accepted the amendment and built more appropriate Brunnen bedding, had the Brunnens suggested it. They made similar amendments for the other breeds. But the Brunnen culture forbade it. They have a rigid sense of decorum. They slept on the platforms for the length of their stay in Einigkeitstadt. But no Wühlenvogel platform would do for their Queen. They demolished it and replaced it with a Brunnen bed, the same chewed-gum indent that held me in my sleep before the celebration.

The walls and floors of the city were dirt, but packed and polished to appear as marble. The floors were not as soft as the sand-like floors of the city above. But an obvious attempt had been made to soften them. So, I commented aloud on how comfortably soft they were. Once the tour was over, and the Brunnens were content that we were appropriately settled, the swan and I were left alone. And I took the opportunity to address my concerns about my curriculum.

I wasted no time gently approaching the topic, but grew increasingly impatient saying, "I've looked at your schedule. It seems that you place a dangerously light emphasis on the skills of battle. I have this sword, Albert's sword, and you don't want me to know how to use it. Am I to walk into battle alone? Because I will never ride a Unicorn in battle if I never learn how."

The Ancient One knew that I had grievances to get off of my chest. He knew I was not done airing them. So, instead of answering me in the long pause that followed, he simply sat on the floor of my sleeping room, settled his feet underneath him and stared into my eyes, inviting me to continue.

"Well, don't we have a war to win? Don't we have cruel enemies surrounding us?"

"Yes," he answered calmly.

"Are my subjects dying every day, in the Shallow Waters and even on the Land?"

"Yes," he answered.

199

I began to gain momentum as my fury built and I rambled on, "Are the monsters of the Deep feeding on Scheriers, Zweigwesens, and Brunnens . . . Unicorns?"

"Yes they are."

"Are there others, sitting in underwater prisons, their wings and arms being torn off and eaten in front of them?"

"I am sure there are."

"Then train me!" I shouted irreverently. "Prepare me for battle. Prepare me for victory."

"Then what!?" he snapped.

He stood and raised his neck tall, so his eyes were at the height of mine.

"If I prepare you only for battle, and we win our victory, what good are you to them then, a warrior with no war? You are the Queen of the Land and Shallow Waters. It's not enough that you achieve our victory. You must deserve it! And you must maintain it."

He calmed a bit, relaxed his stiff, confrontational posture and resumed the soft figure I recognized.

"Winning the war is only a small portion of what you must be prepared to do. I could train you to fight in a few weeks."

My shame began to collect in my face, weighing down the flesh around my mouth and eyes, sinking my expression and dropping my head.

"After you win them peace, freedom, their very lives, they will hold their election and they *will* elect you their Queen, a position you will hold until your death. Do you want this position? Do you want to be ready for the responsibility?"

To my death, here in the Sweeter Realm, away from my family — I had not considered the permanence of my new life here. My ambitions in the Sweeter Realm were immediate, with no vision of a distant future away from my home. A flash of panic at the consideration was washed away quickly and completely by the call of destiny. I thought about Lina and Cort, of Acheriel and Prische, and the many admirable creatures I had encountered. I wanted to be their Queen and Swan Knight, and for the first time, I wanted it more than I wanted to see my home again.

After a long pause, I lifted my shamed face and replied quietly, "Yes . . . I do want to be ready for the responsibility."

"Then put down your sword and sharpen your pen, my love. We have work to do."

I felt strong love behind his sternness, though we had not known each other for more than a couple of months. I came to love him before I met him, from the faithful accounts by the hand of Ludwig, who loved him dearly. *His* connection to *me* was deep and ancient. He had been in love with the Grail Blood since his long conversations with Parsifal and Gütel. The Swan Knights had long been his family, his children, and I felt his paternal love as he lectured me.

As I looked into his eyes, I felt in my own heart much more gratitude than shame. I had so much to learn and I never again challenged in that way my wonderful, wise, loving old teacher. I still wished for more riding lessons. I wanted skills with the sword more than I wanted to understand the many forms of government. But I embraced my classroom schedule and I took pride in my achievements in that arena.

The rest of that day was spent adjusting to life underground. The Ancient One and the Brunnens wanted me to be comfortable, not only comfortable, but happy.

The teacher drew many analogies between me and various mediums of art, "A sculptor must work the clay before sculpting it. He must soften it or harden it, moisten it or dry it, until it is ideal. Such is also the case with your mind."

I was not allowed to fret or mourn, unless a lesson could be learned from it. Scheriers and Friends of the Scheriers became regular inhabitants of the underground village, lightening my spirits and priming my mind to most efficiently receive my lessons. I asked specifically for Lina. I promised her and I promised Rüdiger that I would watch after her. I told The Ancient One that Lina was essential for my training to proceed. He agreed that we should send for her. Lina had not joined us in the Brunnen city after the fall from the cliff. None of us knew where she was.

I asked the swan to send Unicorns to find her.

"No," he said, "*you* send Unicorns to find her."

I stood sharply and he snapped with equal abruptness, "No, send them from here."

I thought about Acheriel, trying to connect with him, but the swan nipped that in the bud, saying, "And not Acheriel or Prische. Find another, one you have never met, one who has been waiting to serve the Queen. Think about Lina. Find her. Connect her to the Unicorn. You must be the link between them. You must learn to link them all."

The idea of being able to link all creatures of the Land and Shallow Waters, to connect each individual in thought with the whole, was an overwhelming prospect. Although it was far beyond any ability I could imagine myself developing, I trusted the teacher and I took small steps to that end.

I closed my eyes and thought about Lina.

"Don't just think about her. Know her. Love her. Find her mind and heart where they stand . . . how they stand."

"I feel strongly about her, but I do not know if I am truly connected with her or if I am simply feeling strongly about her."

"Don't picture her body. Feel her feelings and think her thoughts. Drag her through your mind. You must irritate yourself to arouse this ability in you."

I did just that. I thought about her mind and heart, her sorrow and loneliness. Suddenly, I found her.

I opened my eyes and shouted, "Lina!"

After the fall, Lina could not bear to see me hurt. She also took the loss of Felix terribly. The entire incident dashed her hopes and sank her heart into the sorrows of the past. She left the company and made her way to the cave she shared with her husband. Rüdiger's death still pinched her sweet heart as mercilessly as it did the day he died. She needed to do something. So, she decided to go back to the last place they lived alone together. When I found her, she was alone near the dry lake basin, where I sang the Pfützeschilfs to sleep.

She heard my shout for her and she responded, "Verena!"

I sent simple thoughts to her at first, just that I sought her from the Wühlenvogel constructs beneath St. Hildegard. As I felt the connection thicken, and the complexities of her thoughts read more vividly in my mind, I began to thrill in the ability. I reached deeper and communicated more complex thoughts back to her. I explained that she is not imagining me, that she and I shared each other's thoughts. I thought about how badly I wanted her with me, how I needed her. She responded with a simple thought of acknowledgement, followed by a thought of obedience.

I ordered her to go to the center of the lake basin and wait there for a Unicorn to come to her and bring her to me. Next, I sought the proper Unicorn. I found this difficult. Although my connection to them was already strong, I had not successfully connected with the whole Unicorn collective in vivid and lucid transactions. I read individuals, and they read me. I broadcasted vaguely to the whole. I did not know where to begin to find a Unicorn close to Lina.

The swan interrupted, with an eager and excited glow in his eyes, "Find a thought from Lina, one that speaks to her location. Now, search the Unicorns for a similar thought."

I did it. I found a recent memory of the dry lake basin, resting in the shallow memories of a Unicorn, a sharp-witted, rather philosophical Unicorn named Sinsach. I reached for her and she reached back. She had been waiting for me. Somehow she knew that I would seek her soon. I thought about Lina. I thought about the basin. I thought about the Brunnen city. And I thought about my need for the Scherier. The Unicorn easily connected the dots. She thought her salutations to me, followed by her understanding of my orders. She was off to fetch my sweet Lina and bring her to me.

Within three days, Lina was in my arms. I settled her into my own bedroom. In fact, she slept with me. She ate with me. Only in the heat of my studies was she not with me. The attentions of the Brunnens were exactly what her painful heart needed. Although she spoke often of her lover, she seemed quite her old self. And the success of my endeavor to find her and bring her to me impressed the swan. He even took time away from my language courses to foster my ability to connect to the creatures of my queendom. He always believed that it was that skill, above all others, that would be the savior of us all.

I sneaked into his mind, or rather fell accidentally into it as I pondered the meaning of his strange expression. He was thinking about me, and about the past.

He thought, "She is truly the Swan Knight and Queen. She is going to be the best of Elsa and Kandake, in one sweet and loving child."

My deep red blush drew his attention from his thoughts. I immediately threw the walls up around my mind. But he knew. He knew what I heard from his thoughts. He spent the rest of the day harshly deflating what his unguarded thoughts had puffed up. I loved him all the more for it.

CHAPTER 17

A Benedictine Life

THEOLOGY AND RELIGION WERE IMPORTANT SUBJECTS for me to study. But rather than including them in my underground lessons, The Ancient One passed that responsibility to the Brunnens. Every morning, The Ancient One, Lina, and I joined the Brunnens in their cathedral for prayers and study. In my second week of study, I was introduced to a very special Brunnen, one who answered a question left unanswered in Ludwig's book. She was the companion of Archbishop Conrad, brother of Otto I, The Redhead. She was the Brunnen that Conrad hid among his things when he assumed his position in Mainz, the same Brunnen whose conversations spawned the rumors that Conrad held demonic rituals in his study. Her name is Taufe.

Taufe was not unlike the other Brunnen sisters — just as soft, as beautiful. But a demonstrative uniqueness flowed through her rippling flesh. She had seen so much more, done more, learned more than any other creature in the Land and Shallow Waters, with the exception of the swan. A poignant feminine strength shouted silently from within her. It was wrapped in a cloak of maternal wisdom and devout faith. Her voice was lower than the other Brunnens of the city. It reverberated and haunted the air around her. Her two throats sounded like four, as if truth itself spoke in unison with her voice.

Because of her years with the Archbishop, she was the foremost expert on Christian theology among her kind. In fact, it was she who designed the cathedral in which we met and prayed every morning. After the morning prayers, after the chanting, I remained with Taufe for the first part of my day.

She told me at the beginning of the first lesson, "After the war, after our victory, we will need a Queen, more than a Swan Knight. Each breed has its own laws, its own ways and customs. The Queen's leadership is moral, not governmental. They will turn to you during times of moral need. And they will expect moral decisions from you. It is toward that end that I aim these lessons."

She handed me a book. The cover felt like a soft-barked tree. It was dark brown. The blank pages within were of identical texture, but thinner and much paler, almost white.

"Everything you do, everything you think, everything that you witness, must be poured through the filter of moral reasoning. Write your moral observations in this book. Hold them against the lessons of the Psalms."

I confess that I used the book differently. I included moral reasoning in my writings. But I was inspired by Ludwig to preserve my experiences with a journal. I painstakingly recalled every thought, every conversation, and every experience since coming through the portal. I wrote them in my journal. Without that documentation, much that I have included in this account would not have survived the passage of time. I have remained an avid diarist since. Taufe has grown irreplaceable to me. She has long since forgiven me for my misuse of her first gift and loose interpretatation of her first instructions.

Taufe was among the first of her kind to go through the portal and interact with the Swan Knights. She knew them well and could share stories and insights that even The Ancient One did not know. I was very curious about her life, especially her years with Archbishop Conrad, and the years that followed. She delighted me with many stories, the moral rhetoric of which was direct and obvious.

She taught me, "When Conrad was appointed Archbishop of Mainz by Emperor Friedrich Barbarossa, in 1161, he was introduced to a woman under his charge, a Benedictine nun with a rare gift. Her name was Hildegard."

"St. Hildegard?" I interrupted.

"Yes, well, not yet. Hildegard was already sixty-three years old when the forty-four year old Conrad assumed his clerical title. She was a powerful woman in the church. Since the age of three, she had received visions from God. She kept them to herself, fearing the reaction of a staunchly patriarchal church. She shared her visions with one person, her friend and priest, a man named Volmar. Volmar believed in her and encouraged her to write her visions. In 1148, seven years before the Battle of Verona, where Conrad's brother, Swan Knight Otto I, earned his fame, when Conrad was only thirty-one, Pope Eugenius III read Hildegard's visions. He was moved by them and permitted her to continue writing."

I excitedly interjected, "Wait! Did you meet St. Hildegard?"

"Be patient," she told me with a gentle stroke of the side of my head. "I am getting to that. Hildegard was already quite famous and influential when Conrad became Archbishop. There is a difference between being permitted and being encouraged. Hildegard was busy in the 1150s and 1160s, preaching across the Rhineland. In 1162, just one year after becoming Archbishop, my dear Conrad attended one of her lectures. He invited her to his palace in Aschaffenburg. It was there that I met Hildegard."

"I knew it. I knew you met her."

"Yes. Conrad betrayed his family's ancient oath of secrecy by exposing me to Hildegard. But her holiness was evident, her confidence assured. She shared her visions with Conrad. In her visions, she saw strange creatures in a heavenly land. Conrad knew that Hildegard saw the Sweeter Realm. With his knowledge, he understood many of her visions better than she did. She saw the connections between her own world and a world she could not imagine . . . our world, the Sweeter Realm. He told her everything, all that was taught to him by The Ancient One while he was Second-in-Training. They were both bound to the secrets of the other. Hildegard promised to write nothing that would bring people to the Portal Valley. In 1163, she began work on *Liber Divinorum Operum* (The Book of Divine Works). Hildegard visited us often. She taught us much. In exchange, we taught her the Brunnen language."

"St. Hildegard spoke Brunnen?"

"She spoke it as well as a human throat can. But she wrote it exquisitely. For many reasons, the communications between us required extreme secrecy. Conrad and I wrote to Hildegard in Brunnen, and she wrote back. She referred to the Brunnen language as 'Lingua Ignota', the 'unknown language'. Where her Brunnen vocabulary fell short, she wrote in German or Latin, using the Brunnen alphabet, which she called 'Litterae Ignota'. She composed music for my Brunnen voice, which I gladly sang for her when she visited. Her death in 1179 was devastating to Conrad . . . and to me."

"And she kept your secret to the grave?"

"Of course she did. Hildegard was the most extraordinary human I have ever known. Conrad and I both assumed she had Grail Blood. She came from a noble family. The visions from God were channeled through her Grail Blood, and she saw the Sweeter Realm in her visions.

She was canonized a saint by popular veneration and by the approval of Archbishop Conrad."

Taufe spoke tenderly of Hildegard, tenderly and reverently.

After hearing the story, I told her, "I think St. Hildegard would be very proud to see you today, the spiritual leader of your people, in a church bearing her name. *I* hope to bring *you* that sort of pride someday."

In a soft, reassuring, maternal voice, she replied, "You bring me intense pride now, my dear."

"Maybe someday, many, many years from now, you will be called a saint . . . , St. Taufe."

She quickly denied the honor of the suggestion, "Oh no, my dear, I am quite content to be considered a humble devotee of St. Hildegard, a child of God, and a servant to you."

"I cannot consider you as my servant."

"That is because I serve you in ways and to depths that you cannot yet understand."

She was right. I traveled through many more years of life before I understood the scope of her contribution to me, to the Sweeter Realm, and to mankind.

The city that bore Hildegard's name was in every way a tribute to her. The city was ruled by Benedictine Law. Each week, we sang the Psalter, the one hundred fifty Psalms. Each night, alone with only Lina in my underground room, we sang together the Vespers Hymn, in thanksgiving for the day. We began with the following prayer, which I translate to English verse.

Holy God, we praise thy name;
Lord of all, we bow before thee!
All on earth thy sceptre own,
All in heaven above adore thee.
Infinite thy vast domain,

Everlasting is thy reign.

Hark! The loud celestial hymn,
Angel choirs above are raising;
Cherubim and seraphim,
In unceasing chorus praising,
Fill the heavens with sweet accord:
Holy, holy, holy, Lord.

Holy Father, holy Son,
Holy Spirit, three we name thee.
While in essence only one
Undivided God we claim thee;
And adoring bend the knee,
While we own the mystery.

Spare thy people, Lord, we pray,
By a thousand snares surrounded;
Keep us without sin today;
Never let us be confounded.
Lo, I put my trust in thee;
Never, Lord, abandon me.

I was living two lives in St. Hildegard — the Benedictine life of a Brunnen of St. Hildegard and that of a Swan Knight First-in-Training. Only, there was no portal to protect, no valley to keep peaceful. No, my Swan Knight training sculpted me toward a different end. I was preparing for war and for the moral stability needed afterward.

My time was not my own. Sunday was the only day I did not follow the rigid schedule of my daily training and prayer. On Sunday, after attending mass, presided over by Taufe, I would often copy letters in Brunnen and Zweigwesen for most of the morning, picnic in the afternoon sun, and play with Lina. Guests often came to the city. They came to pray in the cathedral, to receive the soothing attentions of the Brunnens — and to meet me. Those meetings were always on Sunday evenings, so as not to interfere with my training. I met and entertained many guests to St. Hildegard, during my year there. They paid me a cold, cordial, and distant homage until I broke the rigid decorum by some blunder, mortalizing instantly what they had deified in their minds. It was only during the quiet, ending hours of Sundays that I managed to get Taufe to talk about herself.

We were a few months into my training when she revealed her history. She was with the Archbishop when he died near Neustadt, in the year 1200, on the road between Nürnberg and Würzburg. Afraid of being discovered, and no longer having the protection of Conrad of Wittelsbach, she slipped into the river Aisch. She followed the river to Aischquelle, the river's source. She lived there for centuries, alone, with only the native animals for company. When the violence of the Thirty Years War broke out in 1618, she decided to try to get home. She hid in the cover of woods during the day, and walked south all night, until she reached Linderhof.

She found the Grail Valley five years after the death of Milli, the Swan Knight who helped create the Zweigwesen medical manuscript. Milli's nephew, Maximilian was the Swan Knight. He never knew that Conrad's infamous Brunnen had returned to the valley. Taufe joined her people patrolling the valley's perimeter. Maximilian let her through the portal with a host of her own kin, unaware of the one extra Brunnen.

Taufe was ostracized at first, banished from the Brunnen homeland for the breach of decorum, for leaving the valley and living alone with Conrad. She lived with the Queen, Kandake, in her palace on the shore and was happy and useful there for more than two hundred years. When Löwschock killed the Queen, and the war began, Taufe fled into the wilderness. She joined The Ancient One when he made his tour of the Land and Shallow Waters as the King. She accompanied the swan into Brunnen land and reunited with her people. They accepted her back through the stern encouragement of their King.

The knowledge she gained in her years with Conrad was invaluable. She had thorough understanding in a broad range of academic subjects. But she specialized in theology and architecture. Her skills in both areas helped the Brunnens survive the years of war that followed Löwschock's return to the Sweeter Realm. She brought with her the teachings of her friend, St. Hildegard of Bingen. The Brunnens assigned her Benedictine Abbess of the city, and she wasted no time devoting the city to its patron saint.

By the time I met Taufe, she held a position of high esteem among her people. Her appointment as my moral tutor was an honor not lightly given. She was not quite The Ancient One, but she taught the Swan Knight, granting her a rather divine celebrity in the Land and Shallow Waters. Taufe's many experiences, with her kind and mine, afforded her an abundance of examples of moral and immoral behavior. Her intimacy with Hildegard and with Conrad imbibed her with the authority of the Church. Her life was my textbook. Her insights seemed magical and mystical.

One morning I asked her, "Do you think I will ever get home, back to my world?"

Rather defensively, she answered, "This is your world."

"I mean, to the world of humans."

She surprised me with a truth that entirely reshaped me, "Mankind started here."

I thought she spoke in one of her often-confusing metaphors. But there was an earnestness in her expression.

I asked her, "What do you mean? Here? In the Sweeter Realm?"

"I mean just that. Humanity began here. They lived here until they proved themselves unworthy."

"Eden!" I blurted uncontrolled, "The Sweeter Realm is Eden!"

"It would be more accurate to say that the biblical Eden is based on the Sweeter Realm, passed through countless human generations, through countless civilizations, by oral tradition, then written, translated, rewritten, and retranslated."

Fearing the destruction of my entire concept of existence, I asked timidly, "Adam and Eve?"

"Metaphors for the earliest men and women."

"Cain and Abel?"

"They were real. That is to say, there was a first murderer, a first murdered, and we call them Cain and Abel. But Cain and Abel are also metaphors for the first human conflicts . . . You must realize, my dear, that these stories were told when humans thought abstractly, spoke metaphorically. The early tellers of these stories told them to the early audiences using the mode of the day. There was nothing dishonest in their words. They spoke of truth, and they bent the story in a manner to most wholly deliver the truth behind the story. They spoke in abstractions, in metaphors.'

"Metaphors for what?"

"According to our teachings, mankind was made with God's blood. That is to say, they were made with God's divinity inside of them. They were purely divine. The first human to kill another spilled divine blood on the ground and opened the first portal. The murder tainted the blood of humanity. They were drawn to the portal, to the point of

215

the murder, drawn to the violence. Since they all shared the same blood, they all opened the portal upon their approach. They all passed through it, and the decision to do so, to follow the violence, separated them from God. Their blood lost its divinity. When the last man and woman had passed through, the portal closed behind them, banishing the species from the Sweeter Realm. The first covenant between God and humans was broken."

"The first covenant?" I asked.

Taufe sighed at my question, and her face showed her disappointment in my ignorance, as she followed, "The covenant of creation lasted until all people left Eden, until they separated themselves from God. But God had a plan to bring his children back to him. He chose a people and fostered a relationship with them, fertilizing their faith and preparing them to birth the Christ, to bring divine blood back into humanity. He struck his second covenant with them. Christ was born to them, as promised by the second covenant. But Christ struck a new deal with humanity when he consecrated the first Holy Eucharist, when the Holy Grail held the first consecrated Blood of Christ, the Blood of a new and everlasting covenant, which was shed for all mankind. Jesus imbued his followers with the purity of divine blood. When Christ shared his blood during his last supper, he introduced divine blood back into mankind."

Her expression transformed as she spoke those words. It was not an expression of disappointment, of scolding, or even of teaching. It was a look of pitiful, sympathetic sorrow, as if looking at someone in severe pain, or someone doomed to suffer.

With a cracking cry in her voice, she reached to my face and continued, "And soon, my very dear Verena, you must secure that covenant with a sacrifice of your own blood."

I don't know what chilled me more deeply, her words or the way she delivered them. She spoke as if I was already dead, or soon to be, with no chance of escaping. Despite the nurturing caress of Taufe's soft Brunnen palm on my cheek, terror rippled to my extremities, beginning in the deepest center of my being.

We stared deeply into each other, tears welling in our eyes, mine of fear, hers of sympathetic sorrow, until she resumed the conversation, "Although Christ brought divine blood back to humanity, there was no physical connection between worlds until the Grail enchanted blood of Parsifal opened the portal in Linderhof."

"What about Christ? Why did his blood not open a portal when he was crucified?"

"The portals are the passage between God and mankind, between the people and Eden, between love and violence. Christ's blood is purely divine. It would not open a portal. Besides, a portal at the foot of the Cross would have opened Eden to the Romans. It would have been just another land to conquer. Christ forbade it. Also, it was not the time, not the place. Christianity had to seed, it had to sprout and grow before access to the Sweeter Realm could be given to any human."

I thought about the Sweeter Realm, about how it stood then — the war, the violence, the death.

I lowered my head, and with a profound sense of loss, I said, "Eden is not paradise anymore, is it?"

"No it is not," Taufe responded, lowering her head to match mine, "but . . . ," she added, lifting her head slowly to look at me, "this is a wonderful time to be here."

In morbid confusion, thinking about Rüdiger and Felix, about all of the dear creatures who have died violently since I came into the Sweeter Realm, I lowered my face, with scowling eyes glaring through my eyebrows and a wrinkled nose, and leaned into her to ask, "This is a wonderful time to be in the Sweeter Realm? Why is that?"

Taufe reached a hand to me, cupped my chin with her palm, and answered, "Because you are here, and the Grail is here. We will soon witness the fruition of a plan that was set into motion before time itself. Things will happen."

My nerves were whipped into a frenzy by the increasing animation in her voice and gestures as she spoke.

"What things will happen?" I asked, still keenly mindful of her earlier warning.

Taufe stared into the empty space behind me. Her rippling skin went glass-smooth and she began to fade from vision.

In a low, raspy, ghostly half-whisper, she answered, "Great things . . . things that will renew the nature of existence."

In a shudder, that sent ripples across her body, returning her to clarity in my vision, she shook herself from her contemplative trance and looked me in the eyes.

In her quite normal, maternally dulcet voice, she told me, "But I am afraid that my hope might be speaking under the disguise of my faith. I dare not say more."

There was such resolute finality beneath her words. As urgently as I desired elaboration, I did not ask for it — and she did not give it.

She circled the conversation around, saying, "Will you ever go home? I don't see the benefit of pondering such things. God brought you here. Your thoughts should remain here until God brings you elsewhere."

The following moment froze in time. Such a long pause in conversation would have been terribly awkward in most circumstances. But time seemed to decelerate with us, especially in our moments of deep and mutual contemplation.

Taufe broke the silence, saying, "I don't think you will go home. I think your home will come to you."

I don't know if she was trying to clarify things for me, but her last comment only muddied the waters further.

That afternoon, while I studied with The Ancient One, I told him the things that Taufe had said, hinting and prodding for his opinion.

"Taufe is a mystic, with vision and abilities beyond me. I am just an old servant to the Swan Knights."

"I trust your opinion. What big things will happen? What wonderful and great things?"

He grew softer and gravely nurturing as he answered, "All I know is this. If wonderful things do come to us, they will come at the cost of tremendous sorrow."

"Whose sorrow?" I asked, fearing his answer.

He locked eyes with mine and twisted his long neck so that his head sat on its side, and answered me in a tone of immense compassion, "Your sorrow, my dear one."

I could see that it pained him to tell me that. But his duty was to prepare me for my future, and he did not envision a placid and blissful one. To deal with the anticipated sorrow that awaited me, I turned more heavily to prayer. The spiritual routine of my morning, which I had often slept through, became a necessary beginning of my day. It galvanized me to face the rigorous schedule ahead of me and the ominously and encryptically fortold sorrows of my mysterious future.

After morning prayers in the cathedral, I spent about an hour with Taufe. I was grateful for the time above ground, in the magnificence of the cathedral and its many side chambers. I was grateful for Brunnen company. I'm not sure what The Ancient One did during that time. He always left the cathedral in a hurry, and returned in drastically varying moods, but always ready to take me below ground to study and train.

The one course of study that I most heartily protested became my most fascinating class, and spawned the most ferocious debates with the swan. It was my class on governments. The homelands of the Land and Shallow Waters had a loose affiliation, more connected by affection than law. They favored stronger unity, but not centralized government. I laid the examples of historical governments atop the circumstances in my queendom, to imagine and debate how each would work in the Sweeter Realm. The Ancient One and Taufe both warned me, that the breeds of the Sweeter Realm would grant me tremendous power in the wake of a victory. They both knew that their lessons in those early days would dictate how I managed that control. There would be good, moral options at my feet, and horrible, immoral ones. Taufe warned me that I would not necessarily know one from another at first glance. She warned me how a weak mind can twist and misshape selfish motives into the shape of moral ones.

I was greatly comforted by their promises that their counsel would always be at my disposal. I was both intoxicated and poisoned by the thought of such power, both soothed and sickened by it. I wanted to do right by the creatures whose fates had fallen into my lap. But I wanted more to please my teachers, especially The Ancient One. His sternness tempered the rise of my vanity, but always more constructive than destructive.

CHAPTER 18

The Indespensible Skill

AS ONE SO YOUNG AND SO NEWLY THRUST INTO THE LIFE I was living, I often felt lost, not sure who I was or how to act, what to do, be, or say to those around me. The Ancient One always had a connection for me, thick or thin, between the matters at hand and some story or another from the Swan Knight history. For these reasons, I tried to identify with figures from the line of Parsifal. I found delightful any comparison made between a Swan Knight and me.

I was sculpting myself — hand-crafting my own character, with the help of my teachers. Only a small portion of the materials used to sculpt me came from my former life, my former self. At least that is how it felt to me — like I was being entirely rebuilt, to the neglect of everything I had always been. I was physically disconnected from all family and friends from my childhood, all traditions, foods, and locations. My music, my clothes, the path I walked from home to school, everything I had known, everything that pieced together to construct my previous identity was gone from my life. I felt like I was floating in space, drifting farther from the Earth, with nothing near me to grab ahold of, nothing to keep my world from shrinking in my vision.

It was only in the stories from the Swan Knight history that I felt grounded, that I felt like I knew who I was. Those stories were the only chord of connection between Verena Elizabeth Kessler and the Swan Knight Queen living beneath St. Hildegard in the Sweeter Realm. So I kept a jealous grip on them. I squeezed them as if they were all that tethered me to existence.

One morning, as we gathered in the cathedral, a Brunnen who knew Duke Ludwig I, the Crusader, and his son Otto II, stared at me through eyes that were filled with nostalgia.

Before the service began, she came to me and said, "I knew your cousin, Tannhäuser. I met him in the Grail Valley. I did not see him in the Sweeter Realm or meet his daughter. His lover had been a dear friend of mine . . . before her banishment."

I am certain my excitement was evident. I relished all personal accounts of the Swan Knights. They attached me to the image of myself that I was trying to sculpt — a Queen and Swan Knight that would still be recognizable by her mother and father, her brother and her best friend.

"Even if I did not know you are a Swan Knight," she continued, "I would have known you as Tannhäuser's kin. You have his eyes and his hair."

Tannhäuser was not the wisest figure in the Swan Knight history. But he was the most romantic. His transgression brought us Brunhilde. She was the most magnificent member of the illustrious history and the one figure, other than Elsa, that I wished most to be like. If I looked like Tannhäuser, I must also have looked like Brunhilde. I found this thought very appealing.

The stories of Tannhäuser and Brunhilde raised my pulse, even on the one-hundredth retelling. To say that the comparison of my appearance put a spring in my step would be a gross understatement of its effects. I thought of little else all morning. I asked every Brunnen I encountered that morning for confirmation of the likeness. I wanted to ask The Ancient One. But I knew him just well enough to fear the encounter. I sensed a harsh chastisement in response. I waited until I was alone with Taufe to bring it up with her.

My impatient heart leapt directly into the subject, as I leaned eagerly toward her, with bright eyes and fidgeting fingers.

"This morning, one of the sisters told me that I have the hair and eyes of Tannhäuser."

I leaned harder toward her, my heart begging for confirmation from her lips.

"I wouldn't know," she replied nonchalantly, "I spent the span of his life at Aischquelle, with only the company of the wild animals there."

My own dashed hopes combined with my sympathy for her to pull from me a melancholy voice, as I spoke more to myself than to her, "It must have been lonely, with no intelligent communication."

Taufe's eyes stabbed sharply at mine.

She raised one watery eyebrow as she retorted with a distinct flavor of scolding in her voice, "I said they were wild, not unintelligent."

She stared at me for several seconds, frozen in her penetrating gaze. My extremities instinctively withdrew in sheepish shame, seeking shelter against my body.

Taufe's features slowly melted back into their familiar softness, and in the maternal nurturing of her teaching voice, she continued her lesson, "There is a profound, however simple, intelligence in nature. Sadly humans have been out of commincation with that intelligence for a long, long time. During my many years at Aischquelle, I was in full communion with it. Those centuries gave me some of my greatest moments of peace and happiness, some of my greatest sensations of love and admiration. As you walk into the buildings of this city, how often do you touch the trees of the entrances, speak to them, and listen for what wisdom they are willing to impart? How often do you listen to the whispers of the breeze for the ancient secrets they wish to tell? The babbling of a brook is a song of thanksgiving to God. Have you listened to it . . . translated it?"

Those were rhetorical questions. She knew I had never done those things. She also knew that I would begin that very day. I began to see the intelligence, the increasingly obvious design of things I had once thought haphazard — the breeze, when and where it rained, the casting of shadows from the trees, the designs in patches of grass between them. I began to see the intelligence of nature, to look for it in the places my eyes had always drifted over mindlessly. Eventually I saw the truth clearly. Nothing is haphazard. Everything is intentional. And everything is willing to communicate intelligently with those willing to listen.

It tooks months to occur, but the subtle intelligence of nature became demonstrative in my eyes and filled them with wonder at every glance at every inch of my surroundings. Of course, Taufe assisted me and encouraged me. She asked for my translations of nature's voice. I remembered the creaking of the trees during my first few hours in the Sweeter Realm, about the leaves that danced in the swirling wind. I wished hard for the memory to recall those experiences vividly enough to translate. They were lost, along with an entire childhood of intelligent nature ignorantly looked over.

But the poison of regret did not sit long on my lips. I replaced it with the refreshing and exciting tonic of hope. Along with my other lessons, the realization of nature's subtle but profound intelligence gave me great faith in a plan I no longer had to fully understand or see every part of.

As my studies progressed, and the many lessons planted into my head began to fit into a mosaic that began to depict the image of a Queen, my confidence in our ultimate victory increased. As my proficiency in the various subjects began to satisfy the swan, I was granted more time for improving the skill that both of my teachers agreed would be the most powerful weapon against Löwschock, my ability to connect the disconnected minds of my queendom.

It was in this arena that I had the most potential for growth, the ultimate goal being so far above and beyond my abilities at the time. I don't know if he knew or if he only believed, but The Ancient One insisted that I would be able to connect the entire Sweeter Realm in thought, into moments of united consciousness. I truly struggled to wrap my brain around the very notion. The experience was one that I could not have imagined until achieving it.

I made tiny strides toward that goal. I thought about The Ancient One, about the knowledge in that beautiful white head of his.

I thought, "If I could read his thoughts, I could complete my training in weeks."

Rather than suggesting the idea to him, I sought his thoughts on my own. One morning, while I was with Taufe and the swan was out doing whatever he did when he was not with me, I reached for his mind. The moment my thoughts knocked on the door of his, I felt a stern "No!" I fell from my seated position against a wall in a lesser chamber of the cathedral.

I fell to my side and cried, "I'm sorry."

Taufe had enough vision to know that my words were not meant for her.

She knelt beside me and rubbed my temples with those magical Brunnen fingers of hers, for several minutes, until she finally asked, "Are you going to tell me what that was about?"

I struggled to compose a response. Before I could open my mouth, our attention was drawn to the familiar sound of the swan's webbed feet flapping upon the soft cathedral floor. Taufe stood and greeted The Ancient One. From his sad but determined expression, she knew that my abruptly blurted apology was to him. She backed away and allowed the old sage to approach me. There I was before both of my teachers, lying on my side. The Ancient One walked near enough for me to hear him whisper. Taufe took a position beside, to his left, and caressed his long neck with her right hand. They both towered over me.

The Ancient One whispered, "Not me, not yet. There are horrors in my mind that you are not ready to witness, fresh, vibrant, caustic horrors that I could not shield from you. Someday, everything inside of me, all that I am and have been, will be yours to peruse. But not yet. For your sake, my love, not now."

Taufe began humming a quiet but motivational tune that empowered his words like the soundtrack of a movie.

He continued, "There are thousands of minds for you to reach. Seek them. Connect them to others, far away from each other. Be the line of communication between them. Our victory will rely on that ability, much more than on the twisted memories of an old bird."

His words alone would have motivated me. Aggrandized by the accompanying melody, from the sweet, dual voices of Taufe's Brunnen throats, I felt lifted. In fact, I found myself on my feet before I knew that I had moved.

"Think about a creature, one you have never met, one from the history you have learned. Who do you want to meet?"

I had dreamed the previous night about the Eulesängers. In the dream, the Unicorn homeland fell to Löwschock's army. There was nothing to keep them from the Eulesängers. Evil eyes, eyes without bodies, chased the poor little birds through their forests, consuming them into the darkness between their eyes. I awoke with fearful affection for the creatures who sang with Rudolf, who gifted their musical eggs to Nethe. After morning prayers, I had asked Taufe about them. She told me that nobody really knew how they fared.

I told my teachers, "I'd like to meet the Eulesängers."

The swan scratched a crude image of an Eulesänger into the floor. I thought of them. I thought about the many stories of them from the Swan Knight history. I thought about Rudolf, and tried to recall him from the depths of my Grail Blood. I don't know if it was Rudolf, speaking to me through my blood, or the united fear of the Eulesängers, or the wishful prodding from my teachers, but the image of an Eulesänger came to mind, not as I had imagined them before, in vague generalities, but the clear image of a particular bird, not really an image, but the thoughtful and heart-felt perception of one through the thoughts of another.

I called for the Eulesänger, not the one I saw, but the one who thought about the one I saw. I felt his fear, his fear for the safety of the other. It was an old Eulesänger whose mind connected with mine. The one he thought of, feared for, was his daughter. Cort had not made it that far, to the far eastern border of the Eulesänger homeland. This particular bird, a simple and humble male, called Triller, received my thought of introduction. He did not know if I was real or simply the product of his hopeful imagination.

He told his daughter about the experience. As she thought about me, I connected to her too. We connected together, the three of us. When father and daughter shared the experience, they knew it to be real. I sent them thoughts of welcome, and thoughts of the Brunnen city above me. They left immediately.

The Ancient One and Taufe stood as they had, directly in front of me, watching me as I connected to the Eulesängers. They did not know the degree of connection, or the thoughts that had been relayed, but they knew enough to assume my success and celebrate it with a tight embrace of their student.

I was above ground when Triller and Flöte arrived. Nearly a week after reaching for them, they found me riding on Georg, the brown and white Unicorn who volunteered to be the tool of my riding training that day. Triller and Flöte, his daughter, flew directly onto Georg's head. Georg recognized Triller and greeted him immediately with a demand for a sweet Eulesänger song. Triller shouted something, but it was not the song Georg requested. He whistled in animated excitement, gesturing to me. I closed my eyes and tried to read the thoughts that were not being translated to me through the high whistling of the Eulesänger language. Jumbled thoughts of the Swan Knights, of King Ludwig, and of Rudolf were all that came to me.

I thought to him my memories of finding the journal, reading the history, and coming through the portal. I thought about The Ancient One. They were recent memories, memories of the one-winged teacher after he was rescued. Triller obviously did not know that the swan still lived. He looked frantically in all directions. Whistling in language I did not understand, and thinking thoughts so hectic and rapid that I could not grip one long enough to understand it.

I shouted in German, "My friend, he is in the Brunnen cathedral. He is alive and well. He is my teacher. I am his student, his Swan Knight."

The clamorous scene drew the swan's attention. He joined us in the Brunnen forest. Triller and Flöte dove at him from Georg's head. They flew directly under The Ancient One's wing, where he swallowed them both beneath the fanned feathers of his one real wing. Their spirited whistles were muted inside of the tight embrace, but feelings of relief and gratitude came from them into me, not into my ears, not even into my head, but into my chest, where they spread throughout my entire body in the form of warm, lapping waves.

Flöte was born after King Ludwig's death. She had only known war, loss, and sacrifice. Her mother was killed by a sepent of the Deep while visiting the Scherier homeland, when Flöte was still very young. She was raised with two themes running through her head from her father's impassioned and sentimental teachings — her mother's pious goodness and the wise heroics of The Ancient One, their former King. I could not reunite her with her mother. But I did the next best thing. I brought them to The Ancient One, as if I had raised him from the dead, or pulled him right out of a book.

Triller came from a prominent, influential, and ancient family among the Eulesängers. His mother came through the portal on that Christmas night so long ago, while Nethe and Lohengrin held each other's hands and sang the song of the angels, who heralded the coming of the infant Christ. As a child, Triller knew Elsa. He knew Hildemar and Ermenrich. Triller sang to Rudolf and Mechtild, while they ate breakfast after their first night in the valley together. Triller provided many of the details that spun through Rudolf's imagination, and found their way onto his map. His intimacy with the Swan Knights gave him a certain celebrity among all good creatures in the Land and Shallow Waters. Because of those connections, that intimacy, he was of particular interest to me. By that point, my connection to my ancestors, to the heroic Grail Blood that eventually bore me, ran thick, like a rich river of succulent sustenance through my innermost being. The memories, the stories and details that clung to the back of Triller's mind poured into me and thickened that blood further.

The Ancient One encouraged the interaction. He knew that what Triller had to offer me played directly into the swan's aims for my development. As long as I was tightly grasping my heritage, as long as the Grail Blood and its glorious history ran thickly through me, I would remain on task. I would remain engaged. It worked. Triller delighted in providing his Queen and Swan Knight with the desperately desired details of his association with my family. And I ate it up. I ferociously devoured it, letting every story run down my chin until I wiped it with my forearm. He knew the Swan Knights well, especially Ermenrich, Veronika, Rudolf, and Wilhelm IV, father of Albert V. Each detail he provided tattooed those figures to my soul in increasing detail. I loved him for it. I loved Flöte for being his. During his stories, I could almost feel the Grail Blood as it traveled through my veins. It strengthened me and helped me draw upon the abilities of my ancestors.

The Ancient One gave me a break from my studies, a vacation of sorts, spent almost entirely with the Eulesängers. For a full week, I emptied Triller's head of every story he could tell. I was so impatient for what he offered that I invaded his dreams while he slept, desperate for some fragment of a detail long forgotten by his conscious mind. Eulesänger thoughts are fast, and their dreams much faster. I was flung from his rapidly spinning dreams like a toddler from a merry-go-round, and found myself afterwards just as dizzy and disoriented. The experience made me realize how far I was from connecting the entire Sweeter Realm in thought. I spent the last two days of my break trying to strengthen my connection with Triller and Flöte's thoughts. They were patient with me. When they were excited, getting into their thoughts was like trying to hop a freight train. Just as the swan anticipated, my break was no break at all. It was needed. It was refreshing. But my training advanced significantly in that week. I returned to my normal lessons with vigor and with advanced abilities.

The one area of study where my ancestors seemed to abandon me was combat training. I didn't usually train with Albert's sword. It was too precious. When I did, I handled it too delicately to be effective. I usually used sticks. I sparred with Brunnens and Zweigwesens. And I lost. My work on Unicornback was not much more successful. As long as I just held on and the Unicorns just trotted along, I stayed on. As soon as we attempted difficult riding skills, I failed. Despite the encouragement from all directions, the failings frustrated me. I had no doubt of my place in the Sweeter Realm. The abilities growing inside of me were obvious and encouraging. But I began to doubt in my ability to fight. And fight I must.

The need came sooner than I would have liked, much sooner than I expected. The comfort and safety of my first several months in Brunnen land callused my memory against the violence and death I had already witnessed in the Sweeter Realm. I had almost forgotten the terrifying truth — Löwschock knew I was here. He was angry for the loss of his prized prisoner. He still wanted the Grail and assumed that, as a human, I would have it, or know where it could be found. All of these facts stacked heavily against me. Since the rescue, Löwschock had been gathering and plotting.

His greatest force on the Land was the Wühlenvogels. Even with all of the creatures with me at that point, we could not have defeated them. Our only hope was that, when the time came, they would be reluctant to attack their friends. But their oath was binding, and they believed that it belonged to Löwschock.

One day, the Matutini (the Benedictine Morning Prayer service) was interrupted by a flock of Wühlenvogels swooping through the trees of St. Hildegard. The full cathedral was in a panic. Several Brunnens grabbed me and whisked me into a side chamber. A perfectly square stone stood shoved against a wall. They moved the stone to reveal a hole, a hiding place. It was large enough for me and one more. I had not yet donned my armor. That was fortunate, because it left just enough room in the hole for The Ancient One. The two creatures that the King most desperately wanted to see mangled between the teeth of the knobby-headed serpent, me and the swan, huddled together in the small cubby. The Brunnens replaced the stone and the cubby went completely dark.

All it would take is for a single Wühlenvogel to inadvertently fly between the twin trees of a doorway. The Ancient One told me to wall my mind.

"Give them no reason to suspect you are here," he whispered.

"They don't think I'm real," I answered. "They think I am some figure from a dream, some shared phenomenon that none of them speak of."

They did not find the doorways. They flew through the city without entering a single building, almost as if they avoided it. I could not help myself. I thought about the Wühlenvogels, receiving from them some scattered thoughts as they flew through the city. All that I understood was that they were being deceptive. When I described the sensation to The Ancient One, he smiled.

"They are deceiving their King," he said.

"What?" I asked.

"They know these woods. They know this city. They built the village beneath the city, where you sleep every night. I don't think Löwschock has told them about you. I don't think they know that I still live. He fears that their loyalties would return to their rightful place, if the Wühlenvogels knew about either of us."

The thought comforted me. It gave me hope that we would not have to face them in battle. They are the Sweeter Realm's most proficient hunters. Facing them would cost many lives. It was not an issue for that day. The Wühlenvogels were gone without laying an eye on me or any of my friends in St. Hildegard.

The Ancient One and I came out from the cubby. The stone was replaced and we returned to the main hall of the cathedral. Conversations rose, but no higher than a whisper. Nerves were still tattered from the Wühlenvogel flyby. Suddenly, one Brunnen ran into the cathedral from the forest. Her voice rose above the rest, still in a whisper, but a raspy, piercing one.

"The creatures of the Deep are here!" she cried.

They did not scare me as much as the Wühlenvogels did. The Brunnens tried to rush me back to my hiding place.

"No," I demanded. "They will not avoid the entrances as the Wühlenvogels did. They will stumble through them and we must be ready. Where is my armor, my sword?"

In an instant, I was surrounded by Brunnens, each soft hand doing its part to strap me into my armor. A Zweigwesen parted the Brunnen corps. He carried my sword.

"Do not rush into battle. You are not ready. We are not ready to win this fight," the swan instructed.

"I am not rushing anywhere. I will stay right here. But if they stumble into this holy place, they must die here.

233

They cannot find the Brunnen city and return to the Deep with that information."

My argument was logical. But my mind was not. Ever since The Ancient One described his memories as "vibrant horrors", after I tried to enter his mind, my heated wrath for his captors swelled in me, subdued only by prayer and Taufe's moral reasoning. My fury swelled when I knew that they were in our sacred city. I grinded my teeth. My patience and wisdom had a weak control over my body. I leaned forward and rocked back again as reason and vengeance fought a tug-of-war inside of me.

The desperation of the situation focused my abilities. I closed my eyes and reached for every mind in St. Hildegard, every Brunnen, Unicorn, Zweigwesen, Scherier, Friend of the Scheriers, and Eulesänger. I did not just connect their minds to mine. I connected us all together. The thoughts of each were perceived by all. The experience was received differently by each. For some it was overwhelming and they passed out. Most took a few moments to get their bearings, to realize what was happening, before focusing in and receiving their instructions.

The Ancient One was included. Using the path I created, he spoke to the city. He instructed them to set up ambushes against any Deep creature who comes through a doorway. His instructions were relayed just in time. The connection grew quickly hazy. It turned from shared thoughts of clarity to spirally, spinning notions, flying about my head like tiny insects, too fast to swat. The experiences of those in the cathedral with me must have mirrored mine. They became dizzy, swaying and stumbling and shouting random words.

The Ancient One shushed them all and reminded us of the perils at hand. We staged our ambush, comfortable in the knowledge that the rest of the city was doing the same.

The monsters of the Deep did not pass as benignly as did the Wühlenvogels. Buildings were breached. The surprise of finding themselves suddenly in a building, when they had just been walking between the trees of a forest, stunned the monsters, enough to give us a distinct advantage.

As we waited in the cathedral, I reached for the city inhabitants. I could not connect us all again, but I found some individuals, or rather, they found me. In the height of their fear, as the scaled beasts of Löwschock's army entered buildings, their thoughts found me. And they found me in the moments of relief, when the danger ended. Not a single inhabitant of the city was hurt. Four monsters of the Deep stumbled into Brunnen buildings. They were all killed on the spot.

The danger appeared over. I stepped toward the cathedral entrance. Just as The Ancient One said, "Not yet", the most hideous, terrifying creature I had ever seen marched between the trees that opened to the cathedral. It was almost twice my height. It was a thick-scaled, greyish-green serpent. It walked on four limbs. On the front were two clawed wings, clearly not meant to fly through air, but to soar through water. Its back limbs were little more than stubby knuckles, protruding from beneath a long, snake-like tail. Wide, webbed feet capped the stubby legs. Its head was awkwardly large for its body, shaped like a horse's head, but wider, almost square. A row of small horns ran from between its gaping nostrils to the top of its head, where it ended with one giant horn.

The monster appeared through the cathedral entrance, knocking me several yards back to land flat on my butt. It was clearly in shock at its new surroundings. It looked up to the high ceilings, not noticing the armored human it had just knocked over, or the host of creatures ready to do it in.

This creature could have swallowed half of my body in a single bite. But that is not what terrified me. Its eyes, which darted around the room in chaotic fury, those dark eyes, projecting all of the anger and violent, jealous fury in its heart, chilled me to the marrow. I was frozen. Time slowed in my eyes. My host of friends, with whom I had been peacefully praying just twenty minutes earlier, engaged their ambush. They grabbed at the beast, held him down to the floor and yelled for me.

I just watched. The monster shook its tail, sending a couple of Brunnens flying across the chamber. A Zweigwesen stabbed at its eyes with his hard, splintery fingers. But the serpent's eyelids were quick and hard. For several seconds, I thought I was getting to my feet and jumping into the battle, until my hands realized that they still held the floor, still in the spot where I fell.

A voice yelled to the Zweigwesen, "Reinherz, keep stabbing at the eyes."

I remember agreeing, thinking that it was a good idea, before I realized that the voice was mine. Reinherz kept the monster's eyes shut while I got to my feet, marched up to the serpent's head, and drew Albert's sword. Reinherz stepped away. The creature opened its dark, evil, furious eyes and I drove my Unicorn-horned weapon through its right socket, handle-deep into its skull. It writhed and arched, without making a sound, lifting my friends into the air, as they held to the wings and tail. With a wheezing, whining exhale, the monster fell limp. My friends did not let go, and I did not withdraw my sword.

I continued to push forward into its head with all of my strength, until The Ancient One said, "He is dead. Quickly prepare yourselves for another."

I pulled the sword from the monster. My senses were tingling, heightening every sensation. Suddenly, the foul smell of the serpent — the breath of its final exhale, the moldy scales, and the pungent aroma of hate, filled my sinuses. The sloshing, smacking sound of my sword withdrawing from its head, the recesses of each spiral swimming loudly through the monster's brain and out through the eye socket, dove into my ears with disgusting clarity. The light through the stained glass above me danced in my eyes. I heard every inhale and exhale of my friends. I heard their hearts beating, as if I had pressed my ear against every chest in the room simultaneously.

As my friends pulled the dead beast from the doorway, into the center of the chamber, I flicked my sword toward it, flinging blood across the tail and back of the lifeless monster. I stepped forward and waited for the next serpent to come through. None did. I could not focus enough to discern the specific thoughts of the city's inhabitants. But I felt collective relief. I felt no despair, no loss, no increasing fear, nothing from my subjects that would lead me to worry about them.

After several minutes in waiting, a single Brunnen slipped through the doorway, into the forest. I reached my mind specifically for her. The crowd around me did not look at the doorway. They looked at me, waiting for me to relay her thoughts to them. Her thoughts returned to me in the form of a calm and confident relief. I relaxed my guarded position and joined her in the forest. My friends followed behind me. I stood just outside of the cathedral and watched the bodies of Löwschock's minions being dragged from the buildings.

A soft, heavenly Brunnen hand wrapped around my neck. It was Taufe.

"You have killed," she said.

"I had to."

"Of course you did, but the morality of your actions will grow more complicated with reflection. We must study and dissect your feelings."

She was right. I slept very little that night. The morality of killing that beast did haunt me, as Taufe said it would.

237

Killing that sepent was not satisfying. It was strangely tragic. Thank God for the soothing distraction of Brunnen fingers and Brunnen voices. As I fought with the moral ambiguity of the situation, Taufe's fingers through my hair and on my scalp kept my mind on track, with that special sort of magic that only the touch of a Brunnen possesses. And her calm conversation dulled the thorns of my moral struggle.

Each time shivers ran through my body at the thought of ending that life, I thought about Rüdiger. I looked at Lina and stroked the hair along her back.

"Perhaps that was the same monster that twisted and mangled my dear Rüdiger," I thought to myself.

And I thought about those evil eyes. There was nothing of life, nothing of love behind those darting pupils. Only hatred and chaotic fury lived behind those eyes, inside of that brain, until it felt the full length of Albert's sword.

The Ancient One reminded me daily, "Nothing beautiful, nothing Godly died on the floor of the cathedral that morning. Your sword made the Sweeter Realm a safer, lovelier place."

He and Taufe thought very differently on the matter. Both agreed that the monster had to die. But Taufe saw beauty in the beast. She saw the pathetic tragedy of the violent circumstances. The polarity of my thoughts on the matter were pulled further apart by my teachers. The swan's perspective generally won the day. There was always a horrid image, floating shallowly in my mind, to recall my sense of duty — some sweet, soft face never again to light mine with adoring eyes, killed by a monster of the Deep. Nevertheless, each of my magnified senses from that morning linger in my head these many long years later.

CHAPTER 19

The Words of Kandake

THE INVASION OF THE DEEP CREATURES CHANGED ME. It changed us all. And it changed my training. None of us were sure if Löwschock knew where we were. A total of five of his monsters died in Brunnen buildings that morning, including the one I killed. Their bodies were buried with unceremonious expedience. The Ancient One was mortified at the thought of those foul creatures lying forever under Brunnen soil. But we were too afraid to burn them, to send such a beacon into the sky above us.

My academic schedule stayed intact, but was set on edge. Fear guided my studies. A tone of nervous sobriety hung over every lesson. We were more focused, more on task, less jovial, and I'm afraid to say, less loving. I felt like a tool being sharpened, and fear was the stone they used to sharpen me. I no longer felt like a friend, a daughter, or even a Queen. Lina was my only constant comfort. She slept with me each night. She spoke with the tenderness that desperation had stripped from the others.

Acheriel and Prische were rarely in St. Hildegard. They committed themselves to arranging and preparing alternatives to my living quarters and training grounds, should my home in the underground village prove compromised. Triller and Flöte remained in the city. But in the company of the other creatures they could imagine brighter futures for themselves. My company became a reminder of the dangerous times. So they avoided me.

Cort left to continue preparing the Sweeter Realm to receive their Queen. I kept them all near my mind and shared with them their experiences and mine. So, I was the first to know that Prische expected a baby. I knew before Acheriel, the father. She had been pregnant for some time, but she and Acheriel had been apart and Unicorns do not show their pregnancies as other creatures do. When the thoughts reached me from Prische, I was so excited that I reached for Acheriel, spoiling the surprise that his wife had planned for the joyous news.

I begged them to hide away, to find some hidden hole, in some forgotten corner of the Land, to live together and raise their child away from the sacrifice and suffering promised to the rest of us. Like the Rightful Swan Knight, Adolf, Acheriel sent his wife to such a place, to the buried ruins of an ancient Unicorn settlement. He sent her with only a few Zweigwesens. He continued his work for the cause, preparing plans and routes of escape, should our city be again surprised by a swarm of our enemies.

Georg assumed full responsibility for my riding training. He dismissed all others from that duty. Of my tutors, he was harshest of all. He walled his thoughts from me. But in his weary moments, just before he fell asleep, I peered into his mind. It was there that I found confirmation of what I expected. The poor Unicorn was torn between loving me and training me. I saw enough in those moments to tolerate his harshness with an understanding of what motivated it, and what was buried just beneath it.

I found myself quoting Ludwig in my head, asking why I was the Swan Knight now, of all times. Although grateful beyond measure for the honor, I would have loved to have known The Ancient One in a different time, to have laughed with him in the old lodge of the Portal Valley, to have seen him act upon the stage and to have long, meandering conversations about mundane, peaceful topics — to have seen him take flight and soar across the full moon of the Bavarian sky. This was not The Ancient One I knew. His broken stub reminded me of the evil we faced. And the prosthetic that covered it reminded me of Felix and the deadly consequenses of my childish, clumsy, human inadequacies, increasing my fear of my own safety and that of the beautiful creatures who had staked all of their hopes on the seemingly impossible victory I was supposed to deliver to them.

Not a single word passed between the swan and me that did not have a pointed rhetorical purpose. My hours with Taufe were less rigidly regimented. But such was the nature of that subject of study. I treasured my time with her, which became shorter each week, as reports of further incursions from the Deep reached the worried swan. More concern went toward winning the war than toward preparing me to lead in the increasingly unexpected occasion of our victory.

I kept my mind sharp. I remembered each lesson. My skills on Unicornback improved, sufficient enough to fight from that perch. My training with the sword took a larger portion of my day, closer to what I had imagined when my training began. But it was not fun, certainly not playful. I worked with mortal seriousness. My imagination placed me fully into each scenario arranged for me. I allowed my heart to fear for my life as I enacted the battles set before me, many of which had no possible successful outcome.

I never fought alone, but coordinated my attacks between my own sword and the forces at my side, all of whom were volunteers from the city. The Ancient One devised strategies for every imaginable eventuality, in every possible setting, against every known variety of enemy. Although I could not yet connect every mind in the Land and Shallow Waters, far from it, I could connect those nearest me. And I honed that skill in the battle scenarios, coordinating attacks and defenses that were able to adapt based on the thoughts and perceptions of all involved. The Ancient One would not dare admit it, but my progress in that area was beyond his expectations, and it gave him hope.

With the experience of killing still so fresh on my mind, each imagined battle sent memories of the feel in my hand, and the sound in my ears, when I drove my sword into the monster's skull. I completed each lesson equally mortified, equally shaken, and in equal moral ambiguity. The lessons were meant to sharpen preparedness, not to numb my moral reaction to killing.

Every morning, Taufe forced me to recall the violent scenarios of the previous day's training, reminding me of a quotation from St. Hildegard, "Every creature is a glittering, glistening mirror of Divinity."

The Ancient One contradicted that message. He had such disdain for the monsters of the Deep. They disgusted him more than they scared him. He told me often that the immoral can be converted. But the amoral are beyond the reach of the influence of the righteous, and therefore beyond our compassion. He had experiences of Löwschock that none of us could understand — that none of us wanted to understand. He reproached Löwschock bitterly for any and all badness in the Sweeter Realm.

The Ancient One did nothing to connect my combat lessons with any moral responsibility. Taufe made sure that each imagined kill carried the same weight as my actual kill. I slaughtered thousands of imaginary enemies as I trained. The burden on my soul was a heavy one indeed. The integrity of my morality was more important to Taufe than that of my sanity. This brought increasing difficulty into my combat lessons. I was not allowed to hesitate, yet I was expected to bear the moral burden of ending a life, with each swing of my sword. Lina's soft fur was the only sponge that could wash away some of the emotional burden.

I often longed for the warmth of Felix's embrace, but dared not dwell on it. I shoved him from the forefront of my thoughts, deciding that those thoughts would perhaps do me good someday, but not yet. It was excruciating to recall him, but I was terrified of forgetting him — scared to death of losing my ability to clearly focus his image in my memory. I could still remember the feel of his soft feathers. I plunged myself deeply into recollections of him, then chastised myself for such destructive indulgences. So I pictured him, only to shove that picture from my mind. This battle raged on day and night, and often left me weak-kneed, in debilitating sobs.

My sentimental side had to yield. Löwschock called in the loyalty of the Wühlenvogels. They were seen more often, and in larger swarms, flying through the hills, forests, and cities of the Land, always preceding a parade of serpents from the Deep. I feared for the kind creatures of the Shallow Waters, my subjects. I thought about The Ancient One, at his abduction, swimming out onto the Queen's Lake, as King, as the worried and diligent King of the Shallow swimmers. I asked one day if I, as their Queen, should not do the same. In the walled and protected recesses of my mind, where I stored my most precious secrets, I prayed that he would not agree with me and send me out onto the lake to be dragged into an underwater dungeon, as he was. The image of floating onto the great lake alone, conjured at first by my conscious musings, became the plot of recurring nightmares.

The swan dared not risk me as he risked himself.

"Those were troubled times," he said, "but things are worse now. Had I to do it over, I would not have paddled onto the lake that day. I would have brought Ludwig here, as you are here now, and I would have trained him as I train you, not to be a Swan Knight, a protector of the portal, but to be a King. Many lives may have been saved, including his."

He wore the regret of his heroism heavily, not for the great cost to him, but for leaving the creatures without a leader during his century of captivity and for the fate of Ludwig in his absence.

He would never have said it, not then, but from time to time, he allowed his thoughts to scale the walls of his hidden mind and speak to me, "Thank God for you, Verena," he thought openly. "Thank our heavenly God for you."

During the several weeks following the invasion of St. Hildegard, I cried at night. I tried to hold it back, but the sound of my sweet Scherier crying with me when she heard me cry swung the gates of my emotions wide open, and our concerted weeping echoed through the underground village.

In the pauses, I could hear the swan, sometimes with my ears, other times with my mind, crying with us and whimpering, "Poor, sweet girl. God save her."

I heard him beg my ancestors, his students and friends, to come to life inside of me and fight together for my life. He feared terribly for me, and regretted having to throw me so quickly and heartlessly into war. And he tried not to love me. He feared the weakness of his sentimental heart. He knew that if he indulged his own nature, he would hide me away and protect me, robbing from the Land and Shallow Waters what he believed to be the only key to their salvation. So, the paternal figure of the great swan died that day with the monster in the cathedral, to be revived when his love was no longer treacherous.

The Ancient One wanted me to have a healthy amount of fear. His obvious fear for my life pushed my apprehensions a bit further than that. I had many nightmares, one in particular, which echoed in my sleeping mind the realities of my surroundings. From the wardrobe that the Brunnens had made me, that comical variety of fashions, I chose my sleeping clothes — a baggy pair of pants and a large, frilly-cuffed shirt, like what an old pirate might wear. I slept in these clothes because they were appropriately comfortable for sleep and because I would never allow myself to be seen in the city with them. Those were the clothes I wore on that night.

I dreamed that I stood in my pirate shirt and baggy pants, on top of the stone that hides the hole that leads to the underground village. It was nighttime, but the large, full moon above lit the ground well enough for me to see several small figures running through the woods. I strained my eyes to make out their form. They were my poor Shallow Waters creatures, the ones who dove into the lake to save the swan.

They were whispering, mumbling quietly in unison, words I could not understand. I jumped from the stone and ran alongside them. I heard their words.

They were saying, "We will die for the swan and we will die for Verena."

I felt a wave of chills run across me, raising every hair on my body.

I chased them, frantically barking, "No, the swan is already free. Come back."

I could not get their attention, though they were right beside me, around me, and at my feet. Pfützeschilfs rode on the backs of Schildbüffels. Vogelkrötes ran between them, flapping their wings and sailing through the forest as if they were sailing through the water. I ran as hard as I could to catch up with them. But they moved ahead of me, vowing to die for me and for the swan. In a wild frenzy, I screamed at them and flailed my arms. I begged them to stop. One gentle, kind Schildbüffel stopped. I caught up with him and asked him where they were going.

He looked at me, smiled, and spoke in a soft, obedient, reverent tone, "We are going to die in the Queen's Lake."

"No", I ordered, "you don't need to go there. The swan is free."

"We are going to die in the Queen's Lake," he repeated with an eerie joyfulness in his voice.

"Why must you go there? Why do you have to die?"

"Because it is what you wish, my Queen. You want us to die for you and for the swan."

"No I don't! I want you to live."

"We are going to die in the lake," he said one more time before turning and racing after the others.

I chased after him, screaming and crying as he grew smaller in my vision and disappeared over a hill. I was running as fast as I could, but I could not catch them. As I reached the top of the next hill, I saw Taufe standing there. She was covered in deep scratches. Her Brunnen skin rippled downward. As it did, she seemed to melt into the ground.

She pointed to my belly and said simply and calmly, "Use the ring, the one around your waist."

I looked down and saw a thick band of gold, thicker than my arm, wrapped around my waist. I looked back to Taufe. She had melted into the grass of the hilltop, so that only her upper body still stood above the ground.

"Go get them," she whispered. "I have to find my legs."

She looked down and dropped beneath the grass. She was gone. The ring around my waist tightened. It took my breath and began to hurt terribly. I pushed downward at it, trying to force it over my hips and off of my body. As I did, I felt myself being lifted into the air, lifted by the ring around my waist.

Suddenly, I sensed the ability to move at great speeds. I set myself in the direction that the swimmers were moving. I flew. I flew high and I flew quickly. I wanted to fly lower, so I could find my wet friends. But I soared higher. Over a thick band of forest ahead of me, I saw the Queen's Lake. I held tightly to the ring and willed myself to the shore. I flew directly there and landed on the shore of the lake, just a few feet from the water's edge. I stood there, in my baggy sleeping clothes, when I awoke from my dream.

I was not in my sleeping chamber, in the underground village. I was not in the bed at the Brunnen bathhouse. I was standing at the edge of the Queen's Lake, barefoot, cold, alone, and quite awake. For a moment, I thought that I still slept, still dreamed. But there was nothing of the disconnected surrealism of dream in the perceptions of my senses. The notion that I was still dreaming was pushed suddnely and violently from my mind by terrorized confusion.

The air carried a blend of the silvery light of the low but nearly full moon and the first warm rays of the dawn. I grabbed at my waist. There was no large golden ring around me, but my waist hurt, from being squeezed, as if the ring had really been there. Curiosity grew to match my fear and confusion. I didn't recognize my surroundings, that is, I knew it was the Queen's Lake, but I had not seen that portion of the shore, nor did I know on which side of the lake I stood.

I cemented my eyes to the center of the water, looking for any disturbance in the surface that might indicate danger. It was placid. I looked to my right and saw a rather normal stretch of shoreline, with its fine pebble beach. I looked to my left and saw a structure. It was grand — a tall, cone-shaped pyramid. It sparkled with green lights, reflecting from the early morning sun. A triangle-shaped entrance opened to the water. I could see that the lake water flowed into the structure.

"That is the Queen's Palace, Kandake's lakeside palace," I thought to myself.

I wanted to go in. I wanted to see what artifacts remained. Perhaps the letters from Duke Wilhelm were still there, in a neat pile, with a letter atop the pile, Albert's letter, in which he begged for the life of Conrad Gessner. Fear slowly overcame my curiosity, so slowly that I didn't realize it had happened until I was in a full sweat. I was alone, at the gates of my enemy, with no armor, no sword, no Holy Grail, and no friends. I reached my mind for Acheriel. I found him in an instant, and he, in an instant, knew that I was alone, in my sleeping clothes, on the shore of the Queen's Lake. I thought about the Queen's Palace. Acheriel knew exactly where to find me.

"Get into the safety of the forest!" he thought to me.

I took three steps away from the shore, then turned again toward the palace. I was entranced by it.

"It is the Queen's Palace," I spoke softly to myself. "And I after all, am the Queen."

I walked to it. The palace is as tall as a six-floor building. The triangle entranceway is about fifteen feet high. The lake water runs into the entrance and covers the majority of the main hall with four or five inches of water. The floor of the main hall is sand and fine pebbles, the same as the beach. I had to walk on my toes, pressed against the edge of the entrance and along the wall to avoid touching the water. I knew that contact with a single drop of the lake water would alert the King to my presence. At the far end of the hall is an elevated stage, with seven steps leading up from the shallowly submerged floor of the main hall to a tall throne in the center of the stage. The floor rounded up the walls, so that I could carefully shimmy against the wall without touching the water, until reaching the elevated stage.

I walked across the hallowed stage, to the throne. It was a wide chair, too tall for me to easily mount. Although I was Queen, this was Kandake's throne. That is exactly how I saw it. I climbed on and sat, swallowed by the chair like a child sitting at the adult table for the first time. I rubbed my hand along the seat, imagining who had last sat there. There were no letters beside the throne, no artifacts of her queenship at all, just the throne. I sat there, swinging my free-hanging feet, looking down at my hands as I ran them along the armrests. I drifted into a deep trance of imagination. I don't know how long I sat there and mused freely. Incredible visions appeared in my head, as if projected there from behind. I am not certain I was awake the whole time, or if I dozed in and out of fantastic dreams.

A splash drew my attention quickly toward the entrance. There, splashing through the shallow pool of the main floor, bounding toward me, was a single Vogelkröte. There was radiant joy in her face — joy to see me. I stood abruptly and took several quick steps toward her. I looked down at my feet and realized how near I came to the steps that led into the water. When I looked up again, the chamber was darker. A large figure blocked the light that came through the entrance. My little Vogelkröte gasped in horror. She splashed more frantically toward me, but was not fast enough. She was caught in the grasp of a creature of the Deep.

The monster stood about eight feet tall. It looked like a seahorse, whose lower half split into two tails, upon which the beast walked. It had a long, seahorse snout, but with a wide split mouth, so that its snout opened like a beak. Rather than fins, it had bumpy, ridged arms. There were no elbows or wrists. In fact, it did not appear to have any bones in its arms. They moved like hoses, in any and all directions. At the ends of the tubular arms were several, six or seven, spiky digits. The Vogelkröte was being pinched by the wing between two of these digits.

She squirmed and howled the most pathetically fearful plea for help. I was afraid to touch the water, and call forth an army from the Deep. I had no armor or sword. I didn't know how or why I was at the Queen's Lake, how I awoke there from that horrible dream, why my waist was raw and bruised, as if the ring from my dream was real. All of these thoughts came into and out of my mind in a flash. I was determined to save my little friend. I thought about Kandake, controlling the sand, capturing Löwschock, and saving Gessner. I reached toward the sand at the monster's legs. I commanded it to obey me. Nothing happened.

I tried to let out a desperate cry, but what escaped my lips was something much different. It was not German or English. It was an angelically melodic sentence in a language I did not understand. I struggle to reproduce the sounds in writing. They were smacking, gurgling syllables, in swings of musical notes, from very high to very low. Had I not felt the vibrations in my own throat, and felt my jaw move, and recognized the voice to be my own, I would have thought it spoken by someone else. The sand did not grab the monster. But the monster began to sink into the floor. It held its tubular arms high, flailing them about, until nothing remained above the floor of the palace but two spiky hands. Still clamped by one, was the Vogelkröte.

The monster was trapped beneath the floor, unable to move, unable to breathe. The spiky digits went limp and the Vogelkröte fell free. She splashed across the floor, up the stairs, and into my arms. I rubbed her and kissed her. She hummed to me lovingly and gratefully. We continued like that for several minutes, not exchanging a word. I connected with her mind without trying. She and her family lived near the shores of the lake, in constant and perpetual fear of the King. She had witnessed The Ancient One's rescue. And she had lost most of her family in their attempt to assist. She had seen me on the shore that evening, mounted high on a Unicorn. That night cost her many loved ones. But it brought her a glimpse of the Swan Knight and Queen. For her, more hope than sorrow filled the hours that followed the rescue.

My connection with the Vogelkröte was broken when Acheriel ran through the entrance to the palace. He was gasping for breath. His knees wobbled weakly beneath him. He startled the Vogelkröte, who jumped from my arms and splashed her way out of the palace.

"What are you doing here?" Acheriel struggled to demand through his exhausted panting. "Alone, so far from the swan, are you trying to get yourself killed?"

Without a word of response, I hopped on his back and he carried me out of the palace and into the woods, away from the Queen's Lake and toward Brunnen land. By the time we were off of the beach, Acheriel ran at a full sprint, with no signs of having tired himself. While we traveled, I explained to him the circumstances of the strange morning, about my dream and the ring, about waking on the shore of the lake and still feeling the pain around my waist. He could make no more sense of it than I. Acheriel carried me as quickly as he could, back to St. Hildegard and its worried inhabitants. We traveled all day and into the evening. Acheriel rode tirelessly, not stopping once, as the sun crawled across the sky. I had no notion that we could arrive in St. Hildegard on the same day. But Acheriel defied all limitations of his breed. He flew across the Land at the speed of a Wühlenvogel.

The Ancient One, Taufe, and Lina met us at the threshold of the city. I expected to be scolded and have to explain myself as I did to Acheriel. I received no such greeting from my teachers. As I dismounted Acheriel, Taufe warmed me with the caress of her soft Brunnen hands. The swan thanked the Unicorn for bringing me back to him.

Acheriel collapsed onto his buckled legs, nodded, huffed, and said, "A strange thing has happened today."

Taufe rarely followed me into the underground village. But she held me tightly and The Ancient One waddled pressed against me, into the hole and down the steps that led to my sleeping chamber. Lina tried to follow, but The Ancient One told her that the following conference was for the Queen and her teachers. Lina reluctantly obeyed and stayed above ground until called for.

My clothes were dry, but they felt cold and damp to me, so I changed out of them. Taufe served me a grass and bark tea. Once I stopped shaking and started breathing normally, it was time to dissect the day's occurrences.

I told them both all that I knew, every recalled detail about the dream, and how I awoke, how I reached out to Acheriel — dislodging every tiny detail that clung to the back of my skull. I described the palace and my insatiable desire to see it. I spoke with reassuring pride about how careful I was not to step in the water. And I told them about the Vogelkröte and the Deep monster. I paused, leaving them hanging at the most suspenseful part of the story, hesitant and unsure about how to describe the incident with the sand. Did I cause the sand to swallow the serpent? I certainly willed it so. But I was afraid to proclaim such an assumption. I held my breath for a moment, let out a long, slow exhale, and told them what had happened, to the best of my understanding, beginning with the utterance of the strange sentence. I reproduced it as well as I could.

Although there was much astonishment and confusion, there was no doubt, no suspicion. The Ancient One recognized the strange language from my description.

"That is the language of the Wassermönche, Kandake's breed," the swan spoke in a drawn-out, ghostly whisper, "They are gone, all of them, hunted to extinction by Löwschock."

"Lift your shirt," he ordered with clarity and demanding abruptness.

The squeeze of the golden ring left its mark. The skin was red and a deep bruise began to show. The swan's eyes widened at the sight.

His eyes darted from my bruised skin to my eyes, from my eyes to Taufe's, then he said in a dreadfully ominous tone, "I know that mark. You were grabbed by the tail of a Wühlenvogel."

There was no speculation in his voice. He made the proclamation with confident boldness, as if declaring his own beak to be on his face.

Taufe interjected with a great deal more nervous energy than I had ever seen in her, "Why would a Wühlenvogel take her to the Queen's Lake and just leave her there? What was its purpose?"

The Ancient One calmed himself and spoke clearly and slowly, "I believe your dream spoke some truths. I do not know why you left your sleeping chamber, and walked into the forest. But I suspect you ran in your sleep, chasing the ghosts that haunt your nightmares. A Wühlenvogel found you, grabbed you with his tail, and flew you to the lake. In your dream, your mind filled in the facts as well as it could. It placed a ring around you to explain the squeezing sensation. It knew you were flying. And it knew where you were going. You awakened when the Wühlenvogel put you down and flew away."

Taufe repeated more calmly, "What was its purpose?"

The swan conjectured, "Perhaps it too was dreaming, sleepflying. You say that they hear you and they think you are a dream?"

"Yes. They don't know what to make of me. My message is hazy to them, part memory, part dream."

"Maybe your Wühlenvogel was following his own ghosts."

After a moment of pondering the idea, of considering the strange connection, I asked, "Should I reach for him, reach out to the Wühlenvogels again?"

Without a second of thought or hesitation, he answered, "No. . . . no, what you would risk in revealing yourself, in revealing us all, is grander than what could be gained, especially if, as you say, they do not understand the message. There might be a time for that, but not now. We do not want to lead them here to extinguish their shared nightmare."

I recoiled and shivered, having already begun to reach for the connection before asking the question. Fortunately, I rescinded my mind before making contact.

"I am intruiged, I must say," he continued, "by your apparent connection to Kandake and her kind. You spoke her words and commanded the sand."

"I don't know that I commanded anything. I wished it so and it happened, though not exactly as I wished it."

The wise old sage fluffed himself and resumed his post as teacher, saying, "Let us set this matter aside for now. Little can be done beyond speculation. We cannot let it stunt your progress. Your training is going well, my dear. It is nearly time."

Time for what exactly? I didn't know and was afraid to ask. I simply nodded in agreement and began changing into my combat clothes.

"Not yet," Taufe interjected. "You have had a restless night of sleep, a trying morning, and a full day of strenuous travel. Sleep. Then come to me and we will discuss your second kill."

It had been such a strange day. I had not thought much about the creature that suffocated beneath the floor of the palace. I wasn't sure its death was "*my* second kill". But I considered the possibility, and the weight of mortification just started settling on my chest when I thought about the sweet Vogelkröte who lived through the incident. I shook off my guilt and settled into a comfortable sleeping position.

Taufe wished me pleasant dreams as she pushed the reluctant swan out of the room. I heard them speaking as they walked through the alleys of the village. I dared not reach for their minds. The conversation was not meant for me and I didn't want to stifle it. But I was not as sleepy as they thought and my ears were much keener.

Taufe's whisper echoed through the empty passages, "What do you think of this business with the sand. She is not of Kandake's breed. Those talents died with the last of the Wassermönche, during the war. Verena should not have that ability."

"I no longer doubt anything. She has been chosen by the Grail Blood, perhaps by the Grail itself . . . by God. I have spent much time in that palace. The floor did not do that on its own. It obeyed the will of its new Queen. Of that, I am quite confident."

"Her compassion for the creatures of the Land and Shallow Waters is powerful. Who knows what marvels it will pull from her?"

Taufe posed the question, to which they both let out a long and thought hum.

Well, how do I fall asleep after hearing such words? I could not. When the nervous excitement swelled beyond my ability to cage it inside of a still body, I rose to my feet, dressed, and began pouring through the literature of my lessons. Lina joined me, as promised, to find me hard at work.

"Taufe says you should rest," she hesitantly reminded me.

I just looked at her and allowed the truth of Taufe's words to fill me. My love for *Lina* was certainly powerful.

I thought to myself, "If I could sink the sand for the love of that Vogelkröte, I should be able to split the earth with my love for this Scherier."

I could not peel my eyes from her. She lifted her face, then tilted her head in wonder of my adoring gaze. My eyes watered and I confessed my love for her in all of the vocabulary at my disposal. When that well ran dry, I thought my love to her. But even that failed to encompass it fully.

CHAPTER 20

Waiting for Cort

I HELD TIGHTLY TO LINA AS I FELL ASLEEP. I remember no dreams, only comfort and love. I awoke several times, only to run my fingers through Lina's hair and drift back to sleep. Finally, I awoke alone. Lina was gone. I was still sleepy, but without the distracting comfort of my Scherier my mind sought the answers to my many questions. I closed my eyes and tried to clear my mind. When I did, all I heard was The Ancient One's voice, ringing in my memory, saying, "It is nearly time."

I had felt moments of great confidence, when I believed the war and my confrontation of Löwschock to be far off. Now that it appeared to be near, I doubted my readiness, disclaimed my training, and enfeebled my abilities. The tasks ahead of me, the expectations placed upon me, seemed so far beyond my ability to fulfill. I feared for my life. Lying there, alone in my bed, I feared for more than my life.

I didn't wish to be home in Colorado. I didn't desire the embrace of my mother or father. The Brunnen city was my home. The Land and Shallow Waters was my country. In more than a year since I came through the portal, so much had happened to me, so much to alter me, that my memories of my life before had faded. Perhaps if any

257

aspect of my life in the Sweeter Realm resembled in the slightest way my life before, some thin thread of connection would have held me to home. But by then, it was the memories of my former life that seemed like fantasy to me. My reality was here, in the Sweeter Realm.

Cort had seen it in me. I was one of them now, like I had been there for several years, not several months. But I would have been content to remain in St. Hildegard forever, praying in the morning, studying with Taufe and the swan, and riding with Georg. All of that was quite enjoyable when the dangers and despair of our circumstances seemed further off. But The Ancient One was right. Ready or not, the time was coming. The attacks from the Deep creatures on the cities and the settlements of the Land were increasingly brutal. War was upon us.

In the height of my fear, lying in my bed alone, curled into a ball of anxiety, I turned to prayer. I had never prayed so intensely, so gravely. In the depth of my focus on God, I connected with others in equally devoted prayer. I connected with the Brunnen choir in the cathedral. They were singing. I did not hear the singing, but their thoughts were melodic and prayerful. I stood and shouted for Lina. She appeared in a few seconds, startled, but energized by the determination in my voice and posture. I asked her to help me into my armor.

Lina strapped me into my armor. I even wore my helmet, which I rarely wore. I strapped my sword to my side, lifted Lina for a long kiss, set her down, and marched out of my room, through the halls of the underground village, and up the long stairway to the surface of the forest. Lina hopped and skipped behind me like a Scherier half her age.

By the light on the forest floor, I knew it to be late in the afternoon. I had slept through the night and most of the day. This surprised me. My sleep felt like a few restless hours. The Ancient One and Taufe sat against a tree together. Acheriel stood near them. I marched right pass them. The Ancient One saw something in me, a transformation, sudden and dramatic, that I did not yet recognize in myself.

As I walked by them, I heard The Ancient One say to the others, "She is here. The Queen has awakened in her. Bow down my friends."

They all lowered their heads to me as I passed. I continued my pace and direction until I came to the cathedral entrance. I paused before entering. I didn't look back, but I heard the bustle of a growing crowd behind me.

I heard Acheriel instructing others, "Back up. Give her space. Just watch."

With that, I walked into the cathedral. As I marched to the altar, the singing of the Brunnen choir settled to an awkward stop. I knelt before the altar, removed my helmet, and held it under my left arm. In that position, I recommitted to the prayers I had begun in my bed. I clinched my jaw and tensed my muscles in furious concentration, as I begged the Lord to hear me and speak to me. Beads of sweat formed on my brow, and ran down my cheeks and nose, though the cathedral was quite cool.

The Brunnen choir began singing again. As they did, I felt the subtle push and pull of Brunnen hands polishing my armor as I prayed. The air around me got brighter as the light through the stained glass lit the polished armor. I felt my blood gather in my chest and push toward the altar. It was being called, called by the Holy Grail.

The Cup of Christ was telling me, "Now Verena, come to me."

I had never felt so large, and so small, so important and so insignificant. I felt the Grail Blood inside of me. I felt the entire line of Swan Knights. I felt the power God. It was humbling and aggrandizing at the same time. I swelled with zealous commitment. The training, my lessons, the Brunnen city and the underground village, all felt like my past, a past pushing me into the future from behind. It felt stale to me. A powerful drive to push forward, to find the Grail and embrace whatever destiny it has chosen for me, shoved at the bones inside of me. I stood sharply from my kneeling position. I turned on my heels and stormed out of the cathedral, with clinched jaw and fists.

Awaiting me just outside of the cathedral was every inhabitant of the city but the Brunnen choir, who followed me from the cathedral and dispersed into the surrounding crowd. The crowd gathered in a tight semi-circle around the trees that marked the entrance. Their bright figures, so tightly huddled together, looked like a halo, a holy halo over the entrance to a holy place. In the center of them all, standing nearest to me, was Acheriel, Taufe, and The Ancient One. Lina stood on Taufe's shoulders, wrapping her long, flat body around the Brunnen's neck. They all stood in silence, waiting for me to speak, with faces that anticipated something profound.

I walked to The Ancient One and knelt down beside him. I spoke only loudly enough for him to hear, "It is time for me to do as you did, to tour the queendom, to rally the pure and devoted hearts of the Land and Shallow Waters, as you once did . . . and to retrieve the Holy Grail."

"Do you know where it is?" he asked, as the fine feathers of his neck stood erect with excited anticipation of my answer.

"I feel it. It's pulling at me, at the blood inside of me. It will pull me where I need to go. I know this now. Let us follow that pull together, all of us."

"All of us?" he repeated.

"The Grail is not calling me alone. It needs us all. Let's form a new procession, a grand procession, and gather the Grail Army as we go."

With acrobatic agility, he pushed off of my shoulder with his one wing, and vaulted onto Acheriel's back.

He patted the Unicorn's side and said loudly enough for all around us to hear, "It is time to reunite the blood of Parsifal with the Holy Grail."

Among the crowd around us, there was a slow evolution from a few muted gasps to the full and exuberant clamor of hearty cheers and applause.

The city inhabitants would have embarked immediately, if I had suggested it. Even I was ready to march out of the city without a morsel in my belly. Thankfully, more rational minds prevailed. Taufe suggested rest and the gathering of enough of a procession to secure the Grail Blood and to rally the hearts we encountered.

She suggested, "Call to Cort. Bring him here with whomever he can gather along the way. Once they are here, and rested enough to embark, we can leave this city."

No matter how polished was my armor, or how phenomenal my rising abilities, no matter how many creatures gathered around me, bent upon my every word, Taufe was always my teacher. She knew it, and I knew it. There was no second-guessing her mandates, not by me or anyone else. So, I called to Cort, as she directed. He heard me, and he responded as ordered.

It took three weeks for Cort to arrive. That time offered me more leisure than I had known all year. I was still taught, but in short quips, as they came into the minds of my teachers. I sought my own topics of study. I spoke to the city inhabitants. I had never realized how large the city was, how many Zweigwesens call the Brunnen city home. Triller and Flöte had grown as comfortable with their new surroundings as they had been in their old home. I rarely saw them. They flew from building to building, from home to home, dining and bunking with whomever they were visiting when it was time to eat and sleep. Those three weeks gave me time to catch up with them.

About a week before Cort arrived, I was invited to a special event. One of the young Zweigwesens was entering maturity, or what they call "sapping". It is when a young Zweigwesen develops the glands in the fingertips to secrete their binding and healing fluids. As part of the ceremony, the young Zweigwesen must apply the secretion to an adult, usually a friend of the family who serves as a sort of Godparent. I was chosen for that honor. I accompanied the city's Zweigwesens from morning prayers at the cathedral to the main gathering hall, where the ceremony took place.

One of the Zweigwesens, who had just come from Heiligborke to St. Hildegard for the ceremony, told me in a light and carefree voice, "My Queen, you will be happy to hear that your Federman is much improved."

My face formed into a scowl without my control.

I snapped at him bitterly, "What Federman? What are you talking about?"

Rather shaken by the violence of my response, he hesitantly answered, "Your Federman, Your Majesty, Felix . . . your Felix."

The freshest, rawest memories of Felix flooded my brain, as if I had fallen from that cliff just days earlier. Each morsel of regret, each pang of guilt leapt simultaneously from its hiding place in the dark corners of my mind. Panic muted reason.

I scolded him, "Don't talk like that about him. I loved him dearly. How dare you! How dare you talk to me about him?"

I stared at him with angry eyes that both frightened and mortified him. I watched his rough, splintery eyes swell nearly shut. He was broken by my harshness and my compassion overcame my anger.

I apologized for yelling at him and explained myself, saying, "His death was very hard on me. I am not ready to joke about him. I never will be. I killed him. Living with that has been the single most painful part of my existence."

At those words, his eyes returned to normal.

He smiled at me and reached his hands to my temples, as he said, "My dear lady, you did not kill him."

I interrupted, "I know you mean well, but this is a guilt I am not ready to let go of."

"No, my Queen. You do not understand me. Felix is not dead. Have you really believed him dead this whole time?"

The strangest sensation overwhelmed my entire body, tingling and crushing. I don't believe I breathed. I doubt I could have.

I struggled to force enough air from my body to ask the Zweigesen, "My Felix is alive?"

"Oh yes, alive and recovering admirably. He started walking again, just a few days ago."

He softened his exuberance and stared at me inquisitively.

"How is it you did not know?"

I blushed and confessed embarrassingly, "I felt such guilt, and weakness. I couldn't even admit to myself how much I love him. I walled all thoughts of him from those who might judge me . . . and those who would comfort me. I never spoke of him and nobody spoke to me of him."

My creeping doubt needed to hear it one more time, so I asked, "Felix is really alive, alive and recovering?"

"Oh yes, my Queen."

My lungs convulsed, popping air in and out of me in staccato, unpatterned bursts. I began to feel like a Zweigwesen, as my eyes swelled and tears blinded me until I wiped them away. I dropped to sit on the floor.

The Zweigwesen rubbed my cheek with the coarse hair beside his face, as he told me, "You would be so happy to see him. Although he has much painful healing ahead of him still, his spirit brightens Heiligborke."

I demurely asked, "Does he think of me?"

"He speaks of nothing else. When he is not praising you, he is praying for you. After the fall, we took him to our main medical center in Heiligborke. I can tell you now that even our most optimistic feared for his life. But he slowly recovered. He remained unconscious for five weeks. When he awoke, though breathing was laborious and painful, and we begged him not to speak, he uttered a single word, *Verena*. Once we assured him that you were with the Brunnens, already training and riding on Unicorns, a smile bubbled forth from beneath the pain. He held that smile as he slipped from consciousness."

"And how is he now?"

"He is quite his old self. Walking is still difficult, but he improves remarkably every day."

I was the most joyous attendee of the sapping ceremony. That celebration of the Zweigwesens' natural ability to heal held a glorious new meaning for me. When I was asked to serve as the child's first, I felt awkwardly inappropriate for the honor. But as I stood in the gathering hall, receiving the child's first sapping, I believed myself the most grateful recipient of Zweigwesen skills. They brought my Felix back into the world. As the young Zweigwesen wiped her sap on my forehead, lips, and chest, I could not imagine a more appropriate or thankful participant in the ancient ceremony.

Ancient words were spoken, words I understood but do not remember. My mind was elsewhere. It was on the feathered arms that had held me and warmed me when I needed them most. It was on those goofy bowed legs. It was on that floppy nose at the end of that pale face, and on those eyes that looked at me like no other eyes have. I did not know what my future or his held. But I lived in a world

264

where he lived, where he felt the same breezes that blow through my hair. I could focus on recalling him without the pain that those endeavors elicited since the fall that injured him.

I received my ceremonial sapping, grateful beyond measure for the news of Felix. But by the time I left the gathering hall, I felt betrayed, betrayed by anyone who knew that Felix was alive, knew that I thought he was dead, and allowed me to grieve in ignorance. I saw a Brunnen leaving the cathedral.

"Where is The Ancient One?" I asked in a manner to clearly display my determination and displeasure.

The Brunnen bowed her head and pointed between the trees that open into the cathedral.

I stormed into the cathedral and shouted, echoing off of the walls, "Ancient One, did you know Felix was alive?"

By the time the echoes died down, they were replaced by the sound of the swan's steps, emerging from a side chamber to my left.

In a scolding, demanding, teeth-grinding tone, I asked him, "Did you know?"

He stiffened his long neck and lowered his beak, staring at me through the tops of his eyes. He turned away from me and walked back into the chamber from which he had come.

"Don't you walk away from me!" I shouted.

I stared between the two tree trunks of the chamber entrance. Within a few seconds, he returned. A string was clasped in his beak, beneath which hung a bundled stack of letters. I didn't need to probe his thought to know what they were. They were letters from Felix.

In a pathetic, whiny, hurt tone, I asked, "How could you?"

He stared into my eyes and sent me his answer. I met him halfway. His thoughts told me his reasoning, and as much as I wanted to remain angry, I could not help but see that he was right. He imagined a scenario, one in which I knew that Felix had survived the fall. In it, I stayed by his side in the Zweigwesen hospital. I remained with him, nursing him to health, motivated at first by a sense of obligation, but transforming to an ardent love. He saw me so deeply in love with Felix, so cripplingly infatuated, that I never left his side, never trained, never learned, never developed the skills that the last year had brought me.

I felt my face turn bright red. He was probably right. The time and intimacy that more than a year by Felix's side would have nurtured may likely have had such an outcome.

Nevertheless, I refuted, "I am not in love with him. I would not have fallen in . . ."

He interrupted me, "Come now, Verena, we are all in love with him. How could anybody help but love him. His noble heart is the best of us all. But I must say, I am surprised, with all of the minds you touched, all the connections you made, that you did not know sooner."

I answered him with the pathetic truth, "I walled off all thought of him. I tried not to think of him at all, and when I did, I forbade those thoughts from all who shared my mind."

I dropped my head and stared at my own feet through the growing blur of my welling eyes, as I continued through my breaking voice, "I thought I killed him. That noble heart, the best of all of us, I thought I killed him. The guilt and shame was crippling enough inside of my *own* head. To share it with others would have broken me. You are right, my wise old teacher, I do love him. And I thought I killed him."

He swayed his long neck and tilted his head, as he said only, "Oh my love, my sweet treasure."

He waddled to me and threw his one wing around me. His prosthetic wing pushed against my side. I looked down at the wing that Felix had made him, the wing made of Felix's own feathers. I dropped to my knees and cried. The Ancient One squeezed me more tightly to his breast. I fell to my side and curled like a baby on the floor, while my dearest friend and mentor held me and kissed me. He pressed his prosthetic wing against my face, allowing me to place a series of tiny kisses on Felix's feathers. My kisses were expressions of love — deep, subconscious expressions, divided between two recipients — the one who comforted me with those feathers that morning, on the floor of the cathedral, and the one who sacrificed them in what stands in my memory to this day as the noblest act I have ever witnessed from a friend.

He caressed my head and discovered the sap from the ceremony.

"Oh yes, the young Zweigwesen, how was the sapping ceremony? It is a great honor, you know? You are knotted to that child for life."

"They explained the full weight of the honor. I accepted it gladly. If I become the very best possible version of myself, maybe I can be to that child some of what you have been to me."

He said nothing in response, and I did not probe. He simply hummed a low, comfortable note as he continued to caress me.

I wore the sap on my forehead, lips, and chest all day and all night. I was required by tradition to do so. In the morning, when the required day had passed, the sap served as the perfect excuse to receive a Brunnen bathing. The warm water and the soft hands freed my mind, which of course, turned toward Felix. The instinct to reach for his mind was strong. And since my training had ended, and a new journey was about to begin, it probably would have done no harm. But I would not go against the wishes of the swan, so I fought my instincts and I won. I thought of him in my own head only. And I pretended that the warmth of the Brunnen bath came from the embrace of his feathered arms.

The Brunnens who bathed me must have wondered why I cried and giggled, alternating seamlessly between the two. But I would not tell them, and I kept my thoughts within the confines of my own skull. To speak to them would have pulled me from the fictional setting I had allowed my wandering mind to construct. I would linger in that setting as long as I could.

Felix was not the only revelation in the final days before Cort arrived. Prische delivered a healthy goat. That is what they call an infant Unicorn, a title Acheriel's daughter would carry through her first few months, until the tip of her budding horn breaks through the skin. There is much tradition and superstition behind the horn of a Unicorn. The horn is everything to them. It holds their memories. It transfers their thoughts. A goat does not receive a name until the horn breaks through. In fact, it is the horn that is named, not the beast itself. When you call a Unicorn by name, you are actually calling the horn. It is the source of a Unicorn's identity.

The proud father would have forgone his obligations to his wife and goat, had I demanded it. Of course, I would not. I told him to please go to Prische.

"Be with your lover and child."

The Ancient One agreed with me. His duty as a father was paramount. Georg offered to stand in Acheriel's place, to guard me and care for me as Acheriel had. The new father gratefully submitted, but not before I made one request.

"Ride south first, to Heiligborke. I want you to give a message to Felix."

I knew that it was dangerous for me to connect with Felix. To do so would soften me when I needed to be hard, distract me when I needed to focus. I would fall into a well of emotion that I would not be able to climb out of. But I could pass a bit of myself to him and take comfort in his reception of it, even if I did not share in the experience. I took Acheriel by the horn and pulled the tip to my lips. I kissed the horn then pushed it down to press against the center of my chest. I did not permit the full flow of thoughts and emotions that tried to fight their way from me, into the horn. It took exhausting restraint, but I channeled only that which I wanted Felix to have.

I allowed my gratitude to flow from me. I thought about being pulled from the pond and carried in a rush through the woods. I thought about the gift of the wing. I thought about the fall. I gathered my gratitude, only my gratitude, for those heroics, and I allowed *them* to flow from me, into the horn. Just before disconnecting, a single drop of my affection slipped through, one concentrated drop of ardent and adoring love. That single drop spoke clearly of how I longed to see him, how I wanted to be with him, to be held by his strong arms and warm feathers, to hear his voice and gaze into those deep, bright eyes.

It slipped through and I could not pull it back. Acheriel, whose eyes were shut during the transfer, popped his eyes open and lifted his head to look me in the face. The sides of his shaggy beard lifted with his smile. He loved Felix more than anyone. He knew what my message would mean to him and his recovery.

He said, "I am glad to bring your message to one who both deserves and desires it."

I bowed and allowed Acheriel to kiss the top of my head.

"Please kiss Prische for me, and tell her that I love her."

I stepped in closer and whispered into his ear, "And let her know that I will fight to the death to give her baby a better Sweeter Realm."

The horn of a Unicorn puts off no light of its own. But when I whispered the message into Acheriel's ear, his horn seemed to sparkle more brightly and glow from deep within the recesses of the spirals. He reared high, lifting the bright horn so high that I nearly had to look straight up to see it. He huffed and he stomped and he galloped away, south, toward Felix.

CHAPTER 21

Planning the Tour

WHEN CORT FINALLY ARRIVED, he came with an impressive company. He met with eight Unicorns on his journey to St. Hildegard. They joined him, as did many others. Dozens of Zweigwesens, a countless herd of Sheriers, a flock of at least thirty Eulesängers, and every Brunnen he encountered as he passed from the Brunnen border to our city, joined my charismatic little Cort. But before he turned toward Brunnen land, he cut a portion of the Nomadic Belt, gathering twenty or so of his own kind and five Federmensch — two Federmen and three Federwomen. There was nothing in the face to distinguish a Federman from a Federwoman. The distinction came in their figures. The females had pronounced curves — wide hips, a narrow waist, and broader shoulders.

The Federmensch were before me, Felix's people. I could not have born the sight of them, had I still believed that Felix was dead. But knowing that he lived, I was excited to remind my weary eyes of my awkward little friend, of my brave, lovely, and loyal Felix. The Federmensch knew Felix, but they knew nothing of the fall. I explained to them the events that led to his injuries, as well as all of the many attentions he had paid me, and the many times he saved me, body and spirit. They puffed their chests and folded their feathered arms with pride in their fellow Federman. I nearly exploded with affection for him, as I told of his goodness. What did not come across in my guarded words stayed in my head, though I wanted to shout it from the highest hill.

I paraded Cort and his company through the city. Such fierce love enflamed their eyes, such purpose powered their steps that half of the creatures of the Deep would have cowered at their approach. They were greeted into the city like legendary heroes, not just because of their powerful presence, but because everyone knew that their arrival is what we waited for before embarking on my tour of the queendom and the search for the Grail.

We offered Cort and his company a few days' rest and all of the comfortable attentions of the Brunnens. They would have none of that. Cort spoke for them all, declaring them at the Queen's disposal and entirely on her timetable. They were eager and the Grail pulled at my blood. So, after a short meal and the exchange of greetings, they gathered in the heart of the city and awaited instructions

Just knowing that a message, directly from my mind, was likely already received by Felix, lightened my heart and cleared my mind. I was free to stop dwelling on him and start planning the tour of the queendom. The Ancient One kept Ludwig's book hidden securely. It was precious to him. Although I gave it freely, telling the old teacher that it belonged to him more than to me, I had rather hoped that he would refuse it. It was also precious to *me*. I did have access to Rudolf's map. It hung unfolded and framed in The Ancient One's room in the underground village.

The swan and I left the crowd and retreated alone together into his room below ground. There we stood, in front of the map, when we plotted our course of travel. We decided to go north, through the Brunnen capital, a large city called Nährenstadt in German, made of hidden

272

buildings like those in St. Hildegard. The city had been destroyed during Ludwig's lifetime, when The Ancient One was King of the Land and Shallow Waters. The survivors fled into the Brunnen wilderness. They lived there for many years before daring to resettle in the small surviving cities, like the one where I lived and trained all year.

I wanted to see the scale of destruction. I wanted to see *all* of the capitals, all of the shrines and holy places, and all of the monuments. There was still a great deal of fear in the hearts of the creatures, the same fear that had kept them from rebuilding their homes for a century. The violence had been paused for many years. They were afraid of recalling it to full vigor. The entire Land moved slowly and breathed shallowly, knowing that the Waters would not remain calm forever. The recent attacks were evidence of that. All-out war would soon return to their homes. They were as scared as ever.

Standing alone with the swan, in his room, I felt the fears of the creatures in the city. I saw them myself, as I brought their minds to me. When I could not explain it to the swan, who had been so long in captivity and missed much of what the Land and Shallow Waters had suffered, I closed my eyes and connected him to the creatures around us. His head dropped in painful compassion for his friends and former subjects. Every bit of their fear transferred pungently and poignantly to his mind.

He looked at me and said, "Give them a message from me."

"Think your message," I answered, "you have their attention."

"You mean, they see my thoughts as I see theirs?"

"Well, yes. That's the way it works."

He had no shame, nothing to hide. He stiffened his posture and wrapped all of his ambitions for the Sweeter

Realm, all of his wisdom and courage, and all of his love and fear into a tight ball in his head. He let it all go to the connected minds around us. No speech in the entire annals of human motivation could have compared. Creatures who had been too afraid to dream saw his dreams. Those who could not hope received his courage to hope. They saw his vision of me. I saw it with them, that which he had hidden from me until that moment. Nobody knew the Swan Knights like he did. I did not realize it, but nobody knew me like he did. In that quick moment of shared thought, I learned things about me that I would not truly understand for many years.

The swan's hopes were not naïve. We all learned that as well. Every horror of his century of brutal imprisonment came across to us all. The wing, yes, the wing and so much more was bundled in that ball of thoughts. I received, with them all, vivid memories of burying Kandake, on the portal point in Linderhof. Seeing the horrors that The Ancient One had suffered did not add to the fears of the company. It strengthened them to see that he still believed.

They were strengthened further by a long string of memories that went through us all, intentionally tied together and dragged through our heads. They were memories of the Swan Knights — from Parsifal to me. They culminated with that very moment, when my unique ability held our minds together. In the swan's mind, I sat like a crown atop the glorious story of the Swan Knights.

He believed in me and in the creatures who gathered in the city, and in the righteousness of our cause and in the will of God, despite his particularly intimate understanding of the strength and brutality of our enemies. His confidence in our ultimate victory, his faith in the Lord, the Grail, and the Grail Blood was mighty, indeed. All of this, all of his thought, experiences, expectations, doubts, and hope came across to us all in a brief moment, and rallied the hearts of the city. I could hear cheers and fanatical, impassioned hurrahs coming from the forest floor above us.

I took the map off of the wall and carried it to the center of the city. I thought the single command, "Come". The creatures who were not already gathered in the forest appeared from the buildings of the city, walking from seemingly nowhere, between the twin trees of the building entrances, to materialize on the floor of the forest. The Ancient One drew their attention and gave them our plan.

After the Brunnen capital, we planned to continue north, cutting a small corner of Unicorn land, where their fiercest warriors train, and into the Eulesänger homeland. From there, we would continue north, through a thick forest that runs just south of the Eulesänger capital, Eierheim. From Eierheim, we planned to travel northeast, to the eastern edge of a giant marsh. The Scheriers call it Sicherheit Marsh. It has been the refuge of their kind, from all sorts of dangers, for thousands of years. The marsh runs east and west, across the border of the Scherier homeland. It runs against the Scherier capital, a massive system of caves and caverns called Eineklaue. Eineklaue has streets and buildings that run both above and below the ground.

The capital was abandoned. Löwschock's army was savagely ruthless to the Scheriers. Scherier meat was a prized delicacy to the monsters of the Deep, especially to the knobby-headed serpent. The Scherier homeland was almost entirely emptied. Those who were not captured and eaten fled. It was rumored that thousands of Scheriers hid in Sicherheit Marsh. We planned to travel the length of the marsh and gather them, not only to join our army, but to reclaim their cities and holy places. I suspected that the Scheriers were a force, an angry force, viciously loyal to each other and to the Swan Knights. I felt a strong draw to call them from hiding and give them a sense of hope and purpose.

Directly west of Einklaue is a holy place they call Gralkirche. It is a church and theology school dedicated to the study of the Grail and the Swan Knights. The church was run by a holy order of Scherier monks called Die Stiefel von Lohengrin (The Boots of Lohengrin). Their function was to maintain Scherier devotion to the Swan Knights. The church, like the Scherier cities, stood empty, a hollow reminder of better times. It was my intention to see the church functional again, to see the cities bustle.

I thought, "Perhaps The Boots of Lohengrin could be active again, if motivated by his descendant, by a Swan Knight who wears the armor Lohengrin made."

From Gralkirche, we dared not travel farther west, toward Wühlenvogel land. They were an enemy we would need to confront, but not yet. So, we decided to turn directly south, across the border of the Unicorn homeland, through the Wendel Marshes, to Gemeinsam, the Unicorn capital and the holiest place in the Sweeter Realm. Gemeinsam held against the armies of Löwschock. In fact, the sacred site was ferociously protected by the Unicorn collective. Not a single, slimy, scaled fin breached the border of the city. It stood as it had for thousands of years, full of life, ancient rituals, and long-unbroken traditions. It was still a place of pilgrimage for Unicorns across the Sweeter Realm.

In the center of the city rests a great shrine and altar. It is so important to the Unicorns that a replica was made for the Unicorns who lived in the Black Forest city with the Rightful Swan Knights, during The Schism. It is a tall, spiraling, stone obelisk, built to replicate the horn of the most revered figure in ancient Unicorn legend. The obelisk stands at least twenty-five feet tall and is more than five feet wide at the base. In a circle surrounding the base are stones, or small boulders, each with a hole facing away from the obelisk. The Unicorns gather around the altar and insert their horns into the holes for an intimate union with each other and their ancestors.

It was this sacred ceremony that Irmengard, wife of Adolf, Rightful Swan Knight, joined on her first day in Einigkeitstadt, when the Unicorns ran through her childhood memories, and so dissetled the Swan Knight by shouting scenes from his wife's life, through their shaggy, bearded mouths, in the voice of young Irmengard. Of all the wonders in the Sweeter Realm, the Unicorn shrine in Gemeinsam is what I most desired to see.

We hoped to gather enough of an army to travel from Gemeinsam, along the Achima River, through the Achima Mountains, to the Queen's Lake, where we would confront our enemies. God willing, we would find the Holy Grail along the way.

The Ancient One pitched the plan to our friends gathered in St. Hildegard. Each member had a different reason to approve the plan, different things they wished to see or do along the way. It received a unanimous endorsement. Although they were not without apprehensions, and fear lingered in them, putting a peppery sting on their tongues with every "Hurrah" they shouted, my brave devotees committed themselves and each other to the cause with stout pledges of mutual affection. We stood in the forest of the Brunnen city together, shouting and rallying.

Despite the confidence I gained with the brief sharing of the swan's thoughts, I feared desperately for the lives of those dear, sweet, loving and loyal creatures, as I thought in private silence, "I cannot lose a single one of them. The loss of any one would break me."

I am afraid to say, I would need to be much harder than that before the war ended, or I would have broken countless times over. That naïve sentiment came from the last lingering remnants of my parents' daughter, before my life in the Sweeter Realm mercilessly executed what remained of my younger self. I aged a great many years in the months that followed.

There would be no dispersing the crowd, no more delays for rest or refreshment. This was it. The time to leave St. Hildegard, my home and school, was at hand. But before we broke the tight circle in the center of the city, one monumental task had to be performed by The Ancient One. He regained the full attention of the city and gave a quick recap of some of my more surprising accomplishments from the year of training. Next, he asked me to kneel and make the Sign of the Cross. I obeyed with a heart whose increasing rhythm seemed to echo off of the inner walls of my armor. I knew what was coming. The city fell silent. Even the leaves on the trees stopped rustling with the breeze. The Ancient One administered the Swan Knights' oath for the first time since Ludwig.

He altered the parts that mentioned allegiance to the Queen of the Land and Shallow Waters, replacing them with oaths to the Sweeter Realm and its inhabitants. I repeated the words painstakingly, as if a single blunder would send me back through the portal, removed forever from my destiny. Each syllable gilded me, fastening me implacably to the gloriously bejeweled line of people who had knelt before the swan and made those same promises. When I stood and faced the crowd, there were no cheers. I felt altered by the oath, but those who witnessed the ceremony looked at me exactly as they had before. To them, I had always been the Swan Knight. The oath was just a logistical task to be completed before we embark. They nodded their heads and began assembling into our procession.

This new procession was not so meticulously placed as the last. I led, riding on Georg. The Ancient One rode beside me. Taufe walked near us. Other than that, the company was a rather haphazard and shifting mass of creatures. Some walked beside me, some drifted a little ahead only to slow and fall in line. Most followed behind. We did not march with any regal elegance. We were a raucous party, shifting and drifting as we flowed from the city, openly and loudly expressing our hopes and excitement, and equally openly and loudly, our fears and dispairs.

As I mentioned, my life in St. Hildegard had become stale. I was ready to press forward. But when the gathering Brunnen choir stood at the edge of the city and sang their blessings and good-byes, I looked back toward the cathedral and truly felt a sense of loss. I could not see the buildings. I saw nothing of the city but the forest, exactly like the forest ahead of us. But I had come to know St. Hildegard well and could easily imagine it. I was unaware of my spiritual connection to the cathedral — where I first opened my eyes to the lovely form of the Brunnens — until I rode away from it.

As we walked through the thick forest, toward Nährenstadt, the clamor of the crowd crested and waned. When it seemed too low, too settled, I practiced my skills on them. I connected them to me, for just a moment, sending them just a morsel of my faith and love for them.

The first time I did it, I looked toward The Ancient One and grinned. When he asked, "What is it", I looked forward and shared that small taste of my mind with the crowd behind me. The Ancient One, Georg, and Taufe received it with the rest. When the company erupted in simultaneous cheers, The Ancient One simply stared at me and smiled. Georg responded by quickening his steps. I had to remind him to march at a Scherier's pace. Taufe just giggled and looked to the sky, closed her eyes, and mouthed a prayer to God. As we marched on, the crowd settled again, and this process repeated in cycles until we reached the outskirts of Nährenstadt.

CHAPTER 22

Ohhl Ginshass Wahuff

MOST HAD SEEN THE DESTRUCTION OF THEIR CITIES. The remnants of the ravage ransacking of the Brunnen capital did not suprise them. I was struck deeply, not by the damage, or even by the loss of such beauty, but by the errant violence evident in the debris around us. It looked like the Brunnen buildings vomited their interiors between their twin tree entrances and onto the forest floor. The woods were sparse there, much thinner than at St. Hildegard, allowing a clear vision of the damage.

Many of the trees that marked the entrances to the buildings were torn in half or ripped from the ground entirely. The paintings and sculptures, the furnature and other possessions from inside of the buildings were strewn forth from the entranceways, as if the creatures of the Deep turned the buildings inside out, as if they pulled the interiors of the entire city through the twin trees that hid them, crushing everything inside to make it fit through the small doorways and onto the forest floor.

Wreaths, hundreds of them, hung on trees, leaned against stones, and rested flatly on the ground, each memorializing the death of a Brunnen during the city's fight for survival. The darkness, the air of defeat, of death, hung heavily around us, coating the trees, the ground, and the many splintered items across the forest floor. That darkness was fuel for our enemy. The fleshy bark of the city's trees lost its deep, rich vibrance. They wore an ashen jaundice, or in many cases, a cadaverous grey, not from a lack of water or nutirients, but from the absence of love in the city, for the loss of the mystically spiritual relationship between the trees of a healthy Brunnen city and their Brunnen caretakers. Love, Brunnen nurturing, and devotion to God needed to return to the Brunnen capital. Brightness that would take the wind of momentum from Löwschock needed to shine from that sacred place again. I dismounted Georg and began gathering the debris that shot forth from between two trees.

I heard the rise of curious whispers, "What is she doing?" and "Should we be helping?"

When my arms were full of broken pieces of finely molded wood, I stepped between the wilted, sickened trees of the building entrance. I entered nothingness, like standing inside of a glass sphere as it sat at the bottom of the ocean. I dropped the debris and stepped back into the forest. The members of my company had taken up my example. They picked up the broken pieces of the sacred city and made piles of what could be salvaged and what could not.

I seized their attention, intensely thinking the command, "Listen!"

All movement in the city stopped. All eyes found me and held to me.

"We cannot rebuild this city tonight. It may not fully recover during my lifetime. But we can start tonight. We can start with this building."

I pointed behind me, between the trees of the building I had walked through.

"We fix one building, make it inhabitable, and leave behind enough to continue what we begin."

Georg protested, "But we are trying to build an *army*, not a Brunnen city. We should be gathering numbers, not leaving them behind."

As he spoke, I became aware of a circle of Brunnens, gathering toward us from all directions. They perceived my command, "Listen" and they responded. They did not live in the city, but in the woods surrounding it, in huts and small homes, all hidden by Brunnen science, all with twin tree entrances, but small and scattered. All-in-all, there were more than one hundred Brunnens descending upon our party. I could not connect with them all at once, but I found their minds a few at a time. In those brief moments of connection, I envisioned my dream for their rebuilt capital, of an active, prayerful, and welcoming Nährenstadt.

By the time Georg noticed the new additions to our party, they were upon us and among us. One stood at his side. He did not know until the familiar feeling of a Brunnen stroke ran across his shoulder. She walked in front of him, faced him squarely, closed her eyes, looked to the sky, and drew a deep breath, inviting his horn to touch her chest. As he lowered his horn to her, my excited curiosity reached for his mind. I connected with him precisely as his horn made contact with her chest. I witnessed the communion.

Through the horn, she communicated her gratitude to him for bringing them the Queen, for coming with a force large enough and strong enough to protect them so they can come into the open city without fear. She praised him for his beauty and his strength, his kindness and his loyalty. If Unicorn fur could blush, Georg would have turned bright red. Instead, I blushed for him.

When the horn connection ended, Georg began shouting orders to the company, "You heard the Queen.

We start with that building. The reconstruction of this city begins tonight."

We worked halfway through the night fitting up the one building to functionality. The speed of the labor was impressive. Our Zweigwesens applied medicines to the broken trees of the entrance.

"Oh, they will recover nicely in time, my Queen," one of them told me.

The Brunnens sculpted new walls, new furnishings for the building. The Unicorns lifted and pulled all that was too heavy for the others. The Federmensch hoisted heavy beams with their notorious strength. The Zweigwesen connected together to reach high up walls and ceilings. The Scheriers and Friends of the Scheriers searched the city for salvageable items and brought them into our building. Triller and Flöte led the flock of Eulesängers, singing to us all, energizing us after a long day of travel and a long night of work. On occasion, I caught a glimpse of the native Brunnens, admiring the excited, flurrying, whirling energy of their full and recovering city.

Although the Brunnens were not completely satisfied, claiming that it was not yet good enough to house their Queen, I thought the building we fixed to be almost as beautiful as the cathedral in St. Hildegard, lovely in contrast to how we found it, and lovlier still for the united spirit with which it was revived. One Brunnen had been painting while the rest of us worked. She finished as we did and presented me with the first painting to hang in the reconstructed building. It was a scene I knew at first glance, one that had quickly become iconic through spreading rumor. It was me, in Kandake's palace, standing in front of the throne while a sepent of the Deep sank into the floor. Not quite accurately, she painted the Vogelkröte curled between my feet as I stood heroically posed before the throne.

I accepted the gift with pride and hung it myself where the artist instructed me to. I lowered my hands from placing the painting, took two steps back to admire it, and was nearly deafened by the eruption of cheers and applause. It lasted for several minutes. When it finally died down, The Ancient One announced that a long day awaits us all. Most of our company crammed into the building. Many could not fit. So they settled into what remained of the other buildings. The Ancient One ordered us to sleep and we all obeyed. Well, almost all of us obeyed. Georg stood half in, half outside the building, determined to serve as guard for the night. I don't know if he slept, but he was like that when I snuggled up with the swan and fell asleep, and he was like that when I awoke.

We rose to a city almost entirely in ruins — almost. Our one building was a laudable testament to what could be accomplished in half of a night. It gave the Brunnens a glimpse of their recovery. We could not stay to help them. We needed to continue as planned. I recruited thirty of the Brunnens who joined us, leaving the rest to continue the reconstruction of their capital. I left them with two Zweigwesens, for protection and to serve their medical needs, and those of the city's trees.

That one rebuilt Brunnen gathering place gave my company a taste of a bright recovery. They saw the peace and glory of their past through their lenses into the future. And this sense of hope did not come from me or the swan. It came from their own accomplishment, from the clear fruits of their united efforts. We left Nährenstadt with strong faith in its full recovery. The rising of the sun that morning brought a brighter, warmer Sweeter Realm. No doubt Löwschock felt it too, the hope and love pushing down upon his Deep kingdom from above.

I knew that every victory, no matter how small, victories like our one repaired Brunnen building, would double the anger and efforts of our enemies. I knew it, but I tried not to think it. It shot a wave of fear through me, fear that battled against my productive desires, fears that I could not help but project to the minds nearest me. So I covered it. I plastered it with the warmth of confident aspirations rebounding off of the faces around me.

My mind quickly turned to our next destination, the ancient training grounds of Unicorn warriors. It was in those fields that young Unicorns since Elsa's time prepared to serve the Swan Knights, there that they learned how to patrol the hills around Linderhof. It was there that they held their ground in defiant protection of the Eulesänger homeland. We left Nährenstadt in the empowered and laborious hands of those who stayed, and we continued north.

After the good-byes and well-wishes, our traveling company was mostly silent. A strange duality occupied their minds, one which they shared with me in search of reconciliation. On one side was a full consciousness of the brutality of destruction they had just witnessed, the wreaths for the fallen, the loss of life and beauty that the wreaths represented. On the other side was the miracle of their united accomplishment, the remarkable progress that we made in reviving the one building in a single night. I am afraid to say that connecting to my mind did nothing to reconcile the polarity in them. I suffered it with them, exactly as they did, and stood on no good footing to pull them from their internal conflicts. I can only say that their glimpses into my mind legitimized their own conflicts and united us strangely in the universality of our feelings.

After a few hours, our silence was broken. In the midst of a thickly wooded forest, Georg informed me that we were crossing the border from Brunnen land to Unicorn land. Nothing but the words of Georg distinguished one from the other, until, several minutes later, the forest gave way to a wide expanse of open plains. The dirt and patches of grass that covered the forest floor turned to knee-high, bright green grass as far as my eyes could see. The landscape transitioned from the flat forest lands of the Brunnens to the slowly, gently sloping low hills of the Unicorn grasslands.

There was no impediment between the sun and my eyes, no tall trees, no limbs or leaves. The brightness of the grass was almost as hard on the eyes as the sun above. Until I adjusted, I shielded the grass from my eyes with one hand. It was not just the contrast with the darkness of the forest. The Unicorn land was brighter than bright, lit by more than just light. Inherent, native goodness joined the rays from above to scream at my eyes, proclaiming its nobility.

"I used to work here, you know", Georg boasted. "So did your dear Acheriel. In fact, it was on that very hill ahead of us that he introduced himself to me as my tacher."

"Acheriel was your teacher?" I asked with delighted astonishment.

"I doubt that a Unicorn still lives who did not learn from him, from him and Prische."

"Prische was you teacher too?"

"She was our spiritual teacher, much like Taufe has been for you. The Unicorns who train here commit themselves to four things, God, the Holy Grail, the Queen, and the Swan Knights. Half of those are you, my extraordinary young pupil."

If humble gratitude made sound, mine would have injured the ears of all around me.

"I am half of what the Unicorn warriors commit themselves to," I reminded myself repeatedly.

We rode to the top of the hill indicated by Georg.

"Where are they all?" I asked.

"Many are dead, and many defend the Land and Shallow Waters against the current attacks. Acheriel is, as you know, with Prische and their new goat."

"Are there any here training?"

"You tell me."

I slid tentatively from Georg's back, as if usure if the hill would hold my weight. I knelt in the tall grass and ran my fingers through the blades. I began to hear the cloven-hoofsteps of Unicorns, but none around me were in motion. The sounds were not the perceptions of my senses. They were the gatherings of my Grail Blood. I concentrated on the sound and sent it to Georg.

"Those are the sounds of the past you are hearing. This is remarkable. *We* must connect to the shrine in Gemeinsam to see the past. What else do you see?"

I lowered my hands farther and buried my fingertips into the soil. I heard huffing and shouting, then silence.

Then, in an experience similar to the strange sentence I uttered in the palace, I called out, "Ohhl Ginshass Wahuff."

I felt the words come from my mouth in a voice that was not mine. But I shouted with intense passion in my heart, words I had never heard before. I repeated more loudly and with greater desperate emotion, "Ohhl Ginshass Wahuff!"

I continued to repeat the same line, louder and with greater fervor, but I did not know why or what it meant. All I knew was that I needed to shout it, and intense, fiery emotion accompanied the strange words.

I stood, clinched my fists tightly, raised my head and yelled to the hills around me, "Ohhl Ginshass Wahuff!"

The fever left me when I caught, from the corner of my eye, Georg dropping sharply to a front knee, bowing his head to me. The other Unicorns in our company had joined him in a circle around me, all kneeling, all bowing.

"What? What is happeneing to me? What are those words?"

Georg raised his head to me, lifted one bushy eyebrow, and asked, "Do you not know?"

I repeated, "What are those words? Whose voice came from my mouth?"

He answered, studdering in his lingering astonishment, "Ohhl Ginshass Wahuff . . . those are the words of Senische, our great prophet. It is her horn that is replicated by the shrine in Gemeinsam."

"Who is she?"

"She was the one who brought us together. Hers was the first horn to connect one mind to another. She gave birth to the Unicorn collective. Before Senische, the horn was simply an appendage, a tool of defense. According to legend, the spirits of the Unicorns were fading, as we fell into chaos and mindlessness. She traveled all of Unicorn land and collected the spirits of each Unicorns in her horn, preserving them and enriching them with her own goodness. She held them until order was restored. She touched her horn to that of every living Unicorn, returning the spirit revivied and purified to its owner and giving birth to what we call the White Age."

Another bowing Unicorn lifted her head and continued Georg's lesson, "Senische was the first of the Unicorns as you know us to be. As she connected to each Unicorn, and returned the spirit, she spoke those words, Ohhl Ginshass Wahuff. It roughly means, From the Scattered to a United Mind. It is in a language that only survives in a few phrases, passed through vows and oaths. Ohhl Ginshass Wahuff is shouted by the warriors who train in this field, as it has been since before the grass grew here."

"Whose voice came from my mouth?"

The Ancient One suggested possibilities, "Perhaps it was the voice of some young student warrior from many centuries ago, or it may have been the voice of Senische herself."

At the last statement, incredible and astonished thoughts came to me from the Unicorns surrounding me. My connection to the Unicorns was deeper than their connection to each other. It seemed to transcend time. My head was swimming. Between the possession of my voice by another and the significance of the tale I was just told, the significance of the swan's suggestion, I was in a dreamy fog. I descended from the fog to discover the staring, bewildered faces of my entire company, all except for the Unicorns, who still knelt around me with heads lowered in a reverent bow.

The Ancient One was not bewildered, rather confirmed. Nothing I did or said, nothing that happened to me or about me, seemed to surprise him. Oh, he was delighted by my successes, those things that startled me out of my wits. But they seemed to be exactly what he expected, what he envisioned. While the others were dumbfounded by the mythical and magical things that erputed from me unannounced, the swan simply fluffed his feathers with pride.

I suddenly thought about Acheriel and Prische. I recalled the whole surreal experience on the hill and sent my thoughts to them. I did not so much receive thoughts in return, but hope, hope for us and for their new child. One brief notion slipped through, inside of the emotion. It was the belief that they would see me soon. Both of them planned to be with me when I went into battle. They insisted upon it, despite my pleas to the contrary. If I was going to be in danger, they would be there beside me. I don't know if they sent me that idea intentionally, but I got it, hidden inside of their feelings of hope.

We rested on the grassy hills of the Unicorn training ground, eating and conversing leisurely. We did not abound with excited energy. The strange mystery of the Unicorn voice and Unicorn words coming from my mouth laid a thick blanket of thoughtfulness on us all. The talk was low, the fervor subdued. Conversations were more of the past than the future. They talked of glory days gone by, with little thought of what must be done to bring them back — of the perils that were ahead of us. The talk of ancient Unicorn legends spawned their equivalent from the depths of each breed's deepest lore. Ancient stories were told as if for the first time. And the wide, child-like eyes of the listeners lapped up every word.

As the sun fell low in the sky, Taufe and two other Brunnens came to me. I had been sitting alone, deep in imaginative fantasy, obviously putting off an air of desired solitude.

"We should be on our way," Taufe advised with a calm imperative about her voice.

Florenna, one of the Brunnens with her, added, "There is a Brunnen building inside of the Eulesänger border, one that we built for our little friends, as a shelter of refuge during the war."

"We should go there," Taufe added.

My mind had drifted so far from the here-and-now that the dangers of the approaching nighttime were worlds away from my thoughts, until snapped to my immediate presense by the Brunnens.

"How far away is it?" I asked.

Florenna answered, "We could be there in a couple of hours, if we leave now and walk briskly."

I wasted no time with a response. I stood sharply, emitting a wave of energy from my small frame that was felt and acknowledged by the entire company. I announced that it was time to move on, to go into Eulesänger land and sleep peacefully in a Brunnen building.

291

Georg ran to me and whispered, "One moment please, my Queen. They are coming, joining us here. The young warriors are on their way."

I lowered my head and rubbed the pads of my thumbs against my fingertips, thinking, concentrating on the young Unicorn students.

They were shouting in unison, with the vibrancy of youth, "Ohhl Ginshass Wahuff!", as they raced to join us.

They heard the call of their ancient prophet, when I shouted from the hilltop in her voice. They repeated the slogan, over and over as they rode at full gallop to the training ground.

I began mouthing the words with them, then lowly whispering, then vocalizing, getting louder and louder, "Ohhl Ginshass Wahuff!"

The Unicorns in our company heard and joined. The other creatures joined in small pockets at a time, "Ohhl Ginshass Wahuff!"

The hills themselves, the very blades of grass beneath our feet, seemed to shout the old saying that they had heard from many young Unicorns over the centuries. When the shouting reached its zenith, I grabbed Georg and mounted him with all the speed and precision of my training. I drew my Unicorn-horn sword, held it high, and ordered the company to move north.

The shouting died down and was replaced by the bustle and clamor of movement.

Taufe asked, "Aren't we waiting for the warriors?"

Georg stomped his front hooves and huffed a laugh through his beard. He knew what I knew, that I instructed the warriors to meet with us at the quickest point, just north of where we were.

"Where is Cort?" I demanded.

A Zweigwesen ran to my side carrying the Friend of the Scheriers.

"Tonight you ride with me, old friend," I said gently to him, as I rubbed his shiny head.

He radiated with the light of his pride and happiness. The danger ahead, our chances of victory, they meant nothing at all to Cort. He was content to be dead in the belly of a monster of the Deep — dead but right, loyal, noble, and Godly. He was so delighted to be in motion, in persuit of God's will, regardless of what that persuit brought him.

The Ancient One mounted a Unicorn and rode beside me. Georg was ready to run at the speed of his passions. I again reminded him of the stride length of our smaller members.

He answered with an uncharacteristic, adolescent mischieviousness in his voice, "Let us see how fast the company can move. It will be good to know."

He picked up his pace to a hearty trot. Brunnens and Zweigwesens grabbed the Friends of the Scheriers and placed them upon Unicorns. The Federmensch draped Scheriers across their shoulders and ran with their sharply bowed legs. The quicker Scheriers ran on their own hands and feet. The company stayed with us. Georg increased his speed, putting the agility of the party to the test. They stayed directly on our heels.

Suddenly, the sound of galloping hooves came from our left. There they were, two dozen young Unicorn warriors. Cort caught sight of them first.

He yelled from under my left arm, "Ohhl Ginshass Wahuff! The warriors are here."

The entire running company shouted the slogan to the young Unicorns as they came upon us. The Unicorns shouted back, "Ohhl Ginshass Wahuff!"

Twenty-four of the stoutest young Unicorns, with young, pointed horns and smooth, shiny coats, took up positions to the sides and rear of the company, cupping us with their protection.

We ran like that, with Scheriers and Zweigesens, with each of our breeds, throwing an occasional cheer to the warriors beside them, "Ohhl Ginshass Wahuff!" — From the Scattered to a United Mind. Our new warriors always responded in kind.

CHAPTER 23

Crippling Hums and Hairy Bridges

WE CROSSED THE BORDER INTO THE EULESÄNGER HOMELAND as the last of the sunlight kissed the top of the high grass good-night. We ran, without slowing our pace in the slightest, into the cover of a dense Eulesänger forest. In the forest, we slowed to a near crawl. The Brunnens led the way, stopping us finally at the base of two tall trees. They were Brunnen trees, like the ones that grew in St. Hildegard, with their fleshy, deep-brown complexion, not like the thinner, course-barked trees of the Eulesänger forest. Triller and Flöte hovered directly over my head, quickly shifting their eyes in all directions, as if suspicious of the very trees around us. When I peaked into them, I saw irrational fear, not connected with any particular event, enemy, or location. But the Eulesänger woods severly dissettled them.

Taufe shushed the company and walked slowly and silently to the twin trees. She walked between them and disappreared from our sight. Three other Brunnens followed her. From the space between the trees, singing came. At first, it was the comfortable and familiar sound of

Brunnen spiritual chants. It was soon fully orchestrated by the splended whistles of Eulesängers, many Eulesängers.

Taufe stepped through the trees, onto the forest floor and invited me in with a subtle curl of her fingertips. I stepped between the trees, into a chamber larger than any that I had seen in St. Hildegard. It was filled with Eulesängers, hundreds, maybe thousands of birds, as Ludwig described them, "with awkwardly large, thick wings, and bushy tails dragging behind them, like a wolf's tail, covered in such fine feathers that they looked hairy. The birds were deep brown, like the darkest bark in the forest. Their tiny beaks hooked like an owl's and their large, bright-blue eyes expressed both warmth and intelligence."

At the sight of me and my Swan Knight's armor, they surrounded me, running and flying around me so I felt I was drowning in them. They blocked out the light of the room until Taufe whistled to them and they backed away to gather on the floor in a circle around me. They stared at me in silence. I didn't know quite what to say. The awkward moment was broken by another entrance into the room. It was The Ancient One, with Triller and Flöte riding on his back. An Eulesänger whistle flew from them, to bounce off of the silent walls. It did not come from Triller or Flöte. It was the swan's greeting that broke the silence.

The flock at my feet responded with a curt repeat of the same whistle. Triller and Flöte hopped from the swan's back and waddled to the flock, embracing a few, then disappearing among them.

"Introduce yourself," my teacher instructed.

I gazed across the large chamber, at all of the wide, blue eyes, fixed implacably on me. I thought my introduction.

A single bird walked to me from the middle of the flock, dragging her bushy tail behind her. She stood between my feet and rubbed the side of her face against my lower left leg. I bent down and picked her up, and held her to my face, beak to nose. Her eyes had the depth and character of an ancient ocean, with all of the stories and myths of a well-traveled body of water. She closed her eyes and leaned her head into me. I lowered her to my chest and held her against the armor.

She whistled something, but the sounds were muffled inside of the embrace.

I pulled her away from me and asked her, "I'm sorry, what did you say?"

She repeated her announcement. In my studies of Sweeter Realm languages, I learned enough Eulesänger to get the jist.

She said, "Welcome Verena, daughter of Rudolf."

The flock echoed her whistle in unison. I asked the leader if we could stay in their home.

"Our homes are abandoned. We live here now," she whistled.

"All of you?" I asked in clear German, for I could not imitate the Eulesänger whistle, and I would not embarrass myself trying.

She responded in such quick and high-pitched language that I couldn't understand. The Ancient One translated for me. He told me that Eulesänger villages on the ground were passed over by Löwschock's armies, and the towns in the trees were passed under, as if they were unnoticed. The towns and villages of their homeland were entact. But they dared not live in them, not since the Wühlenvogels joined the ranks of the enemy. The serpents of the Deep may not have noticed the Eulesängers and they enjoyed the protection of the Unicorns, but the Wühlenvogels knew them well, and they knew where to find their nests and towns.

Not all of them gathered in the Brunnen building. Many thousands took their chances in the open forest. Nobody knew how they fared. Our hosts were delighted to see Triller and Flöte, and used their appearance as a reason to hope for the survival of the others.

The swan ended his translation, adding, "And yes, they are happy to let us stay here."

We invited the company into the hall. It was snug, to be sure, but we fit. We were hidden in a secret building in a forgotten corner of an obscure forest in the homeland of a breed that was insignificant to our enemies. We slept well. We slept comfortably, and we slept easy, easy enough for me to remove my armor and enjoy the touch of others. I slept sandwiched between Taufe and The Ancient One. Taufe reached her soft Brunnen arms around me to embrace the swan behind me, pulling him more tightly against my back. Other than in the warm, feathered arms of Felix, I have never been so comfortably situated. I fell asleep to a Brunnen lullaby, whispered privately into my ear.

The dream I had that night has remained with me to this day, magnified by my later understanding of its prophetic meaning. The dream, the nightmare came to fruition many years after I had it. In fact, my dream that night fortold the fate of mankind. In the dream, I was in the cathedral at St. Hildegard. Against the wall, on the far end from the entrance, atop the elevated platform, was a tall crucifix. I knelt at its base and prayed for Felix and for my family.

My deep prayers were disturbed by a whisper of my name, coming from above me. I looked up at the crucifix. Jesus stared down at me, still calling to me in the same whisper, as he hung from the cross. I stood and asked him what I could do for him. I asked him if I was where I was supposed to be, doing what he wanted me to do. He looked to his left. My eyes followed his and saw that the nail through his left wrist was gone. He pulled his left hand from the cross and pointed to me. I looked down and saw the nail protruding from my belly.

I looked up in a desperate plea for his help. He was looking at his right hand. The nail was gone. I looked down and saw both nails sticking from my belly, side by side. My shirt had turned red with blood. I slowly lifted my head to the Lord. The nail was gone from his feet. I had not felt the pain of the first two nails, but a sudden cramp in my lower abdomen drew my eyes downward again. This time, I saw the nail sinking into me, beneath the other two. It sank in quick bursts, like it was being hammered into me. The hammering sound accompanied the nail's descent into my body, only it didn't sount like a hammer hitting iron. It sounded like gunshots, a single gunshot associated with each bursting submersion of the nail.

I looked up again to the Lord. He was not on the cross. I saw only the bottoms of his feet as he ascended through a bright beam of light, through the ceiling of the cathedral. I awoke with a jolt, as Taufe did with a similar jolt. She shared my dream. In her dream, she stood just outside of a side room of the cathedral, watching the whole thing in sympathetic horror.

Still lying between Taufe and the sleeping swan, I looked in her eyes and started to cry.

She rubbed my temples and kissed my forehead, my cheeks, and my lips, whispering between kisses, "Whatever this means . . . , whatever the Lord has in store for you . . . , I am with you . . . I will bear it all with you, my love."

I continued crying, returning Taufe's kisses, and reaching behind me to stroke the feathers of The Ancient One, until I fell back to sleep.

In the morning, I was refreshed, with little lingering emotion from the prophetic dream. The Eulesängers served us all breakfast. It was only a sweet, thick, syrup-like nectar, which gathers in abundance inside of the only fruit in the forest. It is not so much fruit. That is, it is not edible, but more like pinecones. But within the core, the nectar grows and sweetens. Breakfast was served in the tiny, half-shells of Eulesänger eggs. Each member of the company received a single portion. Yet, that tiny mouthful satisfied and energized. I wanted more, but only for the sensual pleasure of the nectar's sweet and unique flavor. My stomach craved nothing, though I was quite hungry when I awoke.

After breakfast, The Ancient One wanted me to gather the company and share our plans with our hosts, not just our plans of travel, but also my desire to see the cities and shrines of the Land and Shallow Waters bustling again with life and love. I told the Eulesängers that it was time to return to their capital, time to repopulate their ancient nests. There was a brief moment of apprehension. The Wühlenvogels still frightened them. But the Swan Knight said it and The Ancient One agreed. That was enough for them. After the exchange of puzzled glances, they returned all of their bright eyes to me and sent their cheers flying to my welcoming ears.

They did not cheer long from the floor before taking to the air. They darted and swirled, climbed and dove, all while whistling their excited agreement with their Queen. Triller and Flöte just stood at my side, encouraging the rest. After several minutes of this, the birds all landed and returned their eyes to me. Their whistles turned to a low hum — well, low for an Eulesänger, surprisingly low. They held that low note much longer than I imagined a creature that size could exhale. They were united in a single note that seemed to shake the walls around us. It began to hurt, not just my ears, but my bones and my joints. The Unicorns suffered similarly, as did the Friends of the Scheriers, the

Brunnens, and the Zweigwesens. But the Scheriers were unaffected.

I bent over in pain and Lina yelled, "Stop! You are hurting Verena!"

The humming stopped immediately. So did the pain. In the pain, I had forced every bit of breath from my body.

After a long and slow inhale, I yelled angrily and to no particular target, "What was that?"

Triller rubbed my leg with his wing and apologized for his kind. He continued whistling, but I understood nothing beyond the apology. My mind and body were still recovering from the strange shock.

The Ancient One translated for me, "That is a spiritual ritual, one of thanksgiving. They had no idea it would cause pain. It has never been performed in the company of others. They are mortified to have injured you and they promise never to perform the ritual again."

"No!" I sharply retorted. "This is a weapon, one that can injure both sides. Let us keep this surprise in our pockets and pull it out when we need it."

We arranged a code, a trigger phrase to signal the Eulesängers to produce their hum. At The Ancient One's command "Thank your enemies", spoken in the Eulesänger language, the birds were to reproduce the sound, and hopefully the crippling effects.

"Until then," I requested with a smirk, "a simple thank-you will do."

Recovered and satisfied, we exited the building, onto the forest floor. Not a single Eulesänger stayed behind. None sought the continued protection of the Brunnen building. They were eager to reunite with their nests and towns and the friends and family scattered throughout their homeland.

We headed north, through the center of the band of forest. We traveled less than an hour when our attention was brought suddenly and frighteningly upward, to the top of the forest canopy, where we saw a flock of Wühlenvogels skirting the tips of the trees. They flew quickly, focused, and determined, over our heads and out of sight.

"They are hunting Eulesängers," one of the small birds blurted from his held breath.

"No," The Ancient One responded after several seconds of thought, "they hunt us all. They hunt the Queen. They are not obeying the commands of their stomachs. They are obeying the commands of their King . . . Löwschock."

In the silence of the moment that followed, I could almost hear the crawling skin of the collective company.

Taufe broke the chilled silence, "We are vulnerable in the forest. We stand a better chance in the open fields."

"No, not the fields," Georg huffed low and growling, shaking his head and swaying his long beard. "The mountains. The mountains to the east. That would give us the greatest advantage."

I had not had the greatest of fortune in the mountains of the Land and Shallow Waters. But I had learned and grown so much since the fall. I trusted fully in Georg's tactical expertise, and I had no intention of dismounting his back while the ground was far beneath us. I put my safety on his steady hooves and ordered the company to the east, to the Pfeifen Mountains.

When we exited the eastern edge of the forest, into the open plains beyond, I felt exposed. I felt vulnerable. The others must have felt the same. They drew more tightly to me as we traveled, not to seek my protection, but to protect me, to shield me with their lives if needed. Less than half of the multitude of Eulesängers flew above us. Most walked beside and between us, snuggling their tiny paces tightly against the feet of the others, causing many to stumble and trip to avoid trampling them.

Taufe was right. The Wühlenvogels hunt in the forest. It is in that setting that they are most lethal. The open air would allow us to unleash the skills of the Unicorns, where they live and train, and the moutains would narrow our battle front to one side. Nevertheless, I practiced our secret Eulesänger trigger under my breath, "Thank your enemies", ready to whistle it myself if I had to.

None in the company knew the Pfeifen Mountains well. Our hike through the foothills was slow and took us late into the day. Our plan was to travel north through the western edge of the mountains, ready to return to the plains on our west, or retreat east, deeper into the mountains. The row of low, rounded foothills were not dissimilar to the hills of the Sweeter Realm I had seen so far. But just beyond that, the topography of the mountain range changed drastically. We found a path that rose sharply upward. The peaks along our path were steep, the cliffs abrupt, and the stones sharp and jagged. I could have shaved my legs against the protruding rocks to the mountain side of the narrow path, and fallen for a full minute on the other side, without touching ground.

I commented, more to myself than to any intended recipient, but The Ancient One heard me, "The mountains themselves seem to want to kill us."

"They are not discriminate. They want to kill. And if we hold our ground, they will be more deadly to an attacker than a steady defender. I know these rocks are frightening, much more than the forest. But with our backs to the mountain and the sharp rocks all around us, we can defend ourselves well. The Wühlenvogels would be foolish to attack us here."

"Let us pray it does not come to that."

"Amen, my wise young Queen, amen."

We worked our way slowly and carefully through the mountains. I ardently wished that the Wühlenvogels were friends, not because I feared their attack, but because I was so afraid of the mountains. I wanted to ride one of them safely onto the plains to the west. The Eulesängers hopped and flapped, flew and landed. They were quite safe from the perils of the darkening mountains. But the largest of them were smaller than my head. Their gift of flight was of little use to the rest of us. They scouted ahead and reported the condition of the path, a path which was hardly a path. It was probably some ancient passage, unused for centuries, eroded, weakened, and narrowed. At points, it disappeared entirely, and we crawled across the sharp rocks.

We had traveled all day, non-stop since we left the Brunnen shelter, sometimes at a comfortable walk, but mostly at a rushed, galloping pace. My legs maintained their mindless volley with each other, back and forth, until one would draw my attention by buckling in exhaustion. I muscled through it until the leg resumed its pace and pattern on its own. The path we walked in the mountains offered us several wide and open, flat spaces where we could have rested in shifts. But we pressed past them, desiring the defense of the high, jagged rocks. The sunset found us deep in the mountains, clinging like moss to the rocks around us.

We had hardly turned north — nowhere near where we intended to turn west and head through the plains, to the Eulesänger capital. We dared not proceed in the dark. That would be suicide. Neither could we camp where we were. The Unicorns carried nobody. The path was treacherous even for their steady hooves. There was hardly room to stand, let alone lie and sleep. In the weak light of a partial moon we proceeded, slowly, carefully, and almost blindly, looking for a place to rest. Instead, we came to a ravine, a dead end. The thin path, already sloping slightly downhill, inviting us to fall to our deaths, came to an abrupt stop at the edge of a deep, seemingly bottomless ravine.

We could not press forward. It was too dark to go back. And there was hardly room for us all to stand. I could not even sit. It took every bit of my agility to remain on my tired feet, without sliding down the slope of the path, off of the cliff to our left. Our danger became suddenly and mortally apparent. How long could we remain there, standing like that, before we began falling, one at a time, off of the worn edge of the path? With each pulsing second, my ears expected to hear the desperate scream of some falling friend, sliding from the path and disappearing into the deep blackness to our right. I was so scared, I felt my heartbeat pounding in my jaw and in my ears.

I heard rising activity from the rear of the company, and talking in Zweigwesen. Through the dim light, I could see a parade of Zweigwesens being lifted and passed to the front of the party, over the heads of the others, stepping on Unicorns and Brunnens, scaling along the sharp rocks to our right, until they reached the edge of the ravine. Many surprises have delighted me, have tantilazed my brain and redefined my notions of beauty, since I floated through the portal at Linderhof. The following moment rose above them all. It brought me from intense fear to the warmest of appreciation.

The Zweigwesens began to connect to one another, as Zweigwesens do. They formed a structure, a bridge, connecting to each other one after the last, reaching farther across the ravine, until the very last Zweigwesen in our company grabbed the path on the other side. There they were, a narrow, but well-formed bridge across the ravine, eight to ten Zweigwesens wide.

A single word came from a Zweigwesen mouth, in the middle of the structure, "Well?"

We all stood and stared at them with appreciative hearts until he continued, "Come on. This isn't as easy as it looks."

Without another moment of pause, without any hesitation or testing of the security of the Zweigwesen structure, Georg trotted across the bridge. The Ancient One followed, hopping and shaking his one wing, while his stump held his prosthetic wing high in the air. A group of Scheriers were in front of me. They went next. Taufe and I followed, holding hands *and* breath. I looked down and saw the blinking eyes and widening smiles of the Zweigwesens who saved us.

On the other side, I could see a widening of the path, a safe place for us to rest for the night. I exchanged glances, from the crossing of the company behind me to the place where I knew we could all rest safely until the morning. The entire company made it across the Zweigwesen bridge. I watched as carefully as the dim moonlight allowed, as each Zweigwesen broke the formation, one at a time, beginning at the far end. The bridge appeared to fold up and roll toward me, until every Zweigwesen was safe on our side of the ravine. We moved carefully to the widened portion of the path and rested. My debts to that point had deepened further. I owed my life to so many. Yet such benevolent creditors they are, my subjects, my friends, the sweet creatures of the Land and Shallow Waters.

CHAPTER 24

Nethe's Gift

WE RESTED THROUGH THE NIGHT on the widened and flattened path on the other side of the ravine. There was little room to wiggle, but the tight quarters made me feel safer. The drop from the cliff was steep and long, and the rocks around us were still sharp and jagged. But I felt nothing of that. I was surrounded by soft feathers, fur, and flesh. I was tightly swaddled in the embraces of loyal and loving friends.

I awoke to a bright morning and a circle of astonished eyes, staring at me.

"What? What is it?" I demanded, half asleep and confused.

"You were singing," Cort announced, "soft and lovely hymns."

He hummed in immitation and swayed so grandly to his own voice that he almost fell to his side.

I giggle now, in remembrance of the sight, but at the time I just stared at him in confusion and asked slowly, "I was singing?"

"Yes, my dear one," Taufe answered calmly. "You sang a song I know well, one I learned when I was with Archbishop Conrad. It is a song I never taught you, never sang to you."

"What was it?"

"You sang a hymn written by St. Hildegard. You sang it beautifully, in flawless Latin."

With nostalgic energy in her voice, she recited the words.

O Virtus Sapientie
Que circuiens circuisti
Comprehendendo omnia
In una via que habet vitam
Tres alas habens
Quarum una in altum volat
Et altera de terra sudat
Et tercia undique volat.
Laus tibi sit, sicut te decet, O Sapientia.

I asked her, "What does it mean?"

She glared at me in disappointment, as if to ask, "Weren't you paying attention in your Latin lessons?"

She let out a sigh and translated the Latin loudly, for all to hear. "O Virtus Sapientie — it means *O Wisdom's energy.*"

That was not what I meant by my question. I understood the Latin. I wanted to know what it meant that I sang it in my sleep, this hymn that I never learned, never even heard. But I was so entranced by the foggy familiarity of the words that my real question sat back in my mind, folded its arms, and contented itself to wait while I indulged my tingling curiosity.

She continued her translation.

Whirling, you encircle
And everything embrace
In the single way of life.
Three wings you have:
One soars above into the heights,
One from the earth exudes,
And all about now flies the third.

Praise be to you, as is your due, O Wisdom.

After Taufe's recitation and translation, she began to interpret the meaning, applying the words to me and to the cryptic hints she had already given me concerning my future and the fate of humanity.

I interrupted, "No, that's not what I meant. What does it mean that I was singing the song in my sleep?"

Taufe froze in embarrassment. Her perfectly still body turned silvery, then began to fade from view.

The Ancient One interjected, "You offer us a new delight every day, Swan Knight. What does any of it mean? Our duty is to be with you, to be for you, not to question what it means. You were brought here by God and by the Grail Blood. Once this story is fully written, we will let the historians, the philosophers and theologians debate why you do what you do."

That was good enough for me, and apparently for everyone else as well, all except Taufe, whose struggle to swallow the words that were rising from her heart to her mouth showed clearly with a twisted grimace on her otherwise angelic face. On The Ancient One's last word, the company shook off their wide eyes and frozen stares, and they formed up to continue our journey along the mountain path.

As we traveled, winding and looping through the mountain, toward the north, the path widened and narrowed, but it was never again treacherous. By the early afternoon, the path split, one prong headed up, higher onto the mountain. The other headed down. We took the lower path. It worked us slowly west, from the jagged mountains, into the rolling foothills, and eventually to the plains between the Pfeifen Mountains and the Eulesänger forests. The plains seemed to expand endlessly to the west. Our path from the mountains continued into the plains for about half an hour of walking, then faded and disappeared, leaving us in an open and endless field of grass.

When the sun set, we were in the open plains, exposed and vulnerable. The Scheriers set to burrowing. They are not the Wühlenvogels, who could have sculpted us an underground village with room to spare, while we rested and ate. But many of our Scheriers committed to the cause. As they scratched and dug, they looked like a bubbling fountain of white fur and sharp claws, in constant motion, not exactly synchronized, but like separately moving parts of a single body. The Scheriers worked hard to construct a small cave, only large enough for me, Taufe, and The Ancient One to rest with comfortable room to spare. Before the sky was entirely dark, the cave was ready.

There was no door, no furniture, not even the dirt-mound tables of Rüdiger and Lina's cave. There were no candles or torches. The cave was entirely dark. The Scheriers dug an entrance hole just large enough for us to squeeze through. There was a small flight of six or seven steps steeply down, into a space not much larger than my full-sized bed back home. But it was plenty of room for the three of us and I was happy to be underground again.

The rest of the company slept on the grass of the open plain, most of them gathered tightly near the entrance to the cave.

As the three of us worked our way blindly into the hole, one of the Scheriers shouted, "I wish the Old Digger were here. He could have given you a real nice room to sleep in tonight."

"Hummph. The Old Digger is more mouth than claws," Lina gruffly contested. "I doubt he could have dug a hole big enough for himself."

Then I heard her whisper, or perhaps I felt her thoughts, I really don't remember. In any case, she thought, "But he was right about the swan, wasn't he, my dear husband. You were both right about the swan."

Lina, who had traveled beside the Scheriers, not wishing to draw attention to herself as my particular friend, had little interaction with me since we left St. Hildegard, little more than any of the many creatures with us. Her sentimental confession made me think of dear Rüdiger, of how much I loved them both. I called her into the cave. She slept on Taufe's belly, with my arm draped over her. I can imagine no softer bed than a Brunnen belly — for those creatures small enough to make a bed of a Brunnen's belly. That night Lina had such a bed beneath her. And above her draped an arm willing to suffer anything for her comfort. How very peaceful her dreams must have been that night.

We started early the next morning, with no food and little conversation. The Eulesänger capital lies at the northern edge of the forest, the same forest we abandoned after spying the Wühlenvogels above. We walked for a few hours until only a small, hazy silhouette of the mountains behind us remained. When they disappeared entirely, I had nothing but the sun to set my bearings. The Eulesängers were my best compass. Their excitement, the energy of their movements, and the pitch of their conversations increased proportionately with our proximity to their capital city. But in equal proportion, as we approached the city, my fear of the Wühlenvogels increased. The city was abandoned for a reason. It was open and unprotected.

Ahead of us, I saw a table-top plateau. It seemed to be wearing a hat. As we climbed the shallow slope to the top, I realized what I saw. The entire plateau was capped by a single, enormous nest, made from the dried blades of the same grasses we had been walking through all day. On the nest were hundreds of tiny, straw huts, no larger than a chihuahua's dog house. They looked weak and fragile, yet none were destroyed. None were disturbed. Not a straw was out of place.

The Eulesänger leader, the one who greeted me in the Brunnen building, commented in delighted astonishment, "It is exactly as we left it."

No Wühlenvogels had torn through the city, looking for Eulesängers. No creatures of the Deep had rummaged through in search of food. I could not help but think that the capital would have been a good place for Kandake to hide the Grail. Nobody seems to have paid it any attention.

The Eulesängers, followed by the curious creatures around them, walked slowly and tentatively through the city, looking into the huts and finding everything in perfect order. I walked throught the city with the rest of them, until I reached the city center. I knelt and prayed. I prayed to St. Hildegard, whose spirit seemed to take a maternal interest in me. I prayed that I would find the Grail, or the Grail would find me. I prayed to the line of Swan Knights, to the Grail Blood itself, asking that the Grail reveal itself to me. I felt nothing in response. No tingling beneath my skin, no visions, no possession of my face by someone long dead, nothing to say that the Eulesänger capital was the hiding place of the Grail. I trusted the silence inside of me and abandoned the notion.

The multitude of Eulesängers who had traveled with us filled the city admirably. There was a bustle around us that delighted the entire company with a sense of normalcy. The young Unicorn warriors took no more than a few steps onto the nest. They stationed themselves in a circle along the perimeter, guarding against the Wühlenvogels with their keen eyes. The plateau rested high enough above the plain that the Unicorns could see for miles. This gave the Eulesängers the peace of mind to truly relish their homecoming. Each young Unicorn was thanked by every creature who passed them.

The Eulesänager leader gathered the company to the center of the city. Birds filed out of the many little huts at their leader's command. She gave a speech, but one I struggled to understand. The Ancient One stood near me and translated each time I turned inquisitively toward him. The speech made several references to Duke Rudolf, who she called, "the dearest friend of the Eulesängers".

"Now we have his daughter," she continued, "right here in our own city, a child of Nethe, of Hildemar. I present to her the first gift of the Eulesängers to the Swan Knights."

Two Eulesängers appeared from within a hut to my right. They hopped to me and unfolded their wings. I squatted down and saw what they offered. There, on their outstretched wings, was a collection of their musical eggs, the very sort gifted to Nethe, the same instruments used to lull Elsa to sleep when she was a baby. I put on no airs of humility. I wanted the eggs badly and I took them without coaxing.

The crowd went silent, anticipating my use of the intruments, assuming that the skills slowly and painstakingly developed by Nethe would erupt from me intact after so many dormant centuries. The Eulesänger leader mimed to me the proper way to hold the eggs. Once they were appropriately situated in my hands, she pulled her wings to her beak, instructing me to give them a try. I thought the sound that came from the eggs was quite lovely. The reactions from the company told a different tale. Granted, I did not sound much like an Eulesänger.

I did not realize how unlike their sweet whistles I sounded until The Ancient One knockeded the eggs from my hands and kicked them to Taufe, saying, "Well, that is a skill we will work on, right Taufe?"

Taufe just smiled at him, then turned to me and gave me a sly wink. Her wink diffused the deep blush I felt rising to the surface of my face. Through the evening, I received hints and tips from the Eulesängers. By the time we slept, I had made promising progress.

We stayed for eight days and nine nights in the Eulesänger capital, partly to guard against Wühlenvogels as our little feathered friends settled into their homes, partly because we were all in need of rest. After the second night, there was much debate among the Eulsängers as to who and how many would remain in the capital, keeping it pulsing with life, according to my wishes, and how many would accompany the party on the rest of our journey. Both were desireable to the Eulesängers, both honorable duties. I accepted about seventy birds to continue with the company. Against stauch protests from some, I ordered six of the Unicorn warriors to remain in the capital for protection.

Our company was still much larger than when we embarked from St. Hildegard. Seventy Eulesängers was still plenty to perform their crippling hum with effectiveness. Our next destination, the Sicherheit Marshes, offered protection and, if rumors proved accurate, the chance to gather a significant force of Scheriers. I still believed the Scheriers to be essential to our victory in battle. They suffered heavy losses and had much to fight for — and much to fight against. They were a fiery mix of fierce loyalty, desperate fear, and violent anger.

I also believed that flourishing cities would prove essential. It was something I read in Ludwig's book. When the inhabitants of Einigkeitstadt, the Black Forest city, returned to their families in the Sweeter Realm, "The excitement, the love and unity pushed back any encroachment of hatred and evil from the Deep."

Ludwig continued, writing, "The love of the homecoming pressed against the border to the Deep Waters. The border was still, placid, and peaceful.

Löwschock's dark, cold water had no strength to fight the brightness that pushed down against it."

There was a reason Löwschock's monsters crawled so easily out of the Deep and through the ponds and forests of the Land and Shallow Waters. It was because the good creatures hid. They were scattered. When they gathered, they gathered quietly. In their attempts not to disturb the fragile peace, they left the door open to their enemies. It was time to hold Zweigwesen sapping ceremonies in Zweigwesen city squares, to have Brunnen baptisms in the open pools and streams of Brunnen land, to resume the Scherier games in the open Scherier arenas. It was time for love and friendship, celebrations and rituals, to once again press against the borders of the Deep. I firmly believed in the necessity of it, and I knew Kandake would have agreed. I had only to convince the frightened creatures.

It was not enough to push back with love and normalcy. Battles would be fought. But the revitalizing of the gathering places, the bustling of the cities, the hymns and chants from the holy places, put the wind at our backs and weakened the hatred that powered the enemy. So, although the goal of the tour was to gather an army and find the Grail, it was also to set the queendom to normalcy, and I would see it done at almost any cost.

We left enough Eulesängers in the capital to fully resume the city's former greatness, and enough to spread from there to the nests and shrines throughout their homeland.

The Eulesänger leadership insisted that we stay longer, "At least a month or two", one of them begged. They seemed to have things well in hand. There were no destroyed buildings to reconstruct, no debris to gather and sort. And the situation with the Scheriers was desperate and could not wait. With each day in Eierheim, the Scheriers of our company became increasingly ansy. They were a day

315

away from the marsh that promised long-overdue reunions. I felt them keenly, and after a week I was as eager to press on as they. In the morning after the ninth night, we left the Eulesänger capital.

As we rode from the city, northeast, toward the eastern side of the Sicherheit Marshes, the Eulesängers gathered at the edge of their plateau to bid us farewell. The exuberant cheers as we embarked lifted the spirits of the company. But they were lifted much more once the city was out sight behind us, when I connected my thoughts to the birds we left behind. After the hype of the farewell, the city returned to normal, quite normal, as if Kandake was Queen and Löwschock was just some scary bedtime story, as if the Wühlenvogels were friends and the Swan Knights lived rusticly in the old lodge. They whistled loudly, unafraid of what might be summoned. I could almost feel the warmth of their happiness beating against my back like the afternoon sun as we traveled toward Scherier land.

I tried to unite the minds of the company with those in the Eulesänger capital. I managed only to unite them with The Ancient One and Taufe. But I shared *my* thoughts with the company, my understanding of the power emitting from the revitalized nest, since they could not feel it themselves. The common commotion of a normal Eulesänger city brought a great deal of hope for the future, and quickened the pace of a company well-rested and freshly determined to bring the same normalcy to the battered Scherier homeland.

CHAPTER 25

Broken Bones and Broken Bread

THE SCHERIERS HAVE LONG BEEN the most social creatures
in the Sweeter Realm. They are universally adored. Their
playful spirit, easy manner, yet fierce loyalty and devout
faith have made them the favorite company of all. Other
than the swan, they were the first friends of the Swan
Knights, perpetual inhabitants of the Portal Valley. Many
things had occurred since Conrad Gessner awakened the
ferocity of the Deep, many things that sank hearts and
shattered bodies. But of them all, the devastation suffered
by the Scheriers had the most sinking effect. Compassion
for them ran far, wide, and very deep.

As the company worked toward the Sicherheit Marsh,
where thousands of Scheriers were rumored to be in hiding,
the desire to help them became more tyrannical, permitting
conversation of little else. Spirits were high, but focus was
sharp. The company pulled every fond memory they had of
the Scheriers so near their inner eye that it was all they saw,
not the scenery around us, or even the kind creatures
marching right beside them. They were focused on their
affection for the pleasantest neighbors in the Land and
Shallow Waters. And they were starving to revive the
Scherier cities and sanctuaries.

The march to the Sicherheit Marsh took all day and half of the night. We pushed forward through the dusk and into the blackness of night, more determined than fearful. Although the day was long, seeming to last for weeks, we had few memories of the journey from Eierheim. Love and concern for the Scheriers had placed blinders on us all.

The eastern half of the Sicherheit Marsh is in the Eulesänger homeland. The marsh run west, across the Scherier border, to abut Eineklaue, the Scherier capital. The marsh begin gradually, as low and wet grasslands. It is in that setting that we camped, in ankle-deep water, in knee-high grass. The few hours we permitted ourselves for rest were hardly restful. Only the Brunnens laid comfortably on the wet ground. The Unicorns slept quite well standing. The rest of us sat, leaned, laid, and propped ourselves alternatively, wet and uncomfortable.

The Zweigwesens offered to form themselves into a platform for me to sleep upon. I would have been dry and warm against their thick fur. Holding the connections of their formations is not easy. Yet, they would have held it until morning, and much longer, in the wet grass, had I accepted the offer. Of course, I refused with deeply expressed gratitude. After about an hour of shifting and shivering, I accepted Georg's offer to drape myself across him for a couple of hours of rest. It was by no means a position ideally condusive to sleep. Yet I dozed off immediately. I awoke in the same position, greeted by the first blink of the rising sun, slapping me in my unwilling eyes.

As I slid to my feet and scanned the company, I saw a corps of exhausted creatures. The night had been unkind and unrestful. They moved slowly and spoke low, all except for the Scheriers and Friends of the Scheriers, who gathered and plotted in bouncing, jigging, excited little groups of three or four.

We sipped on the stores of Eulesänger nectar, provided to us when we left their capital. It revived our bodies, and the excitement of the Scheriers to reunite with their lost kind and abandoned cities revived our spirits. Even Lina, still deep in mourning more than a year after the death of her husband, abounded with energy. The Scheriers climbed on top of each other to see into the marsh ahead. There was nothing to see. The wet grasses upon which we stood grew slowly thicker and darker and transitioned into reeds. The water at our feet grew gradually cooler and deeper, the ground softer, and the air more humid. I walked beside Georg, not wishing to sink his narrow hooves too deeply into the mud.

Even if we had wanted to move quickly through the marsh, the conditions forbade it. As the ground became thick mud, it was just one of the obsticles. Another was fear of what wet monsters lingered and lurked. Another yet was our desire to find and liberate any Scherier hiding in the marsh. We moved mostly in silence, broken only by the sloshing and smacking of our feet in the mud and water, and by the occasional whispering by the Scheriers of the names of loved ones believed to be hiding in the Eulesänger portion of the marsh.

It did not take long for the latter to bear fruit. We were not an hour and a half into the morning walk when the first group of Scheriers appeared to the company, crawling out from the reeds like ants from an anthill. There were five of them. Their white hair was coated in mud, but the size, shape, and signature waddle of the Scheriers could be identified through any disguise.

I squatted down beside the nearest of them. He shook his head, flinging mud to his right and left, and revealing the color of his face and the shape of his tiny ears.

He looked right at me and said, "We heard rumors, that a Friend with a name, one who calls himself Cort, travels the Land and Shallow Waters, telling all that the Grail Portal reopened, that a Swan Knight is on our side, that she is the Queen and has great powers. We did not believe it. He says that The Ancient One lives and has been rescued by the Swan Knight, but we did not believe it."

Cort sloshed his way, almost neck-deep in muddy water, to stand beside my left leg. I lifted him with pride and stood him upon my shoulder.

He raised his chin in preparation for his proclamation, then announced, "I am the Friend of the Scheriers with a name. I am Cort, and as you can see, I have brought the swan and the Queen to you."

"Indeed you have, nomad. Today you are a Friend of the Scheriers if ever we had one," the muddy Scherier replied.

The Ancient One recognized the Scherier's voice. He knew the little creature well.

"Prallen!" he shouted excitedly. "You are alive!"

"As I can see, old friend, are you."

"Where is Stossen? Please tell me she lives."

"I am right here, you old bird," a muddy Scherier face proclaimed.

"Of course you are," The Ancient One spoke in a forceful sigh of relief. "You survived Albert's Battle. I should not be surprised to see you here, keeping Prallen on his best behavior."

Rather star-struck, I asked the Scheriers, "You were at Albert's Battle?"

The Ancient One recalled his manners and introduced us, "Prallen, Stossen, this is Verena, child of Lohengrin, Ermenrich, and Rudolf. She is the Swan Knight and the Queen of the Land and Shallow Waters. Verena, these are two ancient friends of your family. They spent more time in the Portal Valley than any tree that lives there now."

In the strength of our large company, Prallen, Stossen, and their friends no longer feared their own white hair. They shook themselves free of the mud that camouflaged them, revealing their radiance. They greeted the other Scheriers of our company, most of whom had been held by Brunnens and Federmensch, or carried on the backs of Unicorns. Prallen knew the marsh well and offered himself as guide. I readily and gratefull accepted. He rode on Georg's back, traveling at my side as we pressed westward, toward the Scherier border.

We had much to discuss, beginning with the most urgent and immediate concerns. Prallen settled my formost fear, assuring me that no monsters of the Deep traveled in the marsh, at least not on the Eulesänger side. He confirmed the rumors that hundreds of Scheriers took refuge in the wetlands, that a broad and thorough sweep through the mud and reeds would yield an army of Scheriers, just waiting for confirmation of the reports that The Ancient One lives and travels with a new Swan Knight. We followed his every navigational suggestion, finding pockets of Scherier settlements, precisely where he said they would be. He knew many of them by name and called them from their hiding places personally.

Our Scherier numbers grew, in bunches of five and six at a time, until they outnumbered all other breeds in the company. More than a hundred fifty joined us as we zig-zagged our way up and down the marsh, in a slow and meandering march toward the Scherier border. It took us four days, yet most of the Sicherheit Marsh remained unexplored by us. We could not linger longer in our search for Scheriers. We needed dry land. Four restless nights in the muddy waters and poking reeds of the Sicherheit Marsh had us desperate for comfort. And we needed to progress in our goal to find the Grail and revive the cities, to gather an army in Gemeinsam and face Löwschock and his monsters.

One thing I had noticed in all of my travels in the Land and Shallow Waters is that there were no fences dividing homelands, no signs, no sentries, nothing to indicate the passing from one territory to another, until we reached the Scherier border. There were no fences or signs to divide the Scheriers from the Eulesängers. The Scherier border was marked differently. Just inside the Scherier border of the Sicherheit Marsh was a party of the foulest creatures I had ever imagined.

Six Deep creatures splashed in the shallow waters of the Scherier marsh, growling, hissing, and striking the most terrifying poses, as if to establish among themselves which was the most hideous and frightening. Two of them looked much like Löwschock, only with longer legs protruding from a much shorter scaled tale. They also had large, bony hooks in place of the lobster-like claws of their King.

One of the monsters had a very human-looking torso, with human-looking arms, rippling with muscle beneath pale-green skin. It was the size of three men. A fleshy cone sat atop its enormous head. As it growled and hissed, its mouth opened wide enough to eat a dozen Scheriers in a single bite, as it no doubt had done. Its long, deep-red tongue curled into a crusty, hooked appendage at the end. Its thick, barreled torso dwindled sharply into a thin tail, like a traditional mermaid. It dragged its tail through the mud by its muscular arms. I did not know what frightened me more, its powerful arms or its wide mouth, with sharp teeth and crusty, hooked tongue.

Two of the beasts were of identical form. They had wide heads and large jaws, like a hippopotamus, with long tusks like a walrus. The eye sockets looked like large knuckles, with bulgy eyes darting about in mindless, spastic agitation. They had long, fish-like bodies, ending with a fish's fin. But the bodies were hairy, not scaled. Four, thick, muscular, stubby arms pushed the monsters around the marsh. Long, sharp claws capped the fingertips.

The sixth monster did not require study by my eyes, nor will it require a description here. It was the knobby-headed serpent, Gessner's knobby-headed serpent, the terror of every Scherier, of every kind and civil creature in the Sweeter Realm.

Fortunately, they caught our attention before we caught theirs. Our company was quite large, and even when we marched without talking, we made quite a bit of noise. True to The Ancient One's prognostication, the ability I inherited from Elsa saved us. The swan spied the creatures first, and he quickly drew my attention to them. I halted the entire company with a single thought. All of them received the command clearly and froze in silence and stillness.

We were not sure how to proceed. Any movement other than a direct retreat would likely have alerted the monsters to us. I connected intimately with The Ancient One, Taufe, and Georg. Without the slightest of movements, this cerebral council debated our options.

"Can't the Brunnens go to them and charm them into an ambush, as your sisters did with the Welf knights in Linderhof?" I asked Taufe.

"We cannot. We have no such powers over the monsters of the Deep. Only one desperate to experience beauty, to experience it and cherish it, is susceptible to our allurements."

The Ancient One added, "Löwschock and his sort are enraged by beauty, enraged and confounded. The sight of our lovely Brunnens would only send them into a frenzy of violence."

Georg presented the only viable option, "A direct attack is our only plan. We are a large company. We would overwhelm them, despite their size and strength. The battlefield is part land, part water, giving both sides advantages and disadvantages. Numbers will prevail, and the numbers are ours."

He had a point. The opportunity to lessen the enemy's number by six, with such a great numerical advantage, was an unexpected opportunity. Still, I knew the monsters would fight hard. I knew how deadly they were, and I knew that losses would be suffered. My spirits were ill-prepared for battle, now that it was upon us.

My eyes remained closed while the council debated, which is why it was the low and angry growl of the

Scheriers, as they crawled through the reeds and mud, toward the enemies, that broke the mental assembly. They were halfway between us and the monsters, in a shared trance, mindless and vengeful. I grabbed their minds and ordered them to stop. They obeyed, but they were too far forward to retreat in silence, and we were too far behind to charge in front of them before the enemies reached them. In a panic, and without discussion or forethought, I drew Albert's sword, hollered an angry cry, and ran toward the Scherier border.

The cry drew the attention of the monsters. They did not charge us. They remained still, staring at me with astonished, confused faces. They clearly did not expect to see the Swan Knight, with a tremendous army of many breeds, running through the marsh, screaming at them. That is exactly what we were. The company followed their Queen into battle. I ran slowly, struggling to pull my feet from the soft mud.

Georg nudged me in the shoulder and huffed, "Get on."

I couldn't pull myself from the mud. The Federmensch hoisted me onto Georg and the company moved admirably toward the Scheriers. Since the monsters stood frozen, we were able to reach the Scheriers before the violence began. Once into a reunited force, we moved together onto the enemies.

Georg was right. We had the numbers to defeat the six monsters. But I was also right. We suffered our own losses. The young Unicorn warriors went straight for the two mermaid-tailed beasts. The older Unicorns were right behind them. The enemies did not stand a chance. One of them struck a Unicorn warrior with a heavy blow of his powerful arm. The Unicorn let out a painful cry and splashed violently to the ground. He struggled. He staggered. But he got to his feet and turned to confront the monster. By the time he did, the rest of the young Unicorns were already withdrawing their bloody horns from the arms, tails, chests, backs, and heads of the two monsters.

Georg and I found ourselves between two of the walrus-tusked creatures. Georg thrusted his horn at one, while the other slashed him in his right hind leg with its sharp claws. Georg growled through his nostrils. I think back with pride in the following moment. In a vivid reenactment of my training, I cartwheeled off of Georg's hips and landed, sword first on the creature's backside. By the time my feet hit its back, my sword was several inches into the back of its neck. It arched harshly, lifting its nose in front of me and its tail behind. I stood on it, like on a canoe, driving my sword deeper into its neck, while it sloshed all four of its stubby arms in the muddy water.

Georg fended off one, while our compliment of Zweigwesens surrounded the third. When the Zweigwesens converged, the monster thrusted forward and caught a young Zweiwesen in its mouth. Her name was Spalte, and I knew her well. I knew her since we gathered in the Zweigwesen city, after rescuing the swan. The mighty, hippopotamus jaws of the monster shattered her into pieces before anybody could prevent it. But before it could draw another breath, the monster was pierced by long, splintery Zweigwesen fingers, through the eyes, the nostrils, and the holes on the back of its jaws, which I assumed were its ears.

Georg continued sparring with the last of the hairy monsters, clashing horn to tusks. A Federfrau mounted the creature's back and wrapped her bowed legs around its neck. It rolled like a crocodile, burying the Federfrau in the mud beneath it. It rolled again and sank a tusk through her chest. The other Federmensch took ahold of the monster's tusks and pulled them apart, ripping them from its head. Large chunks of tissue came with the detatched tusks. The beast tossed and rolled, flinging blood from its face in all

327

directions. Georg, who stood in front of it, was covered in more blood than mud. He took advantage of the monster's disoriented flailing to drive his horn upward, through its open, tuskless mouth, into its skull, and out the back of its head.

While all of this occurred, the Scheriers and Friends of the Scheriers surrounded the knobby-headed serpent. I had no idea how very large it was. When it opened its mouth to scream, I saw a tongue that was longer and thicker than me. It stood high on the base of its tale, towering over all of us. It did not appear scared of the army surrounding it. It seemed hungry and delighted to see its largest meal since the Scheriers left their homeland.

It swung the crusty, arrowhead-shaped tip of its tail, down onto the crowd of Scheriers. Most scurried clear before the tail hit. Some did not. Those who did not were crushed by the flat part of the tip or sliced by the sharp edge. They did not survive. Cort, loyal as ever to his friends, stood first among them. He was not hit by the descending tail, but he was sliced by the edge as the serpent recoiled its tail. The cut was deep across his back. He fell stone-still, facedown into the muddy water. Taufe retrieved him from the water and ran him to the back of the company.

By this time, the other monsters were dead. All attention went to the knobby-headed serpent. Fierce, bloody, shaggy Unicorn faces stared down the serpent. Large and powerful as it was, the odds were not in its favor. It could have killed many more of us, had it fought us to the death. Fortunately, it decided to retreat. We would have hunted it down. But it moved its bulbous, bulky body so quickly, so surprisingly gracefully through the marsh that we had no chance of catching it.

We had lost much. In addition to allowing the knobby-headed serpent to escape, we had to find our missing friends, tend to the injured and honor the dead. But there was also reason to celebrate. Our army won a victory. The only survivor of our enemies in the marsh that day retreated from the Scherier border, opening the passage into Scherier land.

Cort survived. The Zweigwesens gathered plants and mosses, and a thick, purple algae that grew in abundance between the reeds. They concocted their miracles quickly and applied them successfully. The marshlands of the border were not a place to find rest and healing. We carried our dead and injured alike, through the deepest, stickiest part of the marsh, into the Scherier homeland. We left our dead enemies where they fell.

We knew we would be safe from the Wühlenvogels. After the war with the Scheriers, the Wühlenvogels passed strict laws forbidding any damage to be done to a Scherier or any Scherier possession. The creatures of the Deep were our only enemies in the Scherier homeland. This allowed us to keep our eyes focused on the horizon and not in the sky. Still, I wanted out of the marsh. I wanted to be dry, where no secret hole could connect the water I stood in with the Deep.

As we slogged westward, deeper into Scherier land, our injured began showing the signs of Zweigwesen expertize. It was not fast enough for me. Cort was lacerated deeply. His life was not in danger, but he was in pain, and with the eruption of each writhing contortion of his bloodied body, and each cry that accompanied his pain, I wished more ardently for the Holy Grail, to heal my friends as Parsifal was healed. I shared the desire with Taufe.

Ever my moral teacher, she replied in her lecture voice, "The Grail does not exist to save individuals. Even if Cort was certain to die without it, and you held the Grail in your hands, you could not use it so frivolously."

"Frivolous? How can you call a friend's life frivolous? Parsifal used the Grail to save his own life."

"No!" The Ancient One interrupted the conversation, "Parsifal used the Grail to keep the power of the Redeemer out of evil's hands. He knew that the Grail had a holy purpose in the plans of God. Had he died that day, had the poisoned blade of Klingsor's servant completed its task, the Holy Grail of the Messiah would have fallen into Klingsor's hands. Parsifal used the Grail to save the Grail."

His tone of voice began harsh and grew harsher. His personal affection for Parsifal, his first human friend and brother, revealed itself demonstratively. I doubt he intended it, but his tone, not his words, dealt my spirits a blow that manifested as a deep and dull ache in my gut.

Taufe soothed me and chastised the swan simultaneously, saying, "I am sure that Verena would act as she should in any situation, with the sword, with the Grail, and with her tongue, to bring about the will of God. Afterall, old friend, she was taught by you, and she was taught by me, and she has the voices of the Swan Knights, including your Parsifal, reverberating in her veins."

Her words lowered the swan's head, not in shame, but in thought.

"You are right, wise abbess." He looked at me and continued speaking to Taufe, "She has given me more reasons to trust her than to not, more reasons to admire her . . . , more reasons to adore and obey her."

I wanted to kiss him. I wanted to kiss them both.

I kept my eyes on him and mouthed a heart-felt, "Thank you."

He tilted his head, let out a sigh, then followed it with these words, "You want to save them. You want to save us all. It is the Grail Blood that drives that desire. That is why you insisted upon rescuing me, against the advice of the wise, why you risked so much on the word of a Scherier."

I blurted without thought, "I needed you. I could not have done anything without you."

"I agree. You need me. But the prudent would have left me for dead."

In a mock-scolding tone that lightened quickly, he continued, "But you are not prudent, my love. Neither was Lohengrin or Veronika, Otto I or your own dear Ludwig. Neither was Tannhäuser, when he defied the will of all and ran through the portal. But his actions brought the greatest beauty I have ever known."

I continued his thought, "It brought you Brunhilde."

"Yes. And in my lack of foresight, I cursed him for it. He forgave me, as I hope you do."

"Forgive you? Oh my sweet friend, there is nothing to forgive. I am not sure I agree with Taufe, that I would always do what is right. That is why I rely on your scolding, on your teaching and hers, even when it hurts to hear. You have done nothing but serve me selflessly, and I honor you more than . . ."

I saw the futility of trying to fit a world of feelings into the tiny box of language. I closed my eyes and thought my feelings to him. He let out a half-chuckle, half-cry, which repeated randomly over the next couple of hours, as he recalled the connection and the powerful sense of love, admiration, and gratitude that it ushered into his welcoming mind.

The muddy ground beneath us became steadily harder as we pushed through the marsh. We moved more quickly, lighter on our feet. The ground was steady enough and Georg recovered enough to insist that I ride upon him. I denied the offer. The wounds on his leg looked painful and I knew how self-denying he was. He tapped his horn against the shoulder of another Unicorn, transferring in that minute moment an order to carry me. The Unicorn was honored to do so.

I told Georg, "There is a much greater treasure you can carry, greater indeed, and fortunately for you, much lighter."

I sent Georg a single thought of The Ancient One. He drove his horn into the mud beneath the swan and flicked the old bird into the air, catching him high on his shoulders.

In a rather comically bad attempt at fake anger, the swan shouted loudly enough for all around us to hear, "Am I nothing more than cargo, than supplies to be tossed upon a beast-of-burden?"

Georg simply huffed a giggle, shook his head, then mumbled under his breath, "Hmmmff, beast-of-burden."

As the day winded down, the thick reeds of the marsh gave way to thick bladed grasses, which gave way to higher, thinner grasses, as the wetness at our feet transitioned to solid, dry ground. The blades of the grass were bright and soft, crowned with dark bunches of hard seeds. Perhaps it was the relief of the first dry ground in days, or knowing that we could sit and lie in comfort, or that our injured could be properly tended and our dead properly buried, but the grassy field of Scherier land welcomed every inch of my flesh that had the pleasure of brushing against it.

We had made it through the marsh. The Scherier capital, Eineklaue, was supposed to be there, right where we stood.

"Where is the city?" I asked.

Lina ran several steps ahead of me, looked to her right and left, and ran back toward me. She climbed up the front left leg of the Unicorn who held me, over his shoulder and onto my lap. From there, she jumped onto my shoulder for a better view. She repeated her gazes to the left and right. She looked left again and froze, squinting her eyes.

"It is that way!" she shouted, lifting her left hand to point to the south, "We have come out to the north of the city."

The sun was low in the sky and our company was injured and exhausted. Those who had carried our dead were weary of body and spirit. We buried the dead there, under the first solid ground we found. The Scheriers ran off in all directions and returned within several minutes with arms full of grains they had gathered from the tall grasses around us. They set immediately to grinding the grains with their claws, making a large pile of dark flour. One Scherier beconned several Zweigwesens, who responded with an obvious understanding of what was expected of them. The Zweigwesens secreted their sap onto the mound of flour. As soon as the Scheriers were satisfied with the proportions, they took to mixing and kneading the mound into a thick dough.

They portioned the dough into little, Sherier-fist sized balls, set them in a line in front of me, and backed away, as Lina leaned into me, saying, "Watch this."

I still sat high on the Unicorn, with Lina on my shoulder. I looked down at the row of dough balls. They began to take on a slight orange glow. They rose and puffed to loaves as large as the breastplate of my armor.

"Here's the first batch," one of the Scheriers shouted. "Get started without us. We will make more."

Without a moment of hesitation, I dismounted the Unicorn and started passing the bread around the company — but nobody ate. They all just held the bread as if they had decided in advance not to take a bite until they all had a share. Even from those sweet creatures, I was surprised by the politeness. The only thing in their stomachs all day was a tiny sip of Eulesänger nectar.

I continued to pass the bread, breaking portions according to the recipient's size, while the Scheriers and

Zweigwesens made more. When I handed a fistful of bread to the last creature, I looked around the company. Everybody held their bread in their hand, claw, or wing. Nobody had taken a bite. Taufe walked into the center of the company. They situated themselves into circles around her, rings of increasing size from the center. I took a seat in the second ring, holding my portion of bread.

Taufe said a prayer, thanking God for his many gifts, memorializing our dead, and asking that we, our company, may perform the duties required of us to bring about God's will. Next, she lifted her bread high above her head, looked sharply upward at it with her eyes closed. She whispered something. I snuck a quick peak at her thought. She thought on her friend, Conrad of Wittelsbach, the Archbishop of Mainz. She invoked his authority to consecrate the bread. She lowered the bread and ate her portion. She chewed with her eyes closed and her head tilted downward. When she finished chewing, she opened her eyes and lifted her head to the company. On that cue, the company ate their own pieces of bread. I followed their example.

The bread filled me comprehensively, of body, mind, and spirit. Whether the bread or the ceremony, it affected me strongly. I felt stout commitment swell in me. My muscles surged with righteous energy. My mind swam with memories of the past, delight in the moment, and hope for the future. The lovely and loyal creatures around me glowed in my eyes. The orange light of the sunset gave them each a halo, or at least that is how it appeared in my eyes. I thought about the Grail, or perhaps it thought about me.

I felt my blood pushing against the south side of my body, willing me in that direction. I did not ignore it, neither did I indulge it. I set it in the back of my mind, knowing that we needed to rest for the night and would be traveling south in the morning, as Lina directed, toward Eineklaue, the Scherier capital.

The Zweigwesens formed into tree formations, spaced unnaturally evenly in a circle around the company, like pillars in a perfectly round colluseum. The Unicorns, young and old, all but Georg, slept on the perimeter of our camp, each facing outward. The Friends of the Scheriers gathered grass they had picked. They bunched it into a bed for me. After the day we had, the mound of grass felt as comfortable to me as the bed in the Brunnen bathhouse. The Ancient One, Taufe, Lina, and Cort all curled up around me. Georg laid down beside us, near enough for me to reach around Taufe and run my fingertips through the recesses of his spiraling horn. I laid there and silently prayed the Rosary. In the absence of the beeds to mark my progress, I slid my fingertips from one of Georg's spirals to the next, as I worked my way through my recitation of the prayers. I prayed for the dead and I prayed for the injured, and I wondered how many more I would see buried and bandaged before my own death.

CHAPTER 26

Eineklaue

THE COMPANY FELL QUICKLY SILENT. They slept soundly, but I did not. I may have dozed for a few minutes at a time. I couldn't tell when my conscious thoughts dipped into the thinner layers of half-conscious dreams, lulled by my repetitive prayers. The line between thought and dream was thin. My life since I met Cort on the beach that day had distorted the distinction between the grounded and the fantastic. The very battle I had just fought would have been the stuff of my bizarrest dreams just two years earlier.

I am glad the company slept well, glad they were sharp and alert. My wits were not about me in the morning, nor for any significant portion of the day. Georg's injuries looked weeks old. He insisted upon carrying me as we moved south to Eineklaue and I gratefully obliged. We gathered tightly, much more tightly than we had traveled before. The footsteps of those nearest me rang loudly in my ears. The heat of their bodies swaddled me, body and spirit. There was an austerity, a focused preparedness to the group, to a degree that I had not sensed in them before the battle in the marsh.

They feared for me. Somehow, deep in their hearts, beyond the vision of their conscious minds, they knew that I would eventually face the enemy alone. They wanted to embrace me while they could. Those who could not huddle tightly to me huddled to those who could. The collective company held me as we marched. They held me like a cupped palm holding a fragile and precious work of blown glass.

The landscape was still flat, but dry and grassy. The sun was still low in the morning sky when a large, rounded hill appeared before us. As we drew near it, the Scheriers broke ranks and ran ahead of us in a galloping herd of white hair — all except Lina, who ran about twenty feet ahead of us, stopped, looked back, and waited for the marching company to swallow her back into the whole. When Georg walked beside her, she climbed up his front left leg and onto my lap.

"Where are they going?" I askd her.

"They are almost home, returned to the place of their birth. That hill . . . it's the roof of Eineklaue. The city is beneath it."

"Were many of them born there?"

"We were all born there. Every Scherier is born in Eineklaue, then taken to Gralkirche to be baptized and schooled. We live in Gralkirche, raised by the Stiefel von Lohengrin, until our claws come in. Then, we may join our families."

I thought about how very different such traditions are from human culture. In my sleep-deprived stupor, I engaged in a fiery internal debate on the matter, one that shrouded my immediate surroundings from my senses. By the time I snapped myself back to the moment, we stood with the Scherier herd, on the top of the hill.

One of the Scheriers yelled from the center of them, "My Queen, you will want to see this."

I dismounted Georg and walked through the Scherier herd, who parted down the middle for me. As I walked through the herd, I noticed that the hill came to an abrupt

338

end, giving way to a sharp cliff. I could tell immediately that the cliff was not natural, but dug out of the hill. When I got to the edge, I could see a large network of smaller hills, or more like mounds, each cut in half like the hill upon which we stood, much like the hill-cave where I met Lina and Rüdiger, in various sizes from a little smaller than Rüdiger's cave to much, much larger.

We turned hard to our right and ran down the hill, along the edge of the cliff, trying to keep up with the excited Scheriers. At the bootom, we hooked hard to our left, to the entrance of a gigantic cave. I have been back to Eineklaue many times since that day. I struggle now to distinguish between my memories of that sleepy day and those of my many visits since. The hill is merely a hollow shell, a half shell really. No more than ten feet thick. At its highest, in the center, it is at least fifty feet from floor to ceiling. Inside is a giant system of mounds and caves, some with stately, sculpted entrances, and others with mere holes. A complex system of earthen ramps, paths, and slides connect them. On the inner wall of the hill, just as it rounds into the ceiling, a half-circle of torches run, just a few feet from one another. A pathway runs along the row of torches.

Enough of the direct sunlight pushed into the cave for me to see the outlines of the smaller mounds within. One of our Scheriers apologized to me for the darkness and volunteered to light the torches. He broke quickly from the company and ran into the cave.

"Wait!" I ordered. "We don't know what is in there. Take the young warriors with you."

With that command, the young Unicorn warriors trotted after him. They ran deeply into the hill. I could make out the Unicorns, but lost sight of the Scherier. Then I saw a single light, emerging from one of the lesser mounds within. I watched that light travel a ramp, up the inner wall of the hill, to the path that runs along the torches. I watched him light the first several torches, slowly bringing to my eyes the details of the city.

"So this is Eineklaue. It is extraordinary," I spoke revently to Lina.

"No, my dear. Those are the public halls. Eineklaue is there."

She pointed behind us. I turned to see the dozens of smaller hills behind us. Though much smaller, each is a cave, each with a network of caves within. I stared across the landscape, which was pimpled with hills and half-mounds. I tried to imagine it as it once was, teeming with life and activity, with silly Scherier games, wrestling loved ones, theatricals and concerts.

By the time I turned back around, into the main cave, it was brilliantly lit. I watched our volunteer light the last few torches. The cave wore the torches like a flaming half-wreath crown. The lights and shadows revealed a visual in stunning detail, all of the abandoned paths, slopes, and entrances.

Delightlyfull impressed, I turned to Lina and asked, "How far do they go? The tunnels and caves, how deep and how far?"

"Hmmmm, I don't really know. I've been through every step of the city, but I'm not much of a digger, and can't really visualize the whole thing. Rüdiger could have given you a detailed description, God bless him."

After a long pause in contemplation of her last comment, she added, "It stretches far and wide. I can tell you that. You could explore for a year and not see every tunnel."

I tried to imagine the scope of the city underneath and around us, then I added, "So it will take many more Scheriers to revive it."

"Yes, My Queen, it will."

Lina thought for a moment. She sighed deeply a few times then let out a low, almost silent growl. I peered into her thoughts. She was daring the enemies to try to drive us from the city. She swelled with pride in our company and with a ferocious sense of injury for all that the Scheriers had suffered. But it was more maternal and protective than vengeful.

I scooped her up and held her against the top of my armor, just above my collarbones. I rubbed my chin against her back playfully and told her, "This city belongs to the Scheriers. Löwschock will never drive them out again."

I was hearing her with my ears, not seeing her with my mind. So it was a surprise when she looked admiringly at the company around us and said to me, "That's because we are united now, like we were under Kandake, united by you, Verena, the greatest of Queens."

I felt so utterly unbefitting such praise. I knew the truth — that they may have been united *because* of me, but they were not united *by* me. They were united by their own love, and a shared devotion to a common ideal, a common faith, and a long-shared history of devotion to the Swan Knights. I was merely a token, a talisman that symbolized those connections.

I must have thought those thoughts loudly and unguarded, because Georg perceived them and refuted, "Oh no, My Queen, you are much more than that. Surely you must begin to see that."

I hesitated to accept the compliment, but answered back in words that sounded like they came from The Ancient One, "If I were standing here alone, I would hardly be reviving Eineklaue, nor could I have defeated the monsters in the marsh alone, or crossed the ravine without the Zweigwesens. That was done by the wonderful creatures of the Land and Shallow Waters."

341

"Yes!" he returned sharply, "Your subjects! A company of humble creatures made stout by their faith in the Grail Blood, their faith in you . . . , beautiful Swan Knight."

My humility ran out of words to dispute him. So I just scratched the side of his neck and followed it by a rub and a few loving pats. He raised his head and gave a triumphant huff from his shaggy mouth, as I had seen from him many times before and many times since. However small, his argument was a victory over me, and by God, he has always relished those.

We all entered the fully lit city center together. Our injured had healed well. But the Zweigwesens took them to a special cave, where they were tended to until fully recovered. The Brunnens directed the Scheriers in the construction of a Brunnen-style bathhouse. So, the first Brunnen bathhouse in the Scherier homeland was built near the center of the city's main cave. It took a couple of weeks to finish. All breeds contributed their own skills. We were making Eineklaue quite the home for ourselves. After their experiences in Nährenstadt and Eierheim, the company understood the powerful value in reviving the cities. During those first couple of weeks in Eineklaue, there were no debates about pressing onward, about gathering an army and facing Löwschock. We were united in our efforts to bring life to the Scherier capital. Each Scherier room that was lit again, occupied again — each laugh that echoed off of a Scherier wall was a slap across Löwschock's face. That is how we saw it, and we slapped until our hands went numb.

As large as our company had grown, we filled only a small portion of the main cave. Eineklaue needed thousands, maybe tens of thousands to return it to normalcy. I longed to see the whole city bustling. When the bathhouse was finished, and The Ancient One and I were receiving a thorough and relaxing cleaning from our party of Brunnens, the swan drew my attention to him with a clearing of his long throat.

"Achhhemmm, don't you think you should call the rest of them now?"

"Call them? They have had their bathing. It's my turn."

"No, I mean call them to the city. The Scheriers. Call them home to Eineklaue."

I had almost forgotten my ability to do so. Without another word or thought, I closed my eyes and thought of the Scheriers. One thought, one memory of my own interrupted and blocked my connection to the Scheriers who were scattered about the Sweeter Realm. It was a thought of Rüdiger, still painful, still distracting.

"You must set him aside for now," the swan intuitively instructed. "Find the living, not the dead."

After a deep inhale and slow exhale, I tried again. I found them. I found them and connected to them. I could not connect them to each other. They were too scattered, isolated of mind, even if together in body. I sent them my vision of the revived Eineklaue. I let them know that we were there. I felt a rush of excitement, that signature Scherier excitement, return from their minds to me, so sudden, so unexpectedly powerful that I shook myself free of the Brunnen hands that cleaned me.

I apologized, sighed, and set myself to reach farther, to every Scherier in the Sweeter Realm. I don't know if I reached them all, but my thoughts went far and wide — and Deep. My mind left the Land and Shallow Waters. I found Scheriers in the Deep, those imprisoned and dying, and those left for dead. The sensation hit me more powerfully than the celebratory wave of before. It hit me deeper — piercing and biting. I heard cries of pain and cries of loss. My throat felt like it had closed, like I could take no breath. I splashed in the bath. I fought and kicked my way onto the floor, struggling to breathe, struggling to expel the terror that crashed into my head and flooded all other brain functions in a tidal wave of fear, misery, lonliness, despair, and pain.

It left me as quickly as it found me. But in that connection, I had connected every Scherier within my mental reach, even those within the walls of Eineklaue, with the minds of the suffering. They all felt the teeth of the Deep monsters sinking through their thick hair, into their flesh. They all felt the sense of abandonment suffered by those in captivity, those waiting to be eaten in the dark rituals of the Deep. When the horrors left my mind, I could hear the Scheriers of the city. Their moans of pitifully, sorrowful compassion echoed through every cavern and tunnel in Eineklaue's main cave.

The moans pulled me in. Without trying, I connected tightly to the minds of the Scheriers in our company. Their collective sorrow and anguish for the suffering of their kin was almost as debilitating for me to experience as the suffering itself. But the sorrow of the Scheriers quickly changed colors. It rolled and it flipped until it transformed into a deeply driven, passionate, zealous sense of duty and commitment. The Scheriers are an amazing breed. The love and duty inside of them cannot be conquered. Every horrid experience, every nasty feeling that creeps inside of them, becomes a weapon of their love and devotion. It is no wonder that Lohengrin loved them so much. They share his heart. The moans of the city's Scheriers turned to growls, which turned to cheers.

I thought to myself, "The humblest, the lowliest of Scheriers could teach the greatest of humans."

There might be something to their early rearing, all born in the same place, all baptized and schooled by the same religious order. Although each Scherier is unique, abounding with a demonstrative personality, not identical to any other, there is a certain sense of unity and sameness that defines their breed. Their spirits are coated with the same morality, plastered with it from their earliest days.

I crawled back into the bath and allowed the soft hands of the Brunnens to return me to calmness. The call to Eineklaue was answered immediately, answered first by a single, old Scherier, one who was already in the city, hunkered down in one of the peripheral caves.

"Where is she?" I heard in a scratchy Scherier voice, shouted from outside of the bath chamber.

The old Scherier skipped into the bathroom, followed by a young Unicorn warrior and a couple of Brunnens.

"I apologize for the interruption, My Queen," the warrior said reverently, while staring down at the old Scherier, "He was determined, and you know these Scheriers."

"Yes, I believe I do, yet they continue to delight me. It's okay, I called to him and he answered, just like you did."

He acknowledged the truth with a reverently whispered tribute to the referenced moment, "Ohhl Ginshass Wahuff."

I returned the sentiment in kind and he bowed and backed out of the room. The Brunnens who entered with him remained.

I turned my attention to the old Scherier, but he did not look at me. His eyes doubled in size as he stared at The Ancient One.

"I knew it!" the Scherier shouted, "You are alive. I told everyone, but nobody listened. Nobody believed me. But here you are, right here in front of me, our old King and teacher . . . Wait, why are you here? I thought, I thought you were in the Queen's Lake, in the old jail."

The swan answered calmly, with a lofty, academic tone, "I was. I was rescued by the Swan Knight, by our new Queen."

The Ancient One turned to me, then back to the Scherier, and said, "Verena, Swan Knight and Queen, this is the Old Digger, the foremost expert in Scherier constructions. I believe he dug half of this city himself."

The Old Digger's bone-white face turned pink, as he sheepishly answered, "Well, my father dug most of the city, but I dug all the good parts."

"You are the Old Digger?" I interrupted, sitting suddenly erect in the bath.

"I am," he answered, "and I am in your debt for rescuing my old friend."

"No," I told him, "I am in *your* debt. We all are. There was one who believed you, when you said that the swan was alive. My dear friend Rüdiger believed you, and he convinced me to mount the rescue. He led efforts to gather a force of swimmers."

"Good old Rüdiger," he rolled his head and hummed with an air of nostalgia. "How is he?"

I dropped my head, and in a low breath, more thoughtful than communicative, I answered, "My Rüdiger is dead. He died rescuing the swan. He dove into that black water so bravely."

The end of the last sentence became raspy as my throat seized in a flood of emotion.

In a panic, he blurted, "And Lina, please tell me my niece is alive."

"Lina is your niece?"

He nodded with eyes still desperately anticipating my answer.

His question placed in the front of my mind that precious blessing that is my dear Lina. My emotions settled in gratitude for her.

"Your niece is alive and well," I relieved him. "She is in this city, and she is my very special and dear companion."

His sense of relief washed over me in an almost tangible wave. I half expected it to ripple the water of my bath.

I qualified my answer, "She is healthy. But she mourns the loss of her husband deeply."

"Of course she does," the Old Digger mumbled gravely. But picking up his spirits, he proclaimed proudly, "She's an excellent Scherier, and dear Rüdiger is irreplaceable."

I reached my hand to the Old Digger, inviting him into my bath. Without a moment of consideration, he jumped into the water with me.

"Lina will be glad to see you," I assured him, "and we will be able to mourn our Rüdiger together."

He tilted his head downward and stared into my eyes, as if trying to pull the merits of my character from my pupils. He smiled, leaned back against the far end of the bath, near my feet, and he splashed the bathwater in my face. I laughed and splashed him back. The playful game grew wilder, until the splashing spread to the bath next to us, to The Ancient One, hitting him in the head.

"All right!" the swan shouted, "it is good to see you, old friend. Now, go find your niece. I came here to relax."

The Old Digger leapt from my bath to the swan's, creating a tremendous splash with his long, flat body.

When he resurfaced, he cuddled against the base of The Ancient One's neck, threw his short Scherier arms around him, and rubbed the side of his face against the clean, soft feathers, whispering, "Oh things are going to be good again. Oh yes they will. You are with us. The Swan Knight is with us. Things will be good again."

The Ancient One lowered his beak to rest on the back of the Old Digger's neck. They held that embrace for several minues. Then the old Scherier jumped from the swan's bath, turned to me, tilted his head and pressed his ear against the floor in a formal Scherier bow, turned quickly around and left the chamber in search of Lina.

After a lengthy silence, The Ancient One commented, "This is a good thing."

"What is?" I asked.

"The Old Digger is a walking symbol of Scherier traditions, of a glorious past, not so far gone. He will insist on the old rituals and the old games. The Scherier spirit will echo off the walls of Eineklaue again."

CHAPTER 27

The Boots of Lohengrin

THE SCHERIERS IN THE LAND AND SHALLOW WATERS answered my call, pouring into the city in waves. Many came from nearby, from the hidden, obscure little corners of Scherier land. Many came from the Sicherheit Marsh, obviously missed by our zig-zagged sweep of the tall, muddy reeds. They came in small groups and large herds. A group of two would waddle into the main cave, followed by a group of sixty. Thousands of Scheriers came over the following weeks.

I grew impatient to press on, called by some airy, distant, quiet, but urgent whisper into the back of my head. But Taufe and The Ancient One reminded me that the Scheriers were called there by their Queen, and their Queen should be there when they arrive. With the addition of each group of arriving Scheriers, Eineklaue revived, seducing me out of my eagerness to leave with the infectious Scherier character. It was quickly becoming a city again, not just a city, but a Scherier city. As magnificent as St. Hildegard is, with all of its comforts, physical and spiritual, the enrapturing playfulness of the Scheriers gave Eineklaue an exciting youthfulness that endeared the city to me. Every day there felt like a day off of school, with fun and games as the primary order of the day. Spirits were high, and lifted higher with each joyful reunion.

With the help of the Scheriers, the other breeds of our company made themselves as comfortable as I did, suiting up their own caves and buildings, and their own centers for ritual and relaxation. The Brunnen bathhouse was not the only multi-cultural center in Eineklaue. The city became quite the isolated sphere of bliss. It was not easy for the minds and hearts of the city to see beyond the city limits. They did not want to see — to be reminded of the ocean of pain and sorrow whose waves lapped silently against our little island of jubilation and euphoria.

Fortunately, I had no choice. Each time I was numbed by the happy amenities of the city, my mind reached beyond, to thoughts and feelings in the far corners of the Sweeter Realm. While the Scheriers committed their whole hearts to the revitalization of their capital, forgetting much of what drove them back to Eineklaue in the first place, I could not be so forgetful. Each new attack from the monsters of the Deep, across the huddled villages of every homeland, brought new pain to the Land and Shallow Waters. The suffering creatures reached for their Queen. Pinching, piercing, aching, biting thoughts of desperation shot into my head like an arrow from behind, surprising me, taking my breath, and often crippling me.

A band of Federmensch were attacked, traveling the border of the Nomadic Belt and the Unicorn homeland. Only one survived. The pain and sorrow of the survivor found me. Perhaps my affection for Felix magnified the experience. It knocked me unconscious in a convulsing, writhing fit, witnessed by hundreds. I was out for days, screaming loudly in response to the horrors that shook my unconscious mind. The company heard me. They heard my voice and my desperately reaching mind. When I awoke, they had broken themselves free of the seductive grip of blissful normalcy, sobered by the pain of their Queen. They were ready to go wherever I directed.

I did not awaken groggy and lethargic. I jolted into a frenzied ambition with the first blink of my eyes. My mind swirled too uncontrollably to summon the company with thought. I ran, wobbly-kneed through the city, yelling for their attention. Their thoughts were already on me, their eyes and ears keen to my moans and cries as I slept. My frantic hollars as I ran through the city were perceived by all.

I gathered them all at the mouth of the city's main cave and I directed them to Gralkirche, declaring, "All Scheriers born since the war, born away from Eineklaue and kept from the rituals of Gralkirche will go there now and resume the broken traditions."

Lina astonished me with her response, "None have been born away from Eineklaue. None have been born at all since the war."

"None?" I replied with disbelief.

"No, my Queen. Since we abandoned Eineklaue, no Scheriers have been born."

With a heavy heart, I pondered the significance. Many Scheriers had died. None had been born. The loss of the Scherier homeland to the hands of the enemy was disdainful enough before I realized the full scope of the loss. They were not simply driven from their capital, not just stripped of their traditions. Löwschock had squeezed so much more from the dear creatures. The Scheriers were not having children, because they could not have them in Eineklaue. They could not take them to Gralkirche to begin life as a Scherier should. So they did not begin life at all. Eineklaue had sat emptied for more than eighty years. During that time, not a single new Scherier mother sang to a new baby, no Scherier father wrestled with his new child.

My blood boiled as I dwelled on the loss. As if the war had not been hard enough on the Scheriers. I sent my thoughts out to all who might receive them, in the Land and Shallow Waters *and* in the Deep. I wanted the entire Sweeter Realm to know that the good had suffered long enough. Although I felt no connction to the creatures of the Deep Waters, I hoped that they received my message. It was a fierce and furious threat.

The message made it to my immediate surroundings. This time, they did not cheer. They stared, a bit frightened by the fury from my heart. The stout heart of Georg was the only one not taken aback. He began gathering the company, the company that came to Eineklaue with me, plus more than a two hundred of the Scheriers who had joined us since.

The Unicorns, with whom I had shared the earliest and most intimate connections, felt my thoughts from far and wide. They began gathering at Gemeinsam, knowing that I would eventually lead the army there. First thing the next morning, after months in Eineklaue, we left the full and bustling city to its rightful inhabitants, and we traveled west, toward the holy site of Gralkirche.

We were not long on the flat, grassy plain between Eineklaue and Gralkirche before the spire of the holy shrine appeared on the horizon. The Stiefel von Lohengrin had run the holy abbey since shortly after Lohengrin's death. The place and the Scherier's who ran it were devoted to preparing young Scheriers for a life of commitment to the Swan Knights. The members of the Boots of Lohengrin were called "Squires of the Order", but most simply referred to them as "Boots".

I don't know why, but I imagined that we would arrive to a hearty welcome from the Boots, as if they had hunkered down and rode out the wave of war that had decimated the Scherier homeland. Before we entered the holy complex, the eerie stillness of the air around it shattered that notion. It was as lifeless as we had found the Scherier capital.

As we drew near the first row of mounds and caves, the Scheriers of our company ran ahead, in and out of the constructs, in a fit of nostalgia. Some called for the teachers that had raised them. Others recited their old prayers and chants while retracing their childhood steps in a mindless trance. We gathered at the base of the main shrine. It was a typlical Scherier half-mounded cave. But upon it was constructed a tall, hollowed spire, with a spiraling ramp inside that rose to a room near the top, with a set of small, circular windows.

I was dissettled by the eerie quiet. More than any of the devastated and abandoned places I had seen to that point, Gralkirche's emptiness smacked of war and death. There were no bodies, no broken items strewn through doorways. It was just empty. But its emptiness was sickening to me. And the Scheriers of our company felt it too.

"This is wrong," Lina whispered to me, her eyes unnaturally wide, as if they tried to see things that were not there.

I stroked her back and responded, "Yes, sweetheart, it is."

"No, not just that it is empty, but that no Boots have stayed. You see, the law requires that the spire is never empty. One Squire of the Order must remain in the shrine at all times."

I knew enough of the Scherier heart to let such information excite me.

"If that is the law, then there must be a Boot here somewhere. I put Lina on my shoulder and dismounted Georg. Lina gripped tightly to the swan figure on my shoulder as I ran with her to the entrance of the shrine. By the time we stepped inside, she knew what I thought. She leapt from my shoulder and raced up the spiraling ramp of the spire. I crawled after her. The narrow passage could fit a few Scheriers side by side, but it was snug for me and I worked my way slowly, on all-fours.

I had long lost sight of Lina when I heard her cry from far above me.

"Hurry, Verena, please!" she yelled.

I reached the top and found a small room. It reminded me in proportions of the treehouse that our nextdoor neighbor had in his backyard, only it was perfectly round. A circle of tiny windows, like portholes on a ship, let the air into the room and gave a breathtaking view in all directions. In the center of the room stood Lina, crying and staring at an old Scherier. The old Scherier appeared to be dead — worse than dead, emaciated, whithered and drawn, like the only thing beneath his skin was his dried bones.

"I know him," she told me through her tears. "He baptized me."

I stared at his shriveled face and felt a rush of images. I believed them to be my imagination, until the intimate familiarity of a thought connection told me otherwise. He was alive. I saw his memories, thoughts and images floating around his unconscious mind.

"Back up!" I shouted.

Lina obeyed with startled suddenness. I lifted the old Scherier and tucked him beneath one arm. I crawled as quickly as I could down the spire's rampway. At the bottom of the spire, just inside of the shrine, several Scheriers waited. I cleared them out of my way with a harsh command and a wave of my hand and, with a single, shouted thought, commanded the Zweigwesens to meet me at the entrance. I handed the Scherier to the Zweigwesens and begged them to fix him. A group of Zweigwesens rushed the old Scherier into one of the nearby caves, followed by a hoard of desperately attentive Scheriers.

At the mouth of the cave, the Zweigwesens sent the curious Scheriers away. I could tell that they did not hold much hope.

One of them stayed behind and told me, "There is nothing of life in the old Scherier, nothing, no breath, no pulse. He is dead, my Queen."

"No! He thinks. He dreams. I see inside of him. He is in there somewhere. Bring him back."

The Zweigwesen gave me a subtle bow and walked backward for a few steps away from me, toward the cave where they had hurried the old monk, before turning and bringing my command to the other Zweigwesens.

Most of the company explored the complex of Gralkirche. There were many architectural wonders, Scherier mounds that were crowned with spiraling caps, one flawless pyramid, and scultures that told of the site's history. I remained with the bulk of my Scheriers, waiting outside of the cave that held the old Scherier monk. I watched as Zweigwesens came and went, gathering the local herbs and weeds, never in a hurry, never bearing the signs of hope in their expressions.

I reached my mind for the old Scherier. It did not feel like my message was being received, but I continued to sense the life deep inside of him.

I sent the repeated assurance, wrapped in the warmest, most hopeful thoughts possible, "We are here now. You are being cared for. Come back to us."

After a few days with no encouraging results, the Scheriers of the party began to break from the vigil. They assumed the responsibility that was rightfully theirs, as hosts to the company. Only a few of the Scherier leaders remained at the monk's cave. The Old Digger was there, a perpetual ornament hanging on and around the entrance. The Scheriers all knew the holy site well and most of them committed to arranging the company into lodgings that looked to last. They knew that we would not continue until the old Scherier was either recovered or buried. If the shrine were to be revived, as I imagined it, it would need a Stiefel von Lohengrin to run it. I only knew of one, and he was lying as near to death as a living creature could be.

For several days, my mind was bent on the Scherier monk. But as days continued to drag on, my mind drifted to Felix. Thoughts of him blended with those of the monk to encourage me. Afterall, Felix had died, or so I had thought. I felt his body crush beneath me, watched him stop breathing. He was brought back into my world, and recollections of that fact gave me great faith in the miraculous.

Near the end of the first week in Gralkirche, nothing had changed with the old monk. Although he showed no signs of life, he showed no signs of decay. As each day went by without change, the Zweigwesens began to hope.

"Had he been dead when we found him," one of them said to me, "his body would surely have shown the signs of death. But there are no such signs. He simply remains as we found him, with no signs of life or death."

My connection to the monk was weak and one-sided. I tried to share with the Zweigwesens the hints of consciousness coming to me from the old Scherier. I only managed to share *my* thoughts, not the monk's.

The Brunnens turned to their spiritual leader to guide them in whatever contribution they might give. Taufe organized a choir to lead the company in song and prayer. The leaders of each breed gathered in the shrine. The rest of the company flowed out through the entrance to surround us. The shrine rose out from a sea of the faithful. I sat nearest the Brunnen choir, with The Ancient One, Georg, and Lina snuggled tightly to me. Taufe stood among the choir, lending her angelic voice to the cause.

The Brunnen choir sang their Benedictine prayers. Their dual voices, in such prayerful hymns, brought the walls of the old shrine back to life. The walls seemed to join the choir, singing back to the Brunnens who serenaded them. I thought about the old Scherier, and sent my experience of the concert to him. They sang Psalm 85:

Revive us now, God, our helper!
Put an end to your grievance against us.
Will you be angry with us forever,
Will your anger never cease?
Will you not restore again our life
That your people may rejoice in you?

I strained myself to send the musical prayers to the old Boot as directly as I could. It exhausted me and I lost the connection.

Within a few minutes, a Zweigwesen bursted through the company, pushing through the many layers of tightly gathered creatures.

"He lives, my Queen!" he shouted from the entrance of the shrine. "The old monk lives!"

I looked at Taufe and she nodded to me. By the time I looked toward the entrance again, the creatures had formed a corridor for my passage. Taufe, The Ancient One, Lina, and a few Scherier leaders followed me through the crowd and into the cave where the monk was nursed.

By the time we entered the cave, the old Boot was awake and asking the attending Zweigwesens to explain the paste they had smeared upon him and the thick, syrup-like substance he bathed in. He was weak. He was fragile — until he saw me.

"Swan Knight!" he whispered, still staring at me.

He drifted his head directly upward and spoke loudly and clearly, "It is time, Lord. You have sent the Swan Knight. You have put an end to your grievance against us."

He dropped his head, returning his eyes to me, eyes that, though weak and strained, glowed with adoration, and beconned, begged me to approach him. I walked to his side and touched his shriveled hand. It was cold, morbidly so. With the same hand, I ran my fingertips along his back. His body still felt lifeless, but his face glowed with excitement, with the joy of a moment long anticipated, long prayed for. He began whispering, just beneath my ability to understand.

I leaned my ear to him and caught his quotation from the Book of Isaiah, "Open up the gates to let in a nation that is just, one that keeps faith."

When I returned to an upright stance, I was greeted on the shoulder by the hand of Taufe, as she spoke softly and hauntingly to me, in half-song, "He sees what you do not, what you yet cannot, that the gates will be opened soon."

I turned sharply to her and stared at her with eyes of bewilderment.

She continued, "You must stand at those gates . . . and sacrifice your own heart to keep them open."

I did not like the sound of that. I turned to the old Scherier. He smiled and nodded. The Ancient One knew enough to trust the mystic insights of the clerics. But he also knew that such matters were outside of his arena. He saw how dissettled I became. He came to me from behind, drove his head between my waist and my right elbow, and ran his long neck up to my shoulder so that his head nestled just under my jaw. I turned my head and kissed him on his beak.

He snapped me from my fearful thoughts and returned me to the moment, saying, "They do not speak of the here and now. We have many things to accomplish, impossible battles to win. Let us keep our focus there for now."

I thanked him for giving me focus and removing the haunting sense of impending sorrow that swirled around the words of the mystics. My armor, my sword, Georg, and the army I gathered — those were the concerns of the moment, those and the revival of the holy site of Gralkirche, which suddenly bore a greater sense of the probable, with the awakening of the old monk.

I thanked the Zweigwesens for their diligent attendance to their patient. I thanked Taufe for her prayers. I begged the old monk to rest and receive the attentions of his nurses. I led my friends from the cave, allowing the unlikely event of the Scherier's revival to swaddle me in a blanket of faith in the marvelous and incredible. I thought little of Taufe's warnings, but thought heavily of her notions of destiny — my destiny — and of the involvement of Divine Providence, which grew more readily apparent, more tangible with the turn of each page in my life.

CHAPTER 28

Resurrecting the Holy Order

OVER THE NEXT SEVERAL WEEKS, we made a home of Gralkirche. The old Scherier monk recovered quickly, from near death to the excited energy of the hopeful. He spoke in scriptures, a sort of biblical code, never plainly stating his thoughts. From the passages he recited, I gathered that he believed that the will of God would soon be done. There was an apocoliptic finality in his prognostications. His name was Hüter. He was the only Stiefel von Lohengrn left in Gralkirche, the only one left anywhere.

The holy city was abandoned by all but him, either by an intentional exodus or by a scattered retreat, or by violent elimination. In any case, I could find no sign of the order, not through the rigorous search of the mounds, caves, towers, and caverns of the city, nor through my mental search for them. Hüter was the very last.

One morning, I asked him what had happened to his brothers and sisters of the order. He quoted passages from the order's laws, explaining why he remained in the tower, with nothing to eat, alone for who-knows-how-long. I believe that his self-imprisonment in the spire of the shrine, that which almost killed him, may have saved his life. All other Boots of Lohengrin were dead or missing. They were probably eaten by the beasts of the Deep.

Hüter did not step into the leadership role among the Scheriers that was expected of him. The Ancient One and Lina reminded the Scheriers of the trauma suffered by the old monk and begged them for their patience. In Hüter's reluctance, Taufe remained as the spiritual leader of the Scheriers. The Ancient One was the leader of all other matters. I fell in between, expected to give leadership on all things. I was just beginning to trust my own judgment. But I still looked to my mentors for their approval of every decision I made and they passed no opportunity to lay upon me a lasting lesson.

After a couple of months in Gralkirche, with Brunnen voices leading the prayers in the Scherier shrine, and a swan and a human dictating the flow of the city, the Scheriers grew impatient to witness the revival of Scherier traditions in the sacred site. Honestly, I wanted it as much as they did. One night, after the company was settled for sleep, Lina and I went to Hüter. I stressed to him the importance of reviving the order, of continuity in the practices of the Boots of Lohengrin.

"Now, more than ever," I told him, "the Scheriers need to be bound to God and the Grail."

"And the Swan Knights," Lina added.

"Yes," I continued, "and the Swan Knights. Lohengrin, Elsa, Bechtold, they need the loyalty of the Scheriers."

Snapping out of a long dream, Hüter shook himself rapidly, as if trying to shake himself dry.

He stopped as abruptly as he began, froze in absolute stillness for several seconds, turned slowly to me, and responded, "That's me. That's my job, isn't it?"

"I'm afraid so, my righteous brother," Lina answered him.

I simply nodded in agreement.

Lina added, "The order must be rebuilt, the traditions reestablished. And you are the only one left in the Sweeter Realm with the authority to do so."

Hüter surprised us, growing quickly stern and refuting, "No! I am not. I am a servant of the Swan Knights, and now, here, right in front of me, is a Swan Knight. The blood of Lohengrin rides through the Land and Shallow Waters. I have no authority that is not hers by divine right."

The old Scherier knew so much more than I. He knew the Scheriers, their laws, their traditions. I was entirely unprepared to assume the responsibility he tried to thrust on me. But I could not refute him. He honored me so comprehensively. His mind and body still showed signs of weakness. I was afraid of shattering his fragile faith.

I gently reminded him, "And I am nothing but a servant of God and a custodian of the portal. I am your sister in this effort. I need you. I need you to do what I cannot, to say the things I don't know. I can't stay here and revive the order. God has a very different plan for me. Whatever endorsement you need from me to continue you mission, I happily give. Please, brother, you have hundreds of faithful Scheriers, right here in this city. Ordain whomever you choose. Revive the order."

I had to immediately rescind my offer. He looked at Lina and said, "I will begin with her. She is the best of them all."

"Oh no!" I quickly qualified. "I cannot be without her. Her path is the same as mine, wherever mine takes me."

Hüter grimaced, then grinned, as he spoke after some contemplation, "Lina should know best on which path she is meant to march."

Lina gave it little thought. She answered quickly, "I am with the Queen. Rüdiger would be angry with me if I left her side. For my husband, I remain with the Queen."

I was relieved to hear her answer. I could not lose Lina, nor could I have denied the demands of the old monk. In truth, Lina would have served the order well. But she was right. Rüdiger would have wanted her at my side, as he would have been himself, had he lived. I had come to know many of my Scheriers well. I offered nominations, Scheriers I knew to be better suited to prayer, teaching, and the calm but laborious life of a Gralkirche monk than to war. Hüter accepted my list, conducted interviews, and established a seminary. Hüter was the only surviving seed of a devastated spiritual orchard. But from that seed, a new orchard was planted. The ground was fertile and the yield promising.

With Eineklaue active and Gralkirche functional, the Scheriers were free to reproduce, to resume the ancient cycles of their culture. Gralkirche is far into Scherier land, far from the Queen's Lake. But the Achima River, which pours into the lake and sources in the marsh just south of the Scherier border, was an easy avenue for an attack on Gralkirche. I knew that the shrine would not stand long without protection. Few *truly* understood my desire to fill the cities of the Land and Shallow Waters, to revive traditions and grant daily life in the queendom some semblance of normalcy. That normalcy came at the cost of many individuals, of all breeds. Our army was drastically reduced in order to repopulate and protect the cities. Fortunately, those who did not understand were content to obey.

I decided to remain in Gralkirche until the first wave of new Boots graduated from the seminary. The candidates were sequestered. They studied constantly. They had all been baptized and schooled by the order. For these reasons, the process did not take long. Graduation was planned six weeks after they entered the seminary. The first two weeks went swimmingly. I took advantage of the situation to steep myself thoroughly in the history and traditions of the order.

The history of the Boots of Lohengrin, documented in vivid detail in the Gralkirche library, was filled with delightful anecdotes of the Swan Knights, some quaint and some exciting stories about the many centuries that the Scheriers spent in intimate contact with Lohengrin and his decendants. The Ancient One and I frolicked through the pages together, losing ourselves in the past. It was a warm and delightful time for me. The swan's excitement as he pored over the old tomes electrified my spirit. It was the happiest I had seen him. He and I were almost as sequestered as the seminarians. I began to lose mindfulness of everything around me, near and far. I even slept many nights in the library, cradled by loving feathers and by pages of Scherier writing that revived in my heart sensations that reminded me of my early obsession with Ludwig.

At the end of the second week, circumstances changed. The waves of attacks from the Deep increased in number, intensity, and devastation throughout the Land and Shallow Waters. Löwschock began with the shores of the Queen's Lake. The Shallow creatures who had survived near the shore for decades were hunted. Many fled for the Land. Those that did not were killed and eaten. Once the Queen's Lake was entirely his, the King began a calculated sweep of the Nomadic Belt. Every creature living in the belt was run out or killed. The King was particularly brutal to the swimmers who had been living in the shallow pools of the Belt. Those poor creatures he did not kill, were transported to the Deep of the Queen's Lake, where they were tortured and eaten alive, one small body part at a time.

It was only when the refugees of the Shallow Waters and the Nomadic Belt reached Zweigwesen and Unicorn land that I became aware of it. Only then did the minds of the devastated penetrate the fog of cozy study I had created over the library. It came to me at first in thoughts of panic from the Zweigwesens and Unicorns who accepted the refugees, as they heard of the aggressive waves of attackers from the Deep. Many of the survivors witnessed Löwschock himself leading the attacks. As my sympathy sought the suffering, I received the terrors from the captives in the Deep. I received them in the form of vivid dreams, ususally while I slept. But some hit me while I was awake, and pushed me into waking nightmares.

Time seemed to be running short and we did not have the forces to face the creatures of the Deep and the Wühlenvogels. The advancements of the enemy stopped at the edge of the Nomadic Belt. They did not push immediately into Zweigwesen and Unicorn land. Löwschock went to the portal point, on the southeastern portion of the Nomadic Belt. He must have thought the portal in use. Perhaps he expected to catch me passing back and forth from the Sweeter Realm to Linderhof. I was the Swan Knight and the Queen. He knew this. He must have expected that I had the Grail and lived in the palace at Linderhof.

I both desired and feared the Grail. Taufe and The Ancient One insisted that it was my destiny to find it. I delayed any serious attempt. Possession of it would certainly bring the full force of the enemy down upon the peaceful creatures I had come to love dearly and individually. My commitment to Gralkirche and to the Stiefel von Lohengrin was probably my subconscious attempt to avoid progressing toward that destiny. I thought heavily of Parsifal, who was hunted by Klingsor and his enchanted servants. I did not expect to be stabbed by the poisoned blade of a flowermaiden. But Parsifal began the knighthood, and Taufe and Hüter's coded, mystical sermons led me to believe that I would end it, that Parsifal and I would be mirrored bookends, containing between us the entire story of the Swan Knights.

The Zweigwesens and Unicorns had the numbers to secure their borders from the monsters of the Deep. The Brunnens sent hundreds to join the Zweigwesens at their border to the Nomadic Belt, nearest the portal point. The creatures of the Deep flooded the Nomadic Belt but kept themselves contained within it. Georg suggested that the King waited only for the Wühlenvogels. He insisted that a full attack on the Land would come as soon as the Wühlenvogels arrived. All eyes were on the Wühlenvogel border. While they remained mostly inside their own homeland, the forces of the Deep stayed in the Belt.

I did not search for the Grail, nor did I rush to meet the enemy. The young Unicorn warriors recommended attack, before the wave of Wühlenvogels could join from the north. There was wisdom in the idea. But I could not bring myself to give the order. I don't know if it was God, my Grail Blood, or my fear that froze me in Gralkirche, but I refused to leave until the seminarians graduated.

We were all on edge then, as reports of the enemy's movements continued to reach us. The anticipation of war filled the air of the sacred Scherier site. Every one of us reeked of it. There was little talk and no laughter in our company. Even the Scherier history became distasteful to me. Most of the stories were of happy, peaceful times in the valley. The contrast between those blissful tales and the perils of the moment was bold and repugnant. I couldn't look at the library without a constricting sensation in my chest.

The perfect distraction came at the perfect time. Early one evening, one week before graduation, I was in the cave I had claimed as my own. I had already dressed for bed. But instead of laying down, I wandered mindlessly outside of my cave. A single note came from a single Brunnen throat, at the top of the shrine tower. It was soon harmonized by its other half. She sang in Brunnen, the Nativity story from the Gospel of Luke.

I walked toward the song, stopping halfway between my cave and the shrine. Before I realized it, I was surrounded by Brunnens, every Brunnen in the company. With the familiar hand of Taufe draped over my shoulder, I turned to her in time to see her open her mouth and join the Brunnen song. Soon all of the Brunnens sang. The holy city rang out in sacred song. Taufe stopped singing.

She squeezed my shoulder a few times, then stepped directly behind me, wrapped both of her arms around me, kissed my neck, then rested her chin down on my right shoulder and whispered in German, "Happy Christmas, my treasure."

I turned around inside of her embrace, looking upward to face her, intending to ask, "Is it Christmas?"

I didn't need to ask. Upon the first thought of the holiday, I knew. I felt it. It was Christmas Eve. Although the rest of the company still rested ill-at-ease. My spirits rose like a bottle rocket. I woke all who slept and startled the rest with a forceful intrusion into their minds. I ordered them to gather in and around the shrine. They came — curious, not afraid. They sensed the joy in my thoughts.

Hüter, in his condition, had lost all concept of the calendar. He had no idea it was Christmas. But the holiday permiated my thoughts, and by the time they all gathered, the entire company knew the sourse of my sudden joy. Hüter crawled through and over many creatures to find his way onto my lap, in the center of the shrine. He wished me a happy Christmas. I asked if the seminarians could join us.

"Oh, no, Swan Knight," he answered, "they are in their last week. The last week is spent in constant prayer. But now they are aware of the holiday, and they offer a special Christmas prayer for you."

I wanted to hear that special prayer, or at least to sense their thoughts as they prayed. I reached my mind for them but was stopped sharply by Hüter.

"No!" he shouted. "They are sequestered, even from you. Nothing can interrupt their prayers."

I withdrew my mind from the attempt and comforted myself with the knowledge that they prayed together, in such focused, fervent prayers. The Brunnens finished the Nativity Story and the one in the tower joined the company. They treated us all to a repeat performance, singing the Gospel again, but this time in German, for all to understand. The company knew the scriptures. They were thoroughly versed since infancy. Yet, they sat and listened, captivated, as if hearing it for the first time.

After the second rendition, Taufe led the company in prayer. After that, conversations arose and died quite naturally. Not a word was spoken of Löwschock or the Monsters of the Deep. Not a thought of the horns and claws of the Wühlenvogels crossed their minds. They spoke of their Christmas traditions, of loved ones near and far, living and dead. Lina shared her favorite Christmas memories of Rüdiger, who, not surprisingly, always celebrated the day in the grandest style.

As conversations came to a close, more of the company joined to listen to me. They wanted to hear about *my* childhood, about Christmas in the Kessler home. I could not speak loudly enough for the many gathered outside of the shrine. The Ancient One silenced the crowd. Once every mouth was still, he looked at me with smiling eyes. I knew what he wanted. He wanted me to speak to the company together, with thoughts, not words.

With my eyes closed and my mouth still, I gathered their attention to me. I visualized as many images of my childhood Christmases as I could recall, from Christmas Eve mass to the first crack of the sun Christmas morning, from the smell of my parents' strong coffee to start the day to the smell of the pies in the evening. I recalled the rush of the crisp, December Colorado air as I went sledding down a hill near my house. They reveled in every thought I sent to them.

They were particularly fascinated with the Christmas songs I knew. They knew "Silent Night". Of all of the carols I knew, it was the only one they had heard. King Ludwig I, my Ludwig's grandfather, taught it to some Scheriers and Brunnens on Christmas. The song took well to the Land and Shallow Waters, once it crossed the portal.

We sang it together, the entire company, "Stille nacht, heilige nacht . . ."

I taught them many of my favorite Christmas songs in English and translated them. They loved "Angels We Have Heard on High". We sang it several times, once they knew it well. They were a little perplexed by the secular songs, songs about snowmen and sleigh rides, having little reason to associate the snow with the birth of Christ. They enjoyed the songs about Santa Claus. They knew nothing of the Christmas icon, but adored him through the shared memories of my childhood. In the middle of a song, I rose from my seat in the shrine and meandered through the company, working my way outside of the shrine and through the large crowd that gathered around. I saw each member of my company that night. I wished them all a happy Christmas, and I received their holiday prayers and wishes.

In the morning — Christmas morning, the plan solidified in my mind. We would remain in Gralkirche through the twelve days of the holiday. That would give us time to witness and celebrate the ordination of the new Boots of Lohengrin. On the Epiphany, we would leave Gralkirche, travel through the marshlands that cross into the Unicorn homeland, and make our way to the sacred

Unicorn city of Gemeinsam. It seemed right. It seemed Providential. It seemed like an idea coming *to* me, not *from* me.

I delighted Taufe when I told her the plans, quoting St. Hildegard, "I will be a feather on the breath of God. Let him push me where he wills."

Christmas passed joyfully, with games and food befitting the holy holiday. On the Seventh Day of Christmas, we witnessed the ordination of the new Boots. With that extraordinary moment, Gralkirche was whole again. It was again run by a full and complete and committed *Order of the Boots of Lohengrin*. For the next five days, they mingled with us again. They taught us. They prayed with us. They received our earnest promises to visit them as soon as we could.

There was a silent but demonstrative sorrow behind those promises. We all knew what was meant, "We will visit you after the battle . . . if we survive." The Christmas celebrations and the revival of the Stiefel von Lohengrin refreshed our spirits, but did not blind us to the terrifying prospects ahead. We all knew that any one of us could be dead in a matter of weeks. It was likely most of us would be dead. But we all had faith that we would win, that our dead would be martyrs to a Divine plan written before time, and we took great satisfaction in knowing that we would leave behind a bustling Scherier homeland, with its rich and ancient traditions reborn.

CHAPTER 29

Correspondence

AFTER CHRISTMAS, AS PLANNED, we traveled directly south, with a daunting prospect between us and the Unicorn capital of Gemeinsam — the Wendel Marsh. The marsh begins on the southern edge of Scherier land, and opens wider and deeper, thicker and more treacherous in Unicorn land. The Wendel Marsh gives birth to the Achima River, which runs through the Achima Mountains, to the Queen's Lake. This connection to the home of our enemy made traveling through the marsh terrifying.

We were not yet one mile out of Gralkirche when I gathered the minds of the Unicorns in Gemeinsam.

"Go into the marsh," I directed, "and clear us a corridor of safety."

If an ambush were to be staged by Löwschock, it would be in the Wendel Marsh, so easily accessed through the river. The King had the same thought. But there was no legitimate alternative. To avoid the dangerous marsh, we would either have to swing east, almost back to Eierheim, or west, to the foothills of the Achima Mountains. Our best option was the most direct, with the help of the Gemeinsam Unicorns. The Unicorns responded, with full realization of the importance and the danger of their mission.

We reached the northern threshold of the marsh. Although we could see Unicorn land on the horizon, it took us hours to cross the border. The marsh began with sitting water on hard ground, puddles, easily stepped over and walked through. The puddles grew to pools as we progressed. The dry grass of the Scherier plains gave way to firm, sharp, stubby reeds. The hard ground grew softer, clingy, and reluctant to release the feet and hooves of its rare visitors.

Our Scheriers and Friends of the Scheriers were brought to a dead stop. They were hoisted to the arms, shoulder, and backs of the Brunnens, Zweigwesens, Federmensch, and Unicorns. The Brunnens glided smoothly and quickly through the wetlands, but they were jabbed and pierced in their tender feet by the sharp reeds. The Zweigwesens sank ankle-deep with each step, slowing them to a crawl. Each step drew immense energy. Grunting and panting accompanied the sloshing, smacking sound of each withdrawn step. But we dared not stop and rest. We were in for a long night.

The night came quickly, with little of the Wendel Marsh behind us. The darkening sky, pain, and exhaustion wore our spirits thin. The soothing, nurturing sounds of the Brunnen choir were not at our disposal, nor were the spirited whistles of the Eulesängers, whose voices provided our souls with sustenance for much of our travels to that point. Until we reached the protection of the Unicorn escorts from Gemeinsam, silence was our greatest ally. So, we pushed forward in the dark, as quietly as possible, not even allowing ourselves the sighs and gasps that our tired legs and punctured feet demanded of us.

We were a tremendous company. I looked behind me in the dwindling light of the late sunset. I could see no end of the brave creatures following me. I took heart, remembering the monsters we defeated in St. Hildegard and in the Sicherheit Marsh. But then, in those cases, it was the monsters that were surprised. If we were to be ambushed in the Wendel Marsh, surprise would be on the side of our enemy. As these thoughts flew through my drifting mind, my confidence crested and waned, like a tumultuous ocean, tossing my spirits around like a helpless little raft.

To travel the river from the lake to the marsh, the enemy would have to go through the mountain canyon, onto the high plains west of Gemeinsam, pass near the city, and enter the marsh at the southern edge. In other words, they would have to traverse a great deal of Unicorn land, through a collective that was almost constantly connected to my mind. It was this thought that allowed me to fall asleep on Georg's back. I dreamed of the Unicorns — of Unicorn battles, of horns piercing scales, of holy martyrs and fallen loved ones.

When I awoke, the night was black. It was the thoughts of the company that woke me. They were hurting — and they were scared. I thought about my parents. I thought about my brother and Birgit. The thoughts warmed me and I sent that warmth to the minds of my company. I heard the hums of Scheriers and the whistle of Eulesängers as my brightest memories lifted them.

My warm thoughts sank, and the hums and whistles turned to gasps, as we encounted the remains of Löwschock's attempted ambush. The first thing I saw was the bloodied body of a large, thick serpent. It was dead, but recently so. Blood still oozed from the circlular wounds from a Unicorn's horn. The night offered little light for us to see what was around us. Objects, bodies, and beings were right upon us before they came into view. There were no sounds of battle, only the subtle splashing of Unicorns walking through the marsh, which by that point had deepened to sink my poor Zweigwesens to their knees.

I reached for the thoughts of the Unicorns that had come from Gemeinsam, those heroes who faced our ambush and cleared our path. Much pain and loss came through to me. Unguarded at first, I transeferred those thoughts to the entire company, until their gasps and wimpers reminded me to cage them within my own skull. In doing so, I blocked out the thoughts of the Unicorns. My own senses were all that I had to perceive them.

Georg maintained his connection, guiding us to a Unicorn of Gemeinsam. She was the largest Unicorn I had ever seen, dark grey with a black beard and mane. She was wounded. A long, deep and wide gash ran from her back, across her right, rear leg, and down to submerge in the water. I yelled for the Zweigwesens. Several responded and ran toward the Unicorn. They tripped and splashed face-first into the water. Startled and concerned, I looked to them and saw that they had tripped on the body of a fallen Unicorn. They gave the dead hero a few pitiful glances, then began evaluating the wound of the large Unicorn, a retired old warrior named, Schwerthorn.

Her horn was long, with loose spirals. The edges of the spirals looked sharp enough to cut. Blood ran down the deep recesses. Even though I was perched high on Georg, Schwerthorn had to lower her head significantly to touch her horn to my chest. Afraid to touch her sharp spirals, I left my hands flatly at my side and allowed the tip of her horn to tap me gently on my chest.

She sent me all that she knew of the ambush, all that she had planned and experienced. The Unicorns had attempted to form a line of guards, from the southern end of the Wendel Marsh to the Scherier border. By the time they entered the marsh, the enemy had already filled the southern half. The Unicorns found themselves in the throes of battle, too sudden, too violent, too chaotic to call for help. They fought and they won. The marsh was still. But for every slain enemy, a Unicorn body sat half submerged in the marsh.

During the horn connection with Schwerthorn, while her intended information flowed to me, I snuck into her mind from behind, from outside of the horn connection. She had served the Swan Knight Veronika. She was Veronika's intimate friend, playmate, guard, confidant, and ultimately her savior. But that is another story.

The Unicorns who survived the battle joined us, many wounded badly and hardly able to push through the muddy waters on their own. The Zweigwesens attended them with crunchy bars of twig and leaf for them to eat. The bars gave the wounded energy and relieved them of some of their pain. But the marshes are a poor hospital. The flora offered little for the Zweigwesens to use as medicines. It sickens me still to say that we left many behind, those Unicorns who lived but could not travel. There were Zweigwesens in Eulesänger land, not far from the Wendel Marsh. I found their thoughts and directed them to head into the dangerous marsh with what plants they needed to save the Unicorns. Many wounded Unicorns were saved and eventually joined us in Gemeinsam, or were taken to Gralkirche to recover. Many more died where we left them.

The morning sunrise seemed reluctant to show its face. The night dragged as slowly through the marsh as we did. Through the night, we passed the bloody bodies of friend and foe alike, strewn from where we met Schwerthorn to where the water grew shallow and the thorny reeds of the marsh yielded reluctantly to tall grasses, poking through the ankle-deep water.

Before the sun hit us directly, it shone off of a dry, grassy hill ahead of us, too far for *my* eyes, but within the vision of the Unicorns. The beconning hill pulled our spirits quickly through the shallowing marsh. As our hearts lifted higher, the ground got harder, and we found ourselves pulled into a near trot by the anticipation of safety and rest. We hurried like that for hours, quickening as the ground improved. Just after noon, the ground rose at the base of the shallow hill and we left the Wendel Marsh behind us.

When we gathered at the top of the hill, I walked through the company. Their legs were still wet with a rusty-brown liquid — the water of the marsh reddened by the blood of the slain. I imagined what moral words of Taufe must follow, as I saw the blood from friend and enemy, from the faithful and the vile, indistinguishable, dripping into the sea of grass, smeared on the backs of the Unicorns, and dripping down their horns to join the blood of their own wounds. I knew that there was some moral message in the images, placed there for me by God, to be pondered and milked of its wisdom at a more appropriate time.

We rested on the hill for about an hour. It was not nearly long enough for most, but we wanted the marsh far behind us, and the comforts of the sacred Unicorn capital awaited us. The pain of the suffering and dying Unicorns, the ones we left in the muddy, bloody waters, hooked my mind like a fisherman's lure and reeled me into them. The most bitterly acrid connections were made in the last moments of life, when the dying Unicorns sent me their farewells and final blessings. As I suffered the death of each, my lungs stopped when theirs stopped, only to burst back into motion when my weary body demanded air. That is how I spent the hour of rest. In my idleness, the connections were stronger and I could take no more. I achingly gathered our weary company and continued south. We arrived at Gemeinsam before sunset.

There were few structures in the city, no buildings designed for shelter. Large, spiraling, cone-shaped huts were cast about, each filled with items from food to sacred relics. Furniture rose right out of the grass of the city —

tables and platforms, perches and podiums, made from packed grass, saturated in a glue-like paste, molded and hardened. A set of five or six steps led up to a large stage, used for social and religious events. The most prominent feature of the city was the stone obelisk, the altar of the Unicorns and, for me, the most curious sight in the entire Sweeter Realm. But we walked directly and with purpose, not near enough to the obelisk for me to get a good look. I twisted my neck like an Eulesänger, trying not to lose sight of it in the distance as we walked on.

Schwerthorn led us to the southern side of the city, where a large, round, flat disk of the same packed grass covered a hole in the ground. Three Unicorns removed the disk and revealed the sloping passage underground. It led to the Wühlenvogel contructs, built for the Unicorns to acclimate themselves to life beneath the Black Forest. The tunnel opened into a tremendous cavern, already well-lit with torches. It was a wide-open space, with no buildings like those in the cave beneath St. Hildegard. The only structures were the same sort of tables and platforms I saw above ground, and a small replica of the sacred obelisk.

The Unicorns of our company remained on the city surface. Those who brought us down left us there and returned to the city above. Several Zweigwesens remained above ground to attend to the wounds of the injured Unicorns. Most of the rest of the company crammed into the underground Unicorn village. Those who did not fit stayed with the Unicorns. Very few words were passed, very few thoughts to and from me. We nestled tightly to each other and slept, protected beneath one of the only cities in the Land and Shallow Waters never breached by the armies of Löwschock.

I outslept most of my army. By the time I sat up and looked around me, the underground village was almost empty. Some Scheriers slept and Taufe knelt beside me in

379

prayer. I stood and began to creep quietly toward the ramp that led to the surface. My thoughts were on the friends we left behind, and Taufe knew it.

She lifted her head and spoke softly, "Whatever is up there will wait. Dawn in the bloodied waters of the Wendel Marsh is no place for the ceremony of the Psalter. But here, beneath the protected city of Gemeinsam, we may resume our obligations of prayer. Much has happened since we left Gralkirche, and much lies ahead of us. Let us turn to God."

I was eager to see the city above us, to see the many beautiful Unicorns, with their brilliant horns, each with a unique spiral pattern. I wanted to check on the injured and thank our saviors in the marsh. But I knew that Taufe was right. Divine Providence had held my hand through every step and misstep so far. I would not forsake it then.

"Call the choir," Taufe instructed.

I reached to the host of Brunnens in our company, inviting them to join us in prayer. They came. They came with as many creatures as could fit in the underground village. The Ancient One joined us and suggested that we take the rite above ground, in the heart of the city. All agreed, and the company, with the inhabitants of the city and all who visited, gathered around the sacred Unicorn altar.

There it was, exactly as I had imagined it — the tall, spiraling obelisk, with its circle of stones around it, each with a horn-sized hole facing outward. Although the recesses of the obelisk spirals were deep, the sunlight hit every inch of it, as if it was poured on the top and ran down the spirals like a bright, yellow, twisty waterslide.

The Brunnens gathered in the middle, against the shrine. The Unicorn elders encircled them. The rest of us gathered in as tightly as we could. I was just a member of the crowd, not exhalted or specially situated. I appreciated a moment of anonymity, of prayer time when I could speak to God as Verena Beth, not as the Swan Knight, not as the Queen, but as a girl whose faith needed galvanizing before the battle ahead.

Taufe led our recitation of the Psalms. The unity of our combined voices, with our drastically varying vocal tones and ranges, concerted into something truly inspirational. The unity of such diversity gave me hope and drew my mind to the struggles of my own species back home. All of Taufe's words about the connections between humans and the Sweeter Realm swirled around my brain.

"The differences between humans," I thought to myself, "are not as extreme as those between these creatures. Yet here they are, united in affection, in purpose, and in devotion to God."

For the first time in my life, I imagined a truly united humankind as I asked myself, "Is it really so far off, so unreachable?"

I had given little thought to humanity. But Taufe's words echoed in my skull, "Humans began here." "Your home will come to you."

I could not place my finger on it, but the connection between the fate of mankind and the trials of the Sweeter Realm felt near and substantial.

As soon as we finished our morning prayers, two Unicorns parted the crowd and trotted up to me, two wonderfully familiar Unicorns, two beautiful friends. Acheriel and Prische walked up to me, glowing inside of a single aura. A grinning Zweigwesen rode on Acheriel's back.

"Where is the baby?" I asked.

"With my family," Prische answered.

"We have something for you," Acheriel impatiently interjected, "something I know you will treasure."

The Zweigwesen on Acheriel's back stretched his long, splintery fingers toward me. Clutched between them was a folded piece of paper, sealed with a glob of something that looked like amber sap. It was hardened and served as sealing wax.

I am not sure if it was a dominating sense of hope or if I had some mystical insight into the matter, but I knew it to be a letter from Felix. I snatched it with urgent violence and ran from the crowd, behind a cone-shaped storage structure, not much taller than I. I sat down, held the letter against my chest for a few seconds, rubbed it, then broke the seal and read.

> My Dear Queen,
>
> You may be pleased to know that I recover quickly, but not quickly enough, I am afraid, to join you as you go to face Löwschock and his unholy monsters. The skills of the Zweigwesens continue to astound me. But with every physical pain alleviated, a spiritual one replaces it. The nearer I come to full recovery, the more tragic feels the timing. Another few weeks and I would be at your side, where I could be most useful to you.
>
> But I flatter myself. From the reports that reach me, your abilities seem to have developed beyond anything I could presume to assist. All I could offer your greatness is my loyalty, which I can give you from here. But if any harm should befall you in the conflict ahead, anything that I

could have prevented, or in any way lessened, I am not sure I would have the strength to live with it.

Know this, my good and holy knight, while my body is bound by my recovery, my spirit stands near you, admiring and supporting you to the end. Please forgive the impertinence, but I am so unspeakably proud of you, more than I have been of myself or anything I have ever known. If I am proud of myself, it is that I am proud to have served you, proud to be your friend, and proud to be,

Loyally   Your   Adoring   &
Obedient,
Felix

By the time I finished reading the letter, the tears that pooled in drops on my chin fell onto the strange vest-shirt that Taufe had chosen for me to wear that day. I cared nothing for appearances. I wiped my eyes, only to clear my vision from tears so that I could read the letter again. I read it dozens of times consecutively, and nobody disturbed me until I finally composed myself and appreared from behind the storage mound.

I made a bee-line to the entrance to the underground village, exchanging nods and greetings from the smiling faces along the way. Other than that, nobody drew my attention. Nobody engaged me in any way to delay what was clearly a focused and determined mission — to return Felix's letter with one of my own. I could have simply thought my response, and connected it to him. But it would have poured uncontrolled from me and washed over him in an incoherent wave of emotions. So I decided to place my thoughts painstakingly into a letter, a clean and rational expression of what I wanted him to know. I settled into the empty, dimly lit village and I wrote.

> Dear Felix,
>
> Many things have come into my life that I do not deserve, good things and bad things. I have spent little time trying to reconcile myself to them. I have just accepted them, until you. Yours is a degree of goodness that I struggle to understand and cannot believe myself deserving. It is an enigma that haunts my every moment.
>
> Why do you do the things that you do? How can anyone be so pure, so true, and so good? I know what you would say. You would try to project your goodness onto me. But it does not belong there. It does not fit there. In your place, I would not have jumped from that cliff, with no thought of what pain waits at the bottom, thinking entirely of the welfare of another. I would have frozen in fear for my own safety. But not you, my dear Felix, not you.
>
> I ask myself daily, "Does he know his own goodness? Is he

aware that he is entirely unique, among all creatures in any land or water?"

Perhaps, my pure and holy friend, if I continue to seek answers to these questions, if I continue trying to understand how a being can be as constantly and comprehensively good as you are, I might inch myself nearer to you, nearer to deserving the love and loyalty you have bestowed so readily and without cost. Until then, I will strive to be better, more like you, more deserving of you, deserving to be, as I wish to be,

Eternally Yours,
Verena

I held the letter. I read it back to myself many times over, pondering what was too much, what was not enough. I contented myself with it, without making a single alteration. I walked slowly up the ramp to the surface, summoning the same Zweigwesen to meet me at the entrance. I handed him the letter. He folded it in half, sealed it with a secretion from his fingertip, smiled, winked at me and hollered in the Unicorn language. A small, thin, but fast Unicorn answered. The Zweigwesen leapt onto the Unicorn's shoulders and the two of them disappeared in a flash, to the south, to Zweigwesen land, to Felix.

CHAPTER 30

The Lips of Parsifal

MY LETTER FROM FELIX COLORED THE REST OF MY DAY. I saw many beautiful Unicorns. I saw interesting structures, and I saw the sacred Unicorn altar. My eyes had been primed by Felix's letter to receive beauty all the more resplendently. I viewed Gemeinsam and everyone in it through warm, affectionate lenses. I had no mind for time of day. I entirely forgot to eat until food was placed in my hands. The image of Felix healing well, with his flapping nose hanging above his sweet smile and the sparkle of adoration in his eyes, intoxicated the better part of my brain.

As the afternoon grew old, and I strolled in conversation with diverse company, my mood, and that of the entire city, sank abruptly. The afternoon sun was blocked almost entirely by the shadow of a flock of Wühlenvogels. It was more than a flock. There must have been a thousand of them. Before I realized what was happening, Taufe grabbed me by the wrist, more violently and harshly than I would have imagined the soft hands of a Brunnen capable. She yanked me into a coned storage structure and hid with me, covering me like a mother would cover a child in a hail storm.

The Wühlenvogels traveled southwest, toward the mouth of the Achima River, where it empties into the Queen's Lake. It looked like they had come from Eulesänger land, perhaps from the forest south of the capital, the same forest we fled into the dangerous mountains to avoid.

"This is not good," Taufe whispered. "Why would they travel in such a flock to the mouth of the river?"

My eyes seized my thoughts and held them firmly on my surroundings. In the storage hut were dozens of viles and vases, each filled with the same liquid.

I asked frantically, "Is this the Unicorn nectar, the one that gives clarity of thought?"

"I believe it is."

I did not ask permission or even hint at my intentions before plunging my hand into a vase and pulling it out thickly coated in the honey-like substance. I licked and sucked it all desperately from my hand. It worked. It did not give me any information not already in my head. But it gathered and focused what I already knew. I felt like an ant under a magnifying glass in the sun, as my thoughts focused to a painfully searing understanding of the truth. The Wühlenvogels flew to the Queen's Lake, at the base of a river that leads into the Unicorn homeland, just west of Gemeinsam. They may not have seen *me*, but they saw the others. They saw an army of creatures of every breed on the Land gathered in the Unicorn capital. They must have assumed that I was among them.

Löwschock had called them to gather at the lake, gather with the minions of the Deep. They would travel the river and attack the city. In the openness of Gemeinsam, we would not stand a chance against the Wühlenvogels *and* the monsters of the Deep. It would be a battle with two fronts — the ground around us and the air above us. We had to leave the city, and we had to leave soon.

When the Wühlenvogels had passed and were out of sight, Acheriel fetched us from the storage hut. One glance at the contents of the hut, and one look into the sharp focus of my eyes, and he knew that I had sampled the nectar.

"What do your gathered thoughts tell you?" he asked.

I explained all that I knew and all that I suspected.

He closed his eyes and let out a series of forceful huffs before opening his eyes and saying, "We must unite the collective. Come, my queen, witness the sacred ritual. Watch us consult with each other and our ancestors."

I had so desired to see the connection ritual at the altar. But the circumstances drained all mystic wonder from the experience. I marched behind Acheriel as he walked slowly toward the obelisk, his head held high and his eyes closed, silently calling the Unicorns of the city to join him.

A small hint of my curiosity returned as I watched the Unicorns, one by one, approach the altar and insert their horns into the holes of the surrounding stones. The Unicorn nectar still ran through me and a sudden attack of clarity took control of my actions. With only a few holes unoccupied, I ran in front of a Unicorn, just as she was lowering her horn to the stone. I pushed her head aside, drew Albert's sword, and thrust it into the hole.

I did not feel the Unicorns. I did not connect with them or their ancestors. Nor did they run through my childhood, as they did with Irmengard. I connected to Christ, to his Holy Grail. With my outstretched hand still holding tightly to the sword and my head facing directly upward, I screamed. Although I was hardly conscious of it, it was later described to me as a scream of joy and terror, a scream of love and sorrow, a scream of victory and of loss, all rolled together.

Nobody knew quite what to expect when I shoved my Unicorn-horned sword into the sacred altar. But they did not expect that. When my voice died down, there was not a sound in the city. Every breath was held in shock and suspense. My eyes darted from the sky to the base of the obelisk in front of me.

I broke the silence with a loud and excited declaration, "The Holy Grail is here!"

The Ancient One appeared at my left side, staring at me through the tops of his eyes, as he does when he is scolding me.

"The Grail is here? Here in Gemeinsam?"

"No . . . Yes . . ." I stammered, "Here at the end of my sword."

I slowly withdrew my sword from the stone. A Federman reached around me and hoisted the stone from its ancient place of reverence. There was nothing beneath it. The experience with the altar was interacting with the Unicorn nectar still focusing my thoughts. I stepped forward, to the base of the obelisk.

I reached the sword to the stone altar, tapped the tip against the base and said, "The cup of Christ is here."

Without pause, every Unicorn in the circle charged their holy altar together. They toppled the consecrated shrine as if it held no significance to them at all. The obelisk fell to the ground and broke into thousands of pieces. There, under its base, was a small, shallow, circular pit, dug quickly by the arms of Kandake. Inside of it was a bundle of dried seaweed no larger than my head.

The entire circle of creatures around the altar leaned forward, captivated by the very humble ball of light-green weed. There were whispers, speculations. But I did not speculate. I stood frozen in awe of what I knew. I had connected with the Holy Grail. It spoke to me. I knew that the ball of seaweed held the cup of the Messiah.

I felt a bump against my back, the prosthetic wing of The Ancient One, pushing me forward with the feathers from Felix's back, accompanying his soft and fateful words, "Well, Swan Knight, the Grail is in your custody now. Take it."

I sheathed my sword and knelt beside the pit. I lifted the holy package. As I pulled it toward me, the dried seaweed wrapping fell apart. I stood slowly, wanting all around me to witness the moment, a moment whose monumental significance was lost to nobody in our company. By the time I stood erect, the seaweed had broken to tiny pieces and fallen to my feet. In my hands remained the cup of the Redeemer, the Holy Grail.

There it was, in the hands of a Swan Knight, in my hands — a deep-brown, stone bowl, thicker at the bottom than at the rim, with a slightly raised edge crowning the base, and pale-yellow marbling that seemed to dance across it like drops of rain on a windshield. A few flakes of the seaweed casing had fallen into the Grail. I blew into it to clear the flakes. My breath swirled around inside of the cavity lifting and discarding over the rim the last remnants of the Grail's old shrowd. My breath continued to swirl inside of the cup, in a celebratory dance, hesitant to leave, singing back to me in an airy whistle, before escaping the Grail, into the welcoming air of the Unicorn capital. The company around me must have experienced it as I did. They drew long, deep, thoughtful inhales, as if to invite that breath into their lungs to cradle their tender hearts.

I stared at the marbling of the stone cup, as if expecting it to spell some secret message to me. I followed one vein from base to rim, where it met with a single lingering relic — the clear lower lip print of Parsifal. The imprint spoke to me clearly of the desperate moment, when Gütel held the Grail against Parsifal's cold, blue, dying lips. I pulled the Grail slowly to my mouth and pressed my lower lip against the mark left by the first Swan Knight.

Taufe approached my right side and gently caressed the back of my neck with her left thumb, saying, "The last lips to touch the Grail belonged to Parsifal . . . before him, Christ and his Apostles."

Her words were followed by a wave of gasps and hums from a crowd of creatures whole-heartedly in touch with the significance of the moment.

I held my lower lip against the outer rim and gently wrapped my upper lip over the rim, as if to drink from the empty cup. I held it like that, inhaling the air that filled the cavity that once held the first consecrated blood of the Holy Eucharist. Utter silence surrounded me. Not even the breeze dared to make a sound. I pulled the Grail slowly from my lips, with the gentle suction of a loving kiss. The smack of the kiss was the only sound in the city, and it seemed to echo off of everything and everyone around me.

The Ancient One spoke in a raspy whisper from my left, "I have not seen that cup in fifteen hundred years."

His words were followed from his beak by a low, melancholy moan, which pulled my thoughts to him until my mind fell, quite accidentally, into his. The sweet, loyal, tenderly sentimental old bird was flooded with memories, a vivid reliving of every moment he spent with Parsifal and Gütel. In that moment, I came to know Parsifal, the founding patriarch of the Swan Knighthood. I knew him as The Ancient One knew him, as a brother, through the experiences of my dear friend and teacher.

I felt Parsifal's blood in my veins. I felt it rush into my head, where it met with my connection to the swan. The three of us — Parsifal, The Ancient One, and I enjoyed an intimate embrace of thoughts and memories. In that private audience, in that secret meeting between my ears, I stood as witness to the tenderest exchange of sentimental admiration and gratitude. Only then, at that precious reunion, did I come to know The Ancient One. His sense of heart-felt love and duty for the children of Parsifal, from Lohengrin to the silly girl from Centennial Colorado, fifteen hundred years of love and devotion encompassed me as the most profoundly powerful wave of emotion I had ever experienced, shining a bright light on every hidden contours of my teacher's love, fear, and reverent respect for me.

I missed Rüdiger. I mourned him every day. But in that moment in The Ancient One's mind, I knew what Rüdiger knew — that the swan was worth every sacrifice made to free him.

I pulled myself reluctantly from the mind of the swan. The Unicorn nectar still surged inside of me and focused my thoughts where they belonged, to the imminent perils at hand. The recovery of the Grail should have been a celebrated moment. The reverent awe in the minds of the devout, faithful creatures in Gemeinsam should have been allowed to last. But our circumstances forbade such an indulgence and I harshly snapped the minds of the city back to thoughts of fear.

Acheriel, ever concerned for my safety, declared, "They will travel upriver and attack us here. The Wühlenvogels are with them. We must leave here. The underground villages built by the Wühlenvogels are no longer safe. None of the cities are. We must take you into the mountains."

I held the Grail in my left hand and seized Acheriel's horn with my right. I invaded his mind and took control of his mouth.

I connected to every Unicorn in the city, and with my lips sealed, I proclaimed, though their shaggy mouths, in my voice, "No! We did not find the Grail now so we can run into the mountain with it. We found it now because we need it now . . . to face our enemies! Tomorrow, we go to them!"

Creatures across the city stood near Unicorns, hearing my voice come in concert from the many bearded mouths in the city. It simultaneously unsettled them and energized their faith.

The Unicorns in the city turned at my mental command to the Brunnens nearest them, as I continued through their mouths, "And I feel St. Hildegard inside of me. She was a child of Parsifal. I hear her."

The words of St. Hildegard came into my mind and out of the mouths of the Unicorns, in a woman's voice that was not mine.

"It pleased the Lord to touch a small feather, that it flew aloft in wonder. And a strong wind bore it so that it did not sink."

Taufe yelled to the others, "That is her voice, the voice of Hildegard!"

The voice continued through the Unicorns, "She is a feather on the breath of God. Follow her."

With that, I let go of Acheriel's horn and dropped to my knees. I recited the engraving on the wall of the Brunnen cathedral, "Heilige Hildegard, bitte für uns" (St. Hildegard, pray for us).

The Swan Knight had made her declaration. We would attack our enemies, and every thought and effort of that evening and of the following morning were bent upon the preparations. From The Ancient One's description, Lina made me a bag, exactly like the one Parsifal used to carry the Grail into Bavaria.

"The cup of the Messiah must remain at your hip. Guard it as Parsifal did," The Ancient One instructed me.

Since I pulled it from the pit beneath the Unicorn altar, it had not left the jealous embrace of my fingers, until I placed it in the bag and strapped the bag over my shoulder. We did not hide in the underground village that night. The efforts of Wühlenvogel claws seemed an inappropriate venue for our prayers and sleep as we prepared to meet the deadly breed in battle. Primary among my prayers was for their loyalty, for a return of their affections to the Grail Blood of Rudolf. Several times through the night, I was tempted to reach for them. But I dared not risk revealing our plan of attack. If I could manage to turn their loyalties from Löwschock, it would have to be on the field of battle. We had a large army of fiercly loyal creatures. But they were not hunters, with the claws, teeth, and horns of the Wühlenvogels, and the Wühlenvogels numbered in the thousands.

The company slept above ground, among the Unicorns who lived in Gemeinsam. I had lived for more than a year in an underground Wühlenvogel village, beneath St. Hildegard. But the prospect of facing them in battle gave a repugnance to every scatch in the dirt from a Wühlenvogel claw. I slept (if it could be called sleep) as I usually did when not in a bed or underground, sandwiched between Taufe and The Ancient One, with Georg not far away. Acheriel and Prische had spent enough time away from me. They too were near.

Nearest to me, nearer than any creature, was the Holy Grail, napping inside of its bag, nestled into my abdomen. I had imagined that possessing the Grail would make me feel invincible. It did no such thing. I had never felt so vulnerable. The Grail made me feel fragile, and made to seem fragile everything and everyone I loved. In the silence of that night, when all around me were asleep, the Grail spoke no encouraging words to me. It gave me a strong sensation of impending calamity, and a cumbersome sense of responsibility. I bore a burden that no Swan Knight since Parsifal had borne.

That was the night — the last night of preparation. Every night and every day since I saw the lips of Ludwig move on his poster portrait, in my German class in Centennial Colorado, led to that following day, when we would meet the forces of Löwschock. I thought about every moment that I did not train as hard as I could, every lazy moment not spent in study or prayer, as it should have been. I cursed and scorned my weaknesses under the silence of my breath, apologizing to who-knows-whom, begging forgiveness, and praying that those failures would not spell the end of me, or of any of the dear creatures I had grown to love.

I may have slipped into shallow dreams, when my thoughts choose their own path, unguided by the deliberate mind, but when I am still aware of my surroundings. That was it, the closest to sleep that I had that night. It was a tense-muscled, restless several hours, with more moments of panic than of relaxation. The sun seemed particularly unwilling to rise. For the first half of the night, I wanted it to last forever, for the sunrise never to come. For the second half, the torture of lying still, while my mind raced in exhausted desperation, was almost too much to bear. I begged the morning to come. At the first hint of lightness in the sky, I was on my feet, pacing, thinking, praying, and wanting terribly to get on our way. Win or lose, live or die, I wanted to get the day behind us.

The Ancient One was normally a sound sleeper, and rarely the first to rise. He was the first to join me that morning. He jostled Taufe as he rose, waking her and setting her to her morning prayers. One by one, Unicorns, Zweigwesens, Eulesängers, Federmensch, Brunnens, Scheriers, and Friends of Scheriers awoke and rose. Such grave solemnity filled the air. As the waves of creatures took to their feet and moved about, one would have expected the sounds of the city to transform slowly from the soundlessness of night to the bustling clamor of day. No such transformation occurred. By the time the sun was fully above the horizon, every creature in the city was up, with little more noise than I heard in the middle of the night, when only I was awake and the city was still.

396

We all gathered around the shattered remnants of the obelisk. The Ancient One believed that a reminder of the previous day's events would dispel the silent sense of doom that hung over the city and inject in us all the feeling of Providential momentum that had surged through us when I lifted the Grail and when I spoke through the mouths of the Unicorns. I stood on a large broken piece of the obelisk, near the shallow pit that had held the Grail.

"Say something to them," The Ancient One urged me.

I looked around me. Every eye in the city was on me. Their faces begged me for words that would feed their starving confidence. I could think of none. All I could think of was how much I adored them all, and that is all my mouth could manage. I knew that many would not see the sunset of that very day.

I looked out across the crowd and in an apologetic tone, I said, "I love you."

"They did not hear you," The Ancient One told me.

I closed my eyes and began to think my love to them.

"No, no," the swan whispered quickly, leaning his head in to me, "Your thoughts should remain in your head for now. They will reveal more than they should. Let them hear your voice. Let them see that you are here, physically *and* spiritually."

I cleared my throat and repeated, in a voice more emboldened, lined with a thin veneer of bravery and confidence, "I love you all! Sweet friends, good, righteous creatures."

They waited, assuming that more was to come, some gilded words that would send them toward the lake with raucous cheers. Awkwardness stole the silent air that followed.

Taufe's voice broke the tensly still atmosphere, loudly, as she speaks when she is leading prayers in the cathedral.

She bowed her head. I did the same. The other creatures followed. Taufe began with a quotation from St. Hildegard.

Be not lax in celebrating.
Be not lazy in the festive service of God.
Be ablaze with enthusiasm.
Let us be an alive,
A burning offering before the altar of God.

I could almost hear the pulse of the company rise from deep in their chests, to pound against the inside of their skin. Taufe began The Lord's Prayer. After the first few words, the rest of us joined, growing our voices in firmness and volume with each word.

> *Our Father in heaven, hallowed be your name. Your kingdom come, your will be done, on earth as it is in heaven. Give us this day our daily bread, and forgive us our sins, as we also have forgiven those who have sinned against us. And lead us not into temptation, but deliver us from evil.*

At the end of the prayer, Taufe added alone, "Deliver us, oh Lord, from every evil and grant us peace in our days."

The prayer may not have energized the crowd, like the fiery speech they expected, but it galvanized their hearts and united them in resolute purpose, as was evident in their loud, determined, and concerted "Amen!"

There was no confidence in their voices. They did not expect to live. But there was stout determination. They were ready to be *a burning offering*, if that was the fate chosen for them by God. With only a few breaths of recovery from their prayer, the company broke from the crumbled altar into small clusters. The scene was not raucus, nor was it stifled and somber. Fully facing the trials ahead, with eyes opened widely to the dangers, the city assumed an air of normalcy — a matter-of-fact attendance to the final details before we embarked. With the breath of their united "Amen", they released their fears into the crisp breeze of the Unicorn homeland, a breeze honored to wisk those fears far from our hearts.

I sent two young Unicorn warriors to the river to scout the canyon pass through the mountains, to the lake. The rest of us ate and prepared our minds for the day ahead. Nearly a hundred additional Scheriers came into the city, offering themselves for the battle. They were those who had gathered in Eineklaue, and remained to revive the city after we left. As much as I desired the full function of the cities, I welcomed their offer. Among them were the Boots of Lohengrin, including Hüter — all but the one they left in the shrine at Gralkirche. They had rushed east to Eineklaue and joined the band that left from the capital. The Scheriers had sensed my union with the Grail and wanted to share in the historic moment. They left immediately, skirted the eastern edge of the Wendel Marsh and traveled as a herd, through the night in a tireless sprint to Gemeinsam. I thanked the new Boots for their offer, but refused them.

"Your obligations to the Sweeter Realm will be performed some other day," I told them. "And they are as important as what we do today. Please, go back to Gralkirche and be ready to teach the next generation of Scheriers. We will need them. And they will need you."

They obeyed and promised to leave for their sacred shrine the next morning. I assigned five Unicorns to hurry them home to their sacred obligations. But first, they would see us off. My company gathered on the western edge of the city and began following the tracks of the Unicorn warrior scouts, toward the Achima River and the Achima Mountains, toward the Queen's Lake and toward Löwschock.

CHAPTER 31

Battle at the Achima River

OUR ARMY MARCHED WEST, in an unorganized mass at first. But we soon found a united cadence and drifted subconsciously into a more organized formation. We began in segregated bunches of breeds, but as we marched along, and fell into order, the breeds shuffled so that rarely did more than two or three of one breed walk shoulder to shoulder. I rode on Georg, near the rear of the company. I wore my helmet as we left the city but removed it and replaced it several times over the next few hours.

As I watched the army, from my vantage point near the rear, shuffle and blend into a single, diverse body, my spine stiffened. It stiffened with resolution more than confidence, but lined with a firm sense of destiny. The Grail hung in the bag by my hip, tapping gently against my armor as Georg trotted along.

As we neared the river, I reached my mind for the Unicorn scouts. They found nothing in the river, so they followed it west until it dove and cut into the Achima Mountains. They waited there for us, at the mouth of the river-cut canyon, keenly looking downstream for any disturbance in the water, darting their eyes upward for signs of the Wühlenvogels. We met them there, where the river begins slicing its way through the mountains. The afternoon was growing old. We rested and we ate. The last of the dread that hung from them in the morning like swollen fruit on weak branches was shaken off by light conversations.

Moods were as high as could be expected, perhaps a bit higher. They seemed determined to savor each other's company while they could, refusing to let gloom paint what promised for many to be their last day together. The Eulesängers surrounded me as we rested, and laughed with hearty joy in their eyes each time I tried to speak to them in their language. I pulled out my musical eggs, which I kept in a small side pocket of the Grail bag. I played along as they sang their old folk songs. My musical contribution may have been detrimental to the loveliness of the songs, but in its own way, it brought a comical joy to the moment.

We had not rested long when the sun transformed from the intense whiteness of midday to the softer orange of the early evening. Acheriel urged me to press on, warning of the perils of facing the enemy at night — an enemy born and reared in the darkness of the Deep Waters. A darkened sky would tilt the advantage steeply in their favor. I gathered the company in thought, connecting them in bunches and waves to each other, until I had them all united in mind. Each felt me and each other fully.

I reminded them of *our* great advantage, one of which the enemy had no idea — our ability to unite our minds. This gave each in our company a thousand eyes, eyes as low as a Scherier and as high as an Eulesänger in flight, as quick as a Unicorn and as penetrating as a Zweigwesen. They could not reach for each other. They could only connect through me. But I promised to keep them connected as much as I could.

We worked our way into the hills, along the river, whose banks were wide at first as it cut a deep canyon into the hills, allowing us to keep our formation without crossing the river and splitting the army into halves. But as we followed the river, the wide banks were pushed in by the walls of a canyon cut before time, when the river was much larger and mountains much younger. The river was deep at that point. We could not see the bottom. Many suggested that we send half of the army across the river so that we did not trickle down the canyon in single file.

I saw the wisdom in keeping our concentrations, but I would not allow my friends to jump into the water. If the monsters of the Deep were hiding in the river, we needed our feet and hooves on the dry ground. So we stayed on the left side of the river, pressed into few more than four of five side-by-side. This spread the company out so that I, near the rear, could not see the front. The river ran mostly straight. It did not meander through a crooked, mazed canyon. Thank God for that. But the back was so far from the front that the first hundred could have disappeared and I would not have known.

I tried to keep the company connected in mind, but the effort grew exhausting. Instead, I jumped into the minds of five or six at a time. This I could do easily. I kept my mind mostly with the two Unicorn warriors who led the army. While I was connected to the Unicorns, the Eulesängers shouted down to me. They had risen high above the river, passing the tops of the canyon walls. They beconned me to connect with them, to take advantage of their perspective. I did so, and their thoughts gave me an understanding of the surrounding area.

I realized in terror how exposed the Eulesängers were. Had we faced only the creatures of the Deep, their heights would have given us a decided advantage. But we also faced the Wühlenvogels, and the Eulesängers would be easily seen by them. They were a beacon, guiding the Sweeter Realm's most dangerous hunters, like a giant arrow pointing to the army below.

I did something I had never done and have never done since. I took control of an Eulesänger, possessing his mind entirely from him and stearing his thought and decisions. I dove the creature downward, beneath the cover of the canyon walls. As I did, I called for the others to follw me, shouting in their tongue, with the familiar crudeness of their Queen's clumbsy grip on their language. They knew that it was my mind that whistled crudly to them through an Eulesänger beak. They obeyed and followed my lead. I brought my Eulesänger to land on my shoulder before releasing his mind back to his own command.

I could touch the minds of any breed in the Land and Shallow Waters. But only the Unicorns could reach for *me*. It is a good thing that they could. While my mind was in the Eulesäanger's, the front of the army fell under attack. The moment I released the Eulesänger, the Unicorns grabbed me by the mind and forced their thoughts into me. I felt the panic, the rage, the determination, every sensation in the minds of the creatures at the front of the company.

They were strewn thinly by the narrowing pass. They were pressed against the edge of the water by the wall of the canyon, unable to encircle the enemy, who rose out of the water and could retreat and reappear at will. One of the Unicorn warriors was pulled into the river and thrown out, against the wall of the canyon, landing on the creatures beneath him, pushing them into the river. In a few minutes, we had lost more than ten without causing the slightest injury to the enemy.

I ordered the Eulesänger on my shoulder to fly to the point of the battle and scout the areas ahead. The canyon widened, giving room on the banks to concentrate our numbers. The Eulesänger landed on the horn of the other Unicorn scout and I shouted through the Unicorn's mouth an order to rush forward, to the clearing ahead. The company stampeded forward. Many slipped into the river and never emerged.

Had the monsters of the Deep remained where they were, they could have killed half of the company, as we rushed through the narrow pass to the clearing. The river was about twenty feet wide there and deeper than we could see. Fortunately, the monsters followed the front of the company, engaging in a furious pursuit of those they had been fighting. The narrowest, deadliest portion of the canyon was clear and my friends passed safely through it, to gather in greater concetration in the wider part of the canyon.

The battle evened on the wide river beach, where Unicorn horns could swing ferociously and Zweigwesen fingers could thrust, where Scheriers could jump and roll, dive and attack with their burrowing claws and sharp teeth. The battle occurred at eye level, with only the monsters from the Deep Waters. There was no attack from above — from the Wühlenvogels. Momentum swung to our favor. But the majority of the company was still stuck well behind the battle, helplessly unable to engage. They could only look upward for attacks from the sky. Those in the thick of battle looked only at the scales flashing before their eyes, the claws that slashed at them and the tails that swung at them. There was only one thing *I* could do.

I connected the minds of those in the battle. They moved like a single creature, made of diverse and disconnected parts. The enemies were confused. My friends darted, leapt, flew, and fought in choreographed concert. The panicked screams and mourning cries of my company were replaced by the wallows of serpent cries, sounds that would have been wretched and haunting in another circumstance, but delighted my ears as my mind felt the thrust of the Unicorn horns that caused them.

The enemies disengaged from the front of the army and retreated downstream, to a narrower part of the canyon. My company did not follow. We held a position of advantage that we were not keen to give up. The battle was paused. The monsters of the Deep waited, no more than fifty feet from the front of my army. They waited and stared. We continued pushing the back of the company forward, packing the wide beach of the clearing. A few Scheriers took the initiative to cross the river. They made it safely to the other side, while the front creatures stood stone still, daring the monsters to rejoin the battle where the advantage was ours.

The enemy was still in shock of the coordinated fighting of the good creatures. The few Scheriers who crossd the river were followed by a dozen more, then groups of other breeds. This continued down the line, until the army was split in half by the river. This allowed us to gather nearer the front. I was still well behind the clearing. I was wedged in the narrowest part of the canyon, where the initial attack took place. Georg continued to push us forward slowly, as river crossing creatures left vacancies to be filled. Prische managed to work her way near the front. Acheriel crossed to the other side but could push little farther ahead than Georg.

We pushed tighter and tighter until there was no more room for movement. Since we held both sides of the river, the water lost its advantage for the monsters. The river became a funnel of death, waiting to consume them. We were at an impass, neither side willing to give up the advantage of their position. I ordered us to press slowly forward. Although the canyon narrowed and would thin our ranks, we held both sides of the river and could force the enemy to fight on two fronts.

There was fear in the eyes of the serpents, as we inched toward them. Suddenly, Löwschock emerged from the water, at the front of his army. There was no fear in *his* eyes, only determined vengeance. He hollered into the air. It was a chilling, wretched noise, as if every horrible thought in his head, from his centuries of hatred, concentrated into one quick outburst. It froze my advancing army. On their master's command, the monsters left the safety of the river. They filed onto the narrow river beaches, on both sides, creating a line of them, from canyon wall to canyon wall, across the river. We could no longer surround them. Although we had the advantage on the land, our disadvantage in the water was much greater than theirs on solid ground.

They moved clumsily, but powerfully on the land, inching themselves toward us. I anticipated their attack and reconnected the minds of the front line. The advantage of coordination resumed as the fighting did, until we began to suffer losses. In the connection, I felt each serpent claw as it slashed through skin, each serpent tooth as it sank into muscle. I felt it, as did everyone in the connection. The shared pain of our mutilated friends debilitated the coordination, and it broke my concentration. I lost the connection, which was probably for the best. While each wound and each death was felt by them all, it stunned and crippled them.

Knowing that the connection — our greatest advantage — became a liability with the compassion of the survivors, I would not attempt it again. I just pushed the company forward, knowing that we were falling much faster than the enemy. Bright eyes, sweet smiles, and loving hearts were being extinguished by the second. There was a frantic push forward by those desperate to assist their friends and families. The battle was well within sight of me, but well out of reach.

Acheriel, Prische, Georg and I were about forty feet from the wall of monsters. Prische could bear it no longer.

The sounds of battle, the splashes, the screams of pain, and the moans of sorrow echoed inside of her. She jumped into the river and swam downstream, toward the battle. Her horn did her no good as a weapon. She was lucky to keep it above water. It did not stay so for long. Two of the seahorse creatures, like the one I killed in the Queen's Palace, broke their ranks and attacked Prische. They grabbed her with their flailing, hose-like arms. They pulled her under the water and held her, not biting at her, not striking her, just holding her under the water, too deep to be reached by the walls of good creatures that lined the river on both sides.

When Prische went under the water, there was no more battle in my mind — only Prische. I connected intimately to her and Acheriel to me, so that we both lived in her mind. We held our breath as she did. We felt the same ache in the lungs. We battled the same temptation to inhale as her body demanded breath. We both grew weak as she did. And we both inhaled as she did, as she took the water of the river into her lungs. Together we felt the seizing of her body, the burning beneath her ribs, and the extinguishing of her life.

When Prische sank into the darkness of death, the connection ended. The monsters lifted Prische's brilliant white body above the surface for all to see. The wall of serpents opened, allowing the two to retreat with Prische's body, downstream, toward the lake. Acheriel jumped into the river, desperate to save his wife's body from a ceremonious devouring in the depths of the Queen's Lake. I kept my connection to him. I felt the grave urgency of each violent push of his legs through the water.

I felt so strongly for him, for his love and for his loss, for the child he would have to raise without her. In the piercing pain of the moment, my mind reached for the creatures around me. They connected with me, to Acheriel. An eruption of growls and howls rose from the depths of their love. They pushed hard against the enemy line. Friends of the Scheriers ran between the fins and legs of the enemies on land, hitting, kicking, and scratching at their lower extremities, distracting them enough to soften the enemy wall and allow the splintery fingers of the Zweigwesens to find their targets.

Eulesängers pecked at eyes and Scheriers claws at faces. Even the soft, nurturing hands of the Brunnens did their damage. The loss of the most beautiful Unicorn in a thousand years, at the hands of such hideous hatred, put into perspective what was at stake. Our army pushed hard against the enemy. But the serpents of the Deep were larger, stronger, and more vicious.

The direct sunlight had left the canyon entirely. Although the sky above us was still warmly light-blue, the bank of the river, in the depth of the canyon was darkening quickly. Acheriel reached the thick of the fighting. He faced Löwschock directly. The King dwarfed the Unicorn and snapped at his horn with those crusty claws, trying to snap it off of Acheriel's head. It was my place to face Löwschock, not Acheriel's. I raised my sword high and screamed at the King, trying to draw his attention to me. I was too far back and the noise of the battle was deafening.

One sound pierced through the splashes, squeels, and hollers. It was a low howl from above. A flock of hundreds of Wühlenvogels appeared in the sky above us. They swooped down and plucked my friends from the battle, lifting them over the canyon walls and out of sight. Unicorns, Brunnens, Zweigwesens, all were scooped up by the powerful tails and gripping claws of the Wühlenvogels. The former friends of the Swan Knights, who fought beside Rupert and Rudolf at the Battle of Einigkeitstadt, did what Löwschock's serpents could not do all afternoon. They tore through my army like a child pushing through tall grass. Löwschock and the monsters of the Deep sat back and watched. Acheriel swam in place, watching his friends on the shore being scooped up and flown away.

Georg rushed me to The Ancient One. He tried to block me from his mind, but his intentions were clear. He wanted to run me away from the battle, away from the Wühlenvogels. Two Zweigwesens connected to each other, strapping me, binding me to Georg's back. I screamed in protest.

Georg argued, "My Queen, the Wühlenvogels are here. We have lost. We must get you and the Grail to safety, back to Gemeinsam."

"And abandon the others to die?" I challenged.

"They do as they desire. They fight for you, for the Lord, and for the Sweeter Realm."

"No!" I shouted, "Bring me to the front of the battle."

"Certainly not!" he huffed back at me.

I turned my fierce scowl toward The Ancient One. Georg's eyes followed mine.

The revered old King repeated my order, "Take her to the front of the battle."

In his passionate loyalty, Georg yelled at the swan, "Have you lost your mind?"

"**Bring her!**" The Ancient One sternly demanded.

The Wühlenvogels had thinned us substantially. Georg rushed me easily to the front of the line. I stood high on his shoulders and thought to the Wühlenvogels, "Look at me!"

They abandoned their efforts and converged on me, encircling me but not descending on me. They flapped in place with eyes targeted and fixed.

I thought to them, "I am not a dream. I am here . . . a child of Rudolf, a Swan Knight, and successor to King Ludwig. I am your Queen! Your loyalty belongs to me!"

They peeled their eyes from me to look at each other. They looked back to me, staring and flapping in place for what seemed like an eternity. They smiled with their hairy, wolf-like snouts. A few nodded. A few winked at me. They turned on Löwschock and the monsters of the Deep, slashing through their wicked ranks as they had through ours. What remained of our company joined them, piercing, slashing, and biting their way through the retreating enemy.

The Wühlenvogels were as fierce as they were heroic. The brutally violent gifts that God had given them were put on spectacular display. They bludgeoned with their horns, ripped and tore with their claws, and lacerated with the teeth of their long, hairy snouts. While I watched them in motion, decimating my enemies, I could not help but consider how differently I would have perceived the beautiful efficiency of their killing, the majesty of their violence, had their talents still been in play against us.

But they *were* on our side, which liberated me to relish the dynamic duality of their art. The movements of the flock, the acrobatics of the individuals, it was truly a wonder to behold, like a complex corps de ballet, where each dancer is self expressive, yet moving as a part of the synchronized whole. I saw the fall of each monster as the the gift of life to my my friends, a gift given by the Wühlenvogels.

As we pushed forward, the canyon walls were replaced by the rolling foothills of the western slope of the Achima Mountains, where the evening sun still lit the ground. My feet wanted desperately to share the grass with the direct sunlight. Fewer of the enemy fought as more turned toward the lake. Only Löwschock himself and a few of his minions still faced us and fought. The King of the Deep was deadly enough. He pulled Eulesängers out of the air two at a time with his lobster-like claws. With a single swipe of his powerful arm, he knocked half a dozen Zweigwesens unconscious. As he found himself isolated and surrounded, the fury of his fighting swelled.

The last of his monsters dove into the safety of the widening and deepening river. The King of the Deep stood tall in the center of the river, before dropping beneath the surface and fleeing with his subjects.

When the last of the monsters was out of sight and the river looked like a river, with no fighting, no splashing, no bodies being thrown in or pulled under, my sweet friends took a breath. They dropped to the sand where they stood, as if all energy was expelled from them inside of a single exhale. The Wühlenvogels landed and surrounded me. They greeted me with smiles and laughter, as if we had never been enemies, as if we had not lost so many lives. They licked me and rubbed against me. They spoke to me in choppy, antiquated German, expressing their pleasure to meet me and sharing through their laughter their favorite memories of the Swan Knights.

I was in no mood for light reminiscence. The Wühlenvogels had won us the battle, and they saved many of our lives, including mine, Taufe's, The Ancient One's, Lina's, Acheriel's and Georg's. Our debt to them was heavy, heavier still when several of them returned from the canyon with the creatures they had flown off with. They killed none of them. They simply removed them from the battle.

My chest still hurt from experiencing Prische's drowning. My eyes hurt from watching her beautiful body being taken downstream to be eaten. I dismissed myself from my new friends and gathered among my old ones. There was much to decide — but after some mourning and recovery. The evening sun dipped beneath the horizon and we made camp in the foothills to the south of the river, just inside of the Nomadic Belt, away from the treachery of the water.

CHAPTER 32

Flight

THE DAY GAVE US A GREAT VICTORY. Not only did we stop the planned attack on Gemeinsam before the enemy left the mountains. We forced them into a retreat, back to the Queen's Lake. My mind savored the success of the day, categorizing an inventory of reasons to celebrate. But those thoughts were strictly cerebral, forced to pose reluctantly for a victory photo in my mind. My heart spoke very differently. I lost Prische. More painful still, Acheriel and their infant goat lost Prische. Every smile, every word of congratulations and gratitude was pulled downward from below by my heavy heart, a heart that would not allow my mind a purely pleasurable thought. The morbid permanence of our shared losses attached itself to our every word, our every gesture and thought.

To pull me from despair and allow me to be what everyone in camp needed me to be, I weighed our many losses against what was saved and gained. The Wühlenvogels were again on the side of the Swan Knights. And that is no small thing. Many more of us survived the day than even our most optimistic imagined when the day began. Running the monsters of the Deep entirely from the Land was no longer just a hope. It was a probability — and

Löwschock knew it. The blood lost that day yielded a great prize, taking just a little of the pain from our weary hearts.

My entire army gathered on the hill, about half a mile from the western mouth of the river canyon. After eulogizing the dead, and comforting and congratulating the survivors, The Ancient One, Acheriel, Georg, Lina, Taufe, Cort, and I gathered before a large campfire. We had nothing to fear from the warm, bright beacon that night. The Wühlenvogels were clustered on the outskirts of the camp, still guilt-ridden for their contribution to the attacks on the cities while they were under Löwschock's command, still reluctant to integrate with the company they had just saved.

I felt their regret, their lonliness, their desire for my company and goodwill of the kind creatures of the Land and Shallow Waters.

I passed my eyes quickly across those of my dearest friends and simply said, "Excuse me."

I stood abruptly and walked away from the campfire, toward the gathered Wühlenvogels. I dared not think an invitation to join us. This was a moment I could not leave to possible misinterpretation. I walked through the camp, riding a wave of muted conversations as I passed through my good creatures. By the time I reached the Wühlenvogels, all eyes and ears were on me. Many still didn't trust them, so the example was mine to set. I walked through the flock. The leaders stood and stared at me as I approached them, their shaggy snouts hanging open in anticipation.

I touched each Wühlenvogel I walked past, nodding and thanking them. When I reached the leaders, I embraced them warmly and kissed them. I had no fear of them as I stood fully encompassed by the flock. I had seen into their hearts — those feelings of love and commitment that the rest of my company could only hope were there. I invited the Wühlenvogel leaders to join me at the campfire. After I left the flock with the leaders, many other creatures, beginning with the Scheriers, filtered among them, inviting the Wühlenvogels to join them in their celebrations and their mourning. They all blended together, like many colors of paint poured into a single bucket and slowly stirred until they mix into one unique hue. We were one army, one company, one family.

Back at the fire, we had much to decide, whether to pursue the monsters to the Lake and see them fully under water, or to content ourselves with the degree of our victory and tend to the bodies of the dead and the comfort of the mourning. For Acheriel, there was little to consider. Prische's body, along with many others, was taken downstream, wrapped in the cold, scaly, slimy hands and crusty claws of our vile enemies. As exhausted as he was, that thought did not allow Acheriel to settle and recover. He was fidgety and agitated. He paced and huffed and snapped at all who spoke to him. The loss of his wife did not cause that behavior. He would have handled it nobly if he could have buried or burnt her body. The thought of her being torn and eaten by Löwschock brought a savage anger bubbling to his surface, one entirely unfamiliar to those of us who knew him best.

Acheriel did not share his thoughts with many of his fellow Unicorns. He knew the burden they already carried —fears, pains, injuries, and losses of their own. He touched horns with Georg, who insisted upon the connection. And he knew that I peeked into his head. Georg responded as I expected. He wore Acheriel's shared fury plainly on his shiny coat. I felt deeply for Acheriel, but I had so much more to consider. I knew we needed that night, at least one night, for many reasons. I feared a rash decision that would cost lives, and cost our new momentum.

I had my council. The Ancient One, Taufe, Lina, and Georg had their opinions and offered them freely. But the decisions were mine to make. Only my will would dictate our actions. It was a burdensome responsibility, but I was beginning to get used to it.

I told my closest few, "We need this night to evaluate our condition, decide who can press on and who must be treated. We need this night to rally their hearts before throwing them into battle again."

Georg suggested, "We have won the day. Should we ride that wave and chase the monsters back to the Deep?"

"You're right," I conceded, "we have won the day. It is a blessing we should use to its fullest. Had we lost and retreated, we would have no options. Our dead would rot in tomorrow's sun or be eaten. But we did not lose. We won and we have options. Our enemies retreated and we have the river. We can retrieve our dead from the canyon. We can search the banks for survivors. These are unexpected blessings that we should not discard."

They all saw the wisdom in my words and yielded to my decisions. I decided to send four Wühlenvogels, two Unicorns, and two Brunnens back to the river. With a Unicorn on each bank, two Wühlenvogels perched on the rocks on either side, and Brunnens to dip their feet in the water and sense anything coming upstream, I felt confident to reach my mind to the creatures in Gemeinsam and summon each breed to collect their dead. With the entrance to the canyon guarded, the creatures of the Land did just that. I had just enough energy to connect my company with those left in Gemeinsam and those suffering in the canyon, so that they knew who was with me on the hill and who did not make it out of the canyon.

The searchers from Gemeinsam hurried through the night to get to the canyon and travel the scenes of the day's battle in search of their loved ones. The Unicorns, and those who rode on them, came with amazing swiftness and arrived in the canyon while the night was still young. Many found their dead and took them from the canyon. Many searched through the night and morning and left the canyon, assuming that their loved ones were washed away or eaten. Most importantly, some were found alive, brought home and treated.

Many in our company gave in to their exhaustion and slept. My mind and heart were too full to pay the slightest attention to the needs of my body. As I thought about the searchers, crawling the canyon by moonlight, through indescribable carnage, I could not help but connect unwittingly to their thoughts. I found one, then two. As more arrived in the canyon, most suffering either grief or uncertainty, my wandering mind found them and hoisted their sorrows upon its own shoulders.

Some ran quickly and frantically through the canyon, calling out names. Others crept, freezing at the sight of each shadow, each rock that could be a fallen loved one. The reunions of the living with the dead were wretched. Screams reached my mind in concert — not screams from the mouth, but from the heart, from many broken hearts. It was more than my battered soul could handle. The emotional stress showed itself clearly through my expressions and the Wühlenvogels knew what to do. They knew I needed a distraction.

"May I take you to the sky, my Queen?" one of them begged me.

"To the sky?" I asked, assuming a less literal meaning.

"Yes please. May I fly you over the Land?"

I looked to The Ancient One, as if to ask his permission or his assurance.

He responded to my gaze, "You should go with him. There is nothing more beautiful in all of God's creation than the Sweeter Realm from the sky on a moonlit night. I think of it every day, dream of it every night."

Such longing filled his voice as he spoke of his lost ability. It seasoned his words with a richness of tone that I had never heard from him.

The Wühlenvogel added, "It would be the greatest honor, my Queen, if I could fly you over your queendom."

I had no thought of my own desires, of my own curiosity. The rich sadness in the swan's voice consumed me, pushing from my senses even the deepest dispairs in the caynon.

"You may take me to the sky," I answered, "if The Ancient One comes with me."

In a flash, another Wühlenvogel hopped to his feet and volunteered, speaking to me but glancing to The Ancient One, "May I? May I take the swan back to the sky?"

It was settled, two Wühlenvogels, two passangers, and one bright, moonlit night. The grass of our hill was as bright as mid-morning, but with the silver of the moon instead of the gold of the sun. I tried to imagine the view from high above, a whole mountain range, the fields and valleys, the forests and rivers, the surface of the Queen's Lake, all painted silver by the full moon. I tried to hide my excitement, or at least subdue it. I failed. I looked at my dear friend and teacher. One desire stood atop all others — to see that silvery moonlight shining off of his back as the high air rushed through his feathers, just as I imagined it when I read about him, sitting in the Venus Grotto with Ludwig's journal in my hands.

The Ancient One had long resigned to a flightless life. His hesitant heart was slow to imagine the wind beneath him again.

I prodded him, "Well, will you fly with me?"

He stared at me, as if he and I were the only two creatures on the hill.

I added, "Please, do this for me. Let me see you in flight."

In a rare fit of defeated self-pity, he snapped, "I cannot fly. My wing was eaten! I have one fake wing and one that will never be useful again."

I peered into his thoughts. His words may have been of his own loss, but it was the suffering of the Sweeter Realm that he felt so keenly. He felt incapable of giving all that he should to his former kingdom. He would have given his other wing, and both of his legs, if he could see that bright moonlight reflecting from Prische's brillianly white back.

I entered his mind fully and thought to him, "I need this, to see you in flight, if only held by a Wühlenvogel. If Löwschock cannot take flight from you, even though he has taken your wing, then I know he cannot take hope from me."

I left his mind and spoke aloud, "We all need to see you fly. Don't you understand what a victory that would be for us? After all that has been lost, all that has been taken by Löwschock, that you, their former King, the beloved teacher of all, can still soar, with your protective eyes watching over them from high above. Please allow us that victory."

The Ancient One stood abruptly, shook and fluffed himself, and gave an affirmative nod.

I turned to the Wühlenvogels and said, "Let's fly."

Taufe took me by the hand as I walked to my ride, saying, "Fly low. Let them all see you both clearly. The Wühlenvogels are swifter than wind. They can take you far and wide. Fly over the cities, over the shrines. Connect to the breeds. Let them know you are coming. They will gather and cheer, and goodwill will push down against the border of the Deep Waters. The air of the Land, the water of the Shallows, will become repugnantly Godly in the nose of Löwschock. Perhaps it will drive him back to the Deep."

Before I could respond, my Wühlenvogel replied to Taufe, "We will show them to every creature, every tree, and every rock, every pond and pool in the Land and Shallow Waters."

A Wühlenvogel grabbed my armor at the shoulders and took me off the ground. The other wrapped his long tail around The Ancient One and joined us in the sky. Our immediate circle cheered and hollered, catching the attention of the entire camp. The noises were heard echoing in the river canyon, pulling the bereaved searchers from the depths of sorrow. I felt their lifted hearts and knew where we must go first. We flew low, to the mouth of the canyon, then rose high enough for the moonlight to reflect from my armor and the swan's feathers, lighting the canyon beneath us.

No cheers came from the canyon. But a strong, warm sense of hope rose from the banks of the river, up the rocks, and blew against us in wafting warmth, like opening a hot oven in a cool kitchen. Once we cleared the canyon on the east side of the Achima Mountains, we flew directly to Gemeinsam. I called to their minds and they gathered near the city center, where the obelisk once stood. As we flew over them, a wave of vigor rushed through their ranks, as if caused by the wind of our wake.

It seemed like we would backtrack our journey from St. Hildegard. At least that is what I expected. Our Wühlenvogels surprised me with a hard turn to the left — northwest from Gemeinsam, toward the Wühlenvogel homeland. My heart skipped in terror. Such a long time of fearing the Wühlenvogels held the habit of dread near my heart. But the Wühlenvogels adored me, not just because of my family blood, but because my appearance in the Sweeter Realm liberated them from an abhorant, reluctant allegiance to the beast who killed their beloved Queen Kandake, the savior of their cities, and returned them in fellowship-of-arms with the swan, the very creature who pulled them from isolation and joined them in united will and endeavor with their neighbors and the Swan Knights more than seven hundred years earlier.

I did not need to reach into the minds of our two pilots to find expressions of their happy loyalty. I saw it in the shine of their fur, heard it in the flap of their wings, felt it in the squeeze of those powerful, deadly, but ferociously loyal claws. They truly felt liberated from their dispiriting obedience to the King of the Deep by my appearance in the canyon that day. In the hours since I stood high on Georg's shoulders and demanded their allegiance, they had affixed their hearts to me more firmly than they had to Rudolf and his children in all of their years in Einigkeitstadt.

We rose higher as we crossed the northern edge of the Achima Mountains. From that vantage point, I saw the Queen's Lake in the far distance to my left. But a more beautiful sight was to my right — the serene expression on the face of The Ancient One, as the cool, high winds of the Sweeter Realm caressed his feathers for the first time in more than a century and a quarter. His good wing reached far to his right. His artificial wing shook and wobbled, but stretched away from him as far as he could push it with the stub beneath. My thoughts and my eyes had fixated on the crowds we flew over, and on the splendor of the moonlit landscapes. Not until that moment did I savor the beauty at my side. But as the swan's feathers rustled in the breeze, dazzlingly luminous from the moonlight, they appeared magical, holy, as Godly as the Grail itself. Many things have filled my eyes with wonder, since I came through the portal at Linderhof, but the glory of the swan in flight, my memories of him from that night, are the most readily

421

recalled to my mind when I am in need of enlivening thoughts.

My many months of study under Taufe and The Ancient One taught me to be contemplative and philosophical, to see in all situations a chance to improve myself, to see my own flaws in the examples of all failures. Watching the swan in the high moonlight, with his artificial wing, made me think of the story of Icarus. I had always thought that Icarus' wings were to blame for his failure, either their design or materials. Soaring high under the moon with my dear friend, I saw it differently. Icarus' wings were not faulty. His desires were. He wanted the sun. Had he wanted the moon, he would have lived. It is not *that* he desired, or that his desires were ambitious. He was attracted to the wrong heavenly object. I considered and applied this lesson immediately to my own desires. Which of them were the sun and which were the moon? Which would send me plummeting downward? These thoughts and more came into my head, planted their seeds, and left in three flaps of a Wühlenvogel's wings. They were made more vivid, pronounced, and permanent by the fact that they came into my mind off of the moon's reflection from my great mentor. He did not reach the moon. But he became *as* the moon. The silvery light off of his feathers could have lit the eastern half of Centennial, Colorado.

Despite the splendor all around me, my attention remained in admiration of my glorious friend and teacher until we flew over a sacred Wühlenvogel site. It was the place where a Scherier accidentally burrowed into a Wühlenvogel city, launching a bloody war that will remain always as the ugliest stain in Wühlenvogel history. I knew we flew over the site because of the ancient oath that our two Wühlenvogels recited in unison as we approached it. In my studies of Sweeter Realm languages, during my training in St. Hildegard, my study of Wühlenvogel was strenuously pressed upon me. The Ancient One knew that the breed would play a crucial role in the fate of our efforts, one way or another.

As we flew over a monument — two gigantic bone-shaped stones, one representing the Scheriers who died in the conflict, the other for the fallen Wühlenvogels — our flyers recited the following in the Wühlenvogel language.

Under these bones an innocent accident occurred
Fear and ignorance prevailed
Ending the pulsing of a thousand good hearts
The heroism of the Queen brought light to dark eyes
Reflected in the kindness of the tortured and hunted
Never, never, never again
Shall darkness push the light from our eyes?
We swear this oath to the Queen
Our hearts belong to our neighbors
Our horns, our teeth, and our claws
Belong to the Queen of the Land and Shallow Waters

The sentiment translates well, but the eloquence of the poem in the Wühlenvogel language, spoken from Wühlenvogel hearts, through Wühlenvogel mouths, is something remarkably inspiring. As they recited the poem, and reaffirmed their loyalty to the Queen, they remembered Kandake, but their oaths of loyalty were to their new Queen — to me, and to the white-feathered King they thought they had lost to the bellies of the monsters of the Deep.

Our Wühlenvogels remained in deep and somber meditation long after passing the hallowed site. We flew over some sparsely forested, low-rolling hills. I tried to admire the landscape and the beauty of my friend, staying out of the minds of the Wühlenvogels while they meditated and prayed. As the hills flattened into grasslands, we dropped, flying no more than thirty feet from the ground. There was nothing in our vision, nothing above ground to signify our approach to the Wühlenvogel capital — a monstrous cavern they call Steinhörner. Directly over the city, we flew so low that I could have dragged my toes on the ground had I stretched out my legs and pointed my feet.

From our descent, I expected to land, forgetting entirely about the tiny holes that lead into Wühlenvogel cities. Suddenly, we swooped directly upward, flapping higher and higher, until stalling and dropping straight downward. As we picked up speed, I remembered the holes. My heart pounded in a unique blend of curiosity and terror. The Ancient One was pulled downward just as he had flown all night, beside me, to my right.

Through the rushing wind of our accelerated speed, he turned calmly to me and said, "You are the first Swan Knight to enter a Wühlenvogel city this way since Anna, daughter of Rupert, granddaughter of Adolf."

In the moment before we reached the ground, I thought about Adolf, the son of Duke Rudolf, when a Wühlenvogel lifted him from the floor of the Black Forest and took him into the sky, turned upon himself, and dove to the ground, exactly as we were. I thought about Adolf yahooing as he was flown through the underground city. As I read that portion of Ludwig's journal for the first time, in the boat of the Venus Grotto, the notion that I would share that experience with Adolf did not approach the wildest regions of my imagination. Yet there I was, rushing toward the ground in the grasp of a Wühlenvogel, rushing toward a hole too small to fit my index finger.

I did not know what to expect as we passed through the hole, how it would feel or how my mind would try to evaluate the science of the experience. Even now I cannot describe it. It happened in a flash. I was above the ground, being pulled to the grassy field above the capital. Then, I was below ground, held at the ceiling of a tremendous cave, as if I had slept through the transition. The cavern was well-lit with torches, each held by a stone figure attached to the walls and ceiling. So many Wühlenvogels flew the air and walked the ground of the city that the city itself appeared to flap and walk and shift around.

The Wühlenvogel holding me yelled out, barking a high-pitched yelp that I did not recognize from my studies. The floor of the city seemed to react, as every Wühlenvogel walking the surface took to the air. Hundreds of them flew circles around us, creating a funnel of Wühlenvogels, swirling like a whirlpool, blinding us to everthing in the city but its excited inhabitants. I could not tell if we still moved or if we were held in place.

We began to sink into the whirlpool of Wühlenvogels, down the funnel, toward the city floor. I had no notion of the city around us until I felt my feet touch the floor. My Wühlenvogel let go of me and I stood on my own. The one holding The Ancient One released him several feet above the floor, dropping him onto his own two webbed feet. The whirlpool of creatures surrounding us collapsed to the floor around us, revealing the whole of the city and its citizens.

There were no huts or houses within the city, like those in the village beneath St. Hildegard. Steinhörner revealed itself to me, all within the reach of my eyes, in a single, gawking rotation of my body. The scope, the scale of the city was much grander than I had imagined. There was one cavern wall behind me. To the other three sides, the city went on beyond my vision.

One old Wühlenvogel flew to me from high above. Those surrounding me pushed and scooted to make room for her. She clearly carried great weight among her kind. She did not eye me up and down. She did not inspect my armor or my Unicorn-horned sword.

She stared immediately and directly into my eyes and spoke in Wühlenvogel, "They were not dreams. You are not some phantom of our imaginations."

The Ancient One drew her attention, speaking to her in German, "She is real and she is here. Krummzahn, meet Verena, the Swan Knight and the only Queen of the Land and Shallow Waters."

Krummzahn lowered her head in homage, speaking in a reverent half-whisper, "Word of your victory in the canyon has already reached us here. We no longer answer to the snapping claws of Löwschock. Our loyalty has returned to the Queen of the Land and Shallow Waters. Again we fight with the Swan Knights."

At those words, every Wühlenvogel in the city bowed their heads. A traveling ripple of reverent nods waved outward from me, across the ocean of creatures surrounding us.

While they stood bowing I connected to their minds, thinking to them, "I am not a dream. I am here in body, standing among you in your own capital. Thank you. Thank you for your loyalty. Thank you for our victory in the canyon."

The Wühlenvogels slowly lifted their heads. The entire ocean of them fixed their eyes on me in silence. This silence held awkwardly for several long moments, until I thought to them while my lips motioned the words "I love you". Krummzahn looked to the city ceiling and began to howl. In waves, the rest of the city joined her, until the walls, floors, statues and torches seemed to be joining in the celebration.

After several minutes of howling, The Ancient One lifted his wing. The city fell silent.

He yelled, "The Queen and I must continue our flight and rejoin our friends by the river. You may join us, as many as may wish to fight with the Swan Knights again."

Krummzahn stretched her neck forward and kissed my cheek. Two other Wühlenvogels flew from the crowd and assumed the duties of escorts, grabbing me by my shoulders as before, and hoisting The Ancient One with a powerful Wühlenvogel tail. We exited the Wühlenvogel capital they way we entered it, through a tiny hole in the ceiling, leading us back into the open air and under the silvery moon of the Sweeter Realm.

CHAPTER 33

The Soaring Sage

WE FLEW EAST AND QUICKLY PASSED into Scherier land, toward Gralkirche, where we had left the Boots of Lohengrin with the task of reviving the ancient Scherier traditions. Before the tall spire of the shrine came into sight, I called to my Scherier friends. The Boots of Lohengrin had already returned from Gemeinsam, carried home by Unicorns. They mounted the tops of buildings, huts, and statues, where they reveled in the sensation of unified thought and awaited the sight of us flying overhead. As we flew low over the sacred city, they cheered in silence. Their praiseful proclamations were made menatally, while their round eyes looked upward and their wide smiles remained shut.

The Swan Knight's fly-over provided a great spark to the spirits and efforts of a holy order devoted to building and maintaining loyalty to the Swan Knights. No evidence of that spark was spoken to me. It could not have been expressed in words from any language. The fervor of their devotion came to me directly from their hearts. Many used the brief moments of united thought to express gratitude and affection for each other, passing what cannot be encompassed by language. I connected The Ancient One and our two Wühlenvogels with the experience, further endearing them to the Scheriers. Such love and loyalty can only be known by connecting to the minds of the Scheriers. Theirs are the truest hearts of any breed in the Sweeter Realm.

But one heart, one connection I made intimately. I made it briefly and kept it to myself. I saw Hüter standing atop the hut where he was nursed back to life by the Zweigwesens. In the time it took him to wave his hand at me, we ran each other through our memories together — from the moment I first saw his shriveled body in the circular room atop the spire to when I called for his mind from the grip of a Wühlenvogel just a few seconds earlier. I believe that in that moment, while he waved at me, no Scherier had ever been prouder to serve the Swan Knighthood.

We continued east to Eineklaue. Surviving Scheriers had filled the city from the surrounding marshes. It bustled exactly as I had imagined it. The torches were lit and even at that late hour the very ground seemed to ripple with the comings and goings of Scheriers, all on important errands in the middle of the night. As I united them, I realized that such oneness of mind is not only accomplished through my unique abilities. Although they did not see each other's minds, as I do, an undeniable and remarkable unity pulsed in a synchronized rhythm through the hearts of the city. When I connected to them, I felt more like a guest to the connection than like the Master of Ceremonies. They worked as one, they felt as one, even when they did not think as one. God bless them.

Before turning south toward Eierheim, the Eulesänger capital, I swept the Sicherheit Marsh with my mind, searching for any lost, forgotten and forlorn souls. I felt nothing from the marsh but the tiny creatures that have always called it home. Satisfied, we aimed for Eierheim.

The swan and I were both eager to see how they progressed since we left them. Many more birds than we expected filled the city. Most of them flew high to meet us and remained beside us, over us, and under us until we had flown well past the plateau that held the city nest. Many Eulesängers died in the canyon that afternoon. Several from Eierheim had left that night to claim their dead and nurse their wounded. They had not yet arrived in the canyon as we flew over their capital city.

The Eulesängers flying around us asked me to connect them to those who had left for the canyon. I still don't understand why, but I could not make a sound connection. Perhaps it was my exhaustion, or that of the Eulesängers who flapped without rest toward the canyon, but their thoughts came to me in disjointed bursts, in panting, weakened thoughts, like the words of a person who cannot catch his breath. And I was not even able to pass that along as I experienced it. Without intending, I thought about the many Eulesängers who accompanied us out of Gemeinsam, about those who lived and those I watched die. Those thoughts tranfered clearly through the connection that I had kept open. The bright flavor of celebration, as our Eulesänger escorts conducted us over their revived city, was seasoned with a distinct bitterness. But hopes were high, as high as their gratitude for the Wühlenvogels, which they sang in full-throated vigor to their two flying cousins.

Most of the Eulesängers accompanied us through the forest south of their capital, the very same forest we had fled for fear of the Wühlenvogels. Our fear of the Wühlenvogels and our retreat to the mountain east of the forest seemed like ages ago, as the tight but gently loving grip of our friends carried us safely through the forest, toward the building that the Brunnens had built for the Eulesängers. The building was empty. There was no more need of it, nor need to hide the Eulesängers from the vicious preditors that swept through their lands years earlier.

We flew over the abandoned building, across the Unicorn border, to the training fields of the young Unicorn warriors. The fields were empty, of course. All surviving Unicorn warriors, young and old, were camped outside of the canyon with Taufe, Cort, Lina, and the rest of my brave army, or guarding the revitalizing cities of the queendom. But as I scanned my eyes across the rolling fields, my imagination saw the training grounds full. I am not sure if I imagined the past or the future. In any case, the visions illuminated my spirits, while shouts of "Ohhl Ginshass Wahuff" echoed through my fantasy.

The fields yielded to the northern edge of the forest that leads into Brunnen land. I was curious to see the Brunnen capital, to see what progress had been made to the devastated city. We crossed the border and entered the city. In the months since we left it, it had been restored to its stealthy magnificence. At my command, the Wühlenvogels placed us down in the center of the city. The Zweigwesens had healed the trees wonderfully. The younger leaves and branches, smaller, lighter in color, were the only evidence that the old trees had suffered. No paintings or furniture lay strewn between the trunks of the building entrances. Had I never been there, I would have walked right through the city, believeing it nothing but a beautiful forest. However, I had been there, and my memory of it was vivid.

I did not call to them. I wanted to surprise the Brunnens by walking through one of their secret dooways, into one of their spectacular buildings. I ran to the building that we had worked through the night to make habitable. I walked between the twin trunks of the doorway, expecting to revel in the splendor. My eyes were not disappointed by the Brunnen efforts since we left the city — and my heart was not disappointed by the greetings we received by the Brunnens we met inside. Most were asleep when we came to the city. But our presence was not a secret for long. By the time I entered the building, a table had been made ready to receive us and refresh us.

The Brunnens soothed the tired wings of the Wühlenvogels. The touch of Brunnen hands was the perfect welcome for our flying friends, from the tyrannical grasp of Löwschock to the the loving acceptance of the Queen's subjects. The Wühlenvogels savored every moment, both for the sensual pleasures and for the love, trust, and admiration the touch of the Brunnens relayed. I cried when I peered into their minds and felt the sense of welcome, of forgiveness, and of old kinship rekindled. Gaining the Wühlenvogels from Löwschock was essential to us and our goals. But the Wühlenvogels viewed their change of allegiance as entirely their gain. It had taken them thousands of years to join the community of trust with the creatures of the Land and Shallow Waters. Losing it to their allegiance to Löwschock was devastating. Regaining it was the greatest gift they could have received, a gift they say I gave them, when I stood on Georg's shoulders in the canyon proclaiming myself.

The Brunnens were happy to welcome the Wühlenvogels, but happier to see the swan and me. They inquired over their spiritual leader, the venerable Taufe. They begged for details of every moment between our departure from them to the reunion of that night. They were particularly interested in the Holy Grail. They asked about its hiding place beneath the obelisk in Gemeinsam. We all speculated as to how Kandake hid it there without anybody knowing. They wanted to see the Grail, to hold the cup of Christ in their soft and devout hands, but were afraid to make such a presumption.

I did not need to invade their thoughts to read their desires. They wore it plainly on their faces and in the eyes that darted involuntarily toward the bag at my hip. I invited them to remove my armor and inspect the Grail themselves. Not since Parsifal, or the Apostles of the Lord, has the Grail been in more devoutly Christian hands. They held it and caressed it as if they held the fate of all living creatures in their tender palms. They understood the Grail better than I did, had a better understanding of its ultimate purpose. Their pious hearts related to the Grail, to its sense of sacrifice, of selfless rightiousness. I was in awe of the Grail. But they held it with such wonder in their eyes — expressions that I could not yet understand, expressions that betrayed a depth of understanding that was beyond me at the time.

As much as I appreciated the company of the Brunnens, it only made me long to see my home — what I had come to consider my home, St. Hildegard, where I awoke from the fall, met the Brunnens and the Eulesängers, where I killed my first enemy, where I received the first sapping of a young Zweigwesen, where I became a child of Taufe and The Ancient One, where I learned that Felix lives, and where I swore the Swan Knights' oath. The night pressed on and I wanted to return to the camp by sunrise. The Brunnens of Nährenstadt understood. They strapped me back into my armor and saw us on our way, back into the air in the grasp of our Wühlenvogels.

We flew south to St. Hildegard. But the homecoming was not what I expected. The Brunnen choir of St. Hildegard celebrated us with a concert in the cathedral that we could not stay to attend. We exchanged our greetings, received our blessings, and moved on to a destination that squeezed my anticipation more tightly with each thought. I wanted to go into Zweigwesen land and see my dear Felix. As we flew away from St. Hildegard, I connected the holy sisters in thought to their leader. The sudden connection surprised Taufe and pulled her from a solid sleep. But I maintained the link long enough for her to gather her wits, share a prayer with the sisters, and tell me that she loves me.

We flew toward Heiligborke, the main Zweigwesen medical center, where Felix recovered. On the way, I reconnected our minds to the Brunnens in the cathedral, as they sang a private concert directly into our minds. We did not hear the songs. That is not how it works. But we experienced the beauty of the music as perceived by the thoughts of the Brunnens who sang it. We felt the vibrations in our throats while they sang, though no sounds came from us but the flapping of Wühlenvogel wings and our low, almost held breath.

I did not announce our arrival before landing in Heiligborke. This was a surprise I wished to give Felix in person. I longed to see him more than I longed for the air that filled my lungs. But when we got there, he was gone.

"He left yesterday, my Queen," one of the Zweigwesens told me. "He left with a Unicorn, toward Gemeinsam, to meet with you there and help you in any way he can."

"How is he?" I asked.

"We have never seen such a recovery. The Federman's heart is a stout one, motivated by powerful faith and devotion."

I knew what motivated his recovery. He wanted to sacrifice himself more than he already had. In his selfless heroism, he needed to be at my side, serving the Land and Shallow Waters by serving its Queen. I allowed myself for a moment to recall his letter to me, to bend the words to my own desires and imagine that his devotion to me was more personal, more romantic. Still afraid of revealing such thoughts, I pushed them from my mind before I could accidentally transfer them to those minds around me.

I ordered an immediate departure and search for Felix. In the air, I found his mind. I asked where he was and told him that I would come to him.

"No," he thought to me, "it is not your place to come to me. You lead and you fight and you do the business of the Queen. If I wish to be useful to you, then I must seek you out. I must come to you. Please do not divert yourself for me. I will find you, at which point my devoted heart and weak body will be at your disposal."

I begged him, "Please do not put yourself in danger while you are not fully healed. We will fight the next battle without you. Your support is worth more to me than any exertion of your weakened body. I want to see you. But keep yourself from the danger."

"I have no intention of lifting a sword or riding a Unicorn into battle. I would be a hinderence. But I would like to see you, if only to remind you of what is true . . . that God brought you though the portal, called there by the voices in your Grail Blood. You were not brought here to lose. You were not brought here to die. You were not only brought here to achieve our victory, but to celebrate it afterward, and to lead us for countless years to come."

In this free exchange of thoughts, I tried not to be overcome with affection. The particular target of his adoration was still not clear to me. What did he see when he imagined me and what exactly was it that he adored so much — a Queen, a Swan Knight, a girl? Perhaps he saw them all as one, long before I did. I obeyed him, and we ended our long night with a flight back to the camp.

We wasted no time returning to camp, flying so high and so quickly that I could not distinguish any details from the blur of trees, hills, and streams beneath us. The moon had set and the last hours of the night were dark. In our increased speed, my feet — which had hung beneath me as we traveled though the night, as if I walked on the warm, thick air of the Sweeter Realm — lifted behind me, so I was almost horizontal.

As we approached the camp, in the wee hours before dawn, we slowed. The Ancient One stretched his wing and his prosthetic as far he could.

He told his Wühlenvogel, "Let me go."

"No!" I commanded bitterly. "We are too high above the ground."

The Wühlenvogel confessed that he had borne very little of his passenger's weight since the swan stretched out his wings.

"I think he can glide, my Queen."

"I can," The Ancient One insisted. "I cannot flap. I cannot leave the ground on my own. But now that I am in the sky, I think I can glide on my own."

"And if not," the Wühlenvogel added, "I am right above him. I will grab him before he falls."

I gave the swan a hesitant smile that spoke my blessing. The Wühlenvogel unwrapped his tail and The Ancient One began wobbling immediately. He wobbled and shook, but eventually leveled out and smoothed himself into a steady glide — on his own, with his Wühlenvogel hovering a few feet above him. I could not believe my eyes, nor could I believe the sensation in my heart from the sight. The Ancient One was flying, or at least gliding, on his own. Felix's sacrificial gift gained a new preciousness, a value well beyond the beautiful offering made in the Zweigwesen city more than a year and a half earlier.

The Wühlenvogels howled to the creatures in the camp, hoping that Löwschock himself would hear and look up. I don't know about the King of the Deep, but the kind creatures of our camp turned their unbelieving eyes to the sounds of the howling. They looked and saw their former

King, the noblest and most revered creature in the Sweeter Realm, sailing across the sky above them. The first rosy-orange of the new day's light shot from behind the horizon and across his feathers like fingertips across a harp. I heard nothing from the camp as they gawked in disbelief.

A sound rose up slowly from the camp, rising in volume and vigor, a strange sound, a word that none of them quite knew how to say. But they yelled it upward with their best efforts. It was The Ancient One's true name, a long, screeching train of vowels and consonants, the last remnants of a long-forgotten language. The Wühlenvogels and I joined in the cheer. It is difficult to say how much of the swan's glow came from his pride in that moment and how much of it came from the rising sun. But he was resplendent, regal, majestic, ageless and timeless. He wore the experiences and knowledge of his many centuries on each feather that quivered in the breeze.

"Alright," the swan told his Wühlenvogel, "I cannot land since I cannot flap my fake wing. You must bring me to ground."

With that command, the Wühlenvogel wrapped his tail around the swan and escorted him gently to the ground, beside me, in the middle of the camp, near Taufe and Georg, at the exact point from which we were lifted when our night's journey began. In the hearts of our army, over the losses and pain of the previous day, their victory was gilded by the sight of the flying swan, and their determination to defeat their enemies grabbed them by the skeleton and stiffened their posture.

The first light of that new day, the very light that shot across the swan's soaring feathers, could not have have proclaimed a brighter future if the wind had blown through a thousand trumpets. I was right. Seeing their teacher and former King soaring through the air had the effect I expected, bolstered infinitely by the swan's solo flight and the propitious timing of the day's first rays. The creatures shouted and demanded an immediate march on the Queen's Lake.

"No!" Georg shouted. "There is much for us to attend to first, and Verena and her travelers must sleep."

Until Georg's proclamation, I did not feel my own exhaustion. I had traveled through the night and hardly shut my eyes the night before. During the day in between, I fought a hard battle, running my body, heart, and mind through the most rigorous hours of my life. My knees buckled at the realization.

Georg determined that a select few warriors should be assigned to protect me, not just while I slept, but also during the fighting to come, and for the indefinite future. He hand-picked a corps of Unicorns, Zweigwesens, Wühlenvogels, and even a couple of Scheriers to be my personal guards.

"And how shall we denote them as your personal guards, my Queen? How will we distinguish them from the others?" Georg asked.

After giving it a few moments of thought, the perfect solution came to mind, "I can think of only one mark that speaks of protective devotion, of loyalty and sacrifice."

I reached to the ground and grabbed a handful of dirt. I smeared the dirt on the arms and wings of my protective corps, just like the stain on Felix's arm. I called it the "Mark of Sacrifice". My corps wore the mark and its accompanying name with pride and commitment. I fell asleep on the hill outside of the canyon, with The Ancient One and our two Wühlenvogels snuggled tightly to me, while my specially marked corps stood firmly as sentries surrounding us. I slept and I dreamed.

I dreamed of humans, and of Eden. The people were here, in the Sweeter Realm, alongside the native creatures. I thought I saw the past, the very distant past, before people left the Sweeter Realm. But then I saw people I knew, current people, my parents, Karl, Brigit, teachers and friends from school, all walking the paths of my queendom, alongside Taufe and The Ancient One, riding on Georg and Acheriel, and whistling with the Eulesängers.

When I awoke, my special guard still held a tight peremeter around us. They had removed the dirt I had wiped on their arms, or had smudged over it the same permanent, dark, tar-like clay that Felix had wiped from my armor with his feathers. They knew the significance of the "Mark of Sacrifice". They knew the reason I had chosen such an emblem for my special guard. They wanted it to be permanent and visable. They stained their arms and wings with loyal pride.

I told my dream to Taufe. She smiled, but offered none of her interpretations or prognostications, as she used to do. She had a contented expression of accomplishment on her lovely face. I interpreted her response as a validation of my dream, of some profound truth within it. In any case, she felt no need to explain any part of it to me.

I slept through the morning. By the time I was up and had eaten, the river canyon was emptied of searchers. The wounded were attended, the dead removed, and the mourners about the business of mourning. There was nothing to debate, no plans to make. The company went to the mouth of the canyon and met with those who had been dispatched to protect the searchers. Half of the company crossed the river. I remained on the left side, facing downstream. Georg held me. Lina sat on my lap. Acheriel rode near me. Cort and most of the Friends of the Scheriers gathered around me. Many Wühlenvogels flew over the river. Some walked among us. The Scheriers split evenly between banks. The Ancient One and Taufe rode Unicorns on the opposite side. We all marched toward the Queen's Lake, to recover our dead and to push Löwschock from the

Land, and if possible, from the Shallow Waters, back into the Deep, reestablishing the ancient border.

CHAPTER 34

A New Use for an Old Skill

As we walked toward the lake, Brunnens waded through the shallow banks, feeling for any change in temperature that might indicate the presense of Löwschock or his monsters. The river grew wide as we approached its mouth, dividing us by a barrier not easily crossed. It became so wide that we could hardly make out the figures on the other side. The separation worried the company, on both sides, and uneasiness rippled its way to the surface in the form of quickened breaths, wringing hands, and deep sighs.

What we needed was a sense of connection. So I connected us. I brought the minds of the entire company into one pool of thought. Although it strained *me*, it soothed the company instantly. They felt each other's shared anxiety, which morphed quickly into shared hopes and memories that quickened the steps of hooves and the flaps of wings.

A raucus mental rally grew and overflowed into the mouths of the creatures. Inspiring thoughts by one resulted in whistles and hollers by others. Through the unity came a strong sense of destiny, of invinsibility — until the thoughts of a single Brunnen fell upon the entire company at once. Her sensitive Brunnen legs felt the sudden chill of the Deep Waters. The monsters of the Deep were near. The sensation did not break my dear army's will. But it changed their thoughts from celebratory to determined.

My special guard gathered nearer to me. Eyes of every shape and size pierced the waters of the river for signs of violence and hatred. Teeth grinded and fists clinched. Acheriel ran ahead of the company, desperate to find Prische's body. We would not let him stand alone. The entire company on our side of the river matched his pace and raced with him to the edge of the lake.

There is an island in the lake, right where the Achima River drains. It is called Der Mutterleib des Flusses (The River's Womb), or simply Der Leib. Countless centuries of riverbed soil has been carried down from the Wendel Marshes, deposited just inside of the lake, forming the island. During the peaceful times, when the border to the Deep Waters sat placid, the island was a common meeting place between the creatures of the Land and those of the Shallow Waters. Kandake herself spent time there, hosting ceremonies to keep the Land and Shallow Waters united.

From the mouth of the river, we could see that many monsters of the Deep rested on the island's eastern beach. Several of them gathered closely together, hissing, clawing, and shoving at each other, as if fighting over a single meal. The keen Unicorn eyes of Acheriel saw what most of us could not. They *did* fight over a meal. They gathered around the body of Prische, biting and ripping at the remains of what was once the most beautiful Unicorn in generations. Acheriel's fury transmitted from his horn to me, where it reflected and magnified into the minds of the company. He rushed to the edge of the water, mindless of what might creep up through the opaque blackness.

Acheriel screamed at the monsters, drawing their attention from their meal, pulling, as he intended, those vicious claws and teeth from the body of his only lover.

Those thoughtless eyes turned all of their jealous, hateful rage toward us. We were a large company, and the addition of the Wühlenvogels turned the tide steeply in our favor. But the monsters on the island knew no fear. They dove into the water and swam toward us.

Many other monsters appeared beside them, as they resurfaced from the cold darkness of the lake's water. There was no posturing, no setting of opposing forces like the pieces in a chest match. The monsters from the island, still stained with Prische's blood, did not slow their approach until they were upon us.

Acheriel, still transmitting his flaming emotions to us all, rushed at them heroically. The rest of the Unicorns, including Georg and those carrying The Ancient One and Taufe, were swept into a reactive charge at the enemies. While being jostled around on Georg's back and being brought face to face with the blood-stained monsters, I tried to focus my mind to give our company its greatest advantage — united thought. I could not fully unite us, as I had to draw my sword and defend myself from the back of a rearing, jumping, fighting Unicorn. My special guard tried to surround me, but the battle was in full throes and chaos presided.

I jumped from Georg's back, allowing my guards to surround me. We fought together, killing all of the monsters that came at us from the island, but facing tireless waves of reinforcements from the lake. Slimy, scaly Deep monsters immerged, varying in form and dementions. Some I recognized, like the breeds we encountered on the Scherier border. Others were entirely new to my eyes. Most were larger than the Unicorns, but some were small.

One breed of monsters looked like flounder, no larger than a Vogelkröte, but with five or six large scales covering the back. Their gaping, sharp-toothed mouths ran the full width of their bodies. They were deep black, so that we did not see them until they were fully out of the water. Once on the sand, they contrasted with the pale beach, making them easy targets. Three of them gnawed at the armor of my legs before I noticed they were there. I kicked at them, but they were much heavier than their proportion would suggest. My guard fruitlessly kicked and hit at them. They tugged at the monters' bodies but could not pull their wide mouths from their grip on my legs.

They did not penetrate my armor with their teeth. But they held tight and pulled at me as they gnawed. Collectively, small as they were, they outweighed me and began to slide me into the lake. My entire guard surrounded me, trying to free me. I brushed my guard away with a firm command and held the tip of my sword against the back of one of the monsters. My guard piled onto the handle of the sword until their collective weight pushed the sword's tip through the thick scales. The little monster released me as it screamed. When I withdrew my sword and placed it onto the back of another, the other two released me and retreated into the water.

Our friends on the other side of the river fared well. When the scales of the monsters were too thick for the horns of the Wühlenvogels, the fingers of the Zweigwesens found softer targets. Eulesängers pecked at eyes and Scheriers clawed at fins. We lost very few as the waves of monsters crashed and died against us. But they continued to pour onto the shore in a long, ceaseless wave.

The fearful part of my mind suddenly turned to Taufe. My mind sought her and my eyes found her on the other side of the river mouth, grabbed by the hose-like arms of two serpents, the same breed I had buried beneath the floor of the Queen's palace, the same breed that abducted and drowned my dear Prische. Those wild, flailing arms had her tightly in their grip, wrapped several times around her like a boa constrictor. They stood tall upon the curved twin tails they used as legs, as they stood at the water's edge. They pulled Taufe toward their large snapping mouths.

The sight of them reminded me of my encounter with their kind, and my strange control of the sands of the palace floor. With the minutest thought, I grabbed their tails with the sand beneath them. I felt their scaly bodies through the sand, as if I squeezed them with my own fists. In the very same thought, I ordered a Wühlenvogel from my special guard to carry me across the river mouth, to Taufe's abductors.

My Wühlenvogel set me down with his tail while biting through the hose arm of one of the monsters. It hollered a wretched sound, more of anger than pain. I sliced through both arms of the other monster with my sword, so that only one arm remained wrapped around my dear Taufe. Taufe gripped the arm with both of her hands, and with those soft, nurturing, maternal hands, she ripped that arm in half. What remained around her fell limply to her feet.

The monsters continued screaming, armless and held by the sand beneath them. The Wühlenvogel wrapped his tail around the neck of one, and in an effort no more strenuous than a snap of a finger, he popped the creature's head from its body. I held my sword in front of me and ordered the sand to push the other monster forward. I held perfectly still, my sword pointing forward, as the sand slowly pushed the wiggling, screaming serpent to press against the point. I felt the tip of my sword exit through the back of beast. With the last of its dying strength, it snapped its long snout at my head. As its teeth came down toward me, I saw Felix's feathers, attached to the swan's fake wing. He slapped the monster's face with Felix's gift, spinning its head to the side. From that twisted position, it fell lifeless at my feet.

All remaining enemies on my side of the river mouth disengaged. They feared my control of the sand. They joined the continuing waves of attacks on the other side. As swimmers, they had no barriers to divide them, as the river divided us. I looked to the deep water of the river mouth and lifted the sand. Our barrier was bridged. The relentless river water pushed continuously into the lake, overtaking the path I had raised. But it remained shallow enough for us to cross. We flew, swam, ran, and were carried to the other side, to join against the continuing waves of enemies attacking our friends.

We were a reunited company, which made us a concentrated target for the smelliest, foulest creatures of the Deep, those mysterious breeds that had never seen the Shallow Waters, let alone the open air. They broke their ancient isolation on the order of their King, and came up from the depths at the mouth of the river. The air became rancid the moment they surfaced. They were joined by the one monster that I and our many Scheriers most loathed to see. The knobby-headed serpent rose from the surface. It moved toward us, rising from the water as it slinked toward the shore. As its bulbous body came exposed to the air, it stopped, out of the reach of our horns, fingers, claws, and sword. It had no need to come nearer. Its long tail, with its hard and sharp appendage at its end, rose up from the water and crashed down among us. Most got out of its way. But some did not. Some were crushed. Some were split open by the crashing weight of the tail's hard, sharp tip.

I reached for the Grail. My strongest desire was to fill the Grail with the water of the lake and serve it to the dead and dying. I had no time to keep that thought. The tail came crashing down again. The Eulesängers flew around the sepernt's head, trying to distract it from its viciously successful attacks on our tightly huddled company. The beast butted them into the water with its knobby head, where they fell victim to the other monsters. Some avoided the hit and continued to fly around. The Wühlenvogels joined them but fared no better. The scales of the serpent were too thick and hard for the natural weapons of the Wühlenvogels to do much more than distract.

Eulesängers and Wühlenvogels fell by the second. Their sacrifice bore little fruit and I would not have it. I called them back to us. As I did, and the surviving flyers came to shore, we were all met with a terrifying surprise. Two more knobby-headed serpents rose from the water on either side of the first. A fierce howl came from behind them. We looked to the howl and saw the King of the Deep sitting on the shore of the island like a throne.

All fighting stopped. All of our enemies retreated back into the water. There was no need for them. The mighty tails, hard horns, and sharp teeth of the Wühlenvogels had no effect against the thick scales of the knobby-headed serpents. No Unicorn horn could pierce them, no Zweigwesen fingers could reach their eyes. All other enemies joined Löwschock on the island to watch our hopeless fight against the three bulky beasts.

I tried to grab at them with the sand beneath them. They were too far out. The sand beneath them touched only the dark water of the Deep. It is only where the land and water meet in peace and respect that the sands obey the Queen.

The knobby-headed serpents resumed their attacks with their tales. But their hunger for Scherier meat made them blind to the rest of us. They had no interest in serving Löwschock, of defeating our army. They wanted only to satisfy their desire for the flesh of Scheriers. Their tails moved right over and around all other breeds, slapping at Scheriers and flicking their victims high through the air and into their mouths.

We all shared an equal love of the Scheriers, and we all wanted to defend them. But all attempts to break, bend, or even slow the thick, scaly, muscular tails of the knobby-headed serpents failed. I wacked at the tails as they swooped by me in persuit of the scrambling Scheriers. One familiar cry rose above the rest. Lina was hit in the back by a tail and flicked into the air. She landed in the mouth of the knobby-headed serpent on our left. My memory worked better on its own than it did under my conscious command.

Without consideration, I yelled, "Danke deinen Feinden" (Thank your enemies), the code I had arranged to trigger the debilitating hum of the Eulesängers. Just as planned, the Eulesänagers responded with their ancient ritual of thanksgiving. I felt the united tone sieze my gut and rattle my bones as it did before. And just as before, it affected all creatures except the Scheriers — including the knobby-headed serpents and the monsters watching from the island.

As I fell to my knees in pain, the knobby-headed serpent halted the descent of its upper jaw, stopping just short of crushing Lina. It opened its mouth wide again, howling in pain from the musical attack on its body, while Lina draped across a single tooth. The Scheriers of our company united in the strangest strategy. They all swam out to the serpent that held Lina in its mouth. They climbed its writhing body and crawled into its mouth while it howled.

Fifty, sixty, maybe more Scheriers hurdled the monster's row or lower teeth and joined Lina in its mouth. More and more of them joined. A steady flow of Scheriers crawled into the suffering creature's mouth, piled atop each other until the serpent could not have closed its mouth if it wanted to. The Eulesängers stopped their debilitating tones, frozen in astonishment at the actions of the Scheriers.

The knobby-headed serpent tried to bite down on the Scheriers. But such a mass of Scheriers in its mouth held its jaw as wide as it could stretch. They pushed against each other, stretching the monster's jaw beyond its limits. A garbled, muffled moan came from deep within the serpent's throat, accentuated by the cracking and snapping sound of its breaking jaw. The Scheriers broke its jaw completely, so its head flung backward and the top of its knobby skull touched against the back of its neck. The other two serpents were no longer paralized by the hum of the Eulesängers, but remained captured, as we all were, by the strange heroics of the Scheriers.

The broken beast yelled and the Scheriers dove from its mouth, into the lake. I called for a Wühlenvogel, who grabbed me by the shoulders of my armor and delivered me into the unnaturally opened mouth of the screaming serpent. I stood upon its thick tounge. Its mouth still hung open so wide that its upper teeth pointed upward to the sky. I drew my sword, leapt over the deep pit of its gaping throat, onto what was the roof of its mouth. I drove my sword downward, between my feet, through the roof of its mouth, and into its brain. The beast went limp and fell into the water.

The Wühlenvogel plucked me out of the air as I fell and returned me to the shore. The other two knobby-headed serpents began swatting at the swimming Scheriers, who by this point had begun to climb their backs and bellies. They swatted in fear, not in hunger. Every Scherier in our company was either in the water or climbing the serpents. The same strategy would not work again. The Eulesängers resumed their song, but the serpents were not affected as before. Scheriers climbed into their mouths a few at a time and were chewed and swallowed as quickly as they arrived.

One Scherier saw the futility in their efforts and spawned a new idea. He put to use that one skill for which he was famed throughout the Scherier homeland. The Old Digger climbed up the side of a serpent's head, over the top of its knobby skull, and to its eye. The Old Digger began to dig, to burrow as he always had, but not into the ground, not in the construction of a Scherier cave. He dug into the eye of the knobby-headed serpent. The beast screamed and shook. But the old Scherier was quickly waist-deep in the monster's eye.

Soon, the Old Digger disappeared entirely inside of the eye socket. The monster began to sieze and shake. Its howls turned to an airy, high-pitched whistle. It fell forward, toward the shore. Its head flopped on the beach mere feet from where I stood, its hollowed eye socket bleeding onto my feet. In its last moment of life, the serpent opened its mouth, extended its tounge, and let out its last breath.

From between its teeth, out of its mouth, crawled the Old Digger. He had burrowed his way through the eye, into the skull, where he tore through the monster's brain. He immerged from the mouth, with his old white fur drenched in blood, but with a satisfied and somewhat mischevious smile on his face. I shoved my sword through the other eyes and withdrew it with a triumphant and exaggerated fling, tossing a rope of blood in a semi-circle to my right.

The other Scheriers abandoned their attempts to get into the mouth of the last knobby-headed serpent. They all rushed for the eyes. Within seconds, dozens of Scheriers were crawling through its eye sockets and burrowing their way around inside of the creature's head. It fell much like its companion, belly down with its chin on the beach. Some Scheriers crawled out through the mouth, following the Old Digger's example. Some crawled out through the eye sockets, some through the flaring nostrils. The knobby-headed creatures were dead and Löwschock and his surviving minions on the island were in shock.

I took control of the sand beneath the monster nearest me. I lifted the giant knobby-headed, bleeding carcus with the sand and held it high to face Löwschock and the monsters on the island. They stared motionless as the oozing eye sockets stared them down, the monster perched atop a high pilar of sand on gruesome display. Löwschock's expression of hatred morphed into one of terror. I believe he was struck less by the carcus I held on high display, the strangely heroic tactics of the Scheriers, and more by the obedience of the sands beneath him to their Queen. He remembered being captured by Kandake. The incident with Gessner scared him back to the Deep for three hundred years. When a high pillar of sand lifted the knobby carcus at my command, the King and his minions dove from the beach of the island and disappeared into the water. They swam downward, quickly deep and far from the surface. The Shallow Waters grew clear and warm.

A Wühlenvogel circling above shouted, "The water is clear, my Queen! I can see deeply into the lake."

A familiar sight warmed my eyes as I peered into the water. A Schildbüffel came to the surface, followed by a few more, some Pfützeschilfs, Vogelkrötes, Glühenchor, and to my delight, the Queen's old jailor. They had been imprisoned in the Queen's Jail, awaiting execution and a ceremonious devouring. When the Shallow Waters went clear, the jail was abandoned by the cruel jailors. The captives were liberated. A Vogelkröte swam to the shore and crawled to my feet. I lifted my familiar friend to my chest. She was the same Vogelkröte I rescued in the palace. She told me that the Shallow Waters were clear, all the way down to the old border of the Deep Waters.

The old border was restored. The queendom of Kandake, the boundaries established when Queen Achima united the Land and Shallow Waters, were again as they had been. Few heard the soft voice of the Vogelkröte. So her news was passed from mouth to ear across the company. The Unicorns raised their horns high and passed the news to their kind across the Sweeter Realm. I performed the same service to all of the hornless creatures in my queendom.

Smiles widened and opened into cheers and ancient songs of celebration. I did not celebrate. I walked into the lake, waist-deep, and stared toward the center.

Through a half-laugh, Georg urged me, "Come out of the lake, Verena. Your duty here is done. The creatures of the Shallow Waters are liberated. They will come to you. You do not need to go to them."

Taufe ran her hand across Georg's mane and answered for me, "She is not going after them. She is going after Löwschock."

An eruption of protests flew into the air from the surrounding company.

The Ancient One, not fully understanding, but knowing better than to challenge Taufe's wisdom, brought his beak to nearly touch my nose, as he asked, "Do you really need to do this?"

Every creature in the company stood staring, stunned out of their celebratory moods by this surprise development. Only Georg remained animated.

He protested, "No, my Queen. The old borders are restored. Löwschock hides in fear behind the walls of his kingdom. You have done all that is needed of you and more. Now come out of the water and let me carry you back to St. Hildegard, where the Brunnens will soothe you and the Zweigwesens will heal you."

I turned to look sadly and soberly into his eyes. He knew that his arguments had not convinced me.

He continued, but with a cry in his voice that increased as he spoke, "You have the Holy Grail. You are the Queen of the Land and Shallow Waters. There is no reason for you to be in the lake. You have won. You have returned us to the peace we knew under Kandake. It will take a thousand years for Löwschock to rebolster his numbers. You control the sands. You hold the Grail. You have won everything."

I walked up to him, kissed him, pulled his horn to touch against my chest, and I spoke my thoughts through the mouths of the Unicorns in my company, "And then what? I was not led to the portal to restore the old borders. I was not brought here to liberate the creatures of the Shallows, or even to rescue the swan. I came to purify Eden."

As I said this, Taufe's skin rippled upward and she began to glow with a silvery auro. She reached to me, rubbed my neck and whispered, "Now you are beginning to understand your destiny."

I squeezed Georg's horn more tightly and continued speaking through the bearded faces of my Unicorns, "There is much more than a queendom at stake. The Sweeter Realm must be purified and prepared for God's will, for a reunion that has been an eternity in planning. It is true that the Land and Shallow Waters is pure and peaceful. But the Sweeter Realm still suffers hatred and anger in the hidden corners of its Deep Waters. Eden must be made ready. The Sweeter Realm must host a holy reunion. The grievance will be ended and the gate will be opened. Everything that has ever been written, spoken, sung, and performed has been leading to that."

None but Taufe and the Brunnen clerics really understood. The Ancient One connected the dots and allowed his faith to fill in the picture. His faith told him that I was right and that my duty to the Sweeter Realm was not yet completed. He reluctantly accepted, but his fear for me had never been greater.

CHAPTER 35

The Final Confrontation

MOST OF THE COMPANY DID NOT UNDERSTAND what was going on. They did not realize what my words meant for my immediate future, let alone for the ultimate will of God. The realization that the fight against Löwschock was not over dawned upon them gradually. The anxious sobriety of battle preparations returned to their hearts and minds.

My special guard gathered tightly around me, enveloping my dearest ones — The Ancient One, Taufe, Georg, Acheriel, Lina, and Cort.

Lina reminded me, "None of us can dive into the Deep Waters. If we could, we could never defeat Löwschock there. We must rely on our swimmers."

"No," The Ancient One contested, "There are not enough of them, and they are much frailer than our enemy."

In a somber, ghostly tone, I answered, "None of you will go, and neither will the creatures of the Shallow Waters. I will go. I will go alone."

Every member of my special guard dissented emphatically. Too respectful to fight with me, they took their frustrated fear out on each other, snapping, shouting, and blaming. The pathetic spectacle would have nauseated me, had it been possible for me to feel any sicker than I felt then. My mind was trying to resign itself to my own death.

The turmoil within me began to drown all of my senses. The arguments, the questions, the pleas, and the proclamations that swirled around me muffled in my ears. I felt no breeze on my skin. My nose lost the smell of the scene. While I stood stone still in the sand, with the lacerated bodies of friends and the rancid, slimy scales of our vanquished enemies littering the beach, my heart and mind screamed in fear of my own death.

Taufe looked at me with reassuring eyes. He skin smoothed and I began to see the mountains in the background behind her through her fading torso. She stood tall among the chaotic crowd and silenced them with a simple and softly stated question, "She has found the path placed before her by God. Do you believe that the Lord has brought her here to fail?"

"No," The Ancient One answered the question not intended for him, "he has brought her here to succeed, but not necessarily to live. I believe you both, that this must be done, and you have my prayers and support. But I fear for Verena's life. For fifteen hundred years, I have prayed that I would not live to see the end of the Swan Knights. But that is not what pierces my old heart. I would suffer the loss of a hundred Ludwigs, Alberts, Adolfs and Ottos, a hundred Elsas, Lohengrins, and Parsifals, a hundred Brunhildes, before I could bear losing one Verena. Oh my most precious treasure, Verena."

I had no idea that he had come to love me so, that his regard for me could compare with his adoration of Elsa or Parsifal and his love of Brunhilde. Every language on both sides of the portal could combine efforts and still fail to describe my sense of humble honor at his words. My heart swelled and nearly burst for love of him. It pushed the turmoil out of me, so that all that filled me was my love for The Ancient One and the other fine creatures of the Sweeter Realm.

Georg, still more of a friend than a visionary, resumed his protest, "So that is it? We sacrifice Verena? For what? For whom?"

His pitiful cry would have ruptured my spirits just moments before. But the swan's words elevated me. Georg's cries were endearing to me. I saw his waving horn and shaking beard as a display of his love.

He continued, "I refuse to believe that she came through the portal to die at the bottom of the lake. She is our Queen and our most important citizen. What could be more important than her life?"

Taufe climbed upon his back and wrapped her arms around his neck. She slowly ran her nurturing hand up the front of his neck, around the side of his face, to the base of his horn. It seemed to take an hour for her her long fingers to wrap, one at a time, around the horn. She buried her head into his mane and closed her eyes. I connected to them both and received her private message to him. She interrupted his thoughts of bitter regret, as he rebuked himself mercilessly for not crossing the water to the island to kill Löwschock while he was still on the shore. He played the scenario several times through his head. Each time it weighed more. It sat more heavily on his poor, crushed and crippled conscience. He cursed himself for everything he could have done to alter the situation. He blamed himself for what he assumed was my inevitable death.

With her grip on the horn, Taufe thought directly into his mind, "Strong, good, loyal friend, there are countless souls at stake. God's will is being done. Do you think my heart does not break for her? But she, like all of us, is just a tool of God. The tool will serve the purpose of its creation. Let us pray together that it remains unbroken when its work is done."

I saw little chance of that. But Taufe's thought to Georg solidified my sense of destiny and the swan's words filled me with love. I was still afraid to die, deeply regretful for the many things I would never again do and the many people I would never again see. I wished to see Felix one more time, to thank him and confess the love that my conscious mind had avoided embracing. I looked at Lina and Cort. They held each other and cried, alternating between staring at me and burying their faces into each other. I looked at Acheriel. He stood stunned, looking more through me than at me. I dipped slightly into his thoughts and caught a glimpse of his meandering recollections of me. He thought about meeting me outside of Rüdiger's cave, and of discussing me with Felix, in the center of the dry lake basin, while Pfützeschilfs slept on my belly.

I thought about my family. An intense swell of love for my little brother brought the smell of his hair vividly into my memory, as if I had my face pressed against the top of his head in a deep inhale.

"I might not live to see God's reunion with his people," I thought, "but I can die knowing I gave it as my last gift to Karl."

The thought did not alleviate my nauseating fear. But it gave me resolution. I was not in acceptance of my death, but I was in resolution of my course of action.

There was no plan, only that I was to enter the lake alone and face Löwschock. I did not know how I would survive. But I had the Grail. It had done little to serve me to that point. I trusted that it would serve me now. I tried not to think about it. We all did. We trusted that God would guide me to his will.

Several Zweigwesens commited what they feared would be their last duty to me by building a boat to carry me to the center of the lake. They constructed an exact replica of Ludwig's boat in the Venus Grotto. They worked all night to perfect it.

None from my company left the shore of the lake. We camped there that night. During the night, others arrived from across the Land and Shallow Waters. They knew that there was nothing they could do to assist me, that whatever struggles the next day would bring to me were mine and mine alone to bear. But they came to sing to me, to touch me, to kiss me and pray with me while they still could. At Taufe's command, Wühlenvogels carried the entire choir of St. Hildegard from their holy cathedral to the shore of the lake.

I slept little that night. I wanted to savor every moment of their lives and mine. None of us could imagine how I would survive. But their faith in God and the Grail was strong. I tried to raise my faith to match theirs. I fell asleep just a couple of hours before dawn. They let me sleep well into the next day. I said nothing to anyone when I awoke. I allowed the Friends of the Scheriers to silently strap me into my armor, fasten the sword to my hip, and loop the handle to the Grail bag over my shouder.

I began to resolve that my death that day was a certainty, to abandon the last flickering hope that I might survive. I felt my heart pounding in my chest, and I counted the beats silently, wondering how many more it would have. I did not want to die. Small droplets of self-pity trickled from the depths of my heart to my conscious thoughts. What would kill me? How would I die? Would I drown or would the crushing jaws of Löwschock end my life? These were the thoughts that swelled in me, evicting all other thoughts and feelings.

I cried internally, but showed no sign of it for others to see. I blocked my thoughts entirely from them all. One glimpse at my immense fear would have broken them. I refused all offerings of food, knowing I would not be able to keep it down, or even hold it to my lips. I gave no farewells, no kisses that day. I could barely stand to look into their eyes. I wanted to cry on my mother's shoulder, to feel my father's hand cupping the side of my head, to kiss my little brother, to fall asleep in the swan's embrace and awaken in my parents' bed.

I walked alone from the camp toward the water, as if walking to the gallows. The slope of the beach to the water was gentle. But with each step, I felt like I fell fifty feet. Each step toward my assumed death shook my skeleton and echoed demonically in my head. Each breath was harder to draw than the last. I felt my heartbeat in my throat, like each beat closed a shutter in my neck and my breaths had to be drawn in the moments between beats.

The Ancient One waited for me on the edge of the water, strapped to the boat. I mounted the boat and shivered inside of my armor as the swan gracefully pulled me far from shore. I could barely see the silhouette of the land and trees, on any side of me, when we stopped. The Ancient One turned his head, at the end of his beautiful long neck. He opened his beak to speak to me. Before he could make a sound, I leapt from the boat and was deep in the water, sinking quickly from the weight of the armor.

I did not struggle to hold my breath. I felt quite comfortable until I reached what was the clear and distinct border between the Shallow Waters and the Deep. The moment I crossed the border, I sensed that I had crossed from peace into chaos, from goodness into evil. My chest began to ache from my held breath. A wave of violent shivers shot through me as I relived Prische's death. I missed her and I loved her, and I almost inhaled the black water as my sobbing chest begged for the air to cry.

The water of the Deep was thicker, almost syrup-like. I saw nothing but the blackness that began just a few feet in front of me. Instinctively, I held out the Holy Grail. The moment it left he bag, the water around it cleared and warmed, like the water of the Shallows, in a halo around the Grail. My descent slowed. I moved in the direction of the Grail, wherever I held it. I also began to see farther into the Deep, as the halo around the Grail encompassed me and spread farther, to light the way in front of me with clear, bright water. The water surrounding the Holy Grail was as bright and clear and the brook where I met the Glühenchor.

With my focus on the Grail, I felt no impulse to inhale. I descended until my feet hit bottom. The Grail illuminated the lake bed around me to expose the bodies of hundreds of creatures of the Sweeter Realm. There was such fear and despair in their lifeless faces. I stared in a horrified trance until I heard a sound above me. I looked up and saw eyes, dozens of eyes all aimed at me. They swirled and darted around but remained fixed on me, filled with hatred, anger, and a biting, clawing, scratching sense of revenge. Through them all burst suddenly one larger pair of eyes. As it grew closer, I saw that those devilish eyes belonged to a creature horrifyingly familiar to me. It was the beast. The beast that killed my Ludwig. The beast that killed the Queen. It was Löwschock.

He was upon me in a flash, in the very moment that I recognized him. I held the Grail out in front of me with my left hand and drew my sword with my right. I tried to swipe at Löwschock, but my sword moved in slow motion through the water. Löwschock entered the Grail's halo, revealing himself in near, intimate, and horrifying detail. He wrapped himself around me and squeezed all of my held breath out of me. I looked up and saw the last of my breath bubble upward, out of the Grail's bright halo, and disappear into the blackness above me. For a few seconds, I fought against my insticts to inhale. But I knew that I was losing that fight. I beat against the King with the handle of the sword, to which he only tightened the grip of his tail. With one claw, he gripped my shoulder, with the other he drummed tauntingly against the back of my armor.

I felt every fiber of muscle in Löwschock's powerful body, as he wrenched more tightly around me, so tightly that I could feel the scales of his tail through the armor, against my skin. As I felt myself slipping away, I held the Grail to my face and inhaled the water from the cavity of the Holy Cup, as deeply as the monster's grip would allow. If my last breath would be the water of the Deep, it would be from the Cup of Christ. The sensation in my throat and chest was indescribable. It did not feel like water, nor like air. It was shocking but not painful, and it dispelled for a moment my fear of dying. I felt the love of God course through me, a sensation of warmth beyond anything I had ever imagined and far beyond the reach of any linguistic description.

The beast sank his fangs through my armor and into my left upper arm. He released my body with his tail and shook me violently with his teeth embedded in my bone. I lost grip of the Grail and could not see in which direction it went. Löwschock withdrew his fangs from me, spilling from the wound a small river of my blood that streamed from my arm like a ribbon. Löwsckock bit into my opposite shoulder, while I felt the biting, prodding, pulling and squeezing of other monsters all over my body.

Pierced and yanked, jerked about, I did not look at Löwschock or at the other serpents around me. I watched the blood that streamed from the first bite on my arm. The blood pooled into a perfect circle of bright red, a few feet from me. A crackling sound, like that of splitting stone, preceded the transformation of the blood into a hole in the water, into a Grail Blood portal. It put off a bright light, pale blue with traveling waves of dark blue and green rippling across it.

The hole had a strong suction effect, pulling the very darkness into it and lightening the water around it. I laid suspended in the water, unaffected by the pull. The swirling and darting eyes surrounding me were pulled toward the hole. Fangs were ripped from my legs and arms by the pull. The dark, nasty, brutish figures of the Deep's foulest monsters came clear to me just as each flew through the portal and disappeared. I felt a large body brush against me, squirming and fighting the pull of the portal. It was Löwschock. As his tail end went through the portal, he swiped an angry claw at me. In that evil grasp was the Grail. I reached out and pulled the Grail from the swinging claw.

When Löwschock was halfway through the portal, struggling ferociously against the pull, I thought about my lost loved ones. I thought about Rüdiger. Just as my imagination grew so saturatingly real that I could hear his voice ringing in my ears, the portal changed shapes. It transformed into the shape of my first Scherier friend. The Rüdiger shaped portal nodded to me as Löwschock still swam frantically, half consumed by the portal. The Rüdiger shaped portal grew a spiraling horn, then transformed into the silhouette of Prische. It reared its Unicorn head and returned to a perfect circle. A sudden enlightenment fell on me. I had transformed the shape of the portal, as Elsa did, into the shapes of my loved ones.

I stared at the portal and imagined a very different shape, a vicious shape. In accordance with my thoughts, the circular portal grew fangs on the top and bottom. I wished the fanged portal to close on Löwschock. I wished it hard — and it closed. Without moving, using only my desperate desire, I opened and closed the portal repeatedly, watching it chew away at the monster's mid-section. The portal finally snapped completely shut. It disappeared completely and I watched Löwschock's lifeless upper half drift by me, pulling behind a trail of blood, like the tail of a kite. His lower half was nowhere to be seen.

My vision grew dim. But before it went black, I noticed that the water around me was clearing. The clearing waters moved outward from the obvious source, the Holy Grail that I still held in my left hand. The thick, syrup-like water lightened. There was no more distinction between the Deep and Shallow Waters. The creatures on the floor of the lake began to revive and float to the surface. Eden was clean. I smiled and gave up my life to the lake, knowing I had served God and my queendom well. Before I faded, I sent one quick thought to Taufe, not sure if she would receive it.

I simply thought, "I did it."

I awoke on my back, on the shore of the lake, my legs still submerged in the shallow water and being gently licked by the tiny waves that came ashore. There was no pain in my arms and legs, from the bite-wounds I had suffered. My head was turned hard to my right when I opened my eyes. I saw the Scheriers standing there with their low faces, their eyes to my eyes. Behind them were hundreds of inhabitants of the Sweeter Realm, of all different kinds. Beside me was my armor, removed from me and stacked neatly, just as I found it on the day I came through the portal. The Grail was nowhere near me. The empty Grail bag remained strapped to me. I turned to my left and saw The Ancient One. He caressed my cheek with the soft feathers just under his beak.

He pulled away and asked me, "Do you know where you are?"

I answered, "I am by the lake."

He asked, "Do you know *who* you are."

I answered, "I am Verena Beth, . . . a daughter, . . . a friend, . . . a student."

I looked around me at the faces of all of the beautiful and kind creatures of the Sweeter Realm, and I continued,

"And I am Queen of the United Land and Waters of the Sweeter Realm."

A bursting clamor erupted from my last word. With boisterous activity and united singing, the creatures of the Sweeter Realm, my subjects, celebrated their liberation so loudly that I thought it might be heard echoing in the Venus Grotto at Linderhof.

Through the noise, I asked The Ancient One, "The Grail? Where is the Holy Grail?"

"You surfaced without it. It is under the protection of the lake now. And the lake is under your protection, my Queen."

I did not have time to ponder his words. A familiar figure parted the crowd — a feathered figure — a brilliantly bright and beautiful figure, shining and shimmering in the sun. Felix walked slowly, calmly, and gently to my side, silencing the cheers in his wake as he passed through the crowd. I don't remember him reaching for me. I don't remember losing contact with the sand. But suddenly I was cradled in his arms. The small, soft feathers of his chest and arms seemed to individually stroke me, to lovingly caress me. I curled into the smallest dimensions I could manage. He still wore the black stain across his right upper arm. I stroked the stained feathers tenderly and affectionately. To me, those blackened feathers were more beautiful than the most dulcet sunset. He did not wear a stain, but a badge that reminded me of his devoted goodness. I was much more than happy to see him. As I surrendered myself entirely to his arms, his embrace was the very air that kept my lungs in motion, kept my blood pushing through my veins. I rubbed my cheek against the feathers of his chest and shoulder.

He whispered in my ear, "I love you, my Queen."

Without thought, I responded, "I love you, my King."

It was not until the sharp gasps of the surrounding creatures settled into astonished murmurs that I realized what I had said — and what it meant for me, for him, and for the Sweeter Realm. I do love him. I suppose in the depths of my mind, hidden there by the trials we faced together and apart, I have always loved him. I have always thought of him as the other half of me, as my husband and my King, though he has always been so adoringly subordinate. No, not subordinate — supportive, elevating, enriching, improving — everything that a husband is supposed to be.

I would not leave his embrace. By the time the sun set on that day, The Ancient One stood before us, at the threshold of the Queen's lakeside palace, supporting our held hands with his wing, uniting us as wife and husband, as Queen and King. At that moment, I truly treasured my husband. But in treasuring him, I had to take tally of all of the husbands and all of the wives that did not live to see that sunset. Many beautiful creatures had been lost. The constant companionship of my dear friend, the widowed Lina, kept that thought ever on my mind.

I recalled a quotation from St. Benedict, taught to me by Taufe, "He should know that whoever undertakes the government of souls must prepare himself to account for them."

Oh, I accounted for each soul that I lost. The remembrance of each eye that lost the light of life stabbed at my heart ferociously. There was so much to mourn. But there was so much to celebrate. I also accounted for each soul that remained. The shallow water surrounding the entrance to the palace was filled with the wet survivors of Löwschock's cruelty and the appitite of his army. Schildbüffels and Pfützeschilfs, Vogelkrötes and Glühenchor reveled in the clear warmth of the peaceful waters of the Queen's Lake.

As I kissed my husband, it started to rain, the heaviest rain I had ever seen. But between the heavy drops, there was a creamy, soothing sweetness to the air that was peacefully, blissfully nurturing to the nose and lungs. The Sweeter Realm seemed to be smiling through its tears. It accepted its losses without forgetfulness. The Sweeter Realm, like I, adhered itself permanently to the sorrows of the past, while embracing the promises of a bright and peaceful future.

It is with that extreme duality of heart that I stared at the rain as it ran off of the feathers of Felix's chest, neck, and face. The drops seemed to magnify in my eyes as they ran across his feathers like fingers across a piano. Despite all that I had seen, my imagination could never have envisioned such beauty, nor my heart so much love. With gratitude to God that was almost as crippling as it was enlivening, I took my husband into the palace and began our life together. Together we united the Sweeter Realm. Together we reigned over it. And that is how I remained for years — a queen, a wife, a friend, but primarily a Swan Knight, performing the task performed by every Swan Knight before me — protecting the Holy Grail until God recalls it into the service of the righteous.

Glossary
(Warning: Plot points revealed in definitions)
Sweeter Realm Creatures:
Acheriel [a x e: r i: ɛ l] – A Unicorn, light-grey with a salt-and-pepper mane and beard. His horn is brilliant white with blue-grey hints in the depths of the recesses of the spirals. He is the husband of Prische and the first Unicorn Verena meets in the Sweeter Realm. He knew many of the Swan Knights well. He also served as a teacher to the young Unicorn warriors. He is one of the fastest, strongest, and wisest of the Unicorns. He is the best friend of the Federman, Felix.

Bechtold and Hildemar – Two Schildbüffels that Rüdiger called from a shallow lake. They joined Verena's effort to free The Ancient One from the Queen's Jail.

Brunhilde [b r ʊ n h ɪ l d ə] – The daughter of Tannhäuser and his Brunnen lover, born deep in the Brunnen wilderness and raised alone with her parents until her mother died and her father abandoned her. She was adopted by the Swan Knight family and raised by The Ancient One. Among her amazing talents is the ability to jump high into the air and float weightless, and to sense the nature of human hearts. Duke Ludwig I built the castle for her, over the ruins of which King Ludwig II built Neuschwanstein Castle.

Brunnens [b r ʊ n ə n s] – Creatures of the Sweeter Realm, with tall, feminine figures, and almost clear bodies that ripple like water when they move. They have two throats through which they speak in sweet melodic tones.

Cort – A Friend of the Scheriers, a nomadic breed and Verena's first acquaintances in the Sweeter Realm.

Eulesängers [ɔY l ə s ɛ ŋ ɐ s] – Creatures of the Sweeter Realm, brown, ankle-high birds, with awkwardly large wings, a bushy tail, and a hooked beak like an owl's. They communicate in high-pitched, high-spirited whistles. They are the favorite breed of Rudolf I.

Federmensch [f e: d ɐ m ə n ʃ] – A nomadic breed of feathered men and women. They live mostly on the northwestern side of the Queen's Lake. They are slightly shorter than the average human, but renowned for amazing physical strength.

Felix – A Federman, the first of his kind to meet Verena. He is an old friend of the Unicorn Acheriel and spends more time roaming the Land and Shallow Waters with Unicorns than roaming the Nomadic Belt with his own kind.

Florenna – A Brunnen who had been living in the wilderness outside of the Brunnen capital until Verena and her company arrived. She accompanied Verena on the rest of her journey, and stood beside the Queen's Lake while The Ancient One pulled Verena to face Löwschock.

Friends of the Scheriers – A nomadic breed that lives near the shore of the Queen's Lake. They have no names for their breed or their individuals, until Cort, the Friend of the Scheriers who befriended Verena on her first day in the Sweeter Realm.

Glühenchor [g l y: ə n ʃ o: r] – A breed of Shallow Waters creatures native to a particular pond. Each evening, they produce a glow from their bodies and an accompanying musical tone. The corps of them unite in lights and harmony to the delight of visitors from across the Land and Shallow Waters.

Hüter [h y: t ɐ] – Member of the Scherier religious order, the *Stiefel von Lohengrin,* the only monk of the order to survive the war with the Deep. Verena found him in the steeple of the holy temple in Gralkirsche.

Kandake [k a n d a k ə] – The Queen of the Land and Shallow Waters. She followed the Unicorn Achima as

Queen. She is a creature of the Shallow Waters of the breed of Wassermönche.

Knobby-headed Serpent – A creature of the Deep Waters. It has a large, knobby, scaled head. Each scale on its head is larger than a human hand. Its mouth is wide, with its lips wrapping around to nearly meet at the back of its enormous head. It has a bulky, rounded body with no arms or fins and a long, wrapping tail, which begins fat at the base of its bulky torso, and narrows as it winds and wraps, until it comes to a fine point at the tip of a crusty appendage that looks like an arrowhead. It is commanded by the King of the Deep Waters. It has a strong affinity for Scherier meat.

Krummzahn [k r ʊ m ts a: n] – Old Wühlenvogel leader, known well by The Ancient One. She meets Verena after the battle at the Achima River.

Lina [l i: n a] – A Scherier, dear friend of Verena, wife of Rüdiger, niece of the Old Digger.

Löwschock [l œ v ʃ ɔ k]– King of the Deep Waters, a large, clawed, horned water creature with the face of a lion, muscular arms and shoulders, a scaled tail with short, knobby legs and webbed feet.

Pfützeschilfs [pf ʏ ts ə ʃ ɪ l f s] – Creatures of the Shallow Waters of the Sweeter Realm. They are narrow and tubular, one to two inches long, with wings and one single, bulgy eye. They speak in high-pitched squeals. After the war with the Deep, they lived mostly in small puddles on the Land.

Prallen and Stossen [p r a l ə n] [ʃ t o: s ə n] – Two Scheriers that Verena met in the Sicherheit Marshes. They were long-time friends of The Ancient One and of the Swan Knights. They fought in Albert's Battle.

Prische [p r ɪ ʃ ə] – A pure white Unicorn, the most beautiful in a thousand years. She is the wife of Acheriel. She was chosen to carry Verena during the procession to find swimmers to rescue The Ancient One.

Queen/King of the Land and Shallow Waters – the ruler elected by the creatures of the Sweeter Realm to rule the known region on the other side of the portal, excluding the Deep Waters. The Queen from the shallow waters, who ruled during the lives of the Swan Knights was named Kandake. When she was killed by Löwschock, The Ancient One was elected King. After the presumed death of The Ancient One, the Kingship fell to Swan Knight, Ludwig II. When Ludwig died, the Land and Shallow Waters was without a Queen. When Verena came through the portal and resumed the line of Swan Knights, she inherited the title as the presumed heir of Ludwig.

Rüdiger [r y: d ɪ g ɐ] – A Scherier, dear friend of Verena, husband of Lina. He and Lina are the first Scheriers to meet Verena. He is spirited, even for a Scherier, with unlimited faith in the God, the Queen, and the Swan Knights. He is bound more by love than tradition and is remarkably brave.

Scheriers [ʃ e: r i: r s] – Creatures of the Sweeter Realm, with white hair and short, flat bodies. They are social creatures who love to wrestle. After The Ancient One, they were the first breed to meet the Swan Knights. They gifted a boulder of ore from their homeland to Elsa. Lohengrin forged it into Elsa's armor. Verena found the armor on her first day in the Sweeter Realm. The Scheriers are burrowers. They live mostly in caves of their own construction. They are avidly loyal to the Swan Knights and to the Queen of the Land and Shallow Waters.

Schildbüffels [ʃ ɪ l t b ʏ f ə l s] – Creatures of the Shallow Waters, large, with deep shells like turtles. They have wide heads like a buffalo, but with two tightly curled horns, like a ram.

Schwerthorn [ʃ v ɛ r t ɔ r n] – Large Unicorn Verena met in the Wendel Marsh, a retired Unicorn warrior who served Linderhof during Veronika's knighthood.

Senische [z e: n ɪ ʃ ə] – A Unicorn from before recorded history. According to legend, she was the first to use the horn to communicate. She held the spirits of all Unicorns in her horn, protecting them with her own goodness from the chaos that plagued the Unicorns. Once order was restored, she returned the spirits by touching horns with each living Unicorn. It is said that the horn-shaped obelisk that stood in Gemeinsam was a replica of her horn. She is known as the founder of the Unicorn collective.

Sinsach [z ɪ n z a x] - A sharp-witted, rather philosophical Unicorn that Verena sent to the dry lake basin to retrieve Lina and bring her to St. Hildegard.

Spalte [ʃ p a l t ə] – A Zweigwesen who died in the Sicherheit Marsh, killed by one of the Deep creatures that guarded the Scherier border. Verena met her during the weeks she learned the Swan Knight history, in the Zweigwesen city, before the fall from the cliff.

Stiefel von Lohengrin [ʃ t i: f ə l f ɔ n l o: ə n ŋ r ɪ n] – Literally *The Boots of Lohengrin*, an order of ordained Scheriers living in Gralkirche. The order was established shortly after Lohengrin's death. The monks of the order school every Scherier born to the Sweeter Realm. Their primary purpose is to maintain Scherier devotion to the Swan Knights.

Taufe [t aʊ f ə] – A Brunnen who lived for many years with Conrad of Wittelsbach, Archbishop of Mainz and Second-in-Training under Otto I. While with Conrad, she met Hildegard of Bingen, the Benedictine nun who received messages from God that related to the Sweeter Realm. When Conrad died, Taufe lived in the wild near Aischquelle, at the source of the river Aisch. When she returned to the Sweeter Realm, she was eventually granted the title of Abbess at a holy site dedicated to St. Hildegard. She was chosen to be Verena's moral tutor during her training.

The Ancient One – Creature of the Sweeter Realm, a giant swan, the first creature to meet Parsifal. He took the Grail from Parsifal and gave it to the Queen. He is the teacher of the Swan Knight children and the keeper of the Grail Blood history. He taught German to the Queen and the other creatures of the Land and Shallow Waters. He was elected King of the Land and Shallow Waters after the death of Kandake. He was abducted by Löwschock and imprisoned in an underwater jail. Upon his abduction, Ludwig II became King.

Unicorns/ Die Einhörner [d i: aɪ n h œ r n ɐ] – Creatures of the Sweeter Realm, single-horned goat-like creatures, with shaggy, bearded faces, the height of a horse, but with a slightly sloping back and narrow hips. They can communicate with each other and others through a touch of their horns. For many hundreds of years, they were the primary sentries of the portal valley.

Vogelkrötes –[f o: g ɛ l k r ø: t ə s] – Creatures of the Sweeter Realm, literally Bird Toad. They live in the Shallow Waters. They are the first wet creatures encountered by Conrad Gessner. Several of them joined Verena in her efforts to free The Ancient One.

Wassermönchc [v a s ɐ m œ n ç ə] – Breed of Shallow Waters creatures. Queen Kandake was of the breed. Löwschock hunted them to extinction following his return through the portal.

Wühlenvogels [v y: l ə n f o: g ə l s] – Sweeter Realm creatures. They are birds, with long necks and the snouts of wolves and jaws just as powerful, teeth just as sharp. They stand just shorter than The Ancient One. They have two hard, curled horns on their heads, which they use, with the powerful swing of their long necks, to smash the skulls of their enemies. They have large, clawed feet, which they use to burrow into the homes and hideaways they make underground. They have long powerful tails that can wrap and squeeze, with amazing dexterity and strength, whatever they choose to grab. They live in large underground cities, which they burrow with their collective efforts in a few days' time. They are hunters, predators. They built Einigkeitstadt, the city beneath the Black Forest. Their laws demand a fierce oath of loyalty to the Queen/King of the Land and Shallow Waters. Upon the presumed death of The Ancient One and the death of Ludwig II, their oath transferred to the only remaining King in the Sweeter Realm — Löwschock.

Zweigwesens [ts v aɪ g v e: z ə n s] – Creatures of the Sweeter Realm, branch-thin, chest-high, covered from head to toe in soft, almost glowing, coarse, brownish-orange hair. Their hair looks like tree bark on their thin bodies. They have the ability to seamlessly connect to one another and form balances in intricate geometric shapes. When many connect together, they can form into the shape of a tree that nobody could distinguish from a real tree. They are master botanists and they use their knowledge to concoct botanical medicines. For this reason and the medicinal value of the sap-like substance they secrete from their fingertips, they are the Sweeter Realm's most reliable medics.

Sweeter Realm Locations:

Circle Clearing – A circular clearing in a densely forested part of the Nomadic Belt, on the east side of the Queen's Lake. It is about ten yards in diameterand warmly lit day and night. It is covered in short, bright grass. No sound or light escapes the circle of trees that make the clearing peremeter. Verena spent her first two night in the Sweeter Realm there, with Cort and the Friends of the Scheriers.

Deep Waters – A kingdom of the Sweeter Realm consisting of the deep parts of all bodies of water. It is ruled by Löwschock, whose throne is in the deep center of the

Queen's Lake. There is a tangible border between the dark, cold waters of the Deep and the bright, warm waters of the Shallow.

Eierheim [aɪ r h aɪ m] – The Eulesänger capital, a large nest atop a plateau, covered with tiny, Eulesänger huts and houses.

Eineklaue [aɪ n ɛ k l aʊ ə] – Scherier capital city. It is a massave web of hollow mounds, tunnels, roads and arenas. Every Scherier is born in the capital before being taken to the holy site of Gralkirche to be baptized and schooled.

Empty Lake Basin – A dried lake basin in the Land where Verena and her company camped. According to legend, it held the last of the Swimmers until they were all eaten by a land giant, ending the first age of the Waters.

Gralkirche [g r a l k ɪ r ç ə] – A sacred Scherier site, home of the Boots of Lohengrin. All Scheriers are brought there shortly after birth to be baptized, raised, and schooled by the Boots.

Heiligborke [h aɪ l i: g b ɔ r k ə] – A Zweigwesen city and the main Zweigwesen medical center.

Land and Shallow Waters – The known region of the Sweeter Realm, excluding the Deep Waters. It is the jurisdiction of the Queen. It includes in its citizenry all breeds except for the creatures of the Deep.

Pfeifen Mountains [pf aɪ f ə n] – Mountain range on the eastern side of the Eulesänger homeland. It has remained untraveled for centuries because of its sharp, jagged rocks and sudden drops.

Der Mutterleib des Flusses [d e: ɐ m ʊ t t ɐ l aɪ p d ɛ s f l ʊ s ə s] – Literally "The River's Womb". It is an island at the mouth of the Achima River. For countless generations it served as a meeting place between creatures of the Land and creatures of the Shallow Waters. After the union of the Land and Shallow Waters, the island carried a symbolic symbolism and was the site of celebrations in honor of the union.

Nährenstadt [n ɛ: r ə n ʃ t a t] – The Brunnen capital city, destroyed by Löwschock during the war. Verena oversaw the reconstruction of one building. After she left the city, the remaining Brunnens, along with a couple of Zweigwesens, repaired and rebuilt the entire city.

Nomadic Belt/Der Nomadengürtel [d e: r n o: m a: d ə ŋ ɤ r t ə l] – A strip of land in the Sweeter Realm, which wraps around the Queen's Lake. It is where the Nomadic Breeds roam.

The Portal – A passage into the Sweeter Realm from Linderhof valley, opened for the first time when Parsifal's Holy Grail enchanted blood fell to the earth. It opens at the approach of all with Grail Blood —all descendants of Parsifal. It is located at the southeast end of the Nomadic Belt, near Zweigwesen land.

Queen's Lakeside Palace – A palace built for Kandake, Queen of the Land and Shallow Waters. It sits with its entrance dipping into the Queen's Lake, so that the main floor is submerged in a few inches of water. It served as a beacon for the united good-will of the Land Creatures and the Shallow Waters creatures.

Saint Hildegard (city) [z ɛ: n t h ɪ l d ə g a r t] – Religious center of the Brunnen homeland, named after its patron saint, Hildegard of Bingen, friend of Taufe and Conrad Wittelsbach. The site is a cloister, the sisters of which are rarely allowed to leave the city.

Saint Hildegard Cathedral – Primary place of Brunnen worship, a place of religious pilgrimage for all creatures of the Land and Shallow Waters. Its side chambers served as classrooms for Verena's moral schooling.

Sicherheit Marsh [z ɪ ç ɐ h aɪ t] – A large marsh divided in half by the Scherier/Eulesänger border. It runs east-west across the border. Its western edge abuts Eineklaue, the

Scherier capital. Many Scheriers hid there after Löwschock ran them from their cities and shrines.

Steinhörner [ʃ t aɪ n h œ r n ɐ] – Wühlenvogel capital, a tremendous underground cavern, large enough to hold, albiet snuggly, the entire Wühlenvogel population.

Sweeter Realm – The known world on the other side of the portal. It consists of two kingdoms, the Land and Shallow Waters, ruled by the Queen, and the Deep Waters, ruled by Löwschock.

Underground Villages – Villages dug during The Schism by the Wühlenvogels, beneath each homeland of the Land, so that they may acclimate to life in Einigkeitstadt, the city beneath the Black forest.

Unicorn Altar – A monument in the heart of the Unicorn capital of Gemeinsam, in the Sweeter Realm. It is a tall obelisk, in the shape of the horn of the greatest hero in Unicorn history. Around it are several stones, each with a single hole facing outward from the altar. The Unicorns insert their horns into the holes to connect with each other and their ancestors. A replica was built in Einigkeitstadt, the hidden city beneath the Black Forest. It was under this altar that Queen Kandake hid the Holy Grail.

Unicorn Warrior Training Ground – A grassy field with low rolling hills, in a narrow strip of Unicorn land between the Brunnen and Eulesänger homelands.

Wendel Marsh [v ɛ n d ə l] – A wide, deep, and sticky marsh, with sharp, hard reeds protruding through the muddy waters. It runs from Scherier land, south of Gralkirche, south into Unicorn land.

Humans:

Adolf of Wittelsbach, Count Palatine [a: d ɔ l f v ɪ t ə l s b a x] – Swan Knight and ruler of Einigkeitstadt during the Schism. He is the second son of Duke Rudolf I, the Rightful Swan Knight and Mechtild of Nassau. He married

Irmengard of Öttingen, one of the most beloved and respected Swan Knight's spouses. He was assassinated in the Black Forest while celebrating the birth of his daughter.
Conrad of Wittelsbach, Archbishop of Mainz – Brother and Second-in-Training behind Otto I, the Redhead. He was appointed Archbishop by Emperor Friedrich Barbarossa as a reward to Conrad's brother. Conrad was the first to take a Sweeter Realm creature from the valley. He kept a Brunnen as a personal friend when he left Linderhof.

Elsa – The greatest Swan Knight. She was the third Swan Knight, the daughter of Lohengrin and Nethe. She is the only Swan Knight to fully control the behavior of the portal with her mind. She developed telepathic communication with the Unicorns without having to make contact with the horns.

Else of Zweibrücken [ɛ l z ə f ɔ n ts v aɪ b r ʏ k ə n] - The daughter of Stefan, Count of Zweibrücken, son of King Rupert. It is through Else that Verena connects to the Wittelsbach.

First-in-Training/Second-in-Training – The oldest and second oldest children of the reigning Swan Knight, the only two children who may know of the portal and train with The Ancient One, according to the Laws of Ermenrich.

Gessner, Conrad – Friend of Duke Albert V, Swan Knight. He is a biologist and naturalist. Albert V opened the portal for him and he ran through it. He published *Historia Animalium* in 1551, with sketches and descriptions of Sweeter Realm creatures.

Gütel [g yː t ə l] – First Swan Knight spouse. She rescued Parsifal from the enchanted flowermaiden. She is the mother of Lohengrin.

Irmengard of Öttingen [ɪ r m ə ŋ a r t f ɔ n œ t ɪ ŋ ə n] – Swan Knight's wife of Adolf, the Rightful Swan Knight during the Schism. She had an instant connection with the Unicorns and was the first human to share in their collective connection ritual. It was often assumed that she had Grail Blood, but her husband's banishment from the Portal Valley forbade the truth from ever being known.

Lohengrin [l oː ə n ŋ r ɪ n] – Second Swan Knight and only child of Parsifal and Gütel. He married Nethe and was father to Elsa, the greatest Swan Knight. He was the first Swan Knight to train under The Ancient One.

Ludwig I (the Crusader), Duke of Bavaria – Swan Knight and youngest child of Swan Knight Otto I, Duke of Bavaria and his wife Agnes of Loon. Ludwig became Duke at ten years old, when his father died. His mother served as regent until Ludwig came of age. His sister Agnes yielded the Swan Knighthood to Ludwig when he grew strong enough. Ludwig served in the Fifth Crusade as Commander of Imperial Forces.

Ludwig II, King of Bavaria – Swan Knight who faced Löwschock on the banks of Lake Starnberg. He was killed by Löwschock and his body was found in the lake the next day beside that of his friend and psychiatrist, Dr. Bernhard von Gudden. Ludwig constructed Castle Neuschwanstein to be a home and refuge for his friend and teacher, The Ancient One. He built Herrenchiemsee Palace to serve as a hospital for creatures wounded in the war with Löwschock. He recorded the Swan Knight history in a journal left for Verena Elizabeth Kessler, Swan Knight, to find.

Maximiliana "Milli" Maria – Swan Knight and fifth child born to Albert V, Duke of Bavaria. She developed close relations with the Zweigwesens and worked with them on a manuscript of Zweigwesen medicines. The manuscript was acquired in 1912 by Wilfrid Voynich and is now known as the "Voynich Manuscript".

Nethe [n ɛ t ə] – Second wife of Lohengrin and mother of Elsa, the greatest Swan Knight. She died in the house fire with Lohenfrin and their grand-daughter, Birgit.

Otto I (The Redhead), Duke of Bavaria - Swan Knight, first Wittelsbach Duke of Bavaria, known as The Red-Head. He was the hero of the battle of Verona, where enemies attacked the caravan of Emperor Fredrich Barbarosa. He inherited his Grail Blood from his paternal great-great-great grandmother, Elika van Walbeck, who married Berthold of Wittelsbach and attached the Swan Knighthood to the Wittlesbach. Otto's brother was Conrad, who became the Archbishop of Mainz and later of Salzburg.

Otto II, Duke of Bavaria – Swan Knight and only child of Duke Ludwig I and Ludmilla of Bohemia. He married Agnes, daughter of Count Heinrich of the Palatinate on the Rhine. The marriage gave Otto's father, and later Otto, the electorship of the Count Palatine.

Parsifal [p a r z i: f a l] – The First Swan Knight and a keeper of the Holy Grail. His spilled blood created the portal after he drank from the Grail. He and his wife Gütel founded the portal valley. He was father to Lohengrin. He was the first person to enter the portal and the only one to open the portal from the Sweeter Realm and return to the portal valley. He was the first to meet The Ancient One.

Rudolf I, Duke of Bavaria – Swan Knight known during the Schism as the Rightful Swan Knight. He was deposed of the knighthood and the dukedom by his younger brother, Ludwig. He maintained his other hereditary title, Count Palatine of the Rhine, until he yielded that to Ludwig. He was the first to rule Einigkeitstadt, the Wühlenvogel city beneath the Black Forest. He died in England, in a desperate search for the mythical sword Excalibur.

Saint Hildegard of Bingen [z ɛ: n t h ɪ l d ə g a r t f ɔ n b ɪ ŋ ə n] – A twelfth century nun who received visions from God of the Sweeter Realm. She befriended Archbishop Conrad and Taufe, communicating with them in the Brunnen language. Taufe dedicated to her the city and cathedral that bear her name.

Stefan, Count Palatine of Zweibrücken [ts v aɪ b r ʏ k ə n] – Son of King Rupert of Germany, Rightful Swan Knight. He remained ignorant to the Swan Knight legacy. He perpetuated the Grail Blood down his line to Maximilian I, King of Bavaria and great-grandfather of King Ludwig II.

Swan Knights – The line of the descendants of Parsifal, knighted by The Ancient One, whose Grail enchanted blood opens the portal. They are sworn to the protection of the portal and to the service of the Queen of the Land and Shallow Waters.

Tannhäuser [t a n h ɔʏ z ɐ] – A Teutonic Knight with Grail Blood. His name means that he comes from the house of the Lords of Tannhausen. He fought with Duke Ludwig I in the Fifth Crusade. He met Duke Ludwig in the Egyptian prison where the captured crusaders were held. He was unaware of his Grail Blood until he accidentally opened the portal.

Veronika of Welf [f ɛ r o: n ɪ k a f ɔ n v ɛ l f] – Swan Knight and great-granddaughter of Swan Knight Ermenrich. She had an adventurous youth before taking the Swan Knight oath. It was from her adventures that the legend of Tristan and Isolde was born.

Objects:

Albert's Sword – A Unicorn-horned sword fashioned by Duke Alvert V of Bavaria, Swan Knight. The horn was lost during Albert's Battle and gifted to Albert by the Unicorn. Scared of the curious eyes it drew, Albert sent it through the portal. The Ancient One hid it there until he sent Felix to fetch it for Verena.

Elsa's Armor – The armor of the third Swan Knight, Elsa, made for her by her father, second Swan Knight Lohengrin. The armor was made from an ancient Scherier ore with the magical ability to bring a sense of well-being when touched. It consists of a breast plate with attached shoulder plates, upper and lower leg coverings, arm coverings, and a helmet. Small swan figures are on the shoulders and swan wings extend out from the sides of the helmet. Elsa's son gave the armor to The Ancient One to hide it from Elsa. It remained unused until Verena found it on her first day in the Sweeter Realm.

Eulesänger Eggs – Stone replicas of the eggs of the Eulesängers, gifted to Nethe at Elsa's birth, with a hole on one end. When blowing through the hole, the eggs replicate the song of the Eulesängers.

Rudolf's Map – A map of the Sweeter Realm drawn from the descriptions of his Eulesänger friends by Duke Rudolf I when he was a boy. King Ludwig II wedged it into his journal to be found by Verena.

Unicorn Nectar - A thick nectar, the consistency of honey, but salty and bitter. It gives instant clarity of mind when eaten. It reveals no secrets that are not already known, but it clears away peripheral distractions from the subject at hand. The Unicorns consume it when important decisions need to be made.

The Zweigwesen Medical Manuscript – A book of Zweigwesen medicinal plants and recipes, written collaboratively with Swan Knight Maximiliana "Milli" Maria, daughter of Albert V. The plants are all native to the Sweeter Realm. The book is written in Zweigwesen. It has been passed through many owners throughout the centuries. The Swan Knights are the only humans who know the origin language. It has baffled linguists since it left the hands of the Swan Knights. The manuscript was acquired in 1912 by Wilfrid Voynich and is now known as the "Voynich Manuscript". The manuscript has illustrations and descriptions, with specific details, from the collection and storage of the plants to the preparing of the ingredients to the application and dosage of the medicines.

Miscellaneous:

Albert's Battle – A battle at Linderhof between Swan Knight Duke Albert V and hunters and prize seekers who had seen Gessner's book. Involved in the battle were The Ancient One, four Unicorns, six Scheriers, and seventy Zweigwesens.

Battle of Einigkeitstadt – An invasion of the underground city in the Black Forest by the forces of Duke Ludwig IV of Bavaria against the children of his brother, Duke Rudolf, the Rightful Swan Knight. The invaders breached the underground city. Many creatures were killed, including the young twins of Adolf and Irmengard, Rupert and Friedrich. The battle saw the return of Brunhilde, who arrived just in time to save the line of Rudolf I.

Einigkeitstadt [aɪ n ɪ ç k aɪ ts t a t] – Literally "Unity City", an underground city, beneath the northern part of the Black Forest, built during the Schism by the Wühlenvogels for Rudolf I, ruled by the Rightful Swan Knights until the schism sealed with Albert V.

Füssen [f y: s ə n] – Town in southern Bavaria, Germany, on the banks of the Lech River, near the Forggensee. The Romans called it Foetes, a name that evolved over time into its current name. It is where Verena stayed with her family while visiting Bavaria.

Linderhof [l ɪ n d ɐ h o: f] – The name of the portal valley, given by Duke Ludwig II when he was very young. He was trying to say that it was a soft and gentle courtyard compared to the palace at Landshut. The name stuck and it was called Linderhof ever since. By the swan Knight family and the Sweeter Realm creatures, it is also called the Portal Valley, the Grail Valley, Parsifal's Valley, or simply the Valley.

Linderhof Palace – The palace at Linderhof valley that King Ludwig II built where the old lodge stood. He built it so that he could rule Bavaria without leaving the portal valley.

Palatinate of Zweibrücken – An electorship of the Holy Roman Empire, governed by the Counts Palatine of Zweibrücken. Its seat of power is in Mainz. The Wittelsbach gained the title when Rupert II, Count Palatine of the Rhine, came to the financial rescue of the Count Zweibrücken, who had no heirs. Rupert III inherited Zweibrücken. He gave it to his son Stefan. It is from the line of Stefan that Maximilian I, King of Bavaria descended.

Schism, the – The split in the Swan Knighthood after the children of Duke Ludwig II, Rudolf and Ludwig, fought over the dukedom and the knighthood. During the schism, the line of Ludwig remained in the portal valley as Swan Knights there, while the line of Rudolf maintained a simultaneous Swan Knighthood in Einigkeitstadt, a secret city beneath the Black Forest. For most of the Schism, the Rightful Swan Knights in the Black Forest held the title of Counts Palatine on the Rhine.

Venus Grotto – An artificial cave built by King Ludwig II to hide and protect the portal. A mural depicting Tannhäuser and the goddess Venus sits precisely on the portal point. The grotto holds an artificial lake and a boat built to replicate Lohengrin's boat pulled by The Ancient One. The grotto was one of the first places in Bavaria to be lit with electric lights and powered by an electric generator.

487

www.ingramcontent.com/pod-product-compliance
Lightning Source LLC
Chambersburg PA
CBHW071338020726
47502CB00001B/149